TWO WOMEN

Teal and Juniper were twins, genetically identical, but in every other way opposed. They lived in binary: what one was, the other was not.

Juniper was an artist, Teal a technician. Juniper loathed their twinship; Teal was incomplete without it. It was Juniper who felt the call of the endless sea; Teal who stayed human.

Rache might have fallen in love with either one. But Teal held herself celibate, and Juniper's affairs were many and notorious. . . .

Books by Alison Sinclair

Legacies
Blueheart

Published by HarperPrism

ATTENTION: ORGANIZATIONS AND CORPORATIONS

Most HarperPrism books are available at special quantity discounts for bulk purchases for sales promotions, premiums, or fund-raising. For information, please call or write:
Special Markets Department, HarperCollins*Publishers*,
10 East 53rd Street, New York, N.Y. 10022.
Telephone: (212) 207-7528. Fax: (212) 207-7222.

BLUEHEART

ALISON SINCLAIR

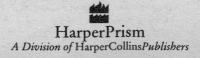

HarperPrism
A Division of HarperCollinsPublishers

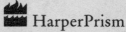 HarperPrism

A Division of HarperCollins*Publishers*
10 East 53rd Street, New York, N.Y. 10022-5299

This is a work of fiction. The characters, incidents, and
dialogues are products of the author's imagination and are not to
be construed as real. Any resemblance to actual events or
persons, living or dead, is entirely coincidental.

A hardcover edition of this book was published
in Great Britain in 1996 by Orion Books.

ISBN 0-06-105820-3

HarperCollins®, 📖 ®, and HarperPrism®
are trademarks of HarperCollins*Publishers*, Inc.

Cover illustration © 1997 by Bruce Jensen

First HarperPrism printing: May 1998

Printed in the United States of America

Visit HarperPrism on the World Wide Web at
http://www.harperprism.com

❖ 10 9 8 7 6 5 4 3 2 1

ONE

They found the body in a tuft of floating forest a half-day's swim from ringsol six. Daven was the first to see it, Rache the first to recognize it for what it was. He stopped Daven's first stroke toward it with a hand on the youth's shoulder, and signaled simply, Look again.

They drifted, ten meters below the surface, in the green-tinged submarine sunlight. The body lay slightly above them, cross-barring the stripes of ribbongrass. Rache felt Daven tense and flinch in recognition. He allowed him time to control his revulsion. He knew the young man's pride. When Daven turned to him, he signaled, Watch for me. Daven nodded, and unshouldered his speargun. Rache indicated that his approach would be circular and oblique, cautious, orthodox. Alone, he might have done otherwise, being already confident he had the measure of the threat. But not while he was responsible for the protection and teaching of a younger.

With Daven flanking him, he circled, swimming slowly, with easy strokes of flippered feet. There was a haze around the body, shimmering slightly. Tiny scavengers, crowding to feast, and fragmenting the rotting flesh. Things decayed quickly in Blueheart's warm seas. No sign of anything larger. Nevertheless . . . he paused a moment, sculling, and then searched in his pouches, drawing out a capsule of repellent, and holding it up for Daven to see. Daven nodded, and did likewise. Rache thought, I'll have to take him hunting. For my own pleasure as much as his education. He had forgotten how much of a pleasure it could be.

This, however . . . repellent capsule in one hand, speargun in the other, he swam slowly toward the body. He slid between strands of ribbongrass, probing ahead with the tip of his speargun, and watching the shadowy depths. This was the moment for caution. Not all these ribbons might be vegetable, and it was not outwith Rache's experience that a medusa might use its own kill for bait. He signaled over his shoulder to Daven, Stay back.

No, no medusa. He scanned the grass twined beside and about the body, automatically cataloging species. No sign of splines, radials, or other dangers. He shouldered the speargun, freeing his hand, and popped the repellent capsule over the body. The cloud burst; despite his anticipation, he flinched at the flicker and slither of small fleeing bodies over his skin. Squinting, he waited until the bright mist began to disperse, and then peered close.

There was, as he had expected, little left of the face. Eyes and fleshy features eaten away, in places to the bone; hands pared to bone and tendon; skin flensed to muscle, bone, fat. She had been a woman. He could not tell the original color of the pulped tissue, but he saw no sign of either clothing or hair. She was likely an adaptive, like himself and Daven modified to live in Blueheart's seas. She wore a wide belt, as he did, with the usual travelers' utilities, knife, clippers, parers, shellcracker. Belt and utilities were decorated with polished shell and very dark olivines. Such dark stones could only come from the outflows beneath the Messnier gyre. Odd: the Messnier gyre was two thousand kilometers away. Across her back she carried a charged speargun, the strap sunk into her disintegrating chest. So death had come on her stealthily. He sculled slowly around her, shouldering aside the grass. He could see no sign of gross injury, no missing limbs, no large bites. Tufts of grass protruded from her clenched fists; he could match them to the torn stubs. She had not died easily.

Carefully, he eased himself from her ribboned cage, and swam back to Daven. He was beginning to feel the need to breathe: he motioned them to the surface.

They broke through into the blazing white of a Blueheart forenoon. Fat cumuli strung across a blue, blue sky. Around them was a slowly shifting sea unbroken by island or shore, though flattened and slightly roughened to the east, by the underside drag of the floating forest. Rache gratefully filled his lungs, and told Daven what he had found and what he thought of it. He said, "We'll have to take her back, and I'd also like to take some clippings of the vegetation for analysis; it might tell us something about why she died."

"You'll take her back to the ringsol?" Daven said. His tone was critical.

Rache said, "We are nearer there than the holdfast. We are due there by this afternoon; in fact, by the time we are done here, we will be overdue." He sculled, riding the swell, waiting. He suspected that the reasons for Daven's displeasure was as obscure and unthinking as most of his reactions to the ringsol. Four months' study under Rache had not changed him.

They were both born to the sea, Rache over fifty years ago, Daven under twenty. Human but adapted to make them viable in Blueheart's brackish sea: their metabolism stabilized against prolonged immersion, their lungs and heart strengthened against water inhalation, their blood and muscle pigments altered and enriched to give them endurance in swimming and diving. Rache's modifications went further, making him so much the sea-creature that it had been a profound shock to his insular community when, in his thirtieth year, he left the sea.

γ Serpens V—familiarly known as Blueheart— was an anomaly amongst the seventeen settled worlds. Humanity, spreading out from Earth, had embarked on a program of survey, settlement, and terraforming of all planets at a workable distance from a suitable star. Human adaptation, to the original or the partially terraformed environment, was always an interim phase. The endpoint was always a planet habitable by primary humans.

But on no other planet had adaptation alone been sufficient for survival: elsewhere, adaptives remained dependent on technological support for food, supplies, information. On Blueheart, intrepid adaptives had tested, and then broken, this dependence. They spread across the shallows and throughout the floating forests, establishing holdfasts around reefs, islands, and rafts, foraging and cultivating native and imported plant and animal life. Their experiment became a way of life, a philosophy, and ultimately, an ideology, with all the rigidity and prescriptions thereof. Rache's family, his home community, were pastorals all; Rache the only dissenter among them. He had thought that Daven might be another; now, he doubted it. There was something deeply conventional about Daven. Most times, Rache respected the effort his nephew had made to have come this far. Sometimes the conventionality irritated him. When Daven said nothing, he reiterated, "We must report back. And her home holdfast must know we have found her. The planetary net would be the most efficient—"

"What about boomer-relay?"

Rache knew himself rebuked, and fairly so. Boomer-relay was the pastorals' long-distance network, using the ocean sound channel as a conduit. It would reach, firsthand, the most insular communities.

"Thank you, Daven." He was pleased to see a flicker of satisfaction in the young man's expression. "But to reach the nearest relay station would take a detour, and we have no time to detour. And when I get back . . . no doubt I will have messages and people wanting attention and scolding me for taking leave when my new vice-admin has been only forty days installed, no matter *how* far ahead I had it planned . . ."

"I could go."

He had been maundering to avert just this suggestion. Daven, he suspected, knew it. "I would rather know what killed her before I let you go off alone."

"I've traveled alone before. I'll be back by night. I'm not afraid."

Rache mused, "Are you that unenthusiastic about returning to ringsol six?" Daven gave him a flat look; Rache's intended humor had too much truth in it. He said, "Daven, I would not hold you there."

"I've got to—" He checked himself, and looked away.

Rache said, "You know I'm grateful for your interest."

The flat look again. "Will you want to wrap her?"

"I should. It is not . . . easy to look at, Daven."

"I'll help you, and then I'll go to the relay station," Daven said, challengingly. "I haven't done anything to make you think I can't, have I?"

Rache sighed. "Don't help me," he said. "Go now so you can be assured of reaching the relay station before dark. Stay there overnight, and come back tomorrow, during daylight." And give me a sleepless night wondering if I did right in yielding to your young pride. He bit his tongue at Daven's evident satisfaction, and held it between his teeth until the youth had dived out of earshot.

Well, he had at least spared Daven the task of wrapping the corpse. He cut ribbons from the weed which enfolded her, and mummified her, rubbing repellent into each strip. The first time he had done this, he had been fifteen, and the body had been his sister's. Athene was the only other one in the holdfast modified as he was; she was his essential companion. They had been two days out from the holdfast when Athene had begun to cough blood. Rache held her face above water while she bled to death from undiagnosed complications of her transfections. Rache had wrapped her body against scavengers and swum with it to the nearest rafttown, looking for a miracle.

He was nearly glad that this body was as macerated as it was. Its look did not remind him. Its feel did not remind him. But its weight, when he roped it to his shoulders, its weight did. It was hard to pull it. The extra exertion and stress increased his need to breathe; he had to swim nearer the surface than he liked, suffering the subsurface drag of waves and the heat of the tropical oceans. He was exhausted in body and spirit by the time he reached the bright buoy and light which marked the ringsol's site.

He sculled, riding the waves, breathing, oxygen-charging his muscles. The formerly clear sky was streaked with fibrous cloud, spreading from the north east and sharp-combed north east to south west. He could feel a certain aggressive pitch to the waves. Blueheart's wide tropics bred storms. Daven might be in for more than one night's wait at the relay station. Rache quietly prayed that the boy did not try to return tonight, ahead of the storm. Swimming under the stars might be glorious—he remembered such nights from the untroubled first years of his marriage—but many of the sea's greatest hazards surfaced at night. A lone swimmer in difficulties would disappear forever. To find a body before it was completely devoured, as he had found this one, was most uncommon.

Rather than entertain such thoughts he exhaled hard, emptying his lungs of reserve volume, and dived. The light went from white, to umber, to blue-green. The warmth peeled away from his skin as he entered the thermocline. He could feel the pressure mounting on skin, eyes, and ears. His right ear, in particular, nagged at the swiftness of the dive. He ignored it. His adaptation permitted him swift descent and ascent; he could dive, with ease, to the limits of sunlight penetration.

Now he could see the station itself, suspended between downwelling sunlight and upwelling artificial light. It was a heavy, shadowy boule outlined by a cage of warning lights. Only its uppermost surface was windowed and bright. A dashed tether dropped away from its base, the conduit to the geothermal tap. A hundred and fifty meters below the ringsol, over two hundred meters below the surface, eight concentric, circular arrays of lights illuminated a square kilometer of sea floor. From the level of the station the floor glowed a dusky blue-green. From the level of the lights, the dusky blue-green would be the deep, rich velvet of abundant growth. As a young man, he had been inspired by the thought of bringing light and fecundity to the dark sea floor, of extending the range of sessile, cultivatable habitat.

He elected to enter through the lock immediately adjacent to medical. The draining of the water left him on hands and knees, like a castaway. He did not try to stand until he heard the inner lock unlatch; he was hauling himself upright when it opened. He was a gregarious man, but he was not quite prepared to be greeted by a crowd.

His right ear was still part blocked, distorting voices and making words unintelligible. Their mood seemed euphoric, a high, somewhat brittle excitement. They seemed to be delighted with him about something. But the stares were abruptly deflected by the sight of the body, the chatter dropped away to silence, and the mood plummeted abruptly to dismay. Someone said, "Oh, Rache. Not . . . Daven—"

"No," he said, at once, appalled that he had let them think that, even for a moment.

His vice administrator pushed out of the crowd and went on one knee, intent on seeing with her own eyes. Meredis was one of the few who seemed to like Daven despite himself. And her training was medical. He said, forcibly, "Leave it. It's *not* Daven. Daven has gone to pass the word on the relay. We think she's adaptive." When she still seemed poised to uncover it, he said, "The body's . . . badly damaged."

She looked up at him, grasping his warning, and got again to her feet. He thought, irrelevantly, that auburn hair, deep ruddy skin, and the blue and black of the survey uniform were an atrocious juxtaposition. "I'll get a float." Paused, smiled. "And, by the way, congratulations."

Rache gazed blankly at her.

She smiled even more widely at his blankness, and said, gently, "Your development proposal has been yellow-striped."

He understood the crowd, and its mood, at last.

In the three hundred years since establishment, Blueheart had been under intense study to develop a complete understanding of its present and past geology, climate, and ecosystem. The results of these surveys were used to refine models of how the planet might be developed. Until very recently, such models concentrated upon Blueheart's transformation to a primary habitat, and the design of the altered ecology. Rache's own was one of the few to advocate leaving the planet unchanged. It had, hitherto, been considered a fringe diversion. No more. It had, abruptly, become a contender.

Someone at the back pitched forward a bundle of cloth; he caught it as it unfolded, and dropped the kaftan over his head. Clad, he felt able to withstand welcome, celebration, and questions. Yes, he was delighted. Yes, he had given some thought to what would need to be done before application for orange-striping. No, he had not thought about whom he would recruit, this had come as something of a surprise, and yes, he promised ringsol six staff would be the first to know. The body rested against his foot, forgotten by all but himself.

And the medics. Meredis returned with the float and the department head of medicine, and Adam de Courcey had the same effect on the enthusiasts that the repellent had on the scavengers: they scattered. The small, fragile-looking man stood regarding Rache with a slightly sour expression. Adam de Courcey disapproved of human adaptation, and to his mind, Rache wore his deformity too lightly. His origin was ε Indi III, one of the two planets to be settled without terraforming.

"I have a body here I need stored," Rache said, letting his hand slide off the bag. De Courcey's fine features tightened; he nudged Rache aside, though Rache outmassed him twofold, crouched, and started to unwind the shrouding weed. The few who had not left before, did now.

"Cause of death?"

"I couldn't say. Her speargun was strapped across her back, her knife in her sheath, so she wasn't aware of danger. There are no wounds from shark or bonecrusher attack. Death wasn't immediate: there is grass clenched in her hands. I would say toxin. She was on the edge of a floating forest, and the forests are home to all kinds of poisonous fauna, though most of those shouldn't kill a human outright."

Adam paused a moment, without looking up, waiting for him to continue. When he did not, Adam said, still without looking at Rache, "It'll take genetics to identify her. I'll survey the missing persons roster."

"No need," Rache said. "Daven's gone to put a message out on the relay. Her home holdfast will know her from descriptions of her and her equipment. If you store the body, they'll contact us."

"Pastoral? You're sure?" He pulled on a pair of gloves and dug in with small fingers, peering close. "Seems pale for an adaptive . . . If you don't want me doing genetics, I can do enough pigment analysis to confirm."

Rache's stomach rolled at the sight of Adam's fingers embedded in the macerated flesh. He swallowed, hard. "No hair, no clothing, and pastoral artifacts. She's pastoral, and she should be returned to her own lab for autopsy."

De Courcey flipped the ribbons of grass back into place, and stood. "But will she be?" Rache let the question go unanswered. This was not the time to argue pastoral compliance with adaptation law. Adam said, "You might like to know what killed her. For your own sake."

"It would be . . . politic to wait on the autopsy, Dr. de Courcey. But . . ." But other adaptives and divers beside himself swam in those waters. He thought of Daven, and said, abruptly, "Do the minimum, but . . as soon as possible."

De Courcey frowned at him, showing no triumph. "You'd better let me look you over, first. Just in case."

Adam was thorough, as always. Half reclining on the examination bed, Rache watched the physician's delicate, economical movements as he specified sample analyses and read their results. Once again, he regretted the barrenness of their relationship. Adam had spent over a hundred years of his career in space—a hundred years extended by relativity and coldsleep to three hundred. One of his first voyages had been on a seeding ship to Blueheart. He had met the heroes and heroines of the stories of Rache's childhood, the first settler/surveyors whose names, deeds, and discoveries were immortalized in pastoral oral tradition. Adam's own stories should have been splendid ones.

But Adam, ε Indi-born and profoundly religious, was opposed to transfection for anything other than therapeutic reasons where there was any alternative. Had he not been, he would never have been grounded. Weightlessness and coldsleep thins human bone. After prolonged debate exploration services ruled that transfection should supersede the original maintenance therapies. Adam refused; for his refusal, he had been discharged from the service, left here on Blueheart.

Adam said, to the screen, "You seem in fair health, though showing signs of mild stress." His glance at Rache was incurious, and did not invite confidence. "No traces of toxin or infection, but if you feel unwell, develop a rash or a fever, nausea or pain, report to me immediately. If I find anything in the autopsy to concern me, I may ask you to wear a monitor for a few days." He cleared the console with a sweep of his hand and turned to face Rache. "Other than that, my concerns are the usual: your weight and your hemodynamics."

Rache said, "I am controlling my weight and you are monitoring my circulation." He eased himself off the bed. Adam's lab was too small and full of breakables for his ease.

Adam let him go. But as Rache reached the door, he said, "I shall be submitting an extensive critique of your proposal."

Rache waited a moment, but Adam did not elaborate. "I shall look forward to reading it," he said. But outside, he smiled to himself. Adam had been as much surprised by the promotion as he himself: that critique was surely intended for the white-to-yellow consideration.

From medical, he went to the operations center, domed atop the base. With self-deprecating humor, the staff had dubbed it the plexus, the organism being insufficiently evolved to be cerebrate. When Rache was appointed, seven years ago, it was a traditional design, with isolated stations, partitions, high screens, and wasted volume above. Now, it was webbed with cables and ladders to suspended platforms and cages harboring life at several levels. It looked a teeming shambles, with all stations occupied and all screens lit and crawling with color. People hunched over the workstations and crowded around the smaller screens, talking, arguing, and, on occasion, throwing things. Rache browsed among them, looking over shoulders, listening in, collecting petitions, updates, promises, alibis, and tidbits of gossip.

"Rache. Hey, Rache!" Oliver, the ringsol's net manager, waved from his cage overhead as though Rache were well offshore and not just below. "Pick up your mail. System's collapsing under it."

"Bad design," Rache rumbled back, and stepped aside to avoid the inevitable beanbag. Oliver, orbitstation born, still had a childish fascination with gravity. Rache lobbed it back into the cage and took the elevator up to his private office, set in a windowed cubicle overlooking the plexus.

Oliver had not exaggerated about the mail. What would it be like when he garnered the whole planet's opinions, and not merely the scientific community's, as he would were his proposal to advance to wider consideration? He scanned those priority-flagged, including a note from Oliver offering him an upgraded scanning and sorting program, and a dryly congratulatory message from the director of the planetary survey service, his own superior. Survey cherished a collective self-image of themselves as scientists, surveyors, and explorers; unblemished by politics. Their mission was purely the acquisition of knowledge for the use of others. The director recognized the absurdity, even as she subscribed to it, and fostered it. Rache viewed the message with the assurance of knowing that, "political diversions" notwithstanding, they had nothing to reproach in his administration, but a little irritation nevertheless. He was doing no more, and no less, than others in his position, if somewhat more successfully. And, he had to admit, more conspicuously. He folded his hands on his stomach and leaned back, frowning at the insignia on the screen, troubled. The proposal would demand more of him, now; and he would become more conspicuous, now.

When the net signaled he had an incoming personal call, the diversion was a relief—until the origin code appeared on screen: Cesar Kamehameha, director of the Adaptation Oversight Committee.

With the oversight committees of survey, development, and resources, the AOC planned and oversaw the accumulation of human, knowledge and physical resources for the task ahead, the terraforming of Blueheart; those four organizations were the powers on Blueheart, and the AOC was the power that most shaped the lives of adaptives and pastorals.

Adaptation was stringently regulated; no variation permitted from those approved by the AOC. The AOC databanks contained the genetic and medical histories of all Blueheart adaptives since settlement. The adaptation laboratories were often the sole contact-point between cultures, pastoral and primary. The natural-born children of adaptive parents were transfected shortly after birth so that they could grow with their modifications. A minority, Rache having been among them, were manipulated prenatally. Once they reached the age of consent, young adults might elect to have their adaptations reversed, or amended; few pastorals elected reversal, and a number, Rache knew, envied such as himself the profundity of his change. For himself, he had never quite overcome his early experiences with the adaptation labs and their director.

Cesar Kamehameha was a compact man. His features were smooth and undersized, even child sized, in an adult face: small, watchful eyes under nearly invisible brows, a straight nose, and a small, secretive mouth. His skin was olive, lightly seamed with age, his hair quite black and his eyes the very dark green of Messnier olivines. He was Earthborn, a hundred and twenty years old. He had lived seventy of these years on Blueheart unchanged, though his work had changed many. He had been principal contributor to four of the Blueheart adaptive lines. The deep adaptation, Rache's adaptation, was his work; he had designed the transfections used on the embryos who had become Rache, and Athene; he had been present during some of their early childhood visits. He had been patient with the impertinence of a three- and four-year-old Rache, a child accustomed to the indulgence of adults, who did not recognize in Cesar an elder, an authority.

He had learned to recognize the authority since. If Survey had a collective self-image to defend, the AOC had an ideology. And Cesar Kamehameha was chief ideologue.

But his views were a paradox. Though unchanged, a primary, Cesar was fascinated by the sea. Behind his image was a single wall of shifting, flickering light, a wall-depth aquarium. The brilliant-hued fish came native from Blueheart and engineered from Earth's tropics. The blacks, yellows, reds, and silvers came from Earth, the golds, blues, grays, and greens from Blueheart. Beautiful as the display was, Rache found it unnatural. He watched the fish trying to swim forward, through the glass.

Cesar said, "Ah, Rache," and paused—and Rache thought that if he did not know better he would have said the powerful Director of the AOC was wondering how best to proceed.

He chose to be direct. "I have some concerns about this proposal of yours."

Not so direct. His concern was the yellow-striping, surely. Rache observed, "It is simply an expansion of something which has been in public domain in various versions for the past five years."

"Not quite," Cesar said. "The strength of this version lies in the extrapolation of adaptive social development over the next two centuries; that is where you have obviously directed your best thought." That was so, and Rache was pleased to have it so acknowledged, even if critically. Cesar must have seen his pleasure, or guessed at it, for his next words were quelling: "At this stage, promotion is simply a recognition of the soundness of the background investigation and the consistency of the extrapolation, and not an approval of the underlying philosophy—"

"I do realize that." Low-level striping was decided within the specialist community. High-level striping was determined by all those who took an interest. The debate was public and planet-wide, and could last for years. At the end, one model would outlast or absorb all the others, and be developed for implementation. "But," Rache said, that it be made plain, "I plan to continue development. I will take this all the way to implementation, if I can."

Cesar's eyes narrowed slightly, but he did not speak.

"Over the years—" Rache hesitated, wondering if explanation conveyed respect or submission. And finding the thought distasteful, continued in defiance of it. "Over the years I have come to see it is wrong to regard Blueheart as we have all the other planets. Nowhere else has so highly evolved an ecosystem. In terraforming we must destroy that ecosystem. Never mind the experience we have in reconstruction and diversification, what we create will not be Blueheart as we know it now. And I cannot be persuaded, that for all human experience, we will do it better."

"I agree." Cesar gestured with a hand to the aquarium just behind him, and the attentive fish, catching the movement, flinched and scattered. "But there is another aspect, one that outweighs concern for the ecosystem, and one you have not addressed. Do you know your history, Rache?"

"Not as well as I would like." The barrage of current information broadcast from system to system—the sunstreams—eclipsed history.

"None of us do. You do not state it explicitly, but I believe you would advocate germ-line adaptation, to create a self-perpetuating aquatic human subtype."

Rache released his breath, as for a steep dive, and had to draw another. "I would rather we be adapted to the seas rather than the seas be adapted to us."

"Historically, the human race nearly perished over differences far smaller than these you would bequeath your descendants. We are the makers of our society; all future generations will be our descendants. It is our responsibility to provide for them wisely. The human race's differences—in characteristics and culture—have been nearly its death many times over."

"And its wealth and survival," Rache said.

"You propose something contrary to the whole tradition of human genetic engineering. You would instate biological differences and inequalities greater than any that ever existed in nature, despite the history of conflict which only ended with the eradication of these inequities."

"I read my history . . . differently," Rache said.

"Difference always looked to me more an excuse for conflict than a cause." He folded his hands on his stomach. "But then, I am an ecologist."

"And a pastoral adaptive."

"I am an ecologist," Rache said again. "It was not pastoralism but science which made me wonder if we should give up our differences. Do we not put ourselves at risk by doing so, by becoming too much alike? We may *need* our diversity." He saw attentiveness, but no engagement in the other man's face. He shook his head slightly. "The proposal in no way excludes primaries. It in no way excludes the creation of as much primary habitat as the Blueheart seas will allow. At the poles, for instance. It does exclude compromising the present ecosystem."

"It is not a matter of degrees of accommodation. It is a matter of principle, and perhaps of survival—"

"Then," Rache said, "you would accept the proposal *without* adaptives?"

Cesar looked out of the screen, keen-eyed. "I might. Would you?"

"No," said Rache.

"You already think of yourselves," Cesar said quietly, "as a race. You already regard yourselves as having an unquestioned right to exist and to perpetuate yourselves—"

"I am one man. I cannot speak for anyone else but myself." His hands had clenched against each other; he could feel the knuckles interlock.

"Your proposal will never be accepted. You are wasting your time and risking your reputation."

"My reputation, such as it is, is that of the highest ranking *pastoral* within the survey service. I am doing what should have been expected of me." He put his hands on the armrests and pulled himself forward slightly. "Are you suggesting I not continue with the proposal?"

"I am asking you to consider that the future might be less gilded than your extrapolations. Study your history." With the barest of courtesies, Cesar broke the connection.

"He is right about you," Adam's voice said from behind Rache. The physician was standing inside the lift. Rache had been so concentrated upon the screen that he had not heard his arrival. "You have a gilded view of human nature. I noticed that you never entertained the possibility of a human cause of death."

"Should I?" Rache said.

"Not in this case." Adam paused. "Nixiaxin."

"No," Rache rumbled.

"Nixiaxin. Traces in the stomach and small intestine. A high enough concentration in the nervous system to paralyze breathing. Lungs were completely collapsed: no water in them, no drowning. She died of asphyxia, due to nixiaxin poisoning. As," he emphasized lightly, "you thought." There was no flattery in the acknowledgment, only precision.

Rache rubbed his face with his fingertips, in intense distress. Red algae coated the upper leaves of ribbon grass. The algae protected the growing tips from over-irradiation. Some species were toxic, some not; the balance was determined by a viral blight which affected the nontoxic species, but to which the toxic were immune. The poison concentrated in anything which fed off the leaves. Blight this far south was unusual, but this year he had mapped reports of blight as far south as Great Diamond seamount, a day's swim away. Had she been from this area, had she had any contact with local people, she would have known.

Adam was saying, "Other than that, she was an adaptive female, age seventeen to eighteen standard years, in excellent health, and with no detectable injury."

"Except," Rache said, ferociously, "that she is dead. Dead of simple ignorance and damnable prejudice." He swung his chair to face Adam. "The information is here. The information is in the *net*. If she had had access to that—" The anger ebbed as suddenly as it had surged.

Adam looked at him with ancient, uncommonly understanding eyes. "Quite," he said.

"Daven knows," Rache said. The boy was safe from that, at least. "Thank you. When someone contacts me about the body, I will let you know."

Adam nodded. "I have a request. I would like to go up to Rossby overnight." Rossby was the rafttown, a floating metropolis which rode the Rossby gyre in a thousand-kilometer track around the southern midlatitudes; it was at present nearing its point of closest approach to ringsol six. Adam's thin face was forbidding, offering neither apology nor explanation. Rache was on the brink of reminding him of regulations when he remembered: Adam's daughter lived in Rossby rafttown. His son, too, but it was the daughter who figured in ringsol gossip: there was some estrangement there. Adam's daughter was in her early twenties, a few years older than the corpse in Adam's store.

After a moment, he said, "Go, then. We'll endeavor not to develop anything exotic for a day."

TWO

Adam de Courcey felt the storm underfoot as he lifted himself out of the summersub. The sensation was less one of motion than of unsettledness, a subtle feeling of having misstepped. Perhaps, he thought, this was also a misstep. But he could not think how else to do this, except in person. Although they represented the most advanced technology developed, starships fostered an oddly archaic human community. There was simply no one aboard whom one could not touch. In a hundred years he had grown unused to sustaining relationships by virtual and distance communications.

Nearly thirty years of still life, he thought, as the tubecapsule carried him toward his daughter, and his habits of thought were still those of a quick-lifer, a spacefarer. She would understand his coming; in their childhood she and Karel had simply accepted his always being there, in substance, unlike other parents. He had had no faith in a virtual presence.

But as to the time it had taken him to come. Perhaps, he thought, he had had intimations of what might happen if he left them behind. He had not forgotten her, but even now, after thirty years, he did not have a still-lifer's sense of time. Four years, he thought, and the number was merely a number, absurdly small, to someone born three hundred and fifteen years ago, and fifty light years distant. Their quarrel, profound and

fundamentally irreconcilable as it was, was not worthy
of so long a silence.

Most non-adaptives, immigrant and native-born,
lived aboard the rafttowns. The smallest were single-
platform structures of a few dozen residents, accessible
only by hoverflight, sail or submersible, and restricted to
the relatively tranquil polar and subpolar oceans. The
largest constituted hundreds of linked platforms,
housed tens of thousands, received orbital dropships,
and outrode tropical storms. Rossby-alpha, so named
for the subtropical gyre beneath it, was the second
largest in the southern hemisphere.

The platforms aged inwards until the centermost,
over a hundred years old. Cybele lived in one of the oldest, below sea-level. She had moved five times in as
many years, each time to quarters smaller, cheaper, and
less well serviced.

Her accommodations block was as grim as any he
had seen. Everything appeared to work; lighting, ventilation, cameras, elevators, public access consoles. But
the lighting and ventilation were outdated, and he saw
his first maintenance spider for a hundred years, slung
beneath a flickering light. Probably the residents had
elected to forgo the expense of replacing their anti-
quated services, beyond what was required for safety.
The decorations dated from the non-terraforming fad of
some twenty-five years ago: stills from the presentations
of an off world artist, immensely influential then, quite
forgotten now. The semicircular wall of the vestibule
was a single panoramic image of the tropical shallows.
The light seemed to shift slightly, the colors to be more
or less glazed with blue. Distinct and dark, a rapier lev-
eled its spike at heart-level.

The decor grew no more subtle as he descended,

level by level. On Cybele's level the walls were rippled and streamered with weed. The floating forests closed him in. He did not look closely, no more than he looked at the tanks in ocean ecology. His perspective on the floating forests was uncharitable, formed by what came to him in medical. Divers were brought in with scarlet weals on hands and face, weeping, spine-filled wounds, and, worst, in crash-hibernation. The hibernation modifications, universal to space-faring humanity, could be life-prolonging, allowing induction of a reversible, extreme hypometabolic state. But the physician was then presented with two potentially fatal conditions, poisoning and hibernation, and he labored to curb its careless use and substitute knowledge of venoms and their antidotes.

He heard laughter behind him, and bare running feet. He stepped out of their way: his bones were no longer dangerously brittle, but they were not as strong as they had once been. They passed without acknowledgment, a man and three young women, all naked, hairless, and daubed from head to toe with poster-hued paint. The woman in the lead shouted over her shoulder, "Come on: we'll be late." They rounded a corner and were gone, but for traces of red, gold, and yellow on the floor and a smeared green hand print on the wall by the corner.

Just around the corner was Cybele's door. He looked at the door, looked at the hand print, took from his pocket a tissue and wiped the wall clean. Only when he had done so did he realize that his rubbing had uncovered a spline, hidden among the ribbon grass. His lip drew back at the detail of the fine, serrated profile of it. His fingers would have been cross-hatched with cuts, seeping blood into the water, attracting flensers and boresnakes. Those would do the killing, most untidily, while the spline spread its fine net napkin and gathered in the scraps.

He did not hear the door open. He did not know until he turned that his daughter was there, watching him.

"Cybele."

"Adam."

He wondered how long, how far, she might have been watching him. Cameras tracked all events in Rossby's public areas. The unedited recordings entered the net, to be accessed at will. And stream-jockeys monitored, edited, and themed the new, the noteworthy, and the diverting, for display on public and private screens. It was reckoned an artform, some argued the highest artform. The transformation of real life, in real time.

At times, in private, he had sought her image on the archives. Seen her coming and going on foot, one of her petty economies. Seen her watching the landing and lifts of the drop ships. Seen her face thin and refine more than it should between the years twenty-one and twenty-five. He had seen the time passing in her face; he had simply not accepted what it meant.

He folded the tissue neatly around the clot of green paint. Folded layer upon layer until the green disappeared and he could clasp it in his hand. "May I come in?"

Her face tightened, but she stepped in and let him follow. He saw that her hands were held stiffly. If he had no power over her now, she remembered when he had, and had used that power to deny her.

Her room was very small. Even its beauties were utilitarian. Against the side wall was a crystalline sculpture, a castle above a waterfall. The castle was translucent white, the waterfall an opalescent blue. Most people who sculpted with crystalmites did so for pleasure. Cybele did so to develop her skills in handling multiple programming tasks. Each one of the tiny motile blocks, less than a millimeter in length, had a picoprocessor. One programmed them to create. If there was any item of luxury in the room, it was the wall-sized image of the wintry indigo wastes of λ Serpens II, newest of the settled worlds. To one side was a portable console, the screen illuminated, and to the other a couch which would serve as a bed. The furthermost wall opened into tiny sanitation and service booths.

The sight was more bitter than he expected. Though he had spent many years in starship quarters no larger, and felt no confinement underseas in ringsol six, he had ensured, while his children were growing up, that they did so in the best surroundings, with space, sunlight, air, security, and the company of other children and adults. The family hall had been on one of the newest outlying platforms, open, low built, with abundant facilities and diversions. Cybele had flourished in it. He would not have expected her to flourish here.

She saw him looking around. "I know it's not the way you brought me up, but it suffices." And when he said nothing, "Can I get you something?"

"Yes," he said, but held the cup she brought him between his hands, not drinking it. "Were you working?"

"Yes."

She serviced the human genetics database of the AOC. She monitored the automatic data-transfer subroutines and reported on irregularities. It was highly confidential work, but menial.

"I'm doing some development work now. It has a bonus attached to it."

She had always had his face, this daughter of his. She looked more like him than he thought a daughter should, ascetic, androgynous. She was wearing a straight, high-collared tunic and trousers in unshaped silk. Neither the color, pale yellow, with a bluish luster, nor the style became her. Her hair was very short, coarse, wavy, lying almost like leaves; his color, light brown, her mother's texture. Her eyes were brown, but could in certain lights and moods look coppery. She was analytical, ambitious, single-minded. She had his face, and his limitations. As she had cast at him, were he now to apply for space-crew, he would be ineligible. As she was ineligible. As anyone who could not support the highest level of neural-cybernetic interfacing was now ineligible.

At twenty-one she had announced her determination to join the space exploration service. She had asked him to help fund the enhancements which would adjust her neuronal circuits to compensate for traits not inborn. Three centuries of exploration salary and bonuses made him more than able. He had refused.

He set his untasted cup on the floor, there being nowhere else to place it. "I am sorry," he said, "so much time has passed." That did not seem enough. "I am sorry," he tried again, "I *let* so much time pass. I do not have a good sense of time." The children had grounded him in time, he thought, with their growing. When they left, he had grown careless.

A ripple of expression passed across her face; he read irony, bitterness, and a kind of satisfaction. "It takes two," she said, directly, and faced him, waiting with a degree of defiance for what he would say next. He was reminded, unusually, of his son, who still confronted him with a childish insistence that it was *his* life, that he was an adult, able to exercise his own judgment. But for all they were of an age, decanted within days of each other, Cybele had always seemed, and acted, the elder. Whatever his regrets, upon her lifestyle at least he felt unentitled to remark. She was right, as an adult, the responsibility was hers as much as it was his.

"Yesterday," he said, "Rache brought a body back to the ringsol. According to him, he had come upon it by chance in the floating forests west of here. She was adaptive."

"She?"

"Yes. Female, age eighteen or so." He went quickly on, "I offered to do the genetics to identify her, but Rache said no. He wanted only the minimum to establish cause of death. I screened for toxins and found nixiaxin. But I noticed some peculiarities in the appearance of the tissues and surveyed the blood and muscle oxygen carriers, and found their binding behavior anomalous." He paused, finding himself suddenly unwilling to confess to this upright daughter of his: "I sequenced the genome." She raised her brows. Genetic information was scrupulously protected. Physicians had a certain privilege, but a full analysis pressed at its limits. He said, "I thought you might be able to tell me whether there are adaptations not included in the public access database."

He held out the fiche, and with it, the unlabeled vial of bone marrow he had drawn from the corpse. "To my understanding," Adam said, "there are eighteen approved variants of the globin locus, and hers is not one of them."

She lifted vial and fiche from his fingers, and stood looking at him. "All the approved adaptations are in the public database. It's law."

Adam said, "I modeled the likelihood of the origin in spontaneous mutation. Without a family tree I could only set lower bounds based upon the age in the population of each of the eighteen variants."

"And?"

"No. And nor are any of the other usual targets for adaptation."

Unapproved adaptation was flagrantly illegal, and the punishments as great as noncapital justice allowed. As were the rewards for information leading to a prosecution.

She turned to the console, loaded the fiche, and slid her hand into the cradle. Transcutaneous fibers synapsed with console input. He remembered her struggle to master the silent interface, and watched her with quiet satisfaction as she brought up his alignments. ". . . oxygen transport . . . ion channels . . . relating expression of oxygen transporters to long-term physiological demands." Symbols danced across the screen. "That's been proposed, but not implemented. You're not supposed to see this, remember: this is the database of proposed modifications . . ." He murmured assent, if that were needed. "Look at the way they've handled iron uptake and storage, relying upon food supplements . . . but yours: intestinal iron transporters are upregulated, ferritin storage is up-regulated, prior to increased synthesis . . ." She sketched a crude simulation, showing the mechanism at work. "Look at the feedbacks. This has to be near the limit of what can be achieved by postnatal transfection . . . There could be a whole laboratory, with medical support, but who . . ." The display flickered as she lost, and then regained control of the interface. "There," she said, with strain in her voice. "These are rejected submissions. No, that's not a

hit; that's not; that might be a rough proposal of the ferritin storage modification . . . Ah, it's going to need more
information. If I could identify her last legitimately modified antecedents—that should be straightforward
enough . . . eighteen years old, you said . . . Do you mind
if I speak to Karel? He . . . might be able to tell me more."

She had matured if she were willing to involve her
brother, whom random genetic chance had gifted their
mother's aptitude for integrated circuitry. Her brother,
who would have been an acceptable recruit to space
exploration, preferred the comforts and diversions of
planetary life. Karel was aide to the director of the AOC
himself, Cesar Kamehameha, who liked his assistants
gifted, but distractible.

"I brought it," Adam said, "to you. To do with as
you thought best."

The display wavered again. She drew her hand from
the cradle and laid it down beside the screen. "I cannot
do this kind of investigation by myself."

"No, but you can analyze the lineage, and the
archives, and perhaps identify who might have done the
work, and where. That in itself will be worth something."

"I thought," she said, in an edged voice, "you
would be more shocked."

"I do not see so large a difference between legal and
illegal adaptation. Both are equally unacceptable in the
eyes of God."

"I . . . don't want to argue religion and morality
with you."

"Nor do I, with you."

She sketched a smile. "What a change."

"Anything you gain from this, you will earn."

"I've had the mineralization enhancements," she
said, abruptly.

The very modifications he had declined. Those were relatively cheap, and simple. He said, neutrally, "Ever hopeful."

She said, "If I were not hopeful, I do not think I would be able to stand this." Her hand took in the small, drab room, the console.

He said, "If I may—" not sure of what he might offer.

"No, you may not," she said, sharply. "You *could* have helped me four years ago. Now I can do it alone."

After a moment, Adam said, "Aboard ship you will spend years in rooms not unlike this one. Your weight allocation is restricted, and personal luxuries are few. If you are on an established route, you have the escape of coldsleep. If you are not, if you are routemapping, then a full watch stays awake throughout to observe. One to seven years of your precious life passes in tedium, irritation, and close confinement. We would not treat social or criminal offenders so poorly. Or," he said, ironically, "are you simply trying to train yourself?"

"No," she said, angry now. "I'm doing it because it is the fastest way that I can achieve my goal. I'm doing it for the same reason you did it: for the exploration. To be among the first to stand on a new planet."

"If you are lucky," Adam said, "you will do that maybe twice in your life. You will stand there in environment suit and helmet, isolated in yourself and from what you have come so far to touch . . ." His fingers spread before him, of their own volition. His body remembered. But that was part of it, the sense of utter isolation, of having stepped away from humanity and its concerns. The holding of the breath and waiting with a mind peeled raw with prayer. He could not tell her that. He did not fear her laughter, or her misunderstanding;

he feared, instead, confirmation that she, too, was damned to listen to the terrible silences of God. He said, "The rest of the time you will spend ferrying settlers and equipment along a route that's not quite established enough to automate."

Her voice was brittle. "But you did it, for a hundred years. Mother did it, does it still, left you, and us, to do it. *Caruso*'s overhead, due to drop and lift tomorrow. You'll be there, won't you? As you've been there before." She flushed suddenly. "I've seen you," she muttered.

"And I," said Adam, his voice uneven, "have seen you."

She stood up from the console, pressing down on it with both hands. "I cannot believe this is happening," she said. "It cannot last; we will argue. You have not changed. And I still want the same as I did before, more than ever, and I will do whatever I must to get it."

There was a silence. Adam said, "You act as though you were exclusively wronged in being frustrated in your desires. You will achieve them anyway, in time. We both knew that, from the very start. All you wanted was to have your way made easier."

"That was not what—"

"You act," Adam said steadily, "as though you were wronged. Yes, I denied you what you wanted. And maybe it seemed to you that I had denied it you forever. Maybe I was, in your eyes, that powerful. But you asked me to sacrifice my beliefs—my faith—for you. To me, it looked as though you wanted me to go against *everything* I believed about the sanctity of the divine plan—that we be able to work out our destiny without interfering with the substance of ourselves and it—for your *whim*, Cybele, which you could realize by your own efforts. I did not realize that what you wanted was a proof of love."

"Wasn't it obvious?" she said bitterly.

"Not to me. Was it to you?"

She sat down in the console chair, hunched in her shapeless tunic, and did not answer.

"Space explorers tend toward romanticism. It is the only way we can last the small rooms and the long, tedious hours. An active fantasy life and a belief in grandness, our own and the universe's. You demand grand sacrifices. I hold to the tenets of an ancient, reactionary faith."

"Don't make fun of yourself." She snatched her head up. "Or are you making fun of me?"

"No. Neither."

"And if—you had understood that what I wanted was a proof of love—would you? No, don't answer that. Don't answer that." The highlights on her tunic shivered as she drew a long breath, and straightened. "When do you have to be back on ringsol six?"

"I asked for the night."

Another deep, steadying breath. "Do you like your work? I would think you do: more like a spaceship than anything else on Blueheart. What do you think of Rache?"

"He's an extraordinarily able administrator, if overly . . . personal in his approach." He recalled the gravity in the administrator's heavy face as he gave him leave. As though there were something Rache understood that he did not. He looked over at the vial of dark red marrow resting beside his daughter's long fingers. It was long past the time that he and Cybele tried to repair their breach. He had merely taken an offered opportunity. What she chose to do with what he had given her was her decision.

The universe had moved on, and all God would have from him was his faith and his grief. He would mourn the passing of God's original creation, man, nature, the stars and planets, as God had first fashioned them and meant them to be. Surely if his grief were great enough, God would be satisfied with that alone.

He was aware of a silence that had fallen. He said, "About everything else, we disagree."

"Do you think *he* could be aware of the illegal adaptation?"

"I did wonder. I have heard conflicting accounts of his relationship with the adaptive community. His kin were evidently opposed to his choice of career; I believe he was estranged for a time. But he goes back now, and the boy Daven has come with him . . . that may indicate an improvement. And then, he is married . . . Whatever that means among adaptives, since it is more usual than not for all the children of one mother to have different fathers."

Cybele gave him a thin smile. "One thing ringsol six has done for you: given you a taste for low gossip."

"I was merely describing the nature of Rache's ties to the adaptive community, as part of the answer to your question. But as to your question—it is hard, very hard, to say." He realized he was tempted to believe it. Some primitive righteousness in him would equate body and soul and say that the adaptive's warped body would house a warped soul. But that was a teaching of a long-ago childhood, unworthy of the man he was now. His experience of humanity was in some ways vast, and in some ways very limited. He had spread his life over three centuries, and over most of inhabited space. Yet he spent most of that life cloistered aboard ship, with companions in handfuls of dozens, for years on end. By journey's end he had known the breadths, the depths, the dissonances, and the harmonies of those few people. He knew what a human being could be. And despite his gross frame and uncouth, tribal manners, Rache was human. He said, "I—tend to believe that what we are expresses itself in the smallest matters as well as the largest."

"That, I know," said the daughter he had reared and disciplined.

"I have never caught Rache in even a small deceit," Adam said.

"Even so," Cybele said, "this has to involve a great many people, adaptive and probably primary. Rache would be ideally placed—"

"Would he? Would he not be better placed in medical? That is where I would look first, among medically trained adaptives, particularly those who were trained after the trouble forty years ago over lack of follow-up of adaptation. Rache's own sister was one of the casualties. So the question, then, is whether that experience would lead Rache to favor all possible safeguards, or whether he would no longer trust primaries to serve his people and support adaptive control. Or whether, as I suspect it would be, it is more complicated than that."

"But he instructed you not to sequence."

"Professional etiquette would demand that the laboratory which did the original adaptation do the autopsy and the sequencing. Rache knows it. I know it."

"But nevertheless," Cybele said, with a half-smile.

"Nevertheless."

Daven returned just before dawn. Rache had spent an unrestful night, not entirely on Daven's account. The return to gravity after a period in the sea always left him aching; no dryland bed could give the repose of the sea. Some time before dawn he turned on the light and began to draft the program of development of the proposal. When the dutynet advised him of Daven's arrival he had to resist the urge to check immediately via the lock camera. *Damn* the boy: coming back through the storm, *and* no doubt diving down here without breath-assist. He would be exhausted: he deserved to be. Rache remembered swimming through storms himself, but never—well, almost never—alone, and never—well, almost never—at night. The effort was unrelenting: one had to surface to breathe, amid spume, rain, and pitching waves, and then dive beneath the surface turmoil to swim. Surface, breathe, dive and swim; surface, breathe, dive and swim, with day scarcely lighter than night, all skymarks obscured, tumbling and struggling in gray twilight or utter blackness. Trusting to an unbroken compass or an undisordered directional sense and a simple faith that one was indeed moving forward. Rache drummed his fingers on the console and tried to think what to say that would discharge his anxieties without rousing Daven's defiance. When he judged the lock should have emptied, he opened a sound channel: "Daven?"

A silence. "Yes."

"Glad to have you back. Come by my quarters, if you're not too tired."

Daven presented himself several minutes later. His very manner said this was a presentation. He had pulled on a shirt and briefs, leaving his legs bare, and still wet. His face was pinched with fatigue, and, Rache thought, the lingering impress of fear. Rache said, "I suggested that you stay over at the relay station."

"Yes."

Rache said, more gently, "Do you now understand why?"

Daven conceded with a single nod, and Rache let it be. The essential lesson here was the stupidity of risk-taking simply to prove one's independence. There was no authority higher or more impersonal than the sea, and if Daven appreciated that, Rache should say no more.

"Did you get the message sent?"

"Yes."

"Any response while you were there?"

"No."

Because you waited no time at all, Rache said to himself. You did not even wait to see how the storm was developing. Was I as much a fool at seventeen? Surely. He suppressed a sigh.

"I've had some unexpected news," he said. "The extrapolation proposal has been yellow-striped."

Daven frowned slightly. "That is good, isn't it?"

"Yes," Rache said, with exaggerated forbearance. "It is good." He was rewarded by a faint apologetic smile.

"What happens now?" Daven asked politely.

"*Now* I will have enough resources to start to develop the proposal properly," Rache said, with enthusiasm. "With the yellow-striping comes an allocation of half a dozen personnel to work directly on supporting research, or detailed simulations—though I'd say we'll be nowhere near having detail enough for simulation before the next round; there's still so much basic research and qualitative development needing done. We'll have to explore the consequences of introduction of offworld species to Blueheart waters. *I* think that if we are going to preserve Blueheart waters then we should preserve them as they are; but I'm in a minority. We'll have to know exactly what we can introduce without endangering Blueheart species or habitats. The difficulty with a marine environment is that it will be impossible to set up preserves for native or imported wildlife—the sea knows no boundaries. We shall have to investigate, in detail, the effect of a full human population on Blueheart, what numbers we might expect the environment to sustain. We shall have to look at the prospective developments in adaptive society, in rafttown/island society, and in the relationship between the two, and that will need a sociologist. That's going to be the difficult appointment. I'll have to tread lightly concerning the issue of human adaptation."

"Why?" Daven said, stiffening. "Aren't you doing this *for* us?"

Fools rush in, thought Rache. He said, "Yes, I am. But not everybody accepts that human adaptation should happen. And those who do think it is a passing thing, which will allow us to settle and explore new environments prior to terraforming. It will take time for them to come to terms with the possibility of having people adapted to Blueheart seas beyond the time of data gathering."

"Why? What is wrong with adaptation? What is wrong," the youth said, nostrils flaring, "with *us*?"

Rache waved a hand, gesturing him toward a chair. "Nothing, as far as I am concerned. But as to their reasons: some think it entails needless suffering and risk. Some people do not want to be obliged to choose for their children. Religious reasons: some believe that adaptation interferes with God's creation and plan. Aesthetic reasons: they find the bodily changes unappealing. Political and social . . . complexities: people make many assumptions based upon your body-type. Investment, social, financial, and intellectual, in a future for Blue-heart that involves changing it to a primary habitat. Concern that the interests of primaries and pastorals cannot, over the long term, be reconciled, and that we will create a divided population." He said, gently, in answer to Daven's expression, "They are all fair and valid reasons."

"Why can't they just leave us alone!"

"It is their planet, too."

"It is their planet, entirely, to them," Daven returned. "They would change it so much that *we* couldn't even live in it."

"I know. That is what I would like to prevent."

Daven gave him a fierce look. "How? You live just like them." He gestured, taking in the bed, the workstation swung over the bed, the wide chair, purpose-built for Rache, the shelves, cupboards, viewscreen, flooring, and walls. "You *like* living just like them. Talking about your studies and your proposal. Working with them, even though you know what they'd do to Blueheart if they could. Doing survey work, even though you know what they're going to do with it."

Rache took a deep breath, willing himself to patience; God knew, he had had need enough to cultivate it. "You're not the first to say this to me, and you will not be the last. And you are not the first to whom I have tried to explain." Daven started to blurt something, and Rache said, forcefully, "*If you will but listen.*"

Daven's eyes widened, and he subsided, but before Rache could say more, he said, sullenly, "It was because of Juniper."

"Juniper?" Rache said, startled.

"The reason you left Scole. The reason you are doing this. Einar told me about Juniper, about you leaving Scole, leaving your marriage, leaving your wife." An ominous flash of dark eyes from lowered brows. Rache had no doubt what Daven had heard, and how. Einar, Daven's elder brother, and for a time Rache's son in all but blood, had never forgiven any of it.

Rache laced thick fingers on his stomach. "Juniper was only the excuse. I left Scole because I wanted to." He let Daven absorb that.

"And Lisel?" Daven said, brittle. "You wanted to leave Lisel."

Though he had known it must come, if old scandals were being stirred, he still flinched within his skin at his wife's name. He said, "I left Scole, yes, and because Lisel would not come with me, I left her. But I did not want to leave her. I thought her my wife still." And did so even now, though it was sixteen years since he had found her gone from Scole. He said, "Juniper Blane Berenice was an artist. Berenici—from β Coma Berenices III. Her speciality was in-time editing, but what they called free-intercalative: she used archived material at will to develop her theme. You'd have to see her work to appreciate it." And have something to compare it with, Rache added silently, because Daven disdained Rossby's documentary art. Though Rache did, too; Juniper had ruined him for it. "When she came to Blueheart, she was already opposed to terraforming. Not out of any love of Blueheart, but rather because she tended to oppose orthodoxy of any and all kinds, and terraforming is the greatest orthodoxy of our age. But Juniper fell in love with the seas, and began to visit pastoral holdfasts, and even nomadic rafts. She was an extremely persistent, persuasive and, when she chose to be, charming woman. And for me, she represented a life beyond the seas."

Daven's face showed a flicker of resentment that he could be so drawn into such an unbecoming story. But he was drawn, Rache saw it.

"I was almost thirty," Rache said. "I thought I had learned everything the seas had to teach. Lisel and I were childless; I did not have a new generation to teach, to absorb me. I did not want to live out the next hundred and seventy years as a neo-primitive; I wanted the experience that the rafttowns had to give. When Juniper came to Scole, I was ready to leave.

"I am not the first to leave a holdfast for the rafttowns; I am merely the first that you know of. I wanted a different life than the one I had. And it was not until I came here that I truly learned to value what I had on Scole, and in the seas. I never thought of the need to work to preserve Blueheart until I left Scole. In Scole, in the seas, there is the sense that the way it is is the way it has always been, and the way it always will be. It is an illusion; our past is a mere two and a half centuries long, and our future, likely not even one."

Daven got suddenly to his feet. "I'm tired," he said.

Rache looked at him a moment. "I'm sorry," he said, not entirely kindly. "You are too young to be learning this; I, after all, was in my thirties." Daven stiffened at the goad. "I wish I understood," Rache said, "why you wanted to come here."

"I wanted to see," Daven said, to his feet, "if what they said about you, and primaries, was true."

"That is a beginning," Rache said. "You were raised, as I was raised, in the expectation of a life in the seas. It was not realistic for me, and that is doubly so for you. Well within your lifetime, the development plan will be decided and implemented. It is a decision which will be made with or without pastorals. You see me as an outcast from Scole. It is, and always has been, more complicated than that. They need me. As I need them. But it is not an easy gyre to swim, not one to be undertaken lightly." He could have said more, much more, but he remembered being seventeen, and received wisdom being about as useful as chlorophyll in the abyss.

"Everyone's so sure. You. Einar. Tove."

Rache grunted, unflattered. Daven's brother was a man in search of a quarrel, and Tove, Rache's grandmother, exerted an influence as subtle, fluid, and inexorable as the equatorial current on the affairs of Scole and the seas beyond. He had always thought of himself as a reasonable man undeserving of such comparisons. "It will come," he said. "It will come in time."

When the boy had gone, Rache lay on his side, looking at the empty chair. Surer than ever that he had done Daven a disservice, perhaps even harm, by encouraging him to come here. Daven only valued what he did not have. Respect from the contemptuous, love from the indifferent. He would never be happy, always be wounded and wounding. He could not make an unpopular choice, and live well in it. His very nature condemned him to orthodoxy, even as it made him look for something more.

I should let him go, Rache thought. The gift of someone's presence is not a gift to keep.

And I was not truthful with him, not about the full price I paid. Sixteen years, and scarcely a day went by when he did not think of Lisel. He had never looked for her, in part because he had no idea where to look, where she might have come from, where she might go. She was, she said lightly, warningly, merely flotsam. He had found her, as he and Daven found the dead girl, adrift in the rubble outside Scole's wave barriers. He had been swimming out to the place where Athene had died, when he heard the clicker slung from her belt. She was sunstruck, Medusa-lashed, delirious, and half strangled by the bubble-weed she had wound around her head and chest. He was awed. He had himself been stung once, and would have drowned in thrashing agony, were it not for his companions. By the time she had recovered, he was deeply in love, with the strength, the stubbornness, the survivor in her. He wanted to know everything about her. But all his curiosity did was convince her that if he knew where she came from he would be over there trying to fix the rift—which he would have been, since then he had no idea that it was possible to live without family and holdfast.

The greatest grief of their marriage was that they were childless. Lisel had utterly refused to seek assistance from the rafttowns. He could go if he wanted, she told him, but he took her as she was, as she came, as he found her. They had been caretakers to Einar, Rache's brother's child, and that had been compensation of a sort.

Their marriage had lasted eight years beyond his leaving. For him, the long separations enriched expectation. From the moment of separation, he accumulated observations, reflections, questions, experiences in anticipation of their next meeting. Nothing he offered her was returned unchanged. Lisel was his third eye. He had thought he had her consent, or if not that, her forgiveness. When they married, they had made promises to each other. Most people made promises they wanted to keep, and thought they could keep. Even at twenty he had known that he and Lisel had taken the harder course: they had made the promises that they feared they could not keep. They had made the subject of their quarrels bind them together. They had not spoken of harmony, fidelity, or children. They had promised the holding of each other's secrets and the realization of each other's dreams. Those seemed the highest promises they could make, and were the very promises they should not have made. For by those promises he had to follow Juniper Blane Berenice, and she had to remain in the sea.

And one day he returned to Scole and she was gone. She had left no message then, but one, and that wordless, and there had been no message since. Einar, bitter at his own abandonment, had utterly refused to tell Rache anything he might have known. Rache knew, from the occasional mention, that Lisel had not died, that she was still alive somewhere out in the seas. And she would know, likewise, that he was still alive; she would know where to find him, should she choose.

When the door chimed, Rache sat up immediately, bolting from his thoughts. "Come!"

The visitor was the net manager, Oliver. He pleated his spindly two-meter height through the door and announced, "I've had an idea!" Oliver had been born on one of the Arcturan orbital colonies, and had never known full gravity before Blueheart's; he still wore a full exoskeleton, despite Adam's insistence that there was no longer any physical need. He had originally signed as a cybernetics expert aboard a Blueheart-bound ramscoop cruiser. By journey's end he was determined that, penalties notwithstanding, he was not reboarding. Some of his considerable debt was repaid by settler's provenance; the remainder he was content to work off over years. He put Rache in mind of a strip of ribbongrass, long, narrow in one dimension, flat in the other. Too insubstantial to loom over people, he curled.

Oliver's ideas were abundant, inventive, and on occasion catastrophic. He said, "It's something from the synthetic intelligence sunstream." Rache jammed pillows at his back and swung the console over to Oliver. Oliver perched on the edge of the bed, grimacing slightly as the exoskeleton resisted his movement. Despite his gangling frame, he had the same thoughtful precision of movement as the diminutive Adam. It was a discipline learned in confined environments. His face managed to be both awkward and delicate, stretched between four sharp points: chin, nose, and cheekbones. After a prolonged flirtation with divers' chic, he had let his hair regrow into a blond thicket. His hand, half the width of Rache's, but nearly twice its length, twitched and shuffled in the cradle as he tried to nudge the interface's adjustment. Symbols flew across the screen. Though he had taken standard cercortex implantation, and stored many of his confidential files internally, Rache had come to it too late to master the internal interface. He had developed a symbolic shorthand. Oliver delighted in the novelty, and had refined it further.

"See," said Oliver, his free hand tapping at symbols in their flight. "This is a simulation. It's extending the design of the immediate dynamic net to the future dynamic net." He regarded Rache with a bright, begging eye. Rache looked back at him, expressionlessly. He had learned that Oliver was ready to seize upon the least encouragement. In all innocence, and with such penitence and abject remorse at any misunderstanding that it was for Rache's own peace of mind that he tried to spare them both. "I see," said Oliver. "You want it from the beginning. Can I leave out the Big Bang and the cooling of the Earth . . . ? In the beginning: information storage was linear, with a direct one-to-one representation of data in storage. Which was fine as long as increases in hardware continued to outstrip demands on the system. Once increases in processing speed turned asymptotic, then the system complexity problem had to be dealt with, which drove the shift from analog to parallel processing.

"In the middle, parallel processing gave rise to the immediate dynamic net, where there is no longer a one-to-one representation, but a reduced representation which references an expansion base: information, instead of being simply lodged, is shifted so it can be accessed as needed. But even that has certain limits, in that the referencing has to be recalled, and the recall takes time.

"So *now* what they've developed on Earth and Chara is a contextually anticipatory dynamic net, and the idea behind it is that you can generally *tell* by what's gone before what should be needed next, and so you scan ahead and start moving everything into place before it's needed. And of course all of this is integrated into the autodidactic systems that we already have so that the system teaches itself from the responses of the user what the requirements have been. But all of this is, of course, extrapolation from past experience, and one of these days someone's going to have to teach computers how to foretell the future. That'd solve all our problems."

"It would?" Rache murmured.

Oliver grinned. "I've downloaded a public domain version of the CADyN installer; I've done some trials in my own area, and it's impressive. I'd like to implement it." A pause, in which Rache, knowing Oliver, waited, and Oliver looked back like a moth caught in a lamp. "The implementation's by tutor virus," he confessed, and rushed on. "And I want to turn it loose in your system, yes, pretty please, Rache. It would take months otherwise. Without committee meetings, and without having to explain to everyone *why* it's an improvement and why their latest lost databyte had nothing to do with the implementation. This way, the worst, the very worst, is that the whole information system crashes hideously, I have to restore from backup, and spend the next three days groveling, snuffling and repenting, and listening to reactionaries complain about over-enthusiastic system operators who think that the net is their personal playground and not a system intended to support serious committed scientific work. And if it does work as the model says it should, everybody will think it just dropped from heaven as a reward for diligence and virtue." He folded his long hands, prayerlike. "So," he said, taking a huge breath, "I thought you could send a memo out telling everyone to offline anything they did not want modified. I've noticed that nobody dares tell you they didn't know about one of your memos."

"I haven't agreed yet," Rache said.

Oliver leaned back against the exo-brace, and folded his arms. "Name your price. Exotic drinks? Exotic artwork? Exotic oligochaeta Serpensa? I know your weaknesses," he finished, slyly.

"The only worms you know are virtual. My price is that you convince me that your tutorial virus will confine its rewriting of our net code to the information systems only and utterly. It will not affect *any* of the instrumentation, life-support and maintenance, or mechanical systems."

"I *knew* you'd say that. Let me show you."

Rache leaned over to study the symbols, more intently than hitherto. Rache's obsessive attention to safety was one of his minor notorieties. And station-born Oliver did not take it lightly; he had come prepared to explain, in more detail than even Rache demanded, how he planned to contain the virus and protect the ringsol's essential systems.

"All right," Rache said, at last, lifted hand parting the space. "I want you to prepare a system-flush followed by an emergency system upload, one which puts the habitat systems in place first."

"I've got an interferon—"

"An emergency is no time for elegance. Prepare a system-flush."

"It won't be an emergency—"

"I always," Rache said, "plan for emergencies."

THREE

In the morning, under the leading edge of the storm, Adam de Courcey and his daughter went to the landing platform on the very outskirts of Rossby to watch *Caruso*'s dropcapsule land. Overhead, in orbit, the ramjet waited to land and lift passengers and payload before boosting outsystem to its next destination. The passengers would be few and the payload small; given the expense of intersystem travel only uniquely skilled individuals and irreproducible artifacts were transported. Following the years of settlement, and the seeding ships, each settled planet had to be self-sufficient in materials. Trade was entirely in the form of information. *Caruso*'s last call had been at λ Serpens II, sixteen years ago. In hibernation, passengers and crew aged but a few months: in this era this was a routine transit, but Adam remembered a five-year shift from two centuries ago.

The drop platform was a thrust-dented, tarnished bowl five hundred meters across. Adam and Cybele leaned shoulder to shoulder against the screen of the gallery on the adjacent platform, five levels up, looking down into the bowl. Other watchers were strung thinly the length of the screen, here, on the two adjacent platforms, and on the walkway adjoining the levels. Most were, like Adam and Cybele, clad and waterproofed. A few stood bare-skinned, melanin-black or ruddy, body-painted and oiled, letting the warm rain pour over them.

Beyond the landing stage, the sea ran heavy and gray green. Adam could feel the pitch, and the slight immediate shock of the waves. Rain blistered the heaving gray water in the channel between the platforms. Warm rain gusted into their faces. Were he alone, Adam might have forgone this drop. Having lived thirty years of still-life, he now wondered whether exploration should ever have been undertaken. When seemingly inevitably it led to this: the blurring and corruption of the original divine design.

He glanced sideways at her expectant, upturned face. She had accused him of being covetous of his God. He had been so many years aboard ship that he had become unaccustomed to sharing worship; he had gone so long unchallenged in his private devotions that he begrudged sharing, and the challenge that it brought. She had challenged him in the past; she would again, and he would regret for a long time the four years he had lost. He saw her catch her breath, gasp in rain, will herself not to cough. He looked up, at the dropcapsule falling near and sudden through the obscuring rain. Cybele's lips stretched back in an expression half-smile, half-grimace. Adam watched her, until he heard the resonance of the dropcapsule's contact with the platform. Hot vapor gouted against the screen. Unseen, deep within the platform, vast stores of compressed air would void into evacuated tanks, providing buoyancy to match the downthrust. The dropcapsule settled, the engines quieted. The channel churned as screw engines controlled the rebound; nevertheless, the platform heaved, and its sheer gray side rose toward them. Vents opened all around the rim of the platform, venting the ballast tanks with a hundred-voiced shriek. The platform gradually receded. Seawater jetted from the rim of the bowl, cooling platform and capsule. Wind and rain and escaping air shredded the steam.

The cooling water drained away; the vented air screamed to silence; beneath their feet the churning abated and the waves trained by. Cybele sighed. Above the lift-stage a hatch opened, and a transparent capsule slid like an immense drop of water down its side. He could see the people within, a dark knot with a feathering of hands reaching out to feel the transparent walls. He had always found the transparent transport capsules unsettling, himself, and never more so than when he was set down for the last time. In the slope of the platform, a door opened; a second capsule emerged. The two circled each other, daintily; the first continued to the door in the platform, and disappeared within, the second crawled up the side of the capsule and was folded away within tarnished metal. Cybele said quietly, "Ah."

A pause, while the buoyancy compensators prepared, and reset, and then the dropcapsule began to lift. To Adam, this was the most breathtaking moment, this meeting of forces: gravity and thrust, thrust and buoyancy. The dropcapsule balanced upon its solid, shimmering column of air, while the screws churned the water to a white lace, and deep within the platform air exploded into water-filled tanks. The platform shuddered, sluggishly, and sank. Cybele, beside him, hands pressed to the screen, held her breath. She watched the dropship, he the platform. As the ship lifted beyond the height of the tallest part of the rafttown, the platform began to rise out of the sea. Screws reversed, vented air shrieked; unheard, the dropcapsule mounted the rain and disappeared, well below the clouds. Cybele wiped rain from her face. Adam felt strangely tranquil. Not unmoved, but tranquil. They stood, side by side, in unbroken silence, while the other watchers dispersed, some moving toward the bridge to the landing platform.

"I suppose," Cybele started, huskily, "you should go back undersea." She cleared her throat. "And I . . . should go to work. I'll come with you down to the docks. Sometimes I forget," an odd smile, "forget there is a city outside my room and the AOC."

"I meant it when I said I would help you with your living expenses."

A dangerous light came into her rain-washed eyes. "And I meant it when I said I did not need your help."

"And I heard," said Adam, and thought better of anything more.

"Look." Cybele pointed past him. "Those must be the people dropped." A straggling line of figures appeared at the far end of the covered bridge which led off the platform. Adam sympathized: reawakening was still disorientating, even without the new environment, and time-lag. They would likely all be expert-voyagers, that rare breed of human accomplished enough in some speciality to be worth transporting across interstellar distance. For most specialists, both expense and time were against them; even in the short transit between λ Serpens II and Blueheart flesh and mind lagged by a decade the information carried at lightspeed on the sun-streams. From Earth to Blueheart, the disparity was over sixty years. To be an expert-voyager, one had to be able to update, reintegrate, and innovate, and to do so more rapidly and effectively than any still-lifer. Those who could were a valued commodity, whose skills—because of the exigencies of travel—were contracted decades in advance. They would be met, they were being met, by representatives of their sponsors, and steered to reorientation and upgrading. Very little of the commonplace would be allowed to trouble or impinge. Their lives would be in many ways not unlike his as it used to be, demanding, attenuated, sheltered.

Cybele said suddenly, "One's been left behind."

Adam shielded his eyes against the rain. He could see the woman now, part way onto the bridge, standing sideways and gripping the hand-rail with both hands. She was in no danger of being blown over—the bridge had mesh sides—but she looked unsteady and disorientated. She was still wearing the paper clothing given her in the dropship: hibernation passengers carried nothing with them. Her trousers were darkening with rain.

Cybele said, "She looks like mother," and started along the balcony, breaking quickly into a run. Adam called after her; she seemed not to hear. Or affected not to hear, as she had at four, five, seven years old. He ran after her. The woman was not Cybele's mother, as Cybele herself would realize if she but paused. Abra mother was still asleep in space, inward bound to η Boötes IV; by the time she returned, if she returned, Adam would be years dead and their children aged. Cybele was going to embarrass herself, and anger a stranger.

But by the time he reached her, Cybele was saying in an ordinary voice, "The bridges get blown about even worse if they're closed." The strange woman still clung to the railing, but one-handed, and had half-turned to face Cybele. As Adam arrived, she said, "This is my father. He's a doctor."

"I don't . . ." the woman said, in a husky voice, "need a doctor. I need somewhere . . . still. Somewhere dry."

Close up, Adam could see how Cybele had been mistaken. Abra had been Berenici: from β Coma

Berenices III. So was this woman, unmistakably. Berenices III was twelve generations past completion of terraforming and reversion to human type, but the descendants of the adaptives remained stocky, deep in the chest, and olive-skinned, to suit an environment still arid and thin-aired. Her hair was as coarse as Cybele's, but glossy black; she wore it in a single heavy plait down her back. She looked to be in her early forties, but a voyager's body aged only in the waking hours. She could be well over a century old.

But there was more. She was not Abra, but she was cerily familiar. "Was someone meeting you?" Her eyes slid past him, unfocusing. They were a peculiarly featureless brown, almost devoid of markings, of texture. He had seen eyes like that before.

He was still staring at her eyes when Cybele said sharply, "Don't do that."

Adam realized what he had seen, and reinforced his daughter's objection with his own authority. "You shouldn't direct-contact the net for a few hours. Not if you're an expert-voyager who usually works in a meditative state. Any slowing of your metabolism could re-trigger some of the hibernation mechanisms."

She dipped her black head, slowly, accepting, but with no humility. Rain lashed across her face, making her jaw tighten. Adam said, "I was an exploration-physician. My daughter is an exploration-aspirant." He made it stand as both explanation and apology.

The woman said nothing, blinking rain from her eyelashes.

"May we do anything for you?"

She looked at him properly for the first time. Before he thought better of it, he said, "Forgive me, but—have we met?"

There was a silence. Cybele was staring at him. The woman's eyes shifted away from him. Adam started to apologize, but in a quiet voice the woman said, "You might have met my twin." She looked up at him again. "Juniper Blane Berenice."

Adam moved a protective step toward Cybele. Caught himself before either noticed. He had indeed met Juniper Blane Berenice.

"But she disappeared—" Cybele checked herself, as she tallied the numbers. Disappeared, presumed drowned, twenty-one years ago. *Caruso*'s last stop was λ Serpens II. Six point five years for a transmission, sixteen years for a ship; no message could have reached her before she left.

"I know."

Just that, a stark assertion of a knowledge only hours old. Adam was one of the few to know what it was to step in and out of time, to land in places where one's fresh griefs were old losses, and one's hoped-for meetings gone to dust. She was soaked from the waist down, the paper clothing crumpled and clinging. Adam found himself moved to a wary compassion. He said, "I am Adam de Courcey Indi. My daughter, Cybele de Courcey Blueheart." He paused, awaiting recognition. To his relief there was none. "Let us see you to shelter."

"I am Teal Blane Berenice. And I thank you."

Cybele led, Teal at her shoulder, Adam followed. Adam could feel his daughter's curiosity, both about his past acquaintanceship, and about Teal's arrival. Let her ask no unseemly or, worse, revealing questions. "Do you need accommodation? Are you here to work?"

"I need accommodation. I am not here to work."

At the end of the bridge was a covered walkway, and within it, a public access terminal. Cybele went to it and fitted her hand into the cradle. Only Adam saw the fleeting hesitation before she did so, in front of the voyager. But the interface was simple enough, and Cybele's handling of it fluent. The expert-voyager stood at her side, watching. Without a word, she laid a finger on the screen, indicating her choice. Cybele withdrew her hand and let Teal take her place. The screen flickered; the visuals smeared into each other. Teal regarded the screen with half-closed eyes, her gaze internalized. Cybele drew breath; Adam laid a hand on her shoulder and she smiled slantwise at him, ruefully. The visuals slowed, returning the introductory schematic. Teal withdrew her hand, and looked around with a new appreciation. She said, "I have downloaded the orientation module. Thank you for your help. Adam. Cybele." She gave them a bare moment to acknowledge her thanks, and recognize the implied farewell. A few steps to the far side of the access terminal was a tubecapsule port. The portal slid aside, showing the small padded interior. She climbed in, and the door closed behind her.

Adam said, amused at Cybele's expression, "Expert-voyagers are not noted for their social graces. Being accustomed to interactions measured in nanoseconds, they find human interactions immeasurably protracted, and replete with redundancy."

"Was Abra like that?"

"She could be. But after nearly a hundred years together, we knew each other so well that we did not need social graces, or redundancy."

"It wasn't a hundred years," she said, rather truculently. "Not awake."

Adam said nothing. He eyed the rain cabling the glassed outer wall and the dark daylight outside. The readiness with which he had let Abra go had, at times, been a stresspoint with his children, usually when his own limitations as man and parent became marked. To the children Abra had appeared as both saint and demon. Saint because in her absence she could do no wrong. Demon because by her absence she had committed every wrong. Adam regretted that he could not better convey to them the flawed, dedicated woman he had known. She could not have stayed, planetbound, any more than he could have continued to travel—until his resources were spent—as a passenger in the ship where he had been crew. She had tried, for his sake. And had left him the best gifts she knew when she no longer could. How these years would have been without them, he did not know.

"You never said you knew Juniper Blane Berenice."

"She traveled to Blueheart with us on the *Maria Callas*."

"You never said you knew her."

"I saw no need."

"You mean you did not want the attention, when she disappeared."

"It was not that intimate a knowledge, Cybele."

Cybele frowned. "You never remember people's faces, Adam. What was she like?"

"Difficult," said Adam. "Clamorous. Charismatic. Extremely talented and confrontational."

"I—see. And she wanted Blueheart kept as it was, which would have involved permanent human adaptation. And you—" She feathered her hands. "She's the one who brought Rache ashore, isn't she? Are you going to tell him you met her sister?"

"No."

"Did you have an affair with her?" she asked, provocatively.

"No," said Adam, with unwanted emphasis. And a little tartly, "Curiosity about my affairs will not compensate you for the lack of your own."

She opened her mouth, closed it sharply, flushed. "I'm not planning to leave anyone behind."

Adam hesitated, and then committed himself to the necessary question. "Does this desire of yours to go into space have anything to do with the possibility of meeting Abra?"

"No," she said, readily. "I'd be curious but no more. I never had anything from her; she left us like a pair of pets so you would not be lonely." She gave him an edged, knowing smile, unsettling him. "Karel has her Berenici aptitudes; I'm your daughter." She fixed on him the clear-eyed appealing look of a much younger child.

"The . . . trouble is," Adam said, moved to a risky candor, "that in a long life one becomes . . . inextricably tangled with other people. Their secrets and burdens become one's own and mean that parts of oneself are no longer to be shared. I might not want to keep things from you, but I might be obliged to."

"That's the . . . kind of condition that makes someone want to uncover secrets. Out of love."

"I have known it happen, in the name of love. But love has little to do with the motivations and nothing to do with the consequences."

"I—see," she said. "I . . . don't want to argue with you again. So I'll take your warning. Only, don't leave it four years before you come again."

With the smallest of gestures he offered an embrace; she rushed forward to accept. He thought as he held her that he could understand Abra's preferring to leave these children in embryo. She knew what it was to do it otherwise, to do it later; she had done it otherwise, nearly a century ago on Berenice.

Cybele found her brother working alone in Cesar Kamehameha's aquarium-lined office at AOC headquarters. He lifted his glossy head, and grinned at her in mischievous delight.

Karel looked Berenici, like their mother, like the woman they had briefly aided by the dropship. He had the olive skin, the stocky build, the coarse, glossy black hair of the Berenici. From Adam, he had only the pale, gray eyes, oddly unsettling against the olive and black. He had inherited the Berenici complexes, product of an old eugenics project on early-settlement Berenice, which made him an optimal host for cortical implantation. He had received his first implants at the age of three; Cybele had been obliged to wait until she was six.

There were times she still bitterly resented his endowment. She was not sure she would resent it more, or less, if he had used it as she would have done. But Karel liked to play, and did so, turning to the world a sunny, feckless face. Only the nature of some of his play hinted at something darker in him. The skin of his wrists was stained with bruises. His clothing would hide the rest of the bruises; and there would be bruises, because he wore his shirt loose and unbelted, but buttoned to the throat. Cybele said, "Adam was on Rossby last night. I suppose I need not feel guilty we did not come and see you." Though she was but days his elder, she had always been the caretaker, the responsible one, the one to rescue him from his dangerous games, and spare him Adam's punishment.

Adulthood had alleviated, but not taken away her responsibility for his irresponsibility.

Karel slid one hand over a bruised wrist. "He's not got a scheduled leave for weeks." And then, belatedly catching himself, "Spare me, Cybele. I'm an adult now."

"People get killed storm-tripping every year."

Karel smiled, forgivingly, stretching and displaying long bruised wrists and fingers. "But he didn't come to see me, so no harm done." Then he straightened, with keen pleasure. "But he came to see you. At *last*. Is it better now?"

"I—don't know," Cybele said truthfully. "God is still his first love and space is still mine. As soon as I can afford it, I'm going to get these enhancements, and he may not forgive me. And I didn't know how much I'd missed him. With that long, distant, Godly perspective that makes me feel so small and scruffy, and yet—well, comforted. He spreads a kind of order around him, or a belief in order. He's the only person I know who acts as though he believes in—well, long terms, wide terms. Everyone else seems to live just for the moment, or at the very best, the end of the week."

Karel's attention was close and thoughtful. He had that from Adam, along with the lucent gray eyes. He said, "He *is* three hundred years old, and he has traveled the length and breadth of explored space; of course he has a different perspective from planet-born juveniles. But he's not the only one. You have it, too. You think about cosmic things. And I suppose I have it, in a warped way, which is why I go looking for excitement." His eyes flickered away, caught on his wrists; his fists closed lightly, flinching. "It's *my* life," he said, "and I do these things because I want to. Not because I have a death wish, or am rebelling, or am asking someone to control me. I want to and I need to. The highs are—astonishing. And almost as good is the feeling afterward. Go outside this afternoon, stand in the sunshine, feel the freshness in the air. That's what I feel like afterward, brilliant and fresh."

Has it begun to frighten you? she thought. She had never heard from him either self-justification—beyond the bare defensive, "it's my life"—or invitation. As Adam with his God, she with her ambition, Karel was covetous of his obsessions. Abra might have donated two ova, but Adam had shaped his children.

In growing feeling of kinship with her brother, she said, "Adam's given me a present. At least, that's what I think he meant." She had intended to tell him the minimum, to ask her questions in the vaguest of terms. She told herself that all she needed to know was whether there were databanks she not only had no access to, but had no knowledge of. But old habits prevailed, of sharing and caretaking. Perhaps Karel needed this as much as she did, for different reasons. She needed prominence and profit; he needed challenge. She said, "Are we private in here? When is Cesar due back?"

"Yes, soon, so come in, Cyb, show!"

"I need you to promise me that you won't tell *any-one* about it. They'll have to know in time, but Adam brought it to me because he wanted me to do as much as I could with it beforehand. If I have it taken out of my hands before I have that chance . . . I'll lose what he wanted to give me. I suppose it was a kind of apology for refusing to support my transfections—"

"Yes, yes . . . you can tell me. I'm your brother, remember."

"You're also assistant to the director of the AOC."

He turned up his wrists, exhibiting bruises. "When

have *I* ever followed the rules or worried about consequences?"

The bravado struck her falsely. He saw that, turned his palms down. "Cybele, you and Adam have my loyalty, first, always and forever."

She said, with lingering reluctance, "You know about the body Rache found."

"Yes. It's been on the nets. There's a party on their way to ringsol six now to claim it."

"Where from?"

"Kense, on Great Diamond."

"Great Diamond . . . ?" Something seemed odd there. She could not quite bring it to mind, yet. Karel was leaning forward with barely restrained impatience. She said, "None of her adaptations appear in the database."

"How d'you know?"

"Adam sequenced."

"*Adam?* He's becoming lawless in his old age."

"I searched," Cybele said, quellingly, "the current, tabled and archived variants, and I found nothing. What I wanted you to tell me—to start with—is whether there are any modifications which have been passed but for some reason are not accessible to someone at my level of clearance. I know settlement adaptations are supposed to be public domain, but I thought if some of them were thought to have future potential as enhancements then there might be a special database reserved for them."

Karel was shaking his head slowly, light eyes grave. "Not a chance. Adaptation development has to be public domain to get the exemptions which make legal implementation easier. Enhancement development is very strict, and *very* confidential. Because it's potentially so profitable." A wry, ingratiating little smile, begging forgiveness for reminding her of her years of self-imposed penury. "Blueheart will not even have the machinery to approve enhancements and maintain confidentiality until after stage III. Anyone who wants to work on enhancement as opposed to adaptation goes to one of the centers: New Boots or Berenice. Or Earth. So, no, there's no such database."

Confirmation of what she and Adam had thought. "Then she was adapted illegally."

Karel went more still than she had ever seen him. "Cyb," he said, on a breath, "that is impossible."

"Not so." Her hand, in her pocket, closed upon the fiche, and held it there. "She was eighteen to nineteen years old, and her globin locus was not one of the approved variants. Iron absorption and storage are both regulated by mechanisms which AOC databanks only describe in the form of unapproved preliminary submissions. Someone has been continuing with unapproved work."

He looked to where her pocketed fist was outlined by the yellow fabric of her tunic. "What have you got?"

"This is a copy," she said, giving it up at last.

He stared down at it. "Cybele, you have to turn this over to the investigators."

"No," she said, harshly. "There are rewards for reports leading to prosecution for unauthorized human genetic engineering." She leaned forward, urging him to understand, to believe. "I can trace the originators of the proposals the modifications are based on. I can trace people who've accessed their references, *and* any related material in the genebanks. Whoever's doing this has to have started with something—with knowledge, with DNA, with vectors. They have to have access to medical monitoring equipment. I haven't worked in database management all these years without knowing how to track information and supply use."

"Cybele, the official investigators can do it faster—"

"What difference will days or weeks matter in something that's been going on for nearly twenty years?"

"It will if the people who're responsible learn of your investigation and close down the labs."

"And then what will they do, when their guilt is written all over the genomes of the people they've modified?"

"And will the adaptives cooperate?"

"They will have to. They rely upon the labhosps. If those services are withheld it will force the illegals to come forward. Remember, that was how the problem of follow-up noncompliance was resolved. Withholding of services and offered amnesty to those who were illegally modified without their knowledge—"

"They'll all claim that—"

"Of course they will. The AOC won't want the victims; it will want the perpetrators. Karel, Adam and I talked about it, all last night. We talked round and round the evidence, the possibilities, the way it could have been done. The reason's apparent enough: independence from the labhosps. This is not the first such violation, but this is major. This is ambitious work, meaning a group, not just an individual, with facilities—"

"All the more reason why you should turn it over—"

She reared up. "You don't think I'm capable—"

"This is not right. You're acting out of greed—"

"Of course I am," Cybele cried out. "You've seen how I live. Do you have any idea how many more years I will have to live like that before I can afford even minimal enhancements? I'll be over thirty then, and every year that passes increases the chance that they won't be as effective as I need them to be. And every year that passes increases the chance of new developments that I can't afford, or new admission standards which I won't be able to meet. *Could any legal punishment be worse?*" She swept tears from her eyes, tried to say lightly, "It's ironic, *you* worried about rules and safety," but the words emerged shrill. She had never expected such a reaction from him. She said again, "If you won't help me, then don't stop me."

He looked down at the copied fiche, lying on the console. "Cybele," he said, almost shamefaced, "I have some savings, and I do earn much more than you. I should have offered then—"

"I wouldn't have taken anything then, and I will not take it now," she said, fiercely.

He looked up, saw her expression, and slumped. His face was a study in unhappiness. "Cybele, have you thought of the danger you could be in, from the people who are doing this?"

"In other words, *you* can get stoned and strap yourself to a railing in the middle of a storm for no good reason except thrillseeking, but *I* cannot put myself at risk to expose a wrong."

He reached up and put a hand on her wrist. "Cybele, think about Adam. It's all over the net that this body was found and by whom. If anyone thinks that he might have done more than a simple autopsy—think about Adam."

"Adam has done nothing illegal. And, you know," hiding the shaking within her, "that makes me even more determined to have as much additional evidence as possible before I turn anything over, to justify what he did, if it should even *need* justification."

"I know what it means to you, but—Cesar!" He snatched at the fiche and fumbled it out of sight; she put her body between him and the opening door. The Director of the AOC smiled benignly upon them. "No need to look so guilty, children; I suspect you of nothing." Cybele gave him a thin smile in return, and glided past him. She glanced back, to see Karel staring after her with all his frustrated arguments in his eyes. Then Cesar moved between them and the door slid closed.

Toward mid-morning, a message came to Rache in his office, with instructions. He was to bring the body to a rendezvous on the surface with a party from Great Diamond seamount, who would then take possession. Daven read it with him and waited, tensely, at his side, while Rache considered the implications. Rache could feel his eyes.

He got to his feet and walked to the window which overlooked the plexus. Oliver sat in his cage, hand webbed, a smile of transcendent bliss on his pointed face, and his beanbags scattered forgotten about his feet. Rache thought, *I may live to regret that,* but the thought did not give him the amusement it had but moments before. Great Diamond simply happened to be the nearest pastoral settlement to the ringsol. If there were a familial connection with the Messnier gyre, it went unexplained. The body would not last two thousand kilometers in the warm seas. It would not be returned to Messnier. The final rites would be said by strangers, and the body given to the sea. The woman's family would have no proper farewell, only memories and second-hand accounts. As his family had, for Athene, when Rache swam her to Rossby, and not home.

He said, without turning, "You did say, in your message, that we were willing and able to preserve the body until her family came for her."

There was a silence; he looked around. Daven's eyes slid away. "I guess they didn't want us to."

Oh, Daven. But surely the holdfast in Messnier would have made their wishes known. Rache said, "Acknowledge the message for me. No—wait."

"What are you going to do?"

"Ask whether they come by request of her hold-fast."

"You will insult them."

"I may." But if they are appropriating the rights of her bereaved, and her last right to be mourned and sea-gifted by her own, simply because it offends them that she lie in storage in a ringsol, then they deserve insult. He considered the liaison who had transferred the message from the net. He did not know him well, not well enough to convey a delicate question obliquely. Rache eased around Daven and half stooped to cradle his hand. He composed the message, asking simply if it were the women's own relatives' directly expressed wish that the body be handed over.

Daven said, "But they're on their way! You have to go and meet them."

"I will, if only to explain why I will not surrender the body without assurances."

"It is none of your business," Daven said.

"Perhaps not."

"You're just making yourself more unpopular," Daven said, in growing agitation. "You have to go up and meet them."

"I will," said Rache. He reminded himself the youth was tired, that the body was a burden on his mind as it was on Rache's. That he might simply want it away. Better think that than think Daven might be right, that it was none of Rache's business, that he was giving needless insult, and that his reactions were contaminated by his own frustrated mourning. Once Athene disappeared into the autopsy lab he had seen her only once more, far too briefly. She was chilled and yellowish, and he had been barred from touching her. He shook his head, heavily. Daven was watching him, alert to his wavering mood. He started to continue the argument; Rache said, roughly, "My decision's made," and turned back to his work. A moment later, he heard the elevator door close.

Confirmation came, only a few minutes before he should have needed to leave. There was no means of telling whether it was a true confirmation, since it was once again relayed, but he had no real grounds for disagreement, and he was tired of argument. He passed through the plexus to promise Oliver that he would try to be back before his experiment. Daven heard his capitulation from the station at which he was seated, but merely gave Rache an expressionless glance, looking entirely too much like his father, Rache's elder brother, in a disapproving mood. Rache had not the patience to sue for forgiveness; he merely nodded to Daven as he passed. He and Adam wrapped the body, still in its seaweed shroud, in a body bag. The flesh was chilled and waxy, the seaweed stiff, dusty with salt. Adam was more taciturn than usual; he, too, looked tired. He helped Rache load and transport the body from medical to the facing dock, and stayed to supervise as Rache sparged the gases from his bloodstream and tissues prior to surfacing. Adaptation did not spare him the consequences of prolonged breathing of pressured air, nor the measures needed to avoid them.

He surfaced into broken sunlight and a choppy sea. He had let the floats in the body bag carry him up, a little too fast for the transition from submarine to surface atmospheres. His hands and feet tingled chidingly. He rested upon a float, breathing hard to vent residual gas, until the sensation eased. He had heard nothing in the ascent to signal arrivals. Once his hands settled, he unlooped the clicker from his belt, wound the spring, and dropped the plumb line. Any nearby adaptive would hear it. But he had no sooner let the line to its fullest extent when, on the crest of a wave, a head broke water. Then two more to his side. They slid down the waves toward him, swimming strongly and purposefully. There were five in all, three men, two women, all his age or older. They formed around him, in a crescent. He could feel the impulse of the one on the horn to flip the tow rope from his shoulder. But the formalities must be observed. "Rache of Scole," he introduced himself.

"Maria of Kense," the woman before him said.

"I am honored," Rache said. Kense was the largest holdfast in Great Diamond, the most influential, and the most conservative. Ringsol six's siting was contentious and his appointment here strategic. That the complaints had become fewer since was not because he was acceptable, but because Kense knew he knew a spurious objection from a valid one.

Maria of Kense said, "Are you? Then this day is not altogether bleak, if we have honored you, Rache."

He felt his expression change, though he tried to prevent it. An adaptive would read its heavy features as primaries might not. He said, "Will you do me the further honor, then, of letting me join you for the sea-gifting?"

"Have you no responsibilities to discharge?"

"Few higher than this."

"It will be a day or so yet. We must correspond with her people as to the form. If they think it seemly, we will let you know."

"You should know that she died of nixiaxin poisoning, and if her people have sent any more of their young into these waters, they should be warned."

"You violated her?" one of the men said.

Maria gave him a black glance. "A simple autopsy and toxicity tests are no violation," she said, quellingly, but her look demanded that Rache explain himself.

Rache said, "Daven of Scole had swum to the relay station, and I wanted to know if I had reason to fear for him. Forgive me," he said, a little more grudgingly than he wanted, "if I acted prematurely."

Maria of Kense forgave, with a gracious nod. "You realize," the other woman said, "that your stations, ships, and machinery are responsible for the spread of this blight."

"The blight spread as widely in the earliest years of settlement. And that information does not come from the net, but from our own tradition."

Suddenly, the man on the horn of the crescent surged forward, gripped the top of the body bag. A knife flashed; he slit the body bag along its length, not in the smooth move he had no doubt planned, but in several impatient jerks. The knife was sharp, but the material was tough; he had to take it in handfuls and drag it along the knife. He sheathed the knife, took the body by its shoulders and heaved it clear. The others watched him. Maria watched Rache.

Without speaking, Rache gathered in the flaccid body bag, and freed the tow rope from the ring. He looped it in his hands and offered it to Maria of Kense. She took it.

"Nevertheless," she said, "it is true that this year the painter algae were sickly even before the blight, and, even so late in the summer, the blight is still spreading polewards. A natural change, perhaps, but a change to our detriment. We can no longer forage as we used to."

"Emissions into the sea are strictly controlled," said Rache, sensing an argument lost before it had begun. "And if you have proof to the contrary, you have two choices: you turn it over to the environmental monitoring agency, or you take action first and justify yourselves after. To let a situation worsen through dislike of imperfect solutions is not only stupid, it is immoral."

He had startled them. Shocked them, even. They looked to the headwoman, to see how she would respond.

She said, calmly, "It has occurred to us that it would be a simple solution to the problem we pastorals present if our food-source became contaminated."

"The blight is natural," Rache said, grittily. He would have said more, but knew he could not do so temperately.

"Can you say so, any more than we can say not?"

"If you have evidence," Rache said, "then you are obliged to present it."

He held her eyes until she said, at last, "We have no such evidence."

"Only distrust," Rache said.

Her black eyes sparked. "And what would you do if you had that evidence?"

"I would make it as public as I could," Rache said, and stopped himself from going on. "If you bring me evidence, I will investigate it. I give you my word, my

word as the grandson of Tove of Scole." Her lips tightened slightly at his reach and his presumption, but
whatever she might have said, or threatened, Tove of
Scole had never disowned him. "If I find evidence, I will
disclose it. But the situation is hypothetical. Within the
next few weeks you will see the blight recede, and next
year it will be minor. I have studied it for two decades."

"I know of your studies," she said. She would have
passed the rope to the man, but he had already har-
nessed the body with his own. She glanced at the rope,
then looped it in her hands and affixed it to her belt.
Taking that little with grace. Rache had the sense that he
had been tested. Whether he had passed, or failed, he
did not know. She said, "Thank you for seeing her
returned to her own." Failed, he thought. "Rache of
Scole," she added, and submerged, leaving him once
again uncertain. Her companions gave him the barest of
farewells and converged upon the body, seizing upon
loops in the ropes. Sunlight splashed across the waves
that closed over them, and briefly blinded Rache. When
his eyes cleared, they were gone.

He rode upon the floats for a while longer, while
shadow and sunlight chased each other across his face.
Their hostility was not unexpected, and yet he wondered at the crudity. From children, or youths Daven's
age, he might expect such goading, but from his peers . . .
was he, he wondered, being provoked to investigate
their suspicions? He could not believe such a thing, even
of the most ardent opponents of adaptation. He thought
of Adam de Courcey, of Cesar Kamehameha; whatever
their beliefs, they had professional ethics to restrain
them, and too much to lose, materially and spiritually,
by violating those ethics. But suppose there were others
with similar convictions, and less to lose. It might not be

difficult to justify, in service of a greater good, human unity and orthodoxy. But still assembling all the little plausible steps, one came up with a gross preposterousness. And yet he knew he would be watching the progress of the blight into autumn and the next year.

He evacuated the floats, and folded the slit body-bag into as small a parcel as he could. A few shards of weed drifted from it. He let them go, though his melancholy impulse was to gather them up. He had to remind himself that Oliver's experiment must have already begun, and he wanted to be there. And Daven would no doubt wish to know about the meeting. Rache sighed, strapped the bag across his back, collapsed his lungs and dived, propelling himself down toward the iridescent glimmer of the plexus.

He was perhaps thirty meters above the ringsol when he saw the lights flicker.

Through the speaker embedded in his mastoid bone, he heard Oliver's thin voice say, "Rache, I've got a problem."

Far below the base, the ringsol's light dimmed. Rache stopped his downward plunge, not believing what he was seeing.

Oliver said, breathless with panic and disbelief, "Rache, I've lost the net!"

FOUR

She had waited long enough.

The physician-explorer was right: there were risks. But there was also the indifference to risk which comes from great loss, and understanding which comes too late.

Teal Blane Berenice stood looking at a closed blind, lit from behind by the afternoon sun, and knew she was too late.

Twenty-one years late. Twenty-four, if she dated it from the first time that Juniper had asked her to come to Blueheart. She had not understood. She thought it one of Juniper's extravagances, a rhetorical conceit, made when Juniper was certain that Teal would never accept it. But if so, the merciless logic of grief observed, why had Juniper never made it before, when they were so much farther apart? Why not when it might indeed be possible that Teal would come?

Why not, unless, finally, she meant it?

They were natural-born twins, genetically identical, but in every other way opposed. They lived, twinned, in binary. Zero; one. What one was, the other was not. Juniper was an artist, Teal a technician. Juniper's affairs were many and notorious; Teal held herself celibate. Juniper loathed their twinship. Teal was incomplete without it.

By Juniper's wish, they had not met for over a century.

At the age of twenty-six, she had taken the first afford-able passage away from their birthplace, β Coma Berenices III. Juniper established a notable career as an artist, while Teal became that rare and valuable special-ist, an expert-voyager in cybernetics. Her work took her from posting to posting, developing and upgrading planetary nets. Teal was the more traveled, but Juniper had undertaken the longest journeys, to Earth at the center of it all, and then to Blueheart, at the very fringe. This was the closest they had been for a hundred years, and Juniper's invitation the first ever.

And she was gone.

She had come to Blueheart for her art, and had become committed to the campaign to preserve Blueheart against terraforming. She had been visiting pastoral communities along the north polar continental shelf. She had been in good health, and her ocean sur-vival gear in good order. It was spring, and the sea calm. She never arrived.

Teal leaned her head back, eyes half closed against the shifting shadows of the room. Twenty years might be long for human memory, but not for the net. All times—nearly four thousand recorded years—and all places were equally near. When she entered the net, she would find embedded in it the net of twenty years ago. If there were an explanation to be had, she would find it there.

She drew in her legs, assuming meditation posture. She withdrew within her skin, exhaling her self in mea-sured breaths. The subroutines flashed clearance. She felt the lengthening and softening of muscles, the bal-ancing of her weight on the fulcrum of her spine. The sensations were a prompt, a consummation. She keyed her transmitter and opened herself to the net.

The essence of perception, one of Teal's instructors once told her, is selection, filtration, and reduction. The brain has no use for raw material; it requires information. It need not acknowledge the millions of photons which glance upon the eye. The impulses are grouped according to shape. The shapes grouped into objects. The objects recognized, given names and attributes. (The first stage of learning to be an artist, Juniper said, is to unlearn perceptual habits.) The net, likewise, comprises photons of information. One cannot examine each and every one. The nets have a standard structure, endpoint of centuries of development, and known to all. The majority of users rely almost exclusively on pre-prepared subroutines, and a limited or externalized interface. But for experts-in-training the first and most difficult task is the building of the internal interface, so that net-input may be apprehended as swiftly as visual. The development of a sixth sense, and the processing hierarchy and symbology associated with that sixth sense.

Teal's symbology was spatial. The net had a structure, was a spectral matrix in space. She was a rarity: most operatives metaphorized net-information in visual, aural or even sensual terms. Some spoke of what they saw, heard, felt. Very privately, she viewed them with a puritanical eye. If she could have dispensed with her envisioned structure, she would have; it was a kind of ascetic yearning for purity in her. But it seemed the human mind demanded a metaphor, however abstract, for the information it processed.

And she had another weakness. The shaped lightlessness was full of whispers. She was haunted by the voices of parents, educators, and acquaintances left far behind. The net technicians on Chara station theorized that it was some aberrant synaptic connection between the artificial cortex and her own. They offered her reimplantation. But her implant was too much part of her; she did not believe any other would be as good. She chose to endure her ghosts.

The one voice she never heard was Juniper's.

Despite the standardizations, each net retained an imprint of its designers. She could recognize the fingerprint, the symmetry and permutations; she could tell who had designed it, or who had programmed its design, and who had taught them. She had to discipline herself not to linger, appreciating that perception. The net had its own kind of relativity; time was different, here. Twenty years would not matter to her, but that she was bound to a weary, mortal body.

She took the time to make small, necessary amendments to her own storage, securing it, readying it for anything she would bring out. Then she initiated the search algorithms, seeking Juniper.

She readily found Juniper's gallery, the encodings of the images, the words and the symbols of her best presentations. It was still live, frequently recalled. She bypassed the vestibule, and used expert's privileges to scan the code. In her latter days, Juniper had moved into emotional-interactive art, poetry, polemic and paean to Blueheart. Teal found limbic address codes, with alternate bioscanning and external feedback functions for the unimplanted. There was also a complex psychometric questionnaire, used to refine the presentations.

She noted the date of the last contribution, three years before Juniper's death, and amended the search to exclude all references prior to the latest date, and all records of that type. But just before she moved on, she thought to extract the listing of all who had viewed the gallery, then, and most recently.

The references thickened. Correspondence from, correspondence to, correspondence concerning, purchases by, travel records for. She mapped Juniper's comings and goings to the last recorded place; the place she already knew. Before she expected, she found herself in the void beyond the end of the references. She extracted the date and time of that last recorded destination, and directed herself toward the access records. She would find out what information Juniper had accessed just beforehand, what final testament she had left.

She found a bewildering barrenness. Juniper herself had not accessed the nets from her point of departure. Nor from any of the four rafttowns she had visited in the previous season. She expanded the search, finding sparse, incomplete entries for the previous year, messages left unanswered, or answered perfunctorily. Even before her death, Juniper had been fading.

Where had she gone? She, like Teal, had been implanted at the age of two, had grown up on and with the net; netspace was the only space wide enough to share; the networld the world in which they could be unalike, untwinned. In the net they were self-creators; and Juniper, the Juniper Teal knew, would not have let that go. Teal saw sheer whiteness and realized that she had unthinkingly opened her eyes, unthinkingly looked after Juniper, outside the net. But she was not ready to follow Juniper there, not yet. Even if Juniper eschewed contribution, her presence and passage would have been marked. Other people's records would outline her. Teal expanded her search protocols and initiated them, and waited, uneasy, for what they might bring.

When she received the first alert messages, she thought they were directed at herself, that she had overdemanded of the net. She interrupted the search protocol, irked that the structure was so primitive, irked that she misjudged. But the alarms continued, intensified. Expert's instincts aroused, she moved toward the source, transferring channel to channel, until she caught up an open connection to a system outside the planet.

It was a delicate, overornate substructure unlike the planet's austere design. This was more characteristic of the pentad. She thought she recognized features of a recent innovation, and briefly regretted having begun her search before seeking updating on the systems and protocols in use in Blueheart. She had not given this frontier world enough respect. But the thought was slow and far out in the borders of thought, for she had other concerns. The structure was disintegrating. Around her, great abeyances opened up. Emptiness cored the framework, branching and extending. During her truncated employment on η Boötes IV, she had seen worm assault from within. Every precaution she had ever learned told her to withdraw, not to risk infection. But the destruction, the *insult* to this creation, and to herself, outraged her. From her own datastore she sent out antibodies and endonucleases. She pulled segments of worms and with each capture, strengthened her own defenses, and refined her antibodies. She spawned repair subroutines, and sent them out to bridge the holes. She worked on a cold, brilliant exhilaration, an entity of abstraction and cerebral reflex.

Then she felt the structure shift. Alert messages clamored. There was *water* damage to the hardware. Absurd, impossible; she was on η Boötes IV, she was on Chara relay station, she was on λ Serpens II. She had forgotten the sea. But even as the last of the worms died under her assault, the structure tilted again beneath her. She did not think, she did not reason, that nothing here could affect her own true body or mind, or that this disintegrating system would be backed up elsewhere. It felt like her last chance, for life, for rescue. She swept up the residue—the fragments, the dead worms, the clinging antibodies—and, holding it together, she fled. She fled into the safe dim haven of her own skull, and there let the fragments spill.

Rache plunged downward. Around him, blue light from the surface lit upon shivering bags of rising air. Adrenaline raged through his blood. One or more of the sea locks was open. He slammed against the surface of the dome. Everything was dim inside. The screens showed darkness, or blizzards, or tumbling shapes. The colors flickered dimly on strained, staring faces, upturned to watch Oliver, straining in his cage. They were good people; they would not panic, but they were technologists, scientists, accustomed to the computer's omniscience. They would waste vital time trying to restore the system. They could not afford to with the sea waiting. He pounded on the dome until they looked up. Daven, sea-wise, had already found a torch. He turned it up toward Rache, bathing him in pale, wavering light. Rache thought, Daven, don't panic; I'm depending on you. He pounded out: Are bulkheads in place? He saw the young man speaking, translating, but he did not await an answer. Put them down manually. NOW.

He could see the "but" in their faces, even Daven's, who knew better. Only half his staff were in the dome. The remainder would be trapped below in the labs and living areas. But the sea did not respect finer sentiments. It did not reward altruism.

Rache hammered: *NOW. NOW. NOW.* He knew he looked half-insane. He felt it. He hoped they could see it and be terrorized into self-preservation.

He glimpsed someone's hand reaching for the lever before everything went dark. Screens, illumination, panels, faces. Everything except the single light in Daven's red-skinned hand.

A terrible darkness welled up behind him. The intense light of the ringsols died more slowly than the dome, but die it did. It simply contracted, shriveling back into the underside of the ringsols, and then out of existence. Rache froze against the side of the dome. The light flashed within, but for the moment he ignored it. Net failed. Power failed. Communications failing. Bulkheads failed. Locks failing. And the sea outside.

These people did not belong to the sea.

He beat upon the dome. *Stay there. I'll close locks.*

He thrust himself away from the dome. There were things he could do, and things he could not. He was not enough of an engineer to worry about the geothermal tap. He would tell himself that the power had been cut off by failsafes. If he were to be boiled alive by eruptions or explosions then so be it. He'd rather not anticipate. He had to believe that six's silence would be noted immediately and investigated. He had to assume that help would come. Trapped air would sustain his trapped people until then. His task was to trap the air and get his people to it.

He could hear the bump and shudder of air freed in great gouts. He could see the pale shuddering envelopes of it rising beyond the hull. He turned his face toward it, and swam, hugging the hull. He dared not risk loss of contact. He swam full speed into some protrusion, dazing himself. Dazed, furious, he thrashed in the water.

Idiot! He was not thinking; he was reverting to reflexes of twenty-five years ago. He had memorized the schematics of this base. He had the wherewithal to know exactly which locks were most urgent. *And* to remember the surface topology between them.

Emergency lights came up at last. Emergency lights, emergency power to catalytic rebreathers and pumps, emergency communications. He thought grimly: It should not have taken them so long. After this, we're having drills as we've never had them before. When I wake up with nightmares from this, I'm going to lie awake planning them. But the air still bloomed and broke upward. *Come on, Oliver.* The nearest was just around the curve of the hull, just beyond the heat-exchange projection he had all but brained himself against. I need those drills as much as anyone.

He approached the lock from above. The turbulence around the air was nearly as dangerous as the flow into the lock from below. He found the lever, jammed his feet beneath it, and exerted all his strength. For a frightening moment, he thought that the lock would not close before the turbulence off-balanced him, and then the gray door slid slowly closed; there was a last blurt of bubbles, and then stillness.

Next! If he could close the two other locks servicing the top five levels that would secure half the base. He could then go in and search the lower halls and rooms. Even as he swam he sorted through faces, recalling those he had just seen in the plexus, and who was likely to be below, and where. He could gauge who would be best able to reach and use survival gear, in the time the water would allow, and who would succumb to useless panic.

The lever to the third lock was jammed. In the chaos of escaping air and inrushing water he could not find what had jammed it. In trying to feel around it, he slid off balance, caught at the lever, missed. Fell briefly through a cavity of unsupporting air. And took the thrust of the inrushing current full in his back. As he was hurled forward, he had a flash of the schematic of the terrain behind the lock. A longish corridor; distance, maybe, for the wave to spend some of its force. He brought his hands vaguely up before him, completely disorientated. He slammed obliquely against a vertical, right leg taking the impact, body swinging into the wall like a sack of wet sand. He had time to decide: Not bad, before he was lifted and bent backward around the turn of a corner, legs pinned to the wall, shoulders and head dragged into the void. Agony. Froth and seawater roared in his mouth and sinuses. Somehow he drew up his legs. Somehow he thrust, and fell back against the edge; somehow he thrust again in terror of his back being broken, and ground off the corner, into the current. He tumbled fleetingly onto his feet, was pulled under and thrown head and shoulder against a bank of equipment. He covered his head and just let himself be battered and borne through thunder and dim churning light.

Sometime later he realized that he was no longer being swept, but being rolled like a stone between rival currents. He kept trying to stand until he fell against a wall. The wall upheld him. The water was chest-height. Shifting, but no longer rising. The light was thin and turbid and the ceiling seemed very close. The sea tasted of salt and iron. His shoulders and hips felt mismated through his spine; he was afraid to shift his weight lest something disconnect. He let himself slide sideways, underwater. This he knew, pain, watery darkness, the proximity of death. This uncovered the core of him. For a lifetime he had lived in the sea, known its bounty and its cruelty. It spoke to him as no deity with a human face ever might. But for twenty-five years he had been safe from it. He had studied it, celebrated it, defended it, and forgotten what it was to fear it. Forgotten that he must defend himself, and his own, against it.

A thin voice was talking to him, unanswered. He had lost a fin. He prized the other off with his toes, rather than bend. Above his head the water's surface pleated and shivered. He could hear the throb of pumps, but there was little difference in the level yet; the locks must still be open. Rache pushed himself toward the central axis. Staircases spiraled north and south of the axial elevator shaft. In the event of inundation, they should be sealed. But as he swam around the last corner, he saw an oval of wavering light welling from below; that, too, had failed. He took a moment to lock the hatch open; he did not want it resealing upon some whim of the malfunctioning net. The stair wound out of the water, up through an oval in the ceiling. He looked up, seeing overhead the underside of the closed bulkhead isolating the plexus. The voice had given him up for the moment. He considered trying the stairs, but there was an aching numbness in his right buttock and leg. Pain he could outface, but he had a visceral dread of paralysis. He surfaced to breathe, then rolled over and propelled himself downward, hand over hand, turn over turn of the spiral staircase. He would go to ocean ecology, on level five, where the divers should have been readying the next day's field trip . . . On the third level, he felt a warning brush of current, turned, twisting his back painfully, and brought up a hand in reflex defense. The diver stalled in his grab, sculled before him. A bristle-headed man, in transparent thin-suit over ragged trousers. Chandar, department head of benthos, and R6's premier diver. "Rache," he signaled, with relief, and a moment later, Rache heard through his implant, "the net's down; I've never seen anything like it. We've got forty-two people up in the plexus, thirty-five responding, fifteen not responding, but taken care of. We've nine suited and mobile, seven more able to reach equipment; they've gone to bring the worst of the known casualties up. We've got seventeen to find, eleven of them primaries—"

Rache signaled an interruption with one large fist outthrust, signaling, "Who?" Chandar hesitated briefly. Rache signaled, water swirling around his hands, "Tell me who and I'll tell you where." Chandar looked askance at some of Rache's guesses, but then, he also looked askance at gossip. He did not know about Noel and Jessie's trysting places, or Synnöve's retreats from her crumbling affair with Anne. Even before he had finished his list, Chandar relayed the first successes. "Who else?"

"Adam—and he's not in Medical."

Brittle-boned Adam, with a century's experience in space; who would certainly have the cool wit to reach and use survival gear, and who would certainly have checked in. Now Rache regretted his dislike of the man; he did not know his habits. "Who else?"

Through the list, guessing and guessing again, while the grid search made its systematic way through the flooded corridors below. Aware all the time of the passage of seconds, minutes, life for those they had not found. Breathing suddenly seemed urgent, though reason argued against it. Some sympathetic asphyxia. He gestured surfaceward and Chandar rose with him. Eight unaccounted for. Full lighting came on, illuminating the grotesquerie of a half-filled room. "The net's restored," Chandar said. "We have pumps and the locks are closed." The level in the flooded hall began to sink. Chandar and Rache moved aside as divers surfaced, dragging the most critical of the casualties with them, lifting them and passing them up the stairs, to the lounge. Chandar said, "They've found Adam."

Rache said, "Good," and Chandar, "No, it's not."

The divers brought him up. He had been in a corridor adjacent to one of the lower locks; he had been struck by the same bludgeon that battered Rache. His head was slack on his body, slack beyond unconsciousness. As Rache reached out to steady it, he felt yielding where none should be, pulped bone of Adam's brow. Adam's face was bone-colored, except for dark blood threading from one ear and the bluish mark, not yet a bruise, above his left eye. They started toward the stairs, and a voice from above said, "I'll take him." He looked up at magenta, gold, auburn: Meredis, with emergency medical kit in hand. He had a moment's relief, which was washed away by a nearly blinding anger. He had seen her in the plexus. He said, "What are you doing here?"

She did not mistake the tone, or misunderstand the question. "Oliver's restored the net; we have control—"

He threw an arm out of the water, spraying her, Adam, Chandar, spattering a wide arc around him. He felt the motion like a knife in the back. "In control of *this*?"

"So courtmartial me later. Stretcher!" she bellowed, roofward. Two more of the plexus staff scrambled down the staircase, a stretcher between them. Meredis helped them strap Adam to it, immobilizing his head. She said, "Tell Arren to intubate and start a crash-hib. I'll be up."

"Is everyone accounted for?" Rache growled at Chandar.

"Three still missing," the diver said, stiff-faced in abstention. Rache caught himself on the brink of a shout, looked from one to the other with the promise of a reckoning in his face, and surged back in the water, meaning to plunge back down through the stairshaft. Black pain rolled up his spine and burst inside his skull. He sank, as bright bubbles dwindled to points before his open eyes.

"Tell me what happened," Rache said.

He lay beached on the drained floor of the lounge. Meredis had said, be reasonable, and he had insisted they help him up the stairs, so he could be where he needed to be. He was in no mood to be reasonable when others were not.

"I don't know what happened," Oliver said, stooped, green-faced, and looking more than ever like a strip of ribbongrass.

"You must know something," Rache ground out, willing himself to gentleness. "You were monitoring your experiment."

Oliver swallowed, a hitch in his long, thin throat. "I'm going to be sick."

"Not over me you aren't."

Oliver nodded, and rubbed at a medicated patch on his left upper arm. His hair was damp, though this was as near as he had come to the waters. "Our net was . . . demolished. The whole thing." His eyes flickered away, jittering over the scene around them; immediately Rache barked, "You're talking to me; look at me," and they jerked back, wide and glassy.

"I may only be a pastoral," Rache said, "but I do know the difference between change and delete."

"There was no power failure. It had to be a virus. I can't see how—"

"It is up to you to find out how," Rache said, each word deliberate. "If we took a virus onboard, then we took it onboard through some external port. Start with these." Oliver caught his breath. Rache said, "Yes?"

"Unless it were something—released from one of our areas. By the modifications of the tutor-virus."

"If somebody had one of those in their area I will chain him to a rock for the fish to eat," Rache said grimly. "Particularly if he had not the wit to realize that our tutor-virus might release it." How he wished he could get up. Move around. Talk to people. Not to ask questions, but for simple animal comfort. The adrenaline had burned itself out, burned him out. There did not seem to be enough air as his stressed system equivocated on gas-balance between enriched blood-stream and pigment-charged muscles. "Use an auxiliary to contact the planet. Find out who was connected to our external ports immediately before the net went down."

Looking less greenish, Oliver dutifully disappeared. Rache rolled his head, looking across the lounge. Beads of water clustered on the amber carpeting, delineating footsteps, smears, shapeless pools. Some people were lying, or sitting huddled, immobilized by shock; others paced purposelessly, unable to rest, from person to person, group to group. The regular and emergency medical staff worked with calm direction; they at least had purpose. They would suffer later. Primaries, Rache thought, were such innocents; they built their safeguards so well that they forgot the threat. It hurt him to see the innocence injured.

As for himself, experience came early. Blueheart's warm waters spawned hurricanes. Storm-barriers, cultivated of natural defenses, surrounded all holdfasts in the storm-belt. Vivid still in Rache's memory, even after nearly fifty years, was the first time the holdfast evacuated. He remembered a noon dark as twilight, a screaming wind, and spume falling in ropes over the rafts. The booming of waves on the barriers was less seen than felt, and already the compound was filling with debris, broken, swept and blown, from the crumbling barriers. He remembered fighting as his uncle strapped him into a rebreather; it was the first time, ever, in a childhood as indulged as the sea would allow, that he had been handled so brutally. The first time, ever, that he knew of such a device. But in Scole the rebreathers were never discussed with children; nobody ever explained that, to survive, the people of Scole must use the disdained primary devices, because no adaptative, however deep, could dive long enough to outlast a hurricane.

Six times since he had strapped the rebreather onto back and face, and swum with his people into water deep enough to shelter them while waves cracked open the barriers and wind and waves shattered Scole. Every time since the first, he had known what to expect, and every time since the first he had wept, at the sight of rafts, barriers, shallow-water crop—his home—merely a shapeless mulch on the shining sea.

Someone was crying, softly, desolately. He moved

his head, but could not see who; it was not a voice he had ever heard weep before. He wondered whether, if he rolled over, he could eventually get to his feet. Meredis said, from above his head, "Don't even think about it." In a shambles of color, she crouched over him. "How do you feel?"

The crying had grown muffled, as though turned against a shoulder. Rache relaxed slightly. "I've felt better," he said. "Casualties?"

The corner of her mobile mouth twisted down. She stooped over him so only he could hear. He blinked against the thready scratch of her hair. "We've lost Adam. Brain didn't respond well to the crash-hib; edema's restricting circulation. He'd be at the limit for resuscitation even without the injury. Knowing his religious beliefs, I wouldn't try. If he has his wishes on record, it'll be straightforward. If not, and his children ask for revival—I hope he's made a will." She rocked back on her heels. "Evac subs are only a few minutes out."

"And?" Rache said.

"We've four others in crash-hibernation. Two will resuscitate, but Elisabet and Micah I'm less sanguine about; they were under too long. Ainsleight's missing. Benedict said she was trying to close one of the locks when he lost sight of her. He thinks she may have been swept out, and she had no diving gear."

"She was always braver than she was lucky," Rache rumbled.

Meredis, who had hardly known Ainsleigh, tilted her head slightly, prepared to listen if he said more. She seemed quite self-possessed in this emergency. He had not expected it of her: she was a laboratory specialist, not a fieldworker, a former director of the adaptation labs on Grayling station. He had supported her application, seeing a willingness to make such changes as an asset. Now, he wondered if he had misjudged her, and she was merely reckless and a hollow risktaker.

He said, "Why did you open the bulkhead?"

She had not been unprepared for the question. She leaned close, keeping her voice low. "Put yourself in my place: watching the clock and counting the minutes . . . You lost Adam, lost Micah—that's your downstairs medical staff. Oliver had the net back on line, we had the locks closed, atmosphere restoring. I *asked* the people whom I knew knew more than I did."

She leaned back slightly to scan his face, saw him unconvinced, said more forcefully, bending less: "For primaries, minutes can mean the difference between straightforward recovery and neuroregeneration and rehab which can take months to years."

His hands fisted at his sides. "I was not forgetting that, but by opening the bulkhead when you had no way yet of knowing that the net was stable, you risked forty-two lives to save a handful. That is not acceptable."

"From your point of view, maybe," she returned.

He became aware of a sudden lull around them, and checked what he might have said. She heard it, too. He looked at her, she at him, with mirrored guilt and grudge at their common lapse. She muttered, "Later, Rache," and he grunted a low promise. "By the way," she said, more loudly, "that was a hell of a search you directed. They told me when I came aboard that you knew everyone's business." Her smile was a little tense, not entirely approving. Rache wondered what business of hers she would rather he not know. She got to her feet, murmuring ruefully, to someone just out of sight, "You did warn me."

Daven's voice said softly, "Yes." His nephew's smooth, round face came into focus as Daven crouched, replacing Meredis.

"You warned her?" Rache said, a little acidly.

"I tried to stop her opening the bulkhead. I knew you would not want it." Rache grunted. Daven leaned closer, lowered his voice, but did not look directly at Rache's face. "The people who're dead. They're really dead? In so little time?" His voice shook.

"Primaries can drown very quickly."

Daven said, "I want to go home."

Rache felt for him, but said, "We need you here. There may not be enough left of the net or the logs to tell what happened. The people who were using the system on or around the time may have noticed something significant. You were one, weren't you?"

Daven's eyes widened; he started to say something, and then jerked around, staring across the lounge . . . *"What's that noise?"*

Rache listened, hearing after a moment the slight reverberation of cycling locks. "The rescue subs."

"I don't want to go with them," Daven said, catching Rache's arm in both hands.

Rache laid a hand over Daven's. "It's going to be all right. I promise. We've survived the worst."

FIVE

An expert-voyager," Rache said. "Nicely done, Oliver."
Early morning, in the docks labhosp on Rossby,
where the casualties of ringsol six had been brought.
Rache, bed bound, was already overfamiliar with his little room: two white walls, one display wall, and one
cylindrical window, curving outward into the dawn-
white sky.

The net manager, seated angularly on a stool beside
his bed, gave him a brilliant, brittle smile. Like the
sparkle of water above the lightless depths. Rache said,
"You've been up all night, haven't you?"

Oliver ignored the question, with undeceptive
blitheness. "So, yes, there was an expert-voyager working on the net, and I managed to track her data stream
through public domain to one of our open ports, and
bring up the logs of her transfers in and out. Which
coincide with the worm assault, as near as I can fix it.
And more of her went out than went in. So the question
is, is our expert-voyager responsible for our demolition,
or did she try to salvage us? I pulled her record off the
sun streams, and it's impeccable, except for an early buy
out from New Boots—which frankly suggests to me that
there's a human being around all that cercortex—you
should see her specifications; I think I'm in love—she's
Berenici, by the way—a slightly early completion of her
latest posting, λ Serpens II—and a request to delay start

of her next contract on, of all places, my own old home, Arcturus—and even more oddly, she was self-financing on her journey here. I *am* deeply envious."

Rache said, suddenly and with certainty, "Teal Blane Berenice."

"Yes—oh, what? You *knew*?" Oliver managed to look entertained, dismayed, and impressed all at once. "And you let me know you knew? Your people-management is slipping, Rache, slipping; but I'll forgive you; I'll ascribe it to your aching back and forgive you."

Rache hardly heard, because the moment he spoke, he knew it to be impossible: for Teal Blane Berenice to be here, now, she must have left before she received the message, his message, telling her of Juniper's death.

"Rache?"

Rache drew a deep breath. "She had a sister. Whom I knew."

Oliver sat upright. "Juniper Blane Berenice! But she died years ago—"

"Yes, she did." But twenty-five years ago Juniper had announced that if anyone could help Rache construct a proper cercortex interface, despite his late start, Teal could. So she would invite her. And Teal, she said, sparkling-eyed, Teal would come. It seemed that Teal had come, all unknowing. He reached for the bed's console; was checked by pain. Though the nerve-field adjusted to compensate, Rache heeded it for the warning it was. He prompted Oliver to move the console low and within reach. The sysop watched with great interest as Rache composed a simple invitation for contact, introducing himself as a friend of Juniper, expressing condolences for Teal's fresh and unexpected grief.

But Oliver said suddenly, "'Surfacing.' That's you."

Rache winced. "It is about as much me as if I took

charcoal and drew your outline on the wall it would be you. Juniper was a great fabulator, and the 'Surfacing' series was pure fable." Oliver still looked impressed, and Rache sighed, remembering long shouted arguments about art and aesthetics. The text was always art and aesthetics, and the subtext the way she perceived and exhibited him. He was at once delighted, and appalled. The delight was pure conceit, belief in his own importance to her. The other was—an instinct, a dread, that he was no more than material.

Oliver said, intensely curious, "Were you lovers?"

"She . . . caused me to leave Scole, to leave the sea. The past twenty-five years of my life might have been entirely different without her." He realized he had answered not the question spoken, but the one intended. Some relationships could be more profound than that between lovers; Oliver had this yet to learn. He said, "We were lovers. For a time." And in swift ellipsis, "Then our convictions took us in different directions." He paused. "We were friends again, eventually."

"What do you think happened to her?"

After she disappeared, he had visited those polar seas, and spoken to the last people to see her alive. They had described her great excitement, her sense that she was thrusting toward some destination. He knew then what had happened to her. When she was assembling piece by piece the elements of a new theme, she only half lived in the world. She was distracted, clumsy with things and people, forgetful. She had always had such an innocent, egoistical delight in the sea; it was to her a vast theme, a vast subject, a vast piece of fluid and matter to be shaped and shown. After all he had tried to teach her, tried to show her, she went out carelessly to the waiting sea. When he realized that, he left her to those polar seas, and swam back to the rafttown.

"An accident." His voice, even after all these years, was harsh.

Oliver climbed back onto his stool, folding limbs and exoskeleton like an untidy pile of driftwood topped by bright eyes. "If she had not died, do you think we'd still be talking about terraforming today?"

Rache grunted a laugh. "She was an artist, not a politician."

"She changed people's attitudes."

"She made the sea fashionable for a while, that is all." Oliver's pointed face became guarded at his tone, and Rache relented, striving for accuracy.

"She was a great artist, yes. But she was not a planner, not a visionary. There is nothing *in* her work that was not of the present. She had no ability to picture Blueheart's *future*, Oliver. And neither she, nor the people whom she inspired, ever understood the difference."

"You did."

He felt his face pull in an expression half smile, half grimace. "And I was a great disappointment to her for my very prosaic and drawn-out approach." The display on his bedside console lit with a message and he turned his attention to it with some relief. And stared.

Instead of answering his communication, the expert-voyager had come in person. She was standing outside the door.

He had anticipated that she would be Juniper's living image. He thought himself prepared. Yet when the door slid open, his heart pulled in on itself, painfully. He saw only Juniper, returned as fresh as she had been taken.

Only for an instant. Then memory and reality split

apart, as Teal stayed where she was, regarding him with impassive eyes. Juniper would have laughed and run to embrace him, or stalked over to stand with hands on hips, demanding what in hell he had done to himself this time. Teal still wore a crumpled, water-damaged drop suit. In the last year he had seldom seen Juniper without diving gear and skin-grease, bare skin beaded with water, or rimed with salt. Or skin-painted with all her artist's skill and flamboyance, in tints which changed with the lighting like a fish's scales.

"I am Teal Blane Berenice."

Her voice had the same low pitch and dark quality as Juniper's, but it was passionless, uninflected.

Rache pushed away both disappointment and relief. "I am Rache Scole Gamma Serpens V; Rache Scole Blueheart. This is Oliver Arcturus Delta."

"You put a trace on me," the expert-voyager said to Oliver. Oliver, most uncharacteristically, was visibly hunting for words; her specifications, Rache thought, amused, must have been impressive. Teal held out her hand. "This, I believe, is yours."

It was a transfer-fiche. Rache nudged his console toward Oliver. Oliver shifted around it, watching the expert-voyager throughout, now like a novice diver encountering his first milk-blister. He found fiche-slot and web by touch, fitted his hand; his eyes widened slightly.

Rache looked back at the expert-voyager. "I suspect you have anticipated our wishes; thank you."

She shook her head slightly, an abrupt, jerky motion, as though begrudged. "There was a limit to what I could do. The salvage was minimal, but I have reconstructed the virus."

"There was a virus, then." He glanced sideways at

the absorbed Oliver. "We were not sure. We were trying a reconfiguration—a CADyN from the sunstreams—Oliver can give you the details."

"Ah," the expert-voyager said, "that explains it. I was going to ask for the schematics of your net, because you should not have sustained such catastrophic damage from so straightforward a virus."

"I . . . see," said Rache.

"The virus was simply intended to delete data from storage. I have seen its form elsewhere, but it is not strictly speaking a derivation. And this is where my limitations come in. I am new to Gamma Serpens V; I do not know the local experts and schools—"

"But this is wonderful!" Oliver said, suddenly resurfacing. He smiled radiantly at the expert-voyager, startling a responsive flicker of warmth in her. Oliver pushed the console at Rache. "I've set up your interface." He was half turned toward Teal, his designs on her attention transparent.

Rache settled his hand and tilted the screen toward himself. Algorithms and annotation rainbow-snowed across it; he slowed the scrolling by half, and by half again. No wonder governments and companies sponsored expert-voyagers across the lightyears. She *could* have created the virus, even in the slight time she had; she knew them that well. But she had not. The style of her commentary suggested nothing withheld. It managed to be both rigorous and informal, unselfconscious. How unlike Juniper, who was always aware of the context, the appearance, the artistic shape of her communications.

She had concentrated on the virus. She had dissected out and analyzed the fragments of the code. She extended the analysis into the damage done the net, and the characteristics of her most successful spun-off defenses, and used those to reconstruct what was missing. She had not been able to determine a site of infection from the residual of the net, but she outlined a strategy for reconstructing the course of the virus through the net. And she added some insider's advice on the legalities of extracting confidential information on planetary net access, should that prove the source of infection.

Rache smile. That, that cunning lawfulness, she had in common with her sister.

He heard Oliver say, "He was over thirty when he was implanted. He couldn't develop the internal interfaces, so he uses visuals. It's rather a pity. He would have been brilliant."

He looked up at the familiar, stranger's face. She had been watching the console from the side, hands clasped behind her back.

"She thinks," Oliver said, blushing, "that the virus took out some of the limiters I'd put in the tutor-virus—to keep it away from the emergency and habitat systems—"

The expert-voyager spoke firmly for herself. "I would have to do a simulation to be sure. What is the state of your investigation?"

"Barely begun. We had no idea that we would have this."

"I can do more." A blunt assertion; she waited to see his reaction. It occurred to him then that she might suspect him as he had her, that she might be as outraged as he and as determined to see it to the end. He said, "I cannot make an official offer of contract until I know my resources."

"Investigation is a professional obligation. However,"

she paused and considered him, "I understand you sent me my sister's informational effects, thereby incurring a substantial debt." She paused. "Consider it overdue repayment of a favor owing."

"I . . . see," Rache said, embarrassed in his turn. He had indeed sent her some of Juniper's effects, though the transmission costs had nearly beggared him. The gesture had been quixotic, and pointless, since she had left before they reached her.

"Then," he said, after a moment, "if we give you schematics of the net, will you go on with your analysis? Find out where it came from?"

She offered her hand. He looked at it, unable to interpret the gesture. She said, "Handshake contract." He took the hand, returned a brief, firm grip, and let it go.

She stepped back, so she could look at them both. "What you could do in the meantime is identify and investigate the background and contacts of trained operators on Blueheart. The virus is relatively straightforward, but the delivery into a relatively safeguarded system such as the ringsol might not be. I do not know. And there are a couple of other matters I should like you to consider." She studied them, hands clasped behind her back. "The ringsol net is of a distinctive design. The virus dispatched it very efficiently. That suggests to me that whoever designed this virus had full specifications and perhaps code. I have verified those are not public domain."

Rache felt a weight settle on his chest. "You mean someone gave it them."

She merely inclined her head slightly, and watched with steady eyes.

"I am sorry," Rache said, leadenly, "I cannot think who might have."

"It might be the start of a productive line of investigation. But it is not knowledge I need, or particularly want. I prefer to proceed without being biased by context."

"You have done this before," Rache said, with grit in his voice.

"Yes."

And not cared for it, he thought. He remembered the terminated contract on New Boots.

"I would rather not do this work on the net."

After a moment, he understood. "Oliver: will you see to it?" Rache caught the console as Oliver went to draw it toward himself, hand lightly overlapping Oliver's. "Not here, Oliver. I have a few words to say to Exper' Blane Berenice." Oliver, startled and intrigued, dawdled from the room.

Teal Blane Berenice had backed away a few steps, and now stood resting her eyes on him. It was arresting: she did not seem to look or gaze. No doubt she already knew everything the net had to offer about him, and perhaps thought it sufficient. He had known high-level experts before, and all were profound introverts, living avidly internalized lives.

He said, "I may have taken advantage of your gratitude for a small favor done long ago . . ."

"Don't," she said, flatly. Silence lay like a stone between them. Since she had laid it there, he let her break it, which she did with an effort. "She contacted me about you. It was you, was it not? She wanted me to come and teach you." She spoke with an edge of quiet mockery. Rache was unoffended. He knew the self-mockery of grief when he heard it. For her, Juniper's loss was still new, still raw.

He said, "When she was declared missing, presumed dead, I sent you everything she would allow. I did not, of course, know you were already on your way. Many of her personal records did not survive her, on her request. But there was an additional proportion of her work, of her records, that she would not let be sent off world. She wanted them held for you . . ."

Something a little like dread came into her face. "Where are they?"

He told her. He had the sense that another woman would have paced. But she seemed set rigid, standing with hands clasped behind her back. He could not tell what she thought, or what she felt. Juniper had been so public in her emotions. Teal withheld everything.

She said, abruptly, "I have lost the habit of talking about her."

"I know." He ventured familiarity. "But she liked to be talked about."

A flicker-glance of appreciation, and then her expression stilled. "I am not like her. People assume."

"I understand," he said. She surprised him with another flicker of expression, wry amusement. He said, "If I may be of any help to you while you are here, in any capacity whatsoever, please ask."

He had no idea how much she knew, might learn, or might perceive of his and Juniper's relationship. He had no idea how much he wanted her to know. He thought it might be simpler if she did not know, and did not accept his offer. But he could not have left it unmade.

"I will come again when I have something to report," she said, and quickly left.

"I am sorry," the counselor said. "Your father's wishes were quite explicit. As a doctor himself, he understood how precisely to specify the conditions under which he did not wish regeneration."

From the screen between them, Adam's image gazed upward, quiet satisfaction in its expression. This was the kind of problem which gave him the greatest delight, lying as it did between his two life-long disciplines, medicine, and theology. He would have worked long and carefully before recording it in its final form, as a kind of prayer to his enigmatic God. Cybele sensed that the counselor was impressed.

"But they could," she said in a thin, angry voice. "They could regenerate."

"Regeneration, in his case, would be tantamount to cloning. The biological structures recording life experience could not be reproduced. He would not be the same man. He would not be himself."

Karel, shivering, said, "Thank you," and half stood.

"No," said Cybele. Karel sat as though his legs had collapsed. His skin bore the traces of paint poorly removed, smears of silver and metallic blue. He looked ill, intoxicant, sobrient, and shock warring in mind and body. He had no sense of what was seemly.

She looked at the console, at Adam's face, embedded in the image plate. Somewhere in one of the earliest stories Adam ever told them, there was a glass coffin, but who was in it, she could not remember.

Beyond the console, she felt the counselor watching her. She did not look up. She wanted, above all, to forget his face.

Karel said, in a stifled voice, "Sorry," and left the room in a stumbling rush, hand to mouth.

The counselor said, "Someone will look after him," though Cybele had not moved.

She said, in a small, chill voice, "He always had an easier time of it with our father than I did."

She felt the attention from across the table warm slightly. He did not say anything condescending, such as, That does not mean you will feel it less. She was glad of that. She risked, at last, a look that saw. He was primary, like herself, though melanin-enhanced to a deep brown, his eyes were white, almost a bluish white, instead of pink. He was large framed, but soft-bodied as an adaptive with his protective layering of fat. Trailing down his cheek from the outside corner of his left eye was a ripple of silver lines, a tattoo, almost hidden by the breadth of his cheek. She said, "You're a Questioner."

They refused to give themselves a name; the most common name given them was the Questioners. They pursued the reconciliation of science and faith, of human engineering and divine plan, with energy, argument, and rigor. They had, Adam said, a blind boundless optimism that God was explicable, and by God, he added with rare irreverent humor, they would get the explanation from Him. Nevertheless, he respected them, as he respected few others who made themselves overfamiliar with God.

She pointed at the console, at Adam's face. "So *you'd* appreciate that."

"Yes," he said, "I do." Considered her a moment. "Do you understand what he is asking?"

"Does it matter?" she said, bitterly, testing him.

"If you applied for an order for regeneration, you would probably lose, given he has so carefully defined what he would wish. The law is always greatly relieved when someone does so in a case like this, because the expression of clear wishes impinges directly upon this issue." His eyes held her. "We might restore life, but not identity. We might recreate mind, but not individuality. There is the person who was your father, making a declaration of personhood, of *choice*."

"And where is my choice?" she said, obdurate.

He said, gently, "Tell me."

It sounded like a yielding, but she felt it as a casting out. As long as she were argued against, she had a hard surface to press upon. Now she foundered, suddenly adrift in grief and darkness. She said, "I want . . . I want . . ." a gobble of sound. He got to his feet, moved quickly for such a large man, and came around to kneel beside her. She rocked, swallowing convulsively. She would not turn to him. She muttered, thoughts in passing, "You'd just be a thing. You'd be nothing to me."

He seemed to find sense in her nonsense and made no other move toward her.

She found, after a time, that she was too tired to struggle any more. She closed her eyes, and the darkness she found there did not frighten her. "I have no choice, do I?"

"Your father made a very clear statement of his wishes."

"And you approve."

A silence. "I have seen too many cases where the bereaved family request regeneration and find themselves—despite their best efforts—with a stranger. The more intense the tie, the greater the hope, the more shattering the final loss."

"I think," she said hopelessly, "I would still like—the chance."

"The one thing," he said, still kneeling beside her, "a religious sense gives one is the knowledge that choice is not something human beings have been newly afflicted with. Many people think it is, they think that it came with technology, and the power of technology, with knowledge and the pushing back of frontiers. But at the core of religion is the knowledge that humankind has always had choice, and will be judged as much on the smallest and most commonplace of choices as on the largest."

The habits of speech sounded so familiar, but the voice was a stranger's, quiet and resonant and a little rough. "Did you know him?"

"We corresponded sometimes."

"It wasn't an accident, then, your being here."

"No. I asked. I thought—I thought we might have a language in common."

She opened her eyes and looked coldly at him. "Adam and I had quarreled. I did not see him for four years until last night. I wanted to go into space, and for that I need transfections—major transfections—transfections which might risk my sacred personhood by restructuring parts of my cortex. He regarded that as meddling with the divine plan." She gasped shallowly, dragged down by pain and confusion, by the knowledge that having barely found him again, she had lost him. "I am *not* religious."

"But it is a language you understand."

She said, "How dare you use it. How *dare* you—!" She pushed the heel of her hand against her mouth to stifle worse. Not for his sake, but for hers. She had nothing else left of Adam. Let her at least behave as she thought he would want her to. She had never seen him grieve, though she knew he had suffered losses. Space. Abra. She said, "Where's my brother?"

She barely perceived his attention shift as he activated his internal node. "One of my colleagues is seeing to him."

"How long can I stay here?"

"As long as you need to."

She cried out soundlessly, No. Lost, floundering, again. She did not want the decision. She did not want to choose how long to stay, whether to go. She did not want willingly to step into the current toward the future. This loss was none of her doing; she wanted to take no part in it.

The counselor said, gently, "What is it?"

"He shouldn't *be* dead. Why is he dead? Why did this happen?"

There was a silence, then the counselor said, "I know someone who might be able to begin to answer those questions, Cybele. Would that help?"

He dreamed of the sea-gifting, that invented ritual by which the dead were given to feed the seas which had fed them. A ritual of great significance to some, as an expression of the spiritual connection between sea and seaborn, and of simple practicality to others. Rache would have allowed the practical readily; his deeper feelings were ones he rarely discussed. In his dream he was attendant and observer both. He could see the sargasso calm of the upper skin of the sea, stippled with the tips of fronds and leaves. He could see the dense subsurface growth, the whorls of leaves, sprays and fans, greedy for sunlight, all with a faint blush of painter algae. He could see them swimming through the green umber shadow below, pressing through the tough cables of kelp, the strong stems of ribbongrass. He could see, in the heavy shadow, the undermatting of the forest, the unique layer of intertwined root, tubule, and worm, which captured the forests' wastage.

Two scouted, four flanked, and two towed the body, wrapped in ribbons coated with repellent. Even so, all along its backtrail, exquisitely sensitive receptors would be waking to its scent. All farewells, all formalities, would have been conducted in the holdfast. Upon a signal, the towers would shed the rope, there might be a pause, and then they would swim away, abandoning her to the sea's disposal. He swam with them, lagging behind, half imagining, half dreaming, the shadowy figures ahead, the barred cables of plantlife, the darkness below. Until they could suddenly see the cables thinning, backed by sunlight. They broke surface in the open sea, and inhaled, with simple gratitude. The leader looked around, to see that they all were with her. He thought it was Maria of Kense, but as she turned toward him, flesh and color melted from her face like a mask; and the face beneath was Juniper's. He jolted awake, and thought for an appalled moment that he had said her name aloud. But the monitoring system made no mention of an outcry.

He scrubbed his face with his hands. He supposed the meaning of the juxtaposition was that Juniper had been sea-gifted, consumed by the sea; he should have been glad that her face were not affixed to the corpse. What else to make of the dream: expression of a fear that Juniper, like Maria of Kense, would not care for what he had become. Probably she would not. She wanted to make Blueheart into something unique in the galaxy. She wanted to make him into something unique. She had been grievously disappointed in his timid, pedestrian approach to her radical vision.

But then, Rache thought, the tribesman in him

believed that uniqueness was a perversion. The ecologist in him knew that the sport was, more often than not, nonviable. In interdependence, in symbiosis, there was survival. More than that, virtue.

Only now did he grasp why Juniper had been so obsessed with uniqueness. He could say, and believe, that genetics was not identity, that she and her twin had been separate entities from conception. But still he must remember that moment of recognition, when Teal walked in the door and he saw Juniper. Juniper's presence overlaid Teal; Teal's would overlay Juniper. Little wonder that she must, above all, be *different*, and why nobody knew of her sister until her death.

He felt feverish, parched, exhausted. The fast-heal given him to knit his cracked bones would excite some inflammatory response. He had been warned; it was nothing to worry about. His fretfulness had nothing to do with his condition. He needed people around him. The holdfast did not teach skill in solitude. He called up the eventstream on the wall display; it would give him some kind of company. Instead, he found himself viewing a report of the disaster at ringsol six. A remote-driven camera crept through the seeping, half-lit corridors. They looked worse than he remembered them; he watched, with a sick fascination, until an overlay advised him he had an incoming message.

"Rache." Michael's close-focus image looked out of the inset, the silvery filigree of his tattoo caught by some strong sidelight. Rache squinted, unable to distinguish the background, bright-colored, shifting. Michael said, "I'm going to visit you later on, but I wanted to ask you if you would talk to a couple of people beforehand. Now I've taken a good look at you I wonder if this was a good idea."

"Fast-heal," said Rache, and swallowed salt and dust. "Who?" he said huskily.

"Adam de Courcey's children, Karel and Cybele. I'm counseling them over their father's revival."

"I thought . . . there was a will."

"There is, and it's a sound one, but they're having difficulties. I can't say whether they're having more than the usual difficulties, or even if I should expect to be further involved . . . but I offered them the chance to talk to you. I know I sound vague, but there's something about them . . ." He threw up his hands. "Before I go any further, how are you?"

"Bearing up," Rache said.

"Do I have to transmit instructions for the care of pastoral tribesmen?" The tone was light, the intent serious. Michael was, among other things, a pastoral-liaison, one of the professional intermediaries between pastoral and primary societies.

"Are you sending me visitors for their good or mine?" Rache said, tartly.

Michael blew out his breath. "Theirs, I swear. I think it would help them to talk to someone who was there. Now, there are some undercurrents, but I'm not sure what they all are. Prejudice against adaptation, likely; they are the children of an old religious, and I have the impression he had fairly exclusive nurture of them. Be patient with them. An element of vengefulness, particularly in the woman." He considered a moment. "This could be hard on you, Rache. Do you feel any responsibility for the people who died?"

"It was the sea," Rache said, expressing in a bare phrase the fundamental submission of the pastoral-born to the will of the sea.

Michael's brows drew together slightly. "Even

though I've worked with pastorals all these years, I still cannot quite *feel* what you feel when you say that." Then he gave him a steady look and said, "Is that all? Are you sure you did everything you could?"

"Michael—" Rache said, warningly, and Michael smiled, his most harmless smile.

"It's a question you need to answer before you are confronted by young Cybele. To yourself, if not to me. As I speak to you it's becoming clearer to me why I needed to speak to you."

"You think she would blame me."

"I think she might. Though she may not know it yet, she is looking for someone to blame."

The young woman led her brother into the room, her stride driving and combative. Rache caught his breath, spooked: but for her eyes, her face was Adam's, barely softened by youth and femininity. A ghost risen from the sea. He hardly saw her brother, who entered uncertainly behind her and paused, just clear of the closing door.

But while she stared down at Rache, he spoke first. "Cybele, he's sick. We shouldn't be doing this."

Rache's gaze shifted to him. He had met Karel before, at least onscreen, as Cesar Kamehameha's assistant. In his face, too, Rache saw the face of the drowned. He started to ask a question, but the question was lost in Cybele's sudden sharp motion. She jerked away from Karel's reaching hand and said to Rache, "He agreed to see us, and I want some answers from someone who was there. From someone who was responsible who was there. You heard them saying that he was the one who directed the rescuers. Why didn't they find Adam before he was beyond help?"

"Don't you listen to *anyone*?" Karel burst out, tears in his raw eyes. "They said probably nothing would have saved Adam."

Rache swallowed, dry-throated. "You are Adam de Courcey's children. Cybele," to the woman, "and Karel," to the man.

"Yes, we are," Cybele said, "And you are Rache of Scole, director of ringsol six. What can you tell us?"

Karel rubbed his eyes. Rache liked him for the openness of the gesture, even as he understood Cybele's tearless, slashing grief. Karel said, "We are sorry to impose on you . . ."

"But you want answers," Rache said, for him. "I will give what answers I can. I must warn you that I am not as alert as I might be. I've had fast-heal, and I'm somewhat feverish."

Cybele's eyelids lifted. Like the unsheathing of spines. As clearly as if it were shouted, Rache heard the thought: Good. She said, "What took you so long to find my father?"

"He was not where he usually was at that time."

"Why was that?"

"Cybele, I did not know your father well."

"You did not like him."

"It is difficult to share a friendship with someone who sees you as an offense to God, no matter how much you respect him. And I *did* respect your father . . . and I would have wished it otherwise, because he was part of the settlement of this planet which is my home."

She shivered slightly with tension. Karel shifted, about to speak. She turned on him. "You know that's not all."

"Well, if you're so sure he knows, *ask him*."

Cybele glared at her brother. Karel slid away from her glance, into a chair. Halfway through the motion he looked up at Rache. "I can sit down, can't I?"

Rache gazed at him. His face seemed to blur into another, one with the same cast of bone, the same olive skin, the same black, coarse hair, rough even when bound back, as Karel wore it, as she had worn it ... "Yes," Rache said vaguely. "Did you ever know Juniper?"

"Juniper?" But of course not, Rache thought, trying to bring his mind into focus. They would have been only four or five years old when Juniper died; they would not have known her. He started to excuse himself, and apologize for Karel's unease. But Cybele forestalled him, saying sharply, "There's a reason Adam could have been wanted dead. Maybe the same reason your ringsol was sabotaged."

Rache was a moment parsing that odd, passive sentence ... "would have been wanted dead" ... and then he understood. He caught himself on the verge of demanding an explanation. This was too important. He said, instead, "Could one of you please get me some cold water?"

The request took Cybele by surprise: it was not the reaction she had expected. She watched him, warily, while Karel obliged, coming around to his side to draw a glass from the bedside tap and offer it to him. Rache poured half of the glass into his palm, and splashed it over his scalp and face. The rest he swallowed in a breath. The effect was purely psychological, a seizure of self-possession after the hours of drifting malaise. "Now, please explain."

He saw that she was reflecting on, or reconsidering,

her bluntness, wondering what she had aroused in this torpid hulk. He said, "If you have any information whatsoever, you *must* tell me—or if not me, if you have some reason not to trust me, you must tell someone who is part of the investigation."

"She doesn't." Karel started back to his feet, gathering a shaky dignity. "I'm—*we're* sorry to have bothered you—"

"Sit down," Rache and Cybele said together. They stared at each other, startled by inadvertent collusion. Then she said, "You are not afraid of what might happen if I tell someone else?"

"I know of no reason to worry."

He saw her face tremble, and settle into a forced stillness. "I can't tell you. I can't trust you—"

"Because I am pastoral?"

Her face stiffened; her eyes fixed, unblinking, on him. This was more than just an unseemly prejudice then. But *what*? He felt as though he were trying to swim in plasma, in a medium fluorescent, insubstantial and inhospitable. "Then go to someone else. Please. For the sake of justice and all of us who survived."

She said nothing, torn, unable to go on and unable to leave.

Karel said, "Sir, do you know anything more about what happened on ringsol six? Other than what is public knowledge. She needs to know. *I* need to know."

His voice subdued Cybele. She moved to stand behind him, thin hands gripping the back of the chair.

"What I know is this," Rache said. "There was an externally introduced virus. Whether it was intended to have the effect it had is doubtful. We were experimenting with a system upgrade at the time, and it seems the two modified each other."

"But who," Cybele said, "and why?"

Karel said, "What else do you know about the virus? Where it came from?" Ah, yes, Rache thought, Karel was a cyberneticist himself. Nowhere near Teal Blane Berenice's standard, though the Berenici complexes gave him the potential.

"Who—we do not know. Why—" He paused, not wanting to voice his next thought. But if he were to obtain their trust, and whatever information they had, he would have to repay in kind. He said, "I wondered if it might have had something to do with my work. If you follow the development of terraforming proposals . . ." Cybele made a little, dismissive headshake, and stopped, midgesture. She looked shocked, and then lost, bereft. She had woven a complicated, supportive pattern of rationales and explanation, but this did not fit.

Karel said in bewilderment, "What would a terraforming proposal have to do—" Then he, too, stopped, appreciated. His reaction was the opposite of Cybele's. He seemed to reach out and embrace the possibility, even as he said, "Surely not."

Rache said, "It may be that the virus was only intended maliciously, to erase data. To register displeasure at the promotion—"

"You said you do not *yet* know," Karel said. "Do you mean you might know soon?"

No, Rache admitted, he was not fit to match wits with Adam's children. He considered his next statement very carefully. "We were able to salvage some material from the ringsol net itself. It is being analyzed."

"By whom?" Cybele said immediately.

"No," said Rache. "I will not tell you yet." "Cannot" might have been safer; he could have camouflaged his own decision behind regulations, instructions, higher authority; but thought what he might have wished for his own children and could not do it.

She heard the difference, looked at him with narrowed eyes. "I want to know who did this."

Rache said, quietly, "We will find out. I give you my word."

"We will wait on that," Adam's daughter said, and turned away.

SIX

Karel's rooms were in the new town, within sight of the family hall of their childhood. The outermost wall was glass, overlooking balcony, the outlying platforms, and the wide, bright sea. Cybele doubted she would have tired of the sea, but Karel did; as they entered, and her face turned toward the light, the window flooded with color. She halted, disorientated, staring into the changing yellow, green, red. She made out at last the shapes, of swimmers flowing together, dancing, copulating, shrinking, and fusing, birth in reverse. Limbs and bodies touched, joined, overlaid, and blended; figures rippled, fissioned, dissolved in green, yellow, and red swirls. She said, harshly, "Turn it off."

She walked forward and laid her palms against the clear panes. Karel's storm-frame stood upright on the balcony; she looked through its struts. Beyond, the view was open to sky and sea. The sun glared upon roofs, roof windows, roof gardens. It reflected dully from the scarred landing bowl. It sparkled bitterly upon the sea. She knew it was real, but it looked like an image of itself, mounted behind glass. Even if she opened the window, and stepped out, felt the wind and the sun, she felt the image would seem no less artificial, the glass no less present. She said, "What was that story Adam used to tell us, about someone in a glass coffin?"

Karel said faintly, with a shudder in his voice, "I don't remember."

Down there, spread like a golden plate upon the sea, was Minaret, where they had grown up. She said, "Do you remember when we decided that Adam was really a space alien?" There was no answer; she did not expect one. She pressed closer to the glass, so that she could see the barrier at the edge of the wide, slanted skirt around Minaret's artificial beach. Minaret had seemed the world entire to her as a child, but then she and Karel and Adam had rarely left it.

She smiled a little, thinking of how, at the age of six, they had decided Adam was an alien. It seemed the only explanation for his quirks. Adam's omnipresence, for instance; unlike other parents, he took such work as came to him on Rossby. Although committed to the principle of the family hall, he was never quite at ease with the practice; he begrudged delegating his children's care. He could be a relentlessly consistent disciplinarian, incapable of the benign inconsistency of other, busier parents. He had little sense of the trivial or the absurd. She leaned her face upon her wrist upon the glass. An alien; of course. She wondered if he ever knew.

She turned to see Karel lying still on the couch, eyes closed. The light was harsh on his face; she could see him as he would be decades hence, grown tired, grim, and older than Adam. She wondered if he were asleep, and how he dared. She knew Adam was dead; she handled the knowledge like something spiny and poisonous; and asleep she knew she would fumble, and be pierced. She watched Karel sleeping, breathing slowly. A little silver paint still streaked his jaw.

"Karel," she said, quietly, not expecting an answer, "what are we going to do now?"

No answer came. She walked stiffly over to the console in the far corner of the room; sophisticated, compared to hers, the hand web supple and very fine. She laid her hand in it, uplinked to the AOC database, and began to work, to resume the searches which she had been conducting when the message arrived, calling her down to the hospital. But the images wavered before her eyes, and she laid her head down on the console to ease her dizziness. Karel's voice said her name; she heard the rustle as he moved. She said, not lifting her head, "I thought you were asleep."

He said, in a very fragile voice, "They've given us Adam's effects. All his files from the net and his cercortex. They're huge."

"Of course they are," Cybele said, lifting her heavy head. "He lived a long time." Lights flashed on the console, protesting her slump; she stared dully at them. "Would you check them and see if there was anything more about that body?"

There was a silence. "I will not," Karel said, shrilly, ending with a gulp. She turned in surprise, and craned her neck to look up at him; her spine felt sodden, unequal to the weight it bore. He was staring whitely at her from across the room. He said, with an effort at conciliation, "You don't need to do anything about that any more, Cybele. Adam's left you more than enough for enhancements."

"How do you know what he's left me?" He checked, pale mouth agape, but she knew. He had always taken such liberties, an innocent presumption—or a retaliation against her dominance; perhaps he did not himself know. He said defensively, "I wanted to be sure he'd left you enough."

"And what would you have done if he had not?"

He sat up, abandoning contact with the net. "You are the one sick with bitterness about what she cannot do, not I. You are the one living like a rat in one of the old quarters because she is desperate to afford enhancement. Not I. You are the one *determined* to pursue this investigation . . ." He choked himself off.

Her spine stiffened. "Are you implying that—that I—caused Adam's death?" she said flatly.

He went so ashen she thought he was going to faint. "No," he whispered.

"Thank you," she said, admitting no sisterly impulse to forgive or comfort. Anger was a blessing, a wellspring of strength, however unholy. She rapped the console. "Stay out of my affairs, Karel."

He gave her a flinching, colorless smile, and looked away. She studied the console. The sight of the fragment of illegal sequence nauseated her; she cleared it away with a sweep of the hand. She did not want to examine Adam's bequests. Karel, she saw with a glance, had had no such inhibitions; he was sitting laxly on the couch, his eyes closed and shifting behind their lids, a mild, quizzical, pained frown on his face. But then he had not been the one who had had to assent to his official death. He had been too distraught, too sick, to either argue or agree. She got to her feet and went to lean against the window. Maybe she would go down to Minaret. Stand with her feet in the water of that gently sloping beach, looking out toward the barriers. Pretend, for a while, that there was no world beyond the one that Adam had chosen for them.

Karel made a wordless sound of exclamation. She lifted her head, and slowly rolled herself around against the glass. He was staring at her with bright, agitated eyes. "Cybele, Abra had other daughters. Juniper Blane Berenice was Abra's *daughter*."

"What do you mean?"

"Exactly what I say—" He stretched out a hand, impulsively, as though to convey knowledge through touch, and then realizing, gestured her impatiently to the console.

She said, "You tell me." Assured he would never know that her refusal was anything more than deference to his superior ability.

He said, avidly, "The last entry in his personal record is about him and you—you never told me about this, Cyb!—meeting Teal Blane Berenice. She's Abra's daughter; so was her twin, Juniper. Juniper met up with them on Earth and signed as passenger aboard the *Callas*—she must have had some kind of wealth to come all the way to Blueheart on her own resources—"

"She was an acclaimed artist," Cybele said, with a slight curl of the lip, thinking of that artist's work gracing the walls of her own broken-down residence; it had, of course, been mounted long after the acclaim had faded.

"Juniper wanted some kind of apology from Abra for leaving her and her sister when she was a child. She wanted to make montages on the theme of an abandoned child. She *plagued* them. Adam blames her for Abra's leaving before you and I were even born. He threw Juniper off Minaret when she tried to visit us; can you imagine that? He said he *rejoiced* at her death." He looked up, eyes wide. "Can you imagine anyone pushing Adam so far? Could you imagine either of *us* making *scenes* with Abra, because she left us? She must have been very passionate—"

"Or very selfish," Cybele said. The animation went out of Karel's face, and protective habits made her yield to charity. "Abra came from a women's enclave. Mothers' ties with their children are sacrosanct. Abra broke all kinds of social prohibitions and several laws by leaving." She could anticipate the next question from the slightly resentful eagerness in his face. "He never told me. I called him an unnatural father once, when I was thirteen or so, and he made me do research on childrearing practices to fit myself to comment. God knows," she said, her voice wavering, "I think that's what he did himself." She clenched her jaw so that she could neither speak nor cry; she could feel both rising in her throat. Karel looked away, his face stricken.

"Karel," she said, at last, in a whisper, "I want to know who killed him."

"Why?" Karel said, sounding stifled. "What point is there?"

When she did not answer, knowing none, he dropped his head almost to his knees. When he spoke, she thought he said, "Don't, Cybele. Don't." But he would not repeat himself when asked. She said, to herself, "Teal Blane Berenice is an expert-voyager." He did not seem to hear. She pushed herself away from the window and returned to the console. She webbed her hand, and asked for whatever information there was to be had on Juniper Blane Berenice, Teal Blane Berenice, and the women's enclaves of their childhood on Berenice.

For the third time that hour, Teal's stress alert gave warning, and, a minute later, detached her node from the net, returning her to her bayside room and a moment later, the thought: Juniper.

She had undertaken this investigation not from professional honor, or a favor due, but from the need for refuge.

Outside the net, there was nowhere to go, but grief.

She should sleep, she thought, in sleep, forget, and after sleep, work again. Sleep was accessible with a simple inner manipulation of implants, a momentary wish.

Instead, she got unsteadily to her feet, and went out onto the balcony. The day had gone, without her knowledge. She was used to that. Years, even decades, had passed her unaware. Only the net, the several nets of her postings and travels, were stable in time.

Juniper, she thought, had loved this place. Loved it as Juniper loved, lavishly, loudly, publicly. It had been a long love, for Juniper. And a mortal one.

She found it incredible that Juniper was dead. Juniper would not have wanted to die, and Juniper did nothing she did not want to do. She might declare herself ready to die . . . of love, frustration, grief, and pure petulant vexation, but to die in truth, in all finality, no, that was not Juniper.

She leaned on the balcony railing, and tried to see it as Juniper would see it.

Her balcony overlooked a miniature bay, with rafttown on three sides and the longest open to the sea. Lights shone on the bay, hazed the darkening distances. The lights turned the water transparent, and she could see the convolutions of the city's reef garden. At the mouth of the bay the reef ended, and the water became black with depths. People were swimming in the bay, and the wind in her face smelled of algae.

That was all. She could perceive shape and movement, she could understand what she saw, but color, imagination, beauty were all Juniper's only. She had given them up to Juniper, many years ago. And she had not missed them, she told herself, she had not missed them. She had her work, and she had Juniper, even at such remove. It had had to be this way. For Teal, twin-ship was profoundly necessary. For Juniper, twinship was profoundly threatening. Throughout their child-hood she had tried persuasiveness, guile, and small cru-elties to persuade Teal to change her face, to lie, to become merely a sister rather than a mirror-self. Juniper, of course, was the original; Juniper, of course, should not be the one to change. Despite reason and entreaties from their mothers and aunts, dismayed at Juniper's spite and Teal's endurance, Juniper had never ceased to struggle. Juniper's was a struggle for existence, and Teal's was not the endurance of weakness, but the patience of strength. Juniper was hers, her half, and Juniper knew it. And Teal wore her possession as lightly as she could. Whatever else Juniper wanted of her, Juniper could have.

She had never, ever expected that Juniper would leave, would buy passage on the slowest, cheapest bot-tom C cruiser to Scarlett's world, and vanish into the silence of cold sleep for thirty-five years.

She dimly recalled that that pain had been even more appalling than this. Perhaps because it had been Juniper's choice. Perhaps because she had expected other people to understand her grief. Instead, they saw it as expression of an unhealthy attachment, from which Juniper had, rightly, fled.

And so she in her turn fled, to Chara station, and the start of her apprenticeship. She had withdrawn into her mind and the nets, and left the living worlds to Juniper. Including this one.

The doorbell chimed. She did not understand what it was until the net advised her she had a visitor. She felt no wish to talk to anyone. She asked to receive an image. It showed a lowered head, folded hands, the opalescent sheen on shrouding veils. She caught her breath, told herself: no. Would Juniper, who had so long denied anything shared, appeal to shared memory? But who else here would know the fashions of century-past Berenice. She could have image-enhanced the hidden face. But she let her heart loose from its tethers and felt its beat shake reason from her. She pushed through into the main room, brought up the lights, said: "Open the door."

The breeze caught the scents of mint and cinnamon. The woman's veils lifted and fanned out on it. She raised gloved hands and lifted the veil from her face. Glass bracelets sparkled and chimed as they slid. Her hair was close-cropped, coarse, lying like leaves around her skull. She could not weave it with glass threads, as Teal and Juniper had done. She wore a crystal-bead scoop beneath her chin, suspended from her earlobes. Her face paint was pearly mauve, with indigo rays from her eyes to her temples, and beneath it her features were austere and fine. Her eyes were huge, coppery, hungry.

She was not Juniper. She was not even Berenici.

And yet as she breathed the mint and cinnamon, Teal's heart continued to outrace her thoughts. Mint and cinnamon scent of her wifmère, Abra, partner to the woman who had given birth to her.

"May I come in?"

Teal merely nodded. The woman walked past her; Teal could hear the slip, slip, slip of legs in silken trousers. A veil unfolded to caress her hand. Mint and cinnamon filled the room.

"We met," the woman said, "yesterday."

Teal remembered, vaguely, rain, a bridge, intrusive, well-meaning presences.

"I was with my father, Adam de Courcey. He is dead."

Teal queried the net. Found Adam de Courcey Indi listed as one of the four casualties of ringsol six. The young woman was staring at her with narrow eyes. The bruising of sleeplessness showed through ill-painted cosmetic. "Someone released a virus into the ringsol six net. It damaged the safety overrides and caused the base to flood. Adam was drowned. As an expert-voyager, you are obliged to help me."

"Help you to do what?"

"Trace the virus. Unless *you* are involved."

"I am an expert-voyager. I take oaths of practice, forbidding me to use my knowledge for malicious or harmful ends. And on η Boötes IV I have seen what even regulated net warfare and piracy does to society and the experts who practice it; I want no part of it."

"You're Juniper Blane Berenice's sister."

Teal turned away, toward the open wall. She had not smelled mint and cinnamon since she, Juniper, and their mother had arrived home to find Abra's parting message. From then on, their names were simply Blane, and Abra's favorite scents were deleted from their home scentorium. She pushed aside the blinds to let the rank sea air roll over her. She could still smell mint and cinnamon. She held onto the rods of the blinds, her shoulders just narrow enough to fit. "Go and wash your face, and take off that costume."

"I'm entitled."

Teal gave a twisted smile and did not turn. "You are entirely too crass to be Berenici." In the women's enclave of a hundred years ago, directness was offensive, even obscene. Interrelations were conducted through a delicate, sophisticated language of indirection, innuendo, and gesture. Words were often the least of it. At the intricate games of manners, Juniper excelled.

"I'm your sister."

Teal felt her shoulders stiffen. She felt the woman directly behind her. "One of your genetic mothers was Abra Collette-Beth Berenice. She left Berenice when you were twelve, aboard the *Maria Callas*. My father was crew. When he was discharged here, she stayed. For a while. She left Adam and us—my brother and me *in vitro*—and took a berth on the *Berling*. She's out there now." She stopped, breathing shallowly. "Your sister found them on Earth."

Abra: mint and cinnamon, and a transparent impression of a face, overlaid on her own image. Abra had been seventy years a sublight navigator before trying to reestablish herself on Berenice. She was a scandal for her bluntness, her impatience with elaborate enclave manners, her liking for outside companionship. Most of all, she was a scandal for her departure before the end of her daughters' years of minority. For that, neither daughter bore her name. Yet her husky, sardonic memory always seemed to have something strengthening to say when Teal found herself most alone. She remembered Abra with some loss, but a much greater understanding.

Juniper, though, Juniper had received Abra's departure as a great, unforgivable wound. Scarcely a day went by in those early years when she did not allude to it, feasting on the sympathy, the outrage, the drama.

She never said that she had met Abra again. Or that Abra had had other children.

Teal said quietly, without turning, "Go and wash your face. Then we'll talk."

She heard slipper-shod feet withdraw. Water running. She uplinked with the net, confirming facts. The woman—and her brother, Karel—were Abra's children. They had been gestated *in vitro* and raised by their father in a family hall on Rossby. Karel was Berenici-apt; Cybele was not. She worked for the adaptation oversight committee in a relatively menial capacity.

When she heard movement behind her, she suspended the link and spoke without turning. "I am already investigating the virus. I happened to contact the net just before the virus assault on ringsol six. I linked though an open port and salvaged fragments of the ringsol net and the viruses which destroyed it." Speaking of her work, her purpose, centered her. "I have reconstructed the virus, and I am now trying to reconstruct the net so that I can examine the path of the virus through the net. From the virus I should, in time, be able to determine a programmer's signature, or at least, a program lineage. From the net forensics, I should be able to track the port of entry, or the point of release." She turned. Cybele had washed all traces of face paint from her skin, unclipped her jewelry, except for her glass bracelets, and held her veils folded small in her hands. Whatever had prompted her to such an absurd masquerade? With Juniper, or sociological treatises her only references perhaps she thought it necessary. Teal said, "I am not inexperienced in this kind of investigation."

Cybele drew breath. Teal, however, was not finished. One of Abra's wisdoms was that every family, every society and subculture, has its own intricate systems of conduct and communication. An outsider must, for survival, be both frank and simple. She said, "I do not see that a genetic relationship should give you any special privileges as regards my investigation. Such things happen, particularly to voyagers. Your father did not introduce us at our meeting. I would rather you take your cue from him." Done, she waited.

Cybele said, "I have some information which might be relevant."

"What kind of information?"

"A possible reason—"

Teal held up a hand. "What I do is pure forensic analysis, without context. Contextual input comes in the next, or higher stages; at this stage it might bias my approach."

Anger flickered across the bare face. "Will you tell me your results, or is that special privilege?"

"The holder of my contract will dictate release."

"Who is that?"

"Rache Scole Blueheart."

"Rache!" Cybele cried out, the first simple outburst Teal had had from her. "He could be right at the heart of it!" Teal heard the small crackle of a breaking bracelet, and thought of Juniper. Teal had been able to wear glass rings and bracelets, but Juniper, never. Cybele raced on, "You may not want context, expert, but you *need* context. Rache is a deep adaptive. He's explicitly anti-terraforming, pro-permanent adaptation—"

Teal said, "Have you cut your wrist?"

She looked down, flinched slightly at the sight of blood and the unfelt cut. When she moved her hand, the curved fragments of two bracelets scattered on the floor. "Take them all off," instructed Teal.

This time she followed Cybele to the san-cubicle and watched her rinse the cuts. Watched the bare, white reflection in the mirror. She said, to the reflection, "It has been a long time since I was on Berenice, and even when I was, I was not good at the games they played." She let it rest there.

Cybele's coppery eyes sought hers. "If you want

information about Juniper—personal information from my father's logs—I have that." She said it with an edge of anger that Teal did not understand; nor did she want to. She sent an instruction to the net; a moment later three sterile bandages dropped into the dispenser slot. She fished them out one-handed. Cybele took them from her, leaving her hand lingering in the air. A moment later, she remembered what she had been waiting for. Juniper always offered her cuts to be bandaged.

"She made people angry," Cybele said. "She made my father very angry, how angry I never knew until I read his logs. My mother would not have left Blueheart so soon if it weren't for Juniper and her demands." She watched Teal's face in the mirror, trying to see how she took this in. Teal did not react. She had been Juniper's proxy for those she offended or discarded for twenty-six years; it seemed she must extend the service to a second generation. They expected likeness, or insight from her. Protest was pointless, and explanation distasteful.

"Are you here to find out what happened to her?"

Teal said nothing, determined now not to discuss Juniper with this unwelcome half-sister. Cybele turned to face her, and said with a shaky chill, "I thought you would understand how I would want to find out about Adam."

"I can understand," Teal conceded, in a rusty voice. "Yes."

Cybele waited. Teal said, "Just that."

"Hey," said Michael, settling himself at Rache's bedside.

Behind him on the screen, the telemetry from ringsol six silently continued, a shifting backdrop of shad-

ter luster of pooled water. Rache

owed rooms, the pewter luster of pooled water. Rache had fallen asleep watching it, uplinked to the salvage teams. Doubtless they had been relieved at his sudden quiet. They had exhibited patience above and beyond the call of duty.

"How are you feeling?"

"Don't ask."

"How'd you do with the de Courceys?"

Rache rubbed his face with a mittened hand. "I could have done better." Michael tilted his head, waiting. Rache told him, word for word. Michael's eyes widened, when Rache mentioned the virus—expanding on what he had told Adam and Cybele—but when he spoke he addressed Rache's concern, first.

"Never mind; I doubt you did any damage, though the survey service would no doubt have preferred that they not know about the virus until some official announcement could be made. You asked some good questions; pity you could not have persuaded them to give you good answers. Those may yet come. By the sound of it, you made a start in getting them to trust you. You may," with a smile, "not go unrewarded in the end."

Rache sighed, frustrated. "I cannot think why they would feel that Adam had some part in this."

"True. Adam's worst enemies were other theologians." He paused. Rache, knowing him, was forewarned of a serious and probably disquieting observation. "Rache, human as it is to speculate, and characteristic as it would be to become involved, *is* the who, what, and why of this virus of your first concern? There are others as committed and better qualified. *You* are best qualified to reestablish ringsol six as a working concern. I am by no means suggesting you have been derelict in your duty to date, but I am suggesting that you not expend precious energy on this investigation."

"You're right, but I . . ."

Michael leaned back, folded his arms. "Of course I'm right. You'd know that for yourself; that is one of your strengths as an administrator: you know your limits and respect other people's competence. And one of your present difficulties is that you do not know the people involved in the investigation. I've noticed you don't take long to decide whether or not you can rely upon someone. I suggest you wait to speak with them, and then decide whether the investigation needs your personal attention."

"Yes, counselor," said Rache, meekly.

Michael leaned forward, slapped his arm lightly. "Michael. This is the hectoring voice of friendship, Rache."

"If," Rache said, "if it should be connected with the yellow-striped proposal—" Michael leaned forward, but said nothing. "Should I not know?"

Michael sat upright. "You'll know, Rache. But that is not what you are asking, is it? What you're asking is, how much am I—are *we*, remember—responsible? How much should we modify our approach, our vision of the future, to consider people for whom our vision of the future is so unbearable as to make them turn criminal—" He checked himself. "Or am I attributing my thoughts to you?"

Rache sighed. "I don't feel responsible for people's sense of threat by our proposal. But if that was the reason, I do feel responsible for what happened to Adam, Micah, Elisabet, Ainsleigh."

"Odd, that," Michael said, mildly, his eyes watchful. "You would take no responsibility for the effect of your actions on strangers, but you do take responsibility

for the effect of a coincidence on your people . . ." He
eased into an inviting silence. Rache did not fill it.

"Come on, Rache," Michael said, "talk to me."

"What about?"

"What you did down there. How you injured your
back. What you feel about the decisions you made."

"Damn you," said Rache, tiredly.

"Surely, but there'll be better company there." He
paused, said simply, "Would you tell me if there were a
reason, Rache?"

"A reason for . . . ? A reason," understanding at last.
A reason for him to feel particularly responsible. A reason to suspect a connection. He appreciated Michael's
skill. Asked as it was, without challenge or apology, it
demanded serious thought, and not reflex denial. He
thought, in a series of flicker-frames, of Juniper, of
Daven, of Einar, of Lisel, of Maria of Kense. Of the ten-
sions between his loyalties. It seemed he could feel them,
suddenly, in his muscle and bone, pulling upon him. If
there were a reason . . . a reason that he should know. If
it were not some faceless stranger, for whom he felt no
connection, but someone of his own . . . He remembered,
again in flickers, his father, his mother, his grandmother,
Tove of Scole; brothers, sisters. He saw, from twenty-five
years ago, the gathering awaiting him in Tove's float to
denounce his leaving. Words scraped into his bones;
when he was sea-gifted, and his flesh eaten away, they
would stand dark on the white bones tangled in the seaweed.

He felt Michael's cool touch on his forehead, on his
shoulder. "Easy," his friend said. "Easy."

He spoke without opening his eyes, "I was thinking . . . if it were someone I knew . . ." His muscles hurt,
as though with pulling. His bones hurt, as though with

scraping. "It would be different." And, knowing the answer even then, "When did they recruit you onto the investigation?"

He felt touch and presence withdraw slightly. "When I asked to be assigned to the de Courceys. It wasn't because of ringsol six that I asked. It was because of them. I thought I could help them."

"And when would you have told me?" Rache said, opening his eyes.

Michael sat down, leaned back: "Before I left here tonight."

Rache considered him in turn. "As you were saying, I need to know and trust the people involved." He spoke mildly, without irony.

"I will make sure you have a chance to meet the others."

"What can I do to satisfy you that I have no reason?" Rache said, an edge in his voice.

"I knew you would never be directly involved, because I know you so well. I cannot know that you would not protect someone who was involved . . . again because I know you so well . . ."

Rache said, "You will be interviewing everyone."

Michael looked quizzical. "As I hope you will be too, since you know these people far better than I."

"I had meant to ask you to," Rache said, with rising anger. "But I had meant to ask you to for *their* good. Three of my people have requested transfer to surface stations. Oliver cannot sleep without full lighting, when he tries to sleep, which is all too seldom. You were the one who was telling me about putting myself to appropriate use. Is this appropriate use of yourself, coming among them as an inquisitor?" His ragged breathing halted him.

Michael was leaning forward, hands dangling from the wrists. He said, "Rache, I am sorry. I did not realize you would have wanted me in that capacity, or yes, I would have declined the invitation. I can yet decline. I shall, if you would prefer."

"No."

"It does not prevent me from doing what I can to help, where help is needed."

"You know better than that," Rache said.

A silence. A sigh. "I do know better than that. I hope not to, but I do. I can see it already happening with you. You've placed me on the other side."

"Why did you agree?"

"Too many of the putative scenarios touch upon primary-pastoral relations. I thought better myself than someone who does not have my specialities. And I thought I could work with you."

Rache jammed an elbow into his pillow. "Explain to me," he said, harshly, "how this touches upon primary-pastoral relations. What is it that I do not know?"

Michael drew breath, hesitated, breathed out with a sigh. "That is difficult to say; the insinuations are nebulous, and it is their very nebulousness that most worries me." He pressed fingertips to his forehead. "I have heard β Coma Berenices III mentioned, more than once, and there the adaptives resisted extinction for nearly fifty years, and their resistance eventually included sabotage and murder. And while my every instinct tells me that Blueheart pastorals are barely awakened to the possibility of resistance, still it worries me that someone is considering the possibility, or trying to create the shadow of that possibility in our minds; indeed, the overreaction worries me more. It seems excessive for what might have been simply maliciousness which mischance turned fatal, and so is it an irrational excess, or a calculated excess . . . ?"

Rache was silent, remembering the six who had come to claim the body. Michael, uncharacteristically imperceptive, continued his own thought, "And you are at the center of it, grandson to Tove of Scole, son of Astrid of Scole, highest placed pastoral in the survey service and author of the first preservationist proposal to be yellow-striped. Whatever the reason for what happened, you will feel the controversy."

"There should," Rache said, "be no controversy. It is a matter of investigating, learning who and why, and returning ringsol six to operation."

"One can but hope," Michael said. The door slid open; Daven started in, and wavered. Michael rose. "Ah, Daven, don't go. I'm done worrying your kinsman. Rache," a wry smile, "good night." With a last, keen glance at Rache and his nephew, he let himself out.

Daven said, forestalling Rache's greeting, "I have to leave."

He wore a silver-shot gray robe, too big on his shoulders. He had overlapped it, tying the sash and forgetting the press-studs. One hand pinned it to his thigh. Beneath it, his legs were bare. Across his back, the loose fabric did not hide the line of a spear-gun. Rache said, "And go where?"

"I have to leave," Daven said. "I have to."

"I did not ask you why, only where."

"No," Daven burst out. "You never asked."

There was a silence. Rache felt the blood pool heavily in heart and stomach. He gestured, leadenly, toward the chair. Daven stiffened, and would not sit. "What have you to tell me, Daven?"

"Someone—someone asked me to come here—"

"Who?"

"I had to receive messages, receive them and move them into the system, and they would—like starfish—take up what they wanted—and I had to send them out—"

Rache caught a guttural breath. Daven plunged on. "I didn't know what they wanted; I didn't think I needed to know because they—I trusted—"

"And," Rache said, "you received and released one of those messages just before the system failed." It was not a question. "Did you know what would happen?"

"No!" One word, heart-rent.

"Did you ask?" The demands, coming with the anger, like surges. "Did you care?"

"I didn't know!" Daven screamed. "I would have cared. I thought they just wanted to know what was being done down here."

"*Who?*"

"I can't tell you. Please don't make me tell you!"

He could not catch the swell for his next words. His first rage was abating. The heat of it came from the certain violation of the first rules he had ever learned, loyalty to tribe, to kin, to those who gave you trust. Never let harm come to the tribe.

He said, "Was it that way from the beginning?"

Daven had not broken those rules. He had simply never considered the ringsol his tribe.

And Rache had known, or should have known. He had worked to set aside his own dislike, his own potential for distrust. He had so wanted someone from Scole, someone from the family, to learn what he had to teach. He had fastened on Daven without knowing Daven. Their relationship had been false to its core. On Rache's side, selfishness; on Daven's treachery. Now this half-formed man would bear the consequences for the rest of his life. Or be less than a man, less than sane.

Rache said, "I'm sorry."

Daven laughed, a chip of sound which nicked Rache and flew away. "If you hadn't invited me—if you hadn't offered me—if they hadn't known—"

"Who?" said Rache, again. Daven shook his head.

"Shall I tell you," Rache said, "what landsman's law holds for you. For me, too, I suspect. If there are any criminal charges to be laid, the trial process will include an interrogation. Painless, comprehensive, and in a way merciful: what the drugs do is suppress all emotional responses. You no longer care about keeping your own secrets."

"Help me," Daven gasped. He half turned, robe flaring, reaching toward a door too far to touch.

Rache growled, "Stop right there." Daven swirled back, stood facing Rache with brittle defiance.

"Who?" said Rache. "Who sent those messages? Where were the outgoing ones to?"

"I don't know; they sent themselves."

His ire rose again as he thought of scavengers ranging unchecked through his net. "So you do not know what was taken. You do not know who it was taken by. You simply let down our barriers."

"You kept saying pastorals had to take greater interest—"

"Pastorals." Rache bore down upon the crack. It would be. Daven would never have so obliged landsmen. But the worm was landsmen's work . . . Pastorals allied with landsmen, but not for exploration, not for creation, but for destruction and death.

Pastorals.

Rache said, "You should go now."

Daven stared at him in forlorn disbelief. Rache

shook his head slowly. "It will," he said, "only postpone it." But I, he thought, do not want to be the one. "Go," he said.

For some time after Daven left, he sat, watching the blank screen and thinking blank thoughts. There was a lot he had to do before the morning. He brought the console on line, and stared at it a while. Then, on a dull impulse, he used the wall-screen to view the nearest docks. He panned unseen over nighttrippers, and star-sailors, readying their boats. He watched an ambulance boat being unloaded; he thought of Adam, Ainsleigh, Elisabet, Micah.

He found it at last, a silver-shot gray robe, lying heaped at the edge of a diving dock. It looked long left, flattened, uninhabited. Out in the dark, color-splashed water, there was nothing to see.

SEVEN

By morning Rache had done not what he thought he needed to do, but what he thought he could do. It would have to be enough. He sent the last of his messages, archived his files, and tried to compose himself for the coming meeting.

Meredis arrived first. Her shirt jarred his tired eyes, gold-sketched flowers, filled in yellow, orange, violet, and green. Gilded insects suspended in the wide black areas between flowers, and he thought of the color-daubed black water the night before. He thanked her for coming; she said, "What is this about, Rache?"

Michael sidestepped through the door, balancing two steaming mugs and wrapped morning rolls. He held out hands, mugs and rolls for Rache to sort, with a sleepy, rueful grin. "I'm not a morning person," he excused himself, taking back the mug and roll Rache handed him, and settling into a chair. Rache sipped his tea, undeceived.

"Please wait for the others," he said to Meredis.

Chandar and Oliver arrived together. The diver's loose tunic clung as though it had been pulled onto a wet body. His day's growth of hair was dewed with fine droplets, and the diving marks were red and fresh on his skin. He said, to Rache, "We'll be reconnecting the geothermal tap this morning. Power up over the day, and reach third-class habitat status by tonight."

"That's good to hear," said Rache, quietly.

"I'd like to be down there for the reconnection."

"I understand that. There's one more to come." He hoped he had not misinterpreted her silence. Michael watched him from beneath lidded eyes. Meredis tapped impatient finger strokes on her portan. Oliver jittered, and Chandar went to the window and squinted out.

The net signaled her arrival outside. He opened the door for her; she stepped through, quite delicately and nearly uncertainly. She stopped short, with an indrawn breath, when she saw the others, and seemed to shrink. Incongruous . . . with his memories of Juniper, he reminded himself ruefully, and said, "Exper' Blane Berenice, please, come in." He was glad to see she had finally exchanged her dropship papers for a trouser-suit in beige and pink swirl.

She said, "Rache," took the few steps needed to bring her to his bedside, and offered him a fiche.

He took it, saying, "Thank you." She gave him a sharp, expressionless look. The blood was suddenly thick and heavy in his heart. In a kind of giddy challenge, he said to them all, "Exper' Blane Berenice was doing a forensic reconstruction of the salvage, trying to determine the source of the infection."

"Did you?" Chandar said.

"Yes," Teal said. She had not turned from Rache. "Judging by the penetration, judging from the pattern of damage, the source was your own area, administrator."

Rache's heart expelled thickened blood in one great winding stroke. Lightheaded, he heard himself say, "Thank you." Thank you for being mercifully swift in your judgment, thank you for giving me that small warning. He leaned his head back against the pillow and ran a glance across them all. Oliver's mouth was open. Michael watched him with keen, knowing eyes. Chandar's face was expressionless, and Meredis's grim.

"Last night, my nephew Daven came to see me. He had been receiving mail containing starfish programs, which packaged and exported confidential material from the ringsol to persons unknown. Just before the disaster, he activated such a package—"

"Where is Daven now?" Michael said. Something about his voice told Rache he would be unsurprised by the answer.

Rache could not help but look away from him. "He left last night."

"Why?" said Chandar and Meredis together.

"It does not matter," Michael said. "He can be brought back." He got to his feet, putting the mug down on the chair behind him, walked to join Teal beside Rache and stood looking down at him, hands in pockets. His expression was sage and sad.

Rache gestured toward his console. "I expect that I will be at least suspended, and I am so advising the staff. Meredis, I have sent you a fuller memo, covering what you will need to do to restore ringsol six to full operation—surveys, regulations, clearances—should you need it. You should arrange for cover, if not replacement, of medical staff as soon as possible. I presume that Exper' Blane Berenice's evidence will help in the reclassification, since it will exonerate the net and system of any flaw." He glanced at Oliver, who was still sitting, staring at Rache, hurt and betrayal in his face. "You should be able to help Meredis, particularly in finding and interpreting regulations."

"And what," Meredis said, paused to clear her throat, "if it happens again?" Rache flinched slightly.

Meredis said, "Since you chose to release one of those involved."

Rache looked in appeal, to Teal Blane Berenice.

She said, "You should put security systems in place, yes."

Meredis started to speak, stopped, and gathered herself. She flicked at the fiche which Rache still held. "What is this?"

"The conclusion of my analysis." Teal directed her gaze to a far corner of the room. Her featureless brown eyes seemed flatter still. Rache had the sense that she was reciting a prepared summary. "The virus originated from the administrative area, but it was not written by the administrator himself, whose style is quite distinctive, nor by the secondary user in that area, who was engaged in the most elementary work. I reviewed the most recent backup of the system, looking for stylistic similarities or even segments of the code. There were none. That suggested an external origin of the virus. That has now been confirmed." The manner of confirmation was unsavory to her purist's heart, Rache thought. Juniper had never cared to have reality intrude upon art. She faced him square. "I have done as much as I can do. I have satisfied our agreement. I regret that it has led to this end."

"It has not led to any end," Meredis said.

Teal turned her face into profile, looking past Meredis. "On the fiche are my outline recommendations. I do not know Blueheart, its concerns, its nets, its personnel. Without that knowledge, I cannot efficiently proceed."

"You cannot withdraw from your contract," Meredis said, half to her and half to Michael. "Not at this stage."

"I am not withdrawing. My contract was with the administrator, and I have done what I undertook to do. I will not agree to another. My reasons, if you must have them, are personal. I find this work, and its outcome, distasteful, and I have other matters to attend to. Personal matters." Having spoken, she did not move.

Michael said, "The expert is a private citizen; she is free to do what she pleases." He leaned forward slightly, the movement catching Teal's eye; involuntarily she looked at him. "But the inquiry may have further questions about the work you have already done, and it would be a great help if you would be prepared to answer them."

Teal stepped back from him. "I will answer such questions as I can."

"Expert," Rache said. "Teal." He was glad she did look at him. He said, "You did what I asked you to do; thank you. The offer I made you stands." She jerked her head, an ambiguous gesture, and turned away. In turning, she caught Oliver's eye, and stopped. "I regret this," she said, starkly, and left before he could react, or answer.

Meredis said, slowly, "In simple justice I must put it on record that I also trusted and assisted Daven. I encouraged his learning, I helped him use the system, and I had no more idea what he was about than Rache."

Oliver burst out, "Did you know anything about what he was doing, Rache?"

"I knew nothing," Rache said. And, with difficulty, "I'm . . . sorry, Oliver."

The young net manager got untidily to his feet, a ragged unfolding of joints. "So am I," he said, to a point on the floor between his feet, and Rache.

Michael seemed abruptly to reach a decision. "Give

me a few minutes with him," he said to the others. "Please."

They did, because they could not think of what better to do.

Michael walked a chair into place and sat down at Rache's elbow. "Talk to me, Rache."

Rache rolled his head tiredly against the pillow.

"Everything is off record."

"And when you are asked what we spoke about?"

"I'm a primary, my memory's poor . . . Talk to me."

"And say what?"

"What exactly happened between you and Daven last night. I want to know what you were thinking, and what you think he was thinking."

"I have never known what Daven thought."

"Maybe I can help."

It would have to go on record anyway, if not now, later. Wearily, Rache obliged. As he listened, Michael got to his feet, and went to the window, standing there, his shoulders filling the narrow frame and his fists curling closed as he became unaware of them, relaxing as he remembered. He turned back to watch Rache as Rache described his search through the public camera records. And as Rache came to the robe lying on the docks, he sat down and laid his face in his hands.

"So," he said, at last, raising his head, "Daven was doing this for a pastoral, or pastorals. Remember when we spoke—yesterday, was it only? You made so strong a distinction between the guilt of strangers and of people you knew . . . I suppose that is why I knew before Teal said anything. The expression on your face was the same . . ." He shook himself slightly. "I might have made a case that your judgment was impaired—we have medical records and the testimony of everyone who saw you yesterday. But there'd be no point to it; you knew what you were doing. And up until just now, I could believe that, like me, you did not believe it could be pastorals." He stopped; that last sentence was as near bitter as he would let himself come. He sat a moment, in silence, looking within. When he spoke again, it was with a shade more care and containment, as though he did not trust himself. "What I would like you to tell me now is who else do you think is involved? Who could have used Daven in such a way, and who would Daven have let himself be used by?"

"I cannot believe—" His voice rasped to silence. Michael, mercifully, left unsaid the obvious: Would you have believed it of Daven? But even unsaid, it lingered in the air. Who, Rache thought, who from Scole?

Michael leaned forward and gripped his shoulder lightly. "I need answers, Rache. Nebulous insinuations are dangerous enough, but this, this could have terrible consequences for primary-pastoral relationships. If you have no answers, then I, or others, will have to find them elsewhere. We will find them, Rache. It will make no difference to the people involved, and will be far better for you, if you can bring yourself to tell us what you know, or suspect, or fear to suspect. There are things the seas cannot hide, and anyone who does this to you does not deserve loyalty of you."

Rache said, "My loyalty is—my loyalty. It is not devalued by what anyone else does. Only what *I* do."

Michael started to say something, changed his mind. "Why do you suppose Daven came to tell you he was leaving?"

"I don't know."

"Rache—" Michael murmured.

"If he wanted to injure me, he has done that. If he wanted forgiveness, he did not get it."

"You caused the boy no end of difficulty, to my mind. He is too young and immature still to reconcile what he admires in you with your deviance. He's angry at you for trusting him so readily, so that he could betray you, so that all this could happen. But I think you know that. Is that why you let him go?"

"Please," said Rache, eyes closed.

"Daven may also have wanted to warn you, in his own way. He wanted to protect you, as you wanted to protect him." Rache heard a rustle of movement, Michael leaning forward. "Whatever happened to Scole in the past, whatever injustices, believe that the boy will have no more than his due. He was a child, and he was used, and he will be treated like a child who was used; I can promise you that. Would you protect the people who used a child that way?"

"No," Rache said, opening his eyes.

"Do you have any idea who might have sent him here?"

"No," said Rache, looking Michael in the face. Michael considered him, and smiled. "But," he said, and it was not a question, "you'll find out."

"Ah, Cybele." Cesar stood to greet her, his small hands placed lightly on either side of his console. But pressed the welcome no farther, gestured her to a chair, and waited until she sat. "How are you?"

"I am fine," she said briefly, and fixed a steady eye upon him. "You wanted to see me?"

He assessed her a moment, a sage, serene figure

against his shifting aquatic backdrop. "I have some news for you and your brother. Rache has been suspended as administrator of ringsol six. There is evidence that the virus was released from his workspace. His nephew, Daven, has disappeared, with, apparently, Rache's consent." He paused. "Depending upon what else the investigation finds, his suspension may become dismissal, and even criminal charges may be laid." He paused again, and said, delicately, "I thought you might want to know before the news became public."

She nodded acceptance. "Daven?" she said.

"The boy is said to be incapable of having done it on his own. Either Rache was himself involved, or Daven had outside help and possibly incentive . . ."

"Who brought up the evidence?"

"An expert-voyager. Ironically, one under some kind of irregular contract to Rache—but the integrity of expert-voyagers is known to be unimpeachable."

"Ah," breathed Cybele.

"I am glad," he said, "to see that you at least are in fair shape. Karel seems to be taking Adam's death very hard."

"He likes to dramatize," she said, trying to put indulgence into her voice; she owed her brother protection, worried and irritated as she was with him. "Please, give him a little time . . . *Then* give him an ultimatum." They exchanged a conspiratorial smile.

"There is one thing Karel said which does concern me. You have some material which your father gave you—material of marginal legality."

She stiffened; he smiled slightly, his expression saying that he trusted her not to do something as silly as deny. She said, at last, "That's right." And looked hard back at him, *daring* him to threaten Adam's posthumous reputation.

He said, "It is material which is pertinent to an ongoing investigation by the AOC."

"You know," she said, before she could stop herself.

"Of course we know," he said, with raised brows. "But I'm sure you can appreciate the delicacy with which we must proceed. Illegals are very efficient at erasing records, and their records are the one thing we must not lose—for the sake of their subjects. We will need those records so we may trace all their subjects for monitoring. It may be another year yet before we can," he gestured evocatively, "close the net and trap all the fish inside. They must have no intimation whatsoever that there is an investigation. I am going to have to ask you for all the material that Adam gave you. It must be transferred into a high-security holding."

She said, "And what about the ringsol six investigation? What could that uncover?"

"Believe me, I am monitoring the ringsol six investigation very closely . . ." He leaned forward slightly. "Which may be why the public version of events may be somewhat different from the version you hear from me. Some of the facts will have to be suppressed or altered to protect our investigation and interests—it will be necessary to downplay the adaptive involvement. Rache's suspension will go on record as a medical leave: he was injured, and has suffered from reactive depression in the past. But justice will be served in the end."

"Anything I can do, I will."

He looked at her, with a raised brow. "I was under the impression that your longterm plans included enhancement and an application to the exploration service . . ."

"Yes."

"Then why delay? As I am sure you know, enhancements involve a year's treatment, followed by several years retraining."

"I want to see this through, first."

He leaned back, studying her in silence, waiting for a satisfactory explanation.

"The treatment will affect my memory. It may also affect my personality. I will not be the same person I am now. I . . ." She hesitated, then, "Adam never wanted me to do this. I want to—I want to discharge a sort of obligation before I go on. Lay him," with a slight waver in her tone, "to rest."

He shook his head slightly. "Then you believe in life after death?"

"No, I—" and checked herself. She did not believe in life after death. But she believed in something after death. She had an obligation to a living presence, and as long as she thought of that obligation, the presence lived on.

"Cybele, I have to warn you that because of the political complications this investigation could continue for years. You know that enhancements are best done before you are thirty. You have just said you do not believe in life after death; how then can Adam's wishes matter? You would have defied them while he lived, as soon as you had the means. Are you being sentimental?"

She shook her head slightly, to clear it. She had again the feeling of being adrift. "I owe it to my father."

A silence, then he said, "I respect that. But I am going to make a suggestion: that you consult a counselor. There are several affiliated with the AOC; one is particularly good."

She said, under her breath, "I thought you understood."

"Pardon?"

She lifted a face darkened with embarrassment. He thought her sense of the persistence of Adam's spirit, of her obligations to the dead, a pathology needing treating. "We had to speak to one about withdrawing life support," she said, shaping the words precisely. "But it is good of you to concern yourself."

"I am only protecting AOC interests. You are valuable employees." But he smiled, to undercut the self-serving disclaimer. "I know who you mean. He has become involved with the R6 investigation. I make the suggestion as much, if not more, for Karel. He might be prepared to go if you were. And as I say, there are several counselors affiliated with the AOC, and those have the advantage that you will be able to discuss confidential subjects with them."

She understood the allusion. "You think that is it, then? Ringsol six was demolished because of that body. Because somebody wanted rid of all possible records."

"It seems likely. When the investigation moves out into the seas—there are some legal permissions needed—then we will have some answers, and I will let you know. Provided," he said, firmly, "I continue to have reason to trust your discretion and judgment."

"I understand."

"And so," he said, "I trust you understand my unease at your holding pertinent evidence. I am going to ask you to go straight back to your quarters and deliver it to me."

"Karel had a copy of Adam's fiche."

"That," Cesar said, "I already have. Will you give me the other?"

She said, "Will you keep me informed about the investigation—the real investigation?"

He smiled a little, at the crudity of her bargaining. She did not care. He said, "Of course," and she flushed. He affected not to notice. "And about Karel—I hesitate to suggest this to you, but it might be best if you did not mention this or other matters discussed in confidence to him, or put too much reliance on things he might say. At least until he is steadier."

"This," said the image of Cesar Kamehameha, "is a great waste."

He had said the same, in nearly the same tone, over Athene's seaweed-shrouded body. Rache remembered his small, proprietary hand lingering and then lighting on her dulled skin. He remembered how that touch and epitaph had extinguished all Rache's hope. That was nearly forty years ago, and they had had frequent contact since, but Rache was never certain that he saw Cesar without distortion.

Not that Cesar had ever been less than generous and gracious. Rache had enjoyed his tacit, and sometimes explicit, support throughout his career. He might, he thought, have anticipated this reaction to his suspension. He heard the weariness in his own voice. "Excuse me, Director, I am not at my best."

"Hardly surprising," the Director of the AOC said. He folded his neat hands on the desk before him. Fish, weed, and coral formed his backdrop. "Since you prefer directness, let me be direct. I presume you want reinstatement, and that as soon as possible." He raised a finely traced brow at Rache's stiffening. "Or is this more complicated even than it appears?"

"I do not see how it is possible."

"Oh, you are not so fresh out of the water as all that. The inquiry has rolled over you and ground you fine, yes, but now it will grind on, and find new meat.

You will cease to seem such a very great sinner. And it will occur to survey—or if it has not occurred to them, it will be pointed out to them—that it hardly serves the cause of primary-pastoral cooperation if the highest ranking pastoral in the scientific survey service languishes in disgrace merely on account of, shall we say . . . unfortunate affiliations."

"I do not want a . . ." he sought out a word, "*political* rehabilitation."

"Do you want any form of rehabilitation?"

Rache kept his eyes on Cesar's face, knowing that his own was unrevealing. He said, "I confess some ambivalence."

"So," Cesar said, dryly, "the scientific survey service is to lose one of its best administrators to injured pride." He left a silence; Rache did not fill it. "I cannot advocate your reinstatement if you are anything less than utterly committed," Cesar said, gently. "You know yourself what you will face: the resentment, the distrust, the rumors. The work of convincing your peers and subordinates that you are competent and trustworthy will be entirely yours. It would not be fair to either of us for you to go into that with less than an absolute determination to succeed . . . But you do realize, I trust, that your next promotion should place you in Survey Central; in thirty years you could be Director of Survey."

"For the same reason as I should be reinstated," Rache said. It was not new to him, that he could be used to build compromise between primaries and adaptives. It was how he had been planning to use himself. But he could find no appeal in the strategy. To be reinstated for purely political purposes, to have to earn again the trust of his peers and subordinates—the former was repugnant and the latter immeasurably saddening. Even without his other concerns he was not sure how readily he would have done it. But this he knew: he would have done it. But now?

He said, "I want to think about it."

"What else would you do with your life and talents?" Cesar said, with an edge of asperity. "You have been out of adaptive society for twenty-five years; you'd never resettle. You didn't settle even when you had never known anything else."

Rache's heart rate stepped up again, preparing for flight. He was not sure that flight might not be wiser. But, if there were even one small part of Cesar which was motivated by simple supportive interest, he owed him a measure of honesty. "I need time to go to Scole."

"That would not be wise. Whatever Daven has done is done; there is nothing you can do for him; and it could make your . . . rehabilitation even more difficult." He shook his head slightly. "I cannot do anything for you if you are going to keep compromising yourself."

"I am responsible for Daven."

Cesar drew breath. "Tell me, how are you getting on with Meredis? She is not particularly experienced in undersea habitats." Rache's logs of the incident had been quite factual, but Cesar had lived long enough on Blueheart to judge Meredis's action in opening the bulkheads.

Rache risked a response to the subtext. "I put nothing in my record."

"Quite so. But you know better. Do you want to leave such an inexperienced administrator in charge of ringsol six in the aftermath of this?"

He'd gone straight into that trap, as into a Medusa's embrace. He said, stiffly, "I am not sure it is up to me."

"Oh," Cesar said, "it is."

"Then you have already . . ." He stopped, rather than ask for confirmation or denial. Cesar tilted his head slightly. Rache felt an upsurge of anger. This morning they had vilified and harrowed him for his associations and his errors of judgment. This afternoon he was suddenly offered absolution. Even as they planned his excoriation, they had arranged this pardon. But while the one had been glaringly public, the other was furtive. He said, grittily, "What use are your arrangements to me when my public record is of an incompetent whose carelessness got four people killed?"

Cesar leaned back, interlacing his fingers. "And set against that the public record of the lives which could have been lost without your actions then and your planning beforehand. Given that we still do not know who is responsible, do you not think that the ringsols remain vulnerable? So I repeat, do you want to leave Meredis in charge of ringsol six?"

"No." He resisted the urge to rub his face, thereby telegraphing his agitation. Cesar's reading of him was flawless. He wanted more than almost anything to re-earn his staff's trust. They were his tribe. And even if he no longer had their trust, he still should not leave them in the aftermath of a crisis. At any other time, Cesar would have *had* him, heart, brain, and body. Cesar would know that. And, like a physicist, he would deduce from Rache's inertia the existence of another force besides his own.

But Cesar decided abruptly to extend mercy. He said, "Contact me when you decide. It would be a great shame if you were to be one more casualty of this." Rache looked at him, but he made no move to conclude. He said, "Tell me about Teal Blane Berenice."

"What . . . about her?"

Cesar spread his hands, a casual gesture which left Rache unnerved. He did not know whether to trust Cesar's innocence. He dared not show distrust.

"She was," Rache said, deliberately, "of great help to the investigation."

"Although she plans no further participation, I gather."

"She had her own reasons for coming to Blueheart. She planned to meet with her sister, after many decades apart; she did not know that Juniper had died."

There was a silence. "I knew Juniper quite well. Well enough to be . . . perturbed by the prospect of her homozygous twin arriving on Blueheart during such a sensitive time."

"They are not at all alike."

"They are homozygotic twins raised in the same environment. Each of them will have been the other's strongest influence."

"You are a determinist," Rache said, too weary for caution or argument.

"And you, I think, discount overmuch the genetic contribution." He looked at Rache a moment with an odd, distracted indecision. "You look tired," he said, abruptly. "I'll leave you now. When you are ready to go back to work, contact me."

She found Karel as she had left him, sprawled on the couch, sunk in Adam's records. The windows were painted over with the dazzling skyless streets of Earth, made spectral by Blueheart's light behind. She turned her eyes from them, to her brother. Before she could speak, he opened his eyes and sat up brightly. "Cyb, you must look into these. It's his first visit to Earth, and it's hilarious; it's a marvelous portrait of the colonial returning to the old world, the innocent abroad. I'd no idea he had such a sense of humor; he's an artist, Cybele; he should publish these." She shivered slightly, hearing the present tense. It was no momentary lapse; in reviewing Adam's life, Karel had left behind Adam's death.

She said, "Karel, I have to talk to you."

He gave her an impish, crafty grin. "I won't talk to you unless you play with me, Cybele." The grin, the voice, the expression, were a child's.

She shuddered, and snapped, "Stop it, Karel." Had there been a palpable connection between him and the net, she would have struck it away; she stood over him, shaking slightly. "You are too old for me to have to be *minding* you like this; I've done it all our lives, and I'm tired of doing it. I have other things that I'd rather be doing." He sat looking up at her, a little blankly, but at least without the happy distraction of the past hours. "I've been to see Cesar Kamehameha. He's going to be patient with you, but his patience will not last forever, and that's all I care to say on that subject; you're an adult, and you can tend your own career. I mean this, Karel: I will not mind you indefinitely." She caught herself, before she blustered into impotence.

Karel said, "I'm sorry, Cyb."

"Don't be." She went to the dispenser and ordered them both cinnamon-chocolate, with sugar. The scent of cinnamon made her cringe, remembering. "I've done some irresponsible things myself these few days."

"I just want to forget," he said, brokenly.

"Yes," she said. "I understand." She paused. "But why didn't you tell me that the AOC already knew about the illegals?" His cup stopped, halfway to his lips; he blanched, and his eyes teared. She said, "I'm not accusing you. If anything, the blame's mine: You tried to warn me, and I did not listen, but I just wish, when I did not listen, you had made the warning more explicit."

"No, you're not to blame," he said, sounding stifled. "You're not to blame at all." She lowered her head, understanding him a little better. Forgiveness was bitter, and he had had more of it than she. Karel said, "What else did he say?"

"He said that the ringsol six investigation was going to have to be subordinated to the AOC investigation, but that he would see justice done in the end."

"Justice!" Karel rocked, spilling a little chocolate on his rumpled overalls, his face twisting with warring laughter and tears. Cybele watched uneasily. "You haven't seen it yet, have you?" he said, turning on her. "He sits there like a Medusa, spreading out his tentacles and waiting, waiting. We could all be dead and damned for the sake of his schemes. How long did he say for you to wait—a year, two years—how many more people do you think will end like that girl, like Adam, like Rache Scole Blueheart—while we wait on Cesar's convenience. *Don't* wait, Cybele. Have your transfections, *forget*, get your training, go into space, leave it all behind you. Listen, Cyb. The best place on Blueheart for this enhancement work is Dernier, at the pole. We'll go to Dernier, you and I; you'll have the enhancements; I'll upgrade my cercortex—if I've got the Berenici complex, I might as well use it—" He shuddered violently. "Use it *right*. I can tutor you; we can work together. We might be able to establish a good enough symbiosis that we could team on navigation: think how valuable that could make us. There are plans to move out to fifty or sixty light-years from Earth. Why not? Why not you and I?"

She felt disorientated, threatened. Some small, childish part of her—which had never forgiven him his easy advantage—was yelling: It's *mine*. *Mine*. "You never wanted to travel."

"I don't want to stay here."

"Karel," she said, "do you know something I don't?"

He caught his breath; the cup in his hand jolted, but did not spill. "I should have done." He closed his eyes, and tears squeezed from between his lids. "I should have known what Cesar was, what the AOC was, what . . ." She put down her cup, and went to take his from him. He caught her hands in a clammy grip. "Karel," she said, "I think you need help. I think you're taking this much, much too hard. There are things you're not responsible for. Justice will be done."

"By Cesar!"

Cybele freed her hands gently and got to her feet. She went to the window, looking out through the dark lattice of his storm-tripping frame to the bright, sea-drenched air, and the sea itself. She felt very tired. She had wanted to believe Cesar's promise. But Karel knew better: Cesar would serve the interests of the AOC and the plans of decades and centuries before he would serve Adam de Courcey. She felt, for the first time, some pity for Rache Scole Blueheart, now she could see he was the least wicked among them. Now he was disgraced, his career ruined, his life's work finished. Yes, Cybele thought, she could see how it would be used. She could even applaud the use. Perhaps that would be Adam's ultimate monument, that Blueheart's uncertain future would be a little less so.

She thought about the sample of bone marrow in its preserving gel, still tucked in its niche in her squalid rooms. Cesar never thought to ask whether Adam had supplied physical evidence.

"What are you thinking?" Karel said. He sounded frightened. Not wanting to, she turned her back on the bright blankness to face him. He looked frightened, hands clenched in each other above his stained clothing.

She said, "I am thinking about what I should do."

"Don't!" he cried, and bit back more words.

She had never seen him like this, though she had long known that he had grave and troubled depths beneath his fecklessness. Adam's death had broken something in him. Was he strong enough to contain it, or endure it? She did not know. She had herself so little experience of loss.

She said, "I owe it to Adam!" and his face went even more frightened and still.

He whispered, "I do not want to lose you, too."

Cybele let out a breath. "I will make you a bargain, then. I do not want to lose you either. I will not do anything; I will wait for the investigation to finish. And you will speak to someone who can help you more than I can. Cesar said there were counselors affiliated with the—"

"No!"

She said, with steel in her voice, "I owe more to the living than to the dead, that I do know. But I will not give so much up and have nothing back from it."

He shuddered again and looked away. "You look, you sound, so like him." With averted eyes, and hands held open in offering or supplication, he said, "Do what you want to do. Do what you have to do. Don't worry about me."

"I do worry about you. You are my brother and I love you."

And she heard Adam on the last night of his life, saying, "You asked me to sacrifice my beliefs—my faith—for you. To prove that I loved you. I did not realize that that was the test, and not the other."

She stood silently clutching at the echoes of memory. She stood so until Karel spoke her name and recalled her to where she was, and when. At last, heavily, she said, "I will stay away from the investigation, Karel. I will stay away. For as long as you need me to."

EIGHT

In the morning, Teal stood on Rossby docks, watching Rache Scole Blueheart at work in a half-flooded berth. Around him, a nearly invisible, dark-threaded film spread like a mantle. He was pleating and pulling it with his hands, bringing it up to his eyes and tilting it until the sun flared on its surface and a white light, like moonlight, lit his face. Such was his concentration, he was unaware of her. She had an opportunity to study him. Knowing now what he had been to Juniper, she was curious.

How very strange that he had attracted Juniper, Juniper who idolized the natural and the beautiful. Teal herself could appreciate the function of him, the logic of all the changes which so suited this large, lumpish red man to the seas. Had it entertained Juniper to lead him out of his born element, to watch him struggle with an alien society, and a belated formal education? She had created a masterpiece in her interpretation of him, the "Surfacing" series, but what had she made of his interpretation of himself? His development proposal was, to her inexpert eye, quality work. And he had been a capable administrator, someone who commanded loyalty, even love.

Until her part of the investigation had ruined him. She thought she had left such work behind her on New Boots.

The shift of her shadow on the water caught Rache's eye; he turned and looked up.

"Exper' Blane Berenice," he said. He kept a hand on the membrane as he turned, and laid the other on the plank beside her feet. She considered a moment, and then sat, cross-legged upon the hot deck. They looked at each other. She could not quite think what best to say. To proceed, baldly, to her purpose seemed ill timed. Let him decide.

But he seemed equally uncertain. Then he spoke, with a kind of resignation. "Were you looking for me?" And, belatedly, it came to her that he would have purposes of his own, out here on the docks. She looked at the film in his hands—which seen from where she sat was an almost invisible membrane, like a slime on the waters, shot through with a purplish mesh. It was stiffer than it looked, stilling, rather than moving with the ripples in the tank. "What is that?"

"This," a hesitation, then resolution, "this is a current-sail." Without thinking, she retrieved the entry from the database even as he explained, "Pastorals use them for long-distance travel. All one needs is a favorable current."

Having grasped the principles, she recalled Rossby's position, and a map of the ocean circulation. She said, "You are traveling south west."

"Yes," he said. "I am going to Scole, my birthplace."

Scole, whence Daven, and possible Daven's instructions, had come. She evaded the subject, pointing. "May I see?" He hesitated, sensing a rough transition, then raised the membrane. The purple was a bioengineered variant of rhodopsin in a semipermeable membrane, coupled to an active water transporter. Light energy pumped water into the mesh, pressurizing a network of sinuses and stiffening the sail. She brushed the tough, slimy surface with her fingertips. "But I am not pastoral. How should I go?" He released his sail, let it spread beneath the surface of the water, and turned to face her, folding both heavy forearms on the edge of the tank. "That depends on where."

"I want to go to Grayling platform."

"Grayling . . ." She thought he might say something about Juniper, but he only said, "Thirty-two south, eighty east . . ." And she remembered that for him Juniper was twenty years gone. She said, abruptly, "Juniper left there, last."

"I remember. But Grayling was in the polar seas then."

"She visited Grayling, several times," Teal said, flatly. He had no right to comment, implicitly or explicitly, on her whims and follies. Grayling had been Juniper's last destination. It would be Teal's first. She did not want to be asked what she was looking for. She did not know. But when she found it, she would know.

"Yes," he said, a little ruefully. "She was minutely interested in details of the adaptation process."

She had merely scanned the personal accounts in Juniper's files. It was not data she understood how to use. But she did remember that many of the personal accounts had been recordings of Rache, talking about his life as a pastoral. He must have given his permission; asking permission was one of the fundamental courtesies. He must know they were there.

She wondered, as she had wondered before, what it must be to be like Juniper, and not be content with the order of facts, the framework of knowledge. To want to wrestle and argue them into an altered form, altered relationships. Juniper did not simply want to know about adaptation, she wanted to make something of it.

"I am a pastoral," Rache said. "So I am biased in favor of unpowered craft. The boomer relay." He paused, giving her time to recall the pertinent information. "One-person skimmers come with full intelligent automation; they navigate and sail themselves. It would take," he paused, calculating, "one and a half days to reach Grayling."

She waited a moment, then said, "There are other ways, aren't there?"

He started to speak, caught himself, said, "Of course, I—I just thought you might appreciate sailing. Juniper . . . I assumed. I'm sorry."

She had a sudden, distinct memory of dune-yachting on the orange sands of Berenice. Of leaning so far out against the haul of wind and sail that the sand seemed like a tsunami poised to fall upon her. Of the sting of sand and sunburn on her bare skin, and the mask of sweat beneath her goggles. She would have been fifteen or sixteen, and Juniper, behind her, would have already been too often beaten to dare her to race.

He braced his hands on the edge, started to heave himself out of the water, then rethought, and waded to the ladder. He climbed stiffly and heavily out. "You could use a powered craft, if you wanted; that would shorten the journey. Or you could go by air."

"As long as I can maintain contact with the planet, I can use those days."

"Rossby council leases craft, of all kinds. Or there are the independent operators, like the partnership who operate this shipyard."

She had been greeted by one on her way in. Adaptive, hairless, melanin, and pigment enhanced. His

tracheal implant—allowing coupling to a rebreather—
ornamented the dark hollow between his collarbones.
She relayed the yard name to the net, and learned his
name, and those of his six partners—a registered marriage as well as a business partnership—and their public
record. Rache waited patiently upon the return of her
attention, then said, chidingly, "They are good people,
and they know the sea."

The partner who walked with them onto the wharf
was a woman, also adaptive, also implanted; a bright
stud closed the tube. She wore a halter-top, shorts, and
a belt hung with tools. She chatted to Rache in a
mélange of local dialect and sea-farer's jargon; he
responded dutifully.

The yacht was a sling-catamaran: two wide-splayed
pontoons, with a capsule rigged between them, and a
long whip of a mast twitching overhead. While Rache
and Teal watched, the docks woman climbed down a
short ladder onto the nearer of the pontoons. Perched
there, her calf hooked on a strut, she unhitched a portan
from her belt and seated her thumb in the recess. A slit
opened at the base of the mat. A thin spar emerged like
a cactus-spike, and between boom and mast sails
bloomed with a coarse rustle, nearly transparent in the
sunlight. Mainsail and jib crawled up the mast, while
the ropes looped free. Then, from the slit, along each
rope, crept a small, sparkling robot. They tracked their
way along the hull, pinning the ropes in place, until they
had secured each rope to its cleat. The woman
crouched, and passed the boom overhead. "All aboard
that's coming aboard," she said.

"Safe journey," said Rache, and held out to her a
package which he had—she had not noticed when—
acquired before they started their walk to the wharf. It

was sealed and looked like hardcopy. On one face of the transparent packet she saw a schematic of the yacht, on the other, a portion of a navigational map. The woman asked. "Rache, I'm hurt. Don't you trust our equipment?"

"I always," Rache said, "plan for emergencies." To Teal he said, "Send me a message when you reach Grayling. I know it is redundant: your journey is logged and filed and you will be tracked all the way to Grayling, but please, send me that message."

"Humor him," the woman advised. "It's simplest and," she glanced toward Rache, "he knows whereof he speaks." She offered Teal a hand, and steadied her into the capsule. Balancing on the float, she pointed out the features: food, water, sanitation; but when she started to explain the console, Teal stopped her. "I presume I can direct-interface," she said. She turned to look the woman in the face. "I am an expert-voyager."

"Say no more," the woman said, a little sourly. She finished, briefly, said, "Safe journey and safe return," and stepped smoothly from pontoon to ladder. Teal saw her shake her head at Rache. She found the interface which she would normally have accessed, and scanned the environment controls, the capsule hatch controls, transparency, temperature. She surveyed the navigation parameters, and the interface with planetary control: Rache had not exaggerated; she would be well watched.

When she looked back at the dock, Rache was alone, sitting on the edge with his feet dangling. They were broad, flat feet, with permanent imprints of fins donned early and worn often. He was not looking at her, but past her, out to sea.

She said, "I will go now." He looked down at her; his expression shifted slowly. "Good hunting, Teal

Blane Berenice," he said, without irony. "If you find out anything more, let me know."

"And good hunting to you."

He started to say something, but in the end, did not. She lowered the capsule over her head. Ropes tightened, the boom drew in, she felt a slight vibration as rudder and keel adjusted, and the skimmer pulled away from the jetty. Rache lifted his hand in farewell. Teal crouched on the bunk, watching docks and boats slide by. The capsule was surprisingly steady, slung as it was from the frame, and supported by the same intelligent ropes as worked the sails. Belatedly she thought to return Rache's gesture, though she was unsure that he could see her. She glimpsed him starting laboriously to his feet, and then the yacht rounded the last of the berths and headed for the breakwaters and the open sea.

Rache left Rossby in the midafternoon, having asked a lift from one of the docks partnership. A restful iconoclastic blend of industry and indolence, they cared only for the sea, not for politics or scandal. Destination was unimportant, merely an excuse for travel. She dropped him overboard during the last hour of daylight, so that he might spread his sail. Once the sail was spread, the current and his drag would hold it open—unless he snarled it by unforgivable carelessness, condemning himself to wait until morning to respread it. He doubted he would.

Before he lost the last light, he caught the edge of the sail and dived with it below the swell, crossing a wind-driven current, sure and strong. The current pulled on the sail; he played out the lines, feeling the tension on them evenly. Fully relaxed, slung behind the sail, he could remain submerged for nearly an hour between soundings.

Twilight had already come to the sea, the last sunset rays too glancing to penetrate. Looking up, he could see a pale underskin, but looking ahead, only dusk. Sound came distorted by the thin, taut membrane, which had a vibration of its own. Through his hands, resting lightly upon the ropes, he sensed through the sail the sea around him. A tautening of one side suggested a thread of stronger current, or a shift of direction; a tremor told him of turbulence, a change in the submarine floor, an obstacle. He knew the route between ringsol six and Scole, knew the submarine contour, the texture of the currents. The touch-compass strapped to his wrist only confirmed what directional sense told him. He sailed on through the dark, surfacing only for air and an admiring glance at the stars. Mere sight had always been sufficient for him. Compared to his astronaut ancestors, compared even to the founders of Scole, he was unadventurous. He thought, as he sailed, of those ancestors. Some had arrived as long as five hundred years ago, others as recently as two and a half centuries. By then the first adaptations had been designed, and the human prototypes had ventured out into the seas. By then they knew that Blueheart was something new in human experience: a planet which allowed, from the outset, complete independence of the adaptive phenotype, experimentation with adaptations which were not biological, but technological and social. From its beginnings, pastoralism had been an alternative. An alternative to the surveillanced order of the rafttowns, to the meticulously detailed developmental models. Pastoral independence was vibrant and proud, pastoral knowledge carefully harbored and transmitted. The experiment became a living culture, with history, learning, and lore all of its own. Pastoral interests diverged from primary, and then conflicted, as both populations grew. In the fifty years before Rache's birth a series of accommodations had to be negotiated, over submarine noise, over contributions of knowledge to the planet, over small-scale tectonic manipulations and citings of establishments. The last controversy had involved Rache himself with Athene's death and the scandal of inadequate monitoring and pastoral noncompliance. Emerald Ridge pastorals had bitterly resented the enforced compliance—enforced on threat of withdrawal of service. Had they chosen to do something about it, after all?

He remembered that he had argued the possibility with Juniper. He had not thought that she was serious, only that she enjoyed provoking him, and proving to him that he was not the desperate radical he feared he was. He wondered if she knew how much she had frightened him, showing him how much further he might go, how much further she might ask him to go.

The message he had received this morning, anonymous, untraceable, said that the woman he had pulled from the sea had been an illegal adaptive, and the virus which had demolished ringsol six's net had been intended to destroy all evidence of that fact.

He felt, through the ropes, a slight change in direction. The current was brushing the rise of the sea-floor toward Emerald Ridge, a long-buried and fertilized old lava outcropping. The whole ridge comprised enchained, extinct volcanoes, most worn to submarine mounts. Scole was centered on one of the few surface residuals, a sea-bitten chip of black rock.

Soon, the current would meet and fray against the first of the storm-barriers. Better sailors than Rache had entangled themselves in those barriers. He played the sail, bringing it and himself to the surface, and let it unfurl beneath the water. There was enough light that he could see it, nearby, a lustrous underskin to the swell, but it was soft enough that he could collapse it. By the time that was done, the sail tight-rolled, wrapped and lashed across his back, the sky overhead was no longer black, but a very dark blue, and along the eastern sky was a thin rim of white. Navigation should be simple, now: he need only sight that rim and swim into it.

He battled the swell until the sun came up, lighting deeper where the swell could not reach. He dived, feeling the current, and swam obliquely across it. The water was more turbid here, with dispersal from the great density of growth and cultivation along the ridge. He swam into the slanting brightness, with powerful strokes of flippered feet and web-gloved hands. The current nudged him along, indifferently, as it passed. Finned bodies bumped him, spinnerfish on their way to daytime feasting-grounds. A dark tangle loomed before him, a detached, becalmed portion of floating forest. Already the ribbongrass was frayed, knotted, splayed. Strips of it jerked away, pulled by spinnerfish. Their bodies piked and spiraled, in the motion which had given them their name, as they tried to tear the tough, still-living grass. Bereft of the forest's body, the fragment was bereft of the forest's protection: the larger forest sheltered ribbon-eels, which fed off, among other prey, scavenging spinnerfish. But the spinnerfish knew their old nemesis had deserted.

He detoured around the clump of ribbongrass, almost immediately found another. He would be among the debris driven onto the barriers by the storm of a few days past. The water was murky: ten meters under he could see a bright haze broken by indigo shadows. Against the haze, he could see the shimmer and flicker of swimming things too small to see. Larger things coalesced slowly, to a moving smudge, or a distinct shape, and slid back into the haze. He was less worried about the swimmers and the scavengers than about the victims of the storm, about splines, radials, and perhaps a medusa cast up with the shredded fragments of the forest. Those would be difficult to see in this haze; difficult to see, dangerous to miss. Carefully, he eased himself to the surface, and rode the sluggish swell, looking west.

And saw what he needed to see, the broken nubbin of Scole Rock, with, to its left, and in the distance, the unmoving low darkness of Mazian island. He narrowed his eyes, picturing the map. To his right, one, maybe two kilometers, the barrier would offer an opening between overlapping arms. Rache turned away from the barrier, and began to swim, surface-ward, head raised and watching for a prickling surface of the swell. When he judged himself clear, he turned south.

The break in the barrier was marked with a submarine buoy and clicker, but the sound was so distorted by the echogenetic clutter that he could take no guidance from it, and had to find the buoy by sight. The channel between the barriers' arms was still thick with debris; he steered carefully through it.

The barriers were adapted from the floating forests' own storm protection. The first was a densely interwound, ligneous growth known as stormwood. Stormwood germinated from encapsulated seeds which had to be broken free before they could sprout; the greater the damage, the more rapid the proliferation. Behind the stormwood was a thick mat of root-algae, which existed in symbiosis with stormwood, and other forest growths. A healthy barrier maintained itself; the work was involved in securing it to its moorings a hundred meters below. Rache remembered dive after dive, day after day, checking kilometer after kilometer of tethering through storm season. Sliding hand over hand down the massive cables, down the dwindling light.

The mat of algae and the water beyond was spiked with broken stormwood. Here, too, he saw the first evidence of industry: fragments netted or roped together, ready to be resettled into thinning stretches of the defense. Rache could see blue-green sprouts and tendrils fringing the shattered ends. In the clearer water behind the mats, he could hear clicker-code and high bubble-voicing; adaptives at work.

He realized, abruptly, now that he was in calmer waters, how very tired he was. He eased himself into a slow, overarm surface-stroke, and worked his way through the winding channel across the second barrier, a mat of yellow pondweed. Pondweed could drown a swimmer as surely as it could dampen a wave. Midway, he passed four teenagers on their way out to the barrier, and recognized three nieces and a nephew. None were Daven, but he did not think they would be. The leading niece was, like himself, deep adapted, with the ruddy skin and body like collapsed clay. He signaled a greeting, and swam on, aware that they looked curiously back down his wake.

On the far side of the barrier were the pastures, the cultivated sea beds. Looking down, he could see green cluttered leaves which shifted slightly with the currents.

At intervals, a bubble freed itself from their undersides and shivered upward. Painter algae grew only in the surface ten meters. During years of severe blight, careful pruning kept the crop below that depth. The shallowest water had to be turned over to white kelp, which did not support the algae. Until his recent visit, Rache had forgotten about the extra work and dietary tedium of the years of worst blight. But even then, he simply accepted it. Painter algae, even the blight, were a necessary part of the ecology; humanity simply had to accommodate. Adaptation engineers had been too occupied in solving the problems of survival in the seas to concern themselves with simple inconveniences. That would have to change. If—when—he could continue on the proposal, he would see that toxin resistance was developed in the proposed adaptations.

Growth of white kelp suddenly barred his way. Rache righted himself, looking over water stippled with rounded white bladders, to find the flagged buoy which marked the passage. Beyond, he could see the boundary floats and float-houses around Scole Rock. Two young girls lounging along the boundary float whistled to him. A woman on a raft shouted a reproof. Whistling was a landman's vulgarity. They gathered themselves up, slanted identical sly glances toward him, and dived neatly into the water. Rache remembered himself and Athene at that age, plotting their escape from the children's compound.

Suspended beneath the boundary floats was a fine-meshed net, which dropped all the way to the sea floor. The net swept the water clean of swimming or floating hazard; the water within was as safe as the adaptives could make it for their vulnerable children. Passage out depended upon being able to prove one's knowledge and competence. Like those two girls, he and Athene had wooed every outgoing adult for a chance to accompany them to the pastures, to the barriers, beyond, a chance to exhibit their learning and responsibility, a chance to gain an advocate for their release.

The children were waiting for him on the other side of the barriers; he saw their dark, slim bodies through the net, marking the opening. He unlaced the slit in the net, slid through, relaced, taking his time and giving them a chance to recognize him. He had recognized them: Einar's two daughters. He said, "Noelle. Ayna."

Ayna, a few months the elder, and by far the more brazen, glanced slyly up at him. "Did you come from Rossby?" she said.

"Did you sail all the way?" Noelle said.

"Yes," Rache said, to both.

Ayna said, "If you're looking for Daven, he's not here."

He looked at her; she looked back, with defiance and a certain triumph. The compound was symbolic of pastoral childhood: children were sheltered, indulged, and kept within boundaries. There were matters for children and matters for adults. Ayna tested the boundaries.

This at least she had told him: the news had preceded him. He said, "And do you know why I should be looking for Daven?"

She inclined her head. "Maybe."

Noelle, floating beside her, looked uneasily awed at such insolence.

Behind the children, his brother's head broke the surface. "Ayna," Bede said, and she swirled to face him. He knew her well, Rache thought, faintly amused, well enough to know without hearing it what had been said.

And she did not argue; when he waved them away, they dived, leaving only twin swirls in the water to mark their passing.

Bede said, "I presume you want to see Daven. He is not here."

Rache reached behind himself, caught a support loop from the barriers, and let himself drift, kicking idly. He leaned his head back against the curved, slimy side of the float. His elder brother was the only other holdfast member to have a landsman's education. In the aftermath of Athene's death, young pastorals had been recruited for training in adaptation monitoring. Bede had been recruited from Scole.

It might have created a certain sympathy between the brothers. Instead, it only enhanced a certain rivalry. Rache would have taken the education, and gladly, but Bede had been the holdfast's choice.

Rache left unasked the obvious: Then how do you know why I am here? But Bede answered it. "It's all over the seas about your dismissal."

"Suspension," said Rache. "I have been suspended."

Bede shook his head slightly. Rache had an impulse to tell him about Cesar's offer of reinstatement, and pushed himself underwater to drown the impulse. Fifty years on and he still thought like a little brother.

"Bede," he said, resurfacing, "I want to talk to Daven. Or to the person who sent Daven. And please, don't tell me Daven is not here."

"He is my son," Bede said. "You cannot expect me to simply turn him over to landsmans' 'justice.'"

Rache let the warm sea close over his head. He had foreseen this. Should he make plain his resort now, in hopes that the threat alone would be sufficient. As he hoped. He resurfaced. "If I am not allowed to see Daven, I am going to lay a charge against him in the seas-court."

The seas-court was the pastoral judiciary, wherein justice between pastorals could be dispatched without involving landsmen, and landsman's law. Much of what passed in the seas was settled without ever breaking the surface, and most of the holdfasts preferred it thus. And the next convention for Emerald Ridge was in but a few days. For a moment, Bede could not find his voice. "This has nothing to do with pastorals."

"I am a pastoral. *I* am the one the boy's actions ruined, and people for whom *I* was responsible died because of what he did."

"You *cannot* use the seas-court to prosecute landsmen's business. You will be flensed, Rache, flensed and tied to the barriers for the fish to eat!"

Rache shook his head slightly, wearily. "You forget, Bede, that I have heard it all before. And if I must, I will bring the matter before the seas-court and *make* them understand how this concerns pastorals. Tell me, Bede, have you ever known of illegal adaptation taking place? Adaptations which have not been approved by the AOC, possibly of people who are not even on record."

Bede snapped a laugh. "That old sea-spume. Yes, I've heard of it, every year since I trained. Nothing's ever come of it. Oh, there are the odd little bits of tinkering, a residue here or there, but if you saw what the AOC do to the little tinkerers, you couldn't imagine that there'd be anything more. The AOC can put a label on your file that follows you forever. As we all know."

Rache ignored the sting. Scole was marked, yes. It was marked because Rache had swum Athene to a raft-town, rather than back to Scole for a quiet sea-gifting and a reported loss at sea. Instead, there had been an autopsy, an uncovering of noncompliance and neglect. Out of this had come the initiative to bring members of the pastoral communities into the monitoring network. Scole chose to believe they had been coerced into giving up one of theirs and probably Bede's life was easier now for his protest then. Rache wondered if he were alone in marking that Bede had pursued far more than the required two years' training: he was no mere technician, but a qualified and competent physician, even within the limitations imposed by a pastoral lifestyle.

Rache said, stubbornly, "Just before all this began, Daven and I retrieved the body of a pastoral woman and took it back to ringsol six. She died of nixiaxin poisoning—of ignorance of the extent of this year's blight. I have been told that the station physician—Adam de Courcey—found that her adaptations were different from any approved. The body was claimed, with some haste, by a party from Great Diamond. I had no sooner given up the body than ringsol six had a complete system failure, jamming open the sea locks and causing the deaths of four of my people, including Adam de Courcey."

"We have not heard half of this."

"Perhaps not yet, but you will, sea and rafttowns alike." There was a resolution in Rache's voice.

Bedevere sculled to Rache's side, caught a trailing loop and glanced around—for his granddaughters, no doubt. "Rache, where is the proof of this? If the body is gone, and your net is erased, and the physician who did the analysis dead, then where is the proof?" He was close enough that Rache could smell his breath, the iron in his blood and the fresh white kelp of his last meal. "Have you yourself seen the gene-scans?"

"Daven," Rache said, harshly, "admitted to me that he had come to ringsol six because he had been asked. He received starfish programs—data extraction subroutines—which exported material from our net. He would not say who asked him, or why, but that person was pastoral. He received and activated one such package just before the destruction of the net. And this one was not a simple data extraction protocol, but a data deletion protocol. It was his, and our great misfortune that we were in the midst of reconfiguring the system. The system failure was caused by an interaction between the deletion protocol and the tutor-virus. I have had it suggested to me that the deletion protocol was meant to remove information about the body."

"Rache," said Bedevere. "Rache, think about this. Daven was on ringsol six well before you found this suspect body. How do you explain that? That he went to the ringsol just in case you might come across a body?"

"That he went," Rache said, tiredly, "for another purpose, and was turned to this one. That is why I want to talk to Daven. All I do know . . ." All I do know is that now, whenever someone tries to argue my conclusions, I wonder if they do so out of clearer insight, or guilt. I should like to believe that Daven was merely a tool. But then I must ask by whom, whom would he trust enough to let them use him as a tool, as I trusted him and let him use me. I would like to believe that Scole is too conscious of the penalties to be involved in this. And that you are simply reacting to the rivalry which has always been between us, older brother and younger, and protecting your son. I thought that the old rift between myself and Scole was hard enough. But this pernicious suspicion begins to feel like a mortal sickness.

He said, "Tell Daven . . . or tell someone who can tell Daven . . . that I would like to speak to him. I will be staying," he considered a moment, "in the guest house." He pushed himself away from the float; Bede caught his arm.

"You will stay with me," he said, unsmiling.

Rather, Rache supplied for himself, than have out of Scole visitors exposed to the prodigal of Scole and his wild tales.

Bedevere's raft was always a surprise. It was not simply that he lived aboard a dry-raft. The platform rode not on natural stormwood, but on a bioengineered, rot-resistant variety. The dividers between rooms, and the sliding outside walls, were of rafttown-grown cane, painted red, white, and ocher, colors most uncommon in tropical seas. The rolled-up screens, against the sudden tropical rains, were synthetic, and not woven ribbon grass. Adults slept on mattresses and children in hammocks slung in air, instead of in the sea. Yet in all other respects, Bedevere had eradicated his years in the rafttowns. The only account of himself he ever gave was that he and his wife could not be bothered with maintenance. And indeed, the usual, sea-gifted material required collection, curing, replacement, and maintenance; indeed, in a raft of this complexity, the work would have been ceaseless. But Rache thought that in truth, it was Bedevere's choice, Bedevere's taste. Keri always seemed a little bewildered, a little apologetic, at the unusual opulence around her.

On Bedevere's raft, the low-roofed domicile was square, with three sides of four small square rooms each, and one central room which filled the fourth side and center. All the rooms opened outward by sliding doors, onto the wide deck, and onto their neighbors by sliding hatches. Bedevere gave him one of the corner rooms, facing away from the Rock and the elder's rafts. He leaned a moment against the open door, looking over the lesser rafts. Mooring order was hierarchical: the elders' rafts ringed the Rock, then the rafts of respected community members, moving outward through the loose network of rings in order of seniority and position. The rafts were not close-moored; there was always space for a little presumption. On his last visit, Rache had been amused to note that Apple's raft had wafted inshore of Bedevere's. Hers was a very proper pastoral raft, a frame deck around a sunken center, made entirely of sea-gifted materials. Rache wondered, idly, where his own raft would have been, had he stayed. The thought brought others more painful, and he pulled the door close. The weave of the cane passed a diffuse breeze and created a pleasantly light-laced shadow. He listened a moment. He had not heard Bedevere dive, but from next door, he could hear small excited whispers: Ayna and Noelle, peering between the weave of the cane. So Bedevere had already gone, no doubt to advise the elders of Rache's return and his intentions. He did not much care what was said without him. He had not said anything that was untrue, or threatened anything that he was not prepared to do. He eased himself down on the bed, suppressing a groan. As he slid into sleep, tickled by the sounds from next door as by small waves, he admitted that he would rather Scole could hide whatever it had to hide from him.

Cybele said, "I am worried about my brother."

"Why," said the man across from her, his dark, tattooed face attentive and calm.

She looked away from him. Orange and yellow streamers on an outside railing caught her eye, she followed their rippling length to its end, and beyond, into space. She said, "I know you cannot help him without his being here. I thought you might help me to help him." A silence. "He's living in Adam's memories. Adam's records," she clarified, at a questioning look. "He has spent the last two days linked to the net, viewing Adam's personal logs. He speaks of Adam in the present tense. He seems to lose track of the fact that Adam is dead." She stopped herself from saying more, from saying, He escapes and I cannot.

"Have you been able to view these records yourself, Cybele?"

"This is not about me," she said, sharply. Took a deep breath. "No, I have not viewed those records; I have not viewed them because I am not ready to view them." She pulled herself upright, defying him to fault her admission.

He smiled slightly. "Well said."

"My father is dead," she said. "I do not know how he died, or why. I need to know these things."

He said, "Is that what you want of me, Cybele?"

She flushed deeply, angry at being found so transparent, and picked at a crimp in her trouser suit. She had worn white, with a pearly finish, an innocent's colors. She had asked to meet him here, in a day rent booth, rather than at his workplace. She feared all her manipulations had been in vain. "I promised Karel," she said, "that I would not press the investigation. That I would wait to be told."

"Was that a promise you wanted to make?"

"No." She looked him hard in the eye to show she was not ashamed. "I promised because my brother was afraid." She held herself very still, concentrating utterly on him, alert to the least change of his face, the smallest flicker of an eye. "He is afraid of what might happen to me should I press for the truth about Adam's death."

He was very good; he let her hold his eyes, and revealed nothing. "And are you yourself afraid?" he said, quietly.

"Should I be?"

He let a beat elapse, still his face did not change. "Do you think the truth will be hard to come by?"

"You tell me."

There was a silence. Then, she could not say how, she felt the change in him. "I have come to fear," he said, quietly, "that it might."

She felt the ground shift beneath her, as with the sudden removal of an obstacle.

"As of yesterday," Michael said, "I am no longer involved in the investigation."

She swallowed. "Why?"

He drew himself together again. "I am not sure I should be telling you this; I am not sure I have good reasons for telling you this. You came to me for a consultation, about your brother, and I would like to help both your brother and you, but I sense you want more from me than that, and that is something I am not sure I can give. I withdrew from the investigation because I became aware that what I had believed was an asset was in fact a liability, and I found myself being led into a conflict of loyalties."

She listened intently to him, matching subtext with her own knowledge. How, she thought, to elicit more without revealing what she herself knew. She said, "You are Rache's friend, and a pastoral liaison."

His face became guarded. "Yes."

"So this," she said, keeping her voice light, "has something to do with pastorals."

"It seems it may."

"So you," she said, "withdrew because you were afraid of your divided loyalties. And yet you say truth might be difficult to come by. Are there other people who don't have your sense of honor?"

He sighed. "I have no right discussing this with you, even in the most general terms; and I have no business even trying to assuage my conscience by proclaiming I have no right talking to you. Except that I am deeply concerned for the people who may be affected by this investigation. Please, Cybele, tell me what you know. When you spoke to Rache, you gave him the impression that you believed something particular about your father's death."

She felt cold, with the knowledge of her own part in it. "I know that he died on account of a pastoral secret."

He leaned forward slightly. "What secret?"

She leaned back, quite deliberately, and laid a hand flat between them. She was learning the alchemy of turning the lead of remorse to the gold of anger. "No, you tell me something, now. Tell me whether you believe that the people who caused my father's death will be brought to justice."

"Cybele," he said, "if I promised you that, I would be lying. Man's justice is deeply flawed, though we do the best we can; that I can promise. But if you want perfect justice, wait on God's."

"And you think," she said, quietly, "that my father must wait on God."

"I think, in the end, we must all wait on God."

A little shakily, she got to her feet. "I want—to think about what you've said. Can I come back to see you . . . bring Karel if I can persuade him to come?" At the door, she turned, looked back at him. "Thank you," she said, "for having the decency not to lie."

Sometime on the second day of her voyage, Teal had the rare thought that if she were ever to settle on a planet, she might choose this one. It suited her. Here on the open sea the external world was pared to essentials, the sky, the pitch of the waves, and the thrust of the wind. Her human needs were meager, food, water, sanitation, a bunk to lie on, light at night, and a shade from the sun. The sea's distinctive odor was less offensive as she grew intimate with it. She had never been troubled with nausea before, and was not now.

In the early stages of the voyage she had toyed with the idea of sailing the boat by hand as she had sailed the dune-skimmers so well on Berenice. She examined the AI's algorithms in detail, drawing on old, organic knowledge for expansion. Then she accessed the net and surveyed all the different types of small watercraft used on Blueheart, and concluded that if she wanted to sail, she would need a different craft; this one was stable, not agile. Lying on her bunk, she idly considered what it would be like to redevelop so old a skill.

As the skimmer carried her on, she continued to explore Juniper's last year. Though she had entered little of note herself, Juniper had remained a presence in other people's lives until her death, and in their recollections thereafter. Her doings and concerns had been recorded, and from them, and the archival data, Teal built a context, a backdrop, around Juniper's empty outline.

But there was still so much missing, because Juniper

had spent the greater part of that year at sea, among pastorals, traveling between holdfasts and nomadic flotillas, now so well known that she no longer need appeal to the primary-pastoral liaisons to arrange introductions and ease her visits. One had remarked, in a memoir, that the holdfasts had come to receive her with the stoicism they reserved for the caprices of the sea; some frankly solicited her accounts of the more reclusive holdfasts who had yielded to her. When she came ashore it was to pursue her sporadic, vehement argument with the advocates of terraforming, and to delve into the subject of adaptation.

That, too, was as unlike the Juniper Teal had known as was her relationship with Rache. Berenici society enshrined the natural; Juniper had, in that respect, been utterly orthodox. Teal thought both absurd: Berenici history featured adaptation, eugenics, and a near monopoly in certain enhancements; and she and Juniper were conceived of an ovum-ovum fusion. Nevertheless, even their natural twinship pained Juniper, lest they be suspected of being clone sisters. Her ignorance about adaptation had been carefully cultivated and lovingly maintained. But from the time she had brought Rache from the seas she had corresponded with people involved in adaptation development, vigorously pressing them for speculation as to the possibilities. She had incorporated her explorations into the controversial series "Transformations," a series of twelve montages of a subject undergoing adaptation to the marine environment. The final transformations were far beyond anything which would have been allowed by the AOC; by the final frames their subject was no longer even recognizably human.

The subject was Juniper herself.

"Transformations" was eventually placed in a

restricted area of the gallery, along with all the critique and rejections of the piece, and Juniper never again made adaptation the subject of a major work. But her interest in it and its ultimate potential had continued, tempered but unabated. She had, by the time of her death, achieved a minor expertise on the subject, and the best documented movements of her final year were between smaller platforms working on adaptation, although she had never, even on a whim, expressed the slightest interest in being herself adapted. And that Teal thought uncommon; Juniper had expressed most whims, if only for effect.

She found her explorations oddly pleasurable. As ever, the net filled the absence that Juniper had left. At the same time, it brought her closer to Juniper than she had been since Berenice. She could see that her sister's life had been a full one, and she could begin to see what of this planet Juniper had found to love. For the first time in decades of lived time she was at liberty to pursue her own whims, and discover whatever pleased her to discover. She had left behind the investigation, with its unhappy likeness to η Boötes IV. She had no wish to be a judge, and even less to be an instrument of judges, and certainly not against someone who had loved Juniper well. Juniper had been widely loved, but rarely well loved; Teal had been rarely loved, and never well.

She browsed, meditated, dozed, and woke to browse again. In her meditation and her sleep, she retained her uplink, carefully leaving uploading inactive, carelessly leaving downloading active. She listened to the net whisper in her dreams, promising more riches.

In the high noon, she was jarred from sleep by the hammering of her heart. She slammed upright, not knowing where she was, seeing only the brightness of the sun, the harsh sparkle of the sea. Gasping, she reached for the access to her autonomic implants. There was no response. She pressed her arms against her ribs, braced them against the violence within. She could feel the arteries vibrating in her temples. She knew, in terror, that she was malfunctioning, and this malfunction could be fatal. She sent to the net, but met the barrier she herself had raised. She could not organize the instructions to bring it down. She rolled out of the bunk, and crawled toward the console. Blood burst from her nose, splattering her hands and the deck. She pressed a bloody hand to the interface, and scrambled symbols crawled away from her fingers. She laid a second hand beside the other, shaking violently, choking on blood and air, beyond thought or deed, beyond anything but waiting for an end.

Her heart suddenly stalled. She felt it like a void in her chest. Her blood drained into that hollow center. She started to draw back her hands, and found that she was slumping forward, that they were all that had kept her upright. Her face met the screen, not hard, but decisively. She thought, but there should be no barrier . . . and felt absurdly cheated. Before her eyes, gray went to red went to black.

Bedevere woke Rache, with word that his grandmother wanted to see him. Rache lay a moment, collecting his wits. The heat of noon stunned him.

He eased himself up to sitting, and then to standing, cautiously shifting his weight, and waiting for pain. None came. Bedevere said, "Tove is waiting for you."

Tove was grandmother to Rache and Bedevere on

their father's side, and a hundred and forty-eight years old. She was the acknowledged matriarch of Rache's family, and oldest of the eighteen elders of Scole. Rache felt suddenly lighter in spirit. Tove was the child of a time when pastoralism was simply a bold experiment in settlement. She held it in no great reverence. If she had had some bitter words to say to him about his leaving, they had nothing to do with ideology, and everything to do with his failed human obligations.

Her raft was, like Bedevere's, a dry-deck raft, though made entirely of natural materials, maintained and repaired by her many descendants, who numbered a quarter of Scole. Pastoral society had become matrilineal in resistance to genetic paternity typing, and in recognition of human frailties. Tove of Scole had had eleven children, by five different fathers. Her third son, Rache's father, had been lost at sea before his younger son was born.

Seeing her, Rache always thought of a burned-out candle. Beneath her wizened skin, between her wiry muscles, the fat in her had flowed downward, draining from arms, shoulders, and breasts into her hips, thighs, and ankles. With dignified vanity, out of the water she always wore a colored wrap around her waist. Her face was as finely defined as a primary's. Her eyes, though shrunk in pronounced sockets, were candle-bright.

"Thank you, Bedevere," she said, and Bede went with a slight, unconscious obeisance. Bede had always been very deferential to the elders of Scole.

As was Rache, as child and youth. The elders governed Scole. They mediated disputes, approved marriages and the adaptations of the unconceived or newborn. They were Scole's representatives to the larger world.

But Rache's deference now was conditional, not ingrained; he had experience of leadership, in several forms, and knew its quality or lack. He lowered himself into the sling seat before she could tell him to do so.

She ran him over with a bright eye, and said, simply, "Tell me."

Rache did, but with measured succinctness. Seaclad he might be, offered audience with one of the eldest elders of Scole, but he came as an authority in his own right, administrator of ringsol six. He told her of the finding of the body, of its surrender to the party from Kense, of the inundation of ringsol six and the investigation, of the findings and culmination.

"You tell it like a landsman," she observed.

"I know."

She folded her hands on her bright wrap. "I have heard his part from Daven already," she said. She compressed her lips, eloquently. "A pity that wisdom cannot be transfected in. Or that fools were not left to the sea. Your generation shelters its young too much. The pastoral pioneers did not leave behind the cradle of civilization for their descendants to build playpens and raise fools."

"The sea does not cull out every kind of folly," Rache said, mildly.

She slapped hands palms down. "The trouble that child has caused. Hardly any of it intended, that I will tell you. He was an innocent, and a dupe . . . and a coward, for leaving you as he left you."

"I think," Rache said, "I made him leave."

"Oh, that idiocy about chemical interrogation," Tove said, astringently. "Very noble of you, Rache, very noble. You should have children of your own. I do not say you would not breed a fool or two, but rearing your own would leave you proof against this soft-heartedness about the young. They are not worth it."

"I was afraid, you see—"

"Afraid. What of?" But a moment's thought answered her own question. "Then more fool you for sending him away. More fool you for trying to protect those very people with whom you have argued these twenty-five years from the consequences of their criminal acts. More fool you for thinking you might be thanked, or for thinking there might be some virtue in your deed. They would have hated you and you would have hated yourself."

"Daven is very young," Rache said, shakily. "He is too young to be caught so in a quarrel so much older than himself."

"As you were caught? You survived. Grant also that he might."

"I remember how it felt." He remembered too that when the investigators came, when the questions started, she was one of the few who did not blame him for what he had begun.

He said, "What did he say to you?"

"He told me what you and he had said to each other, of course. He told me who had asked him to go aboard ringsol six, and what reason they had given—"

"Who was it?"

"I have sent," she said, "for that one to come and give an accounting of themselves to me. Then I will send that person to you, so that they may give an accounting of themselves to you."

"I am administrator of ringsol six," he said, intemperately.

She leaned back, eyes glinting like chipped obsidian. "And I am elder of Scole, *the* elder of Scole. This touches upon my charge as much as it touches upon yours. You will have your hour, and I hope you do not rue that hour."

"It is someone I know," Rache said, heavy-hearted. She did not answer.

"Tove," he said, "did Daven say why the virus was released?"

"He said he knew nothing about a virus. He said that to him, the package was like any other."

"Just before I left to come here, I received a message. Someone had taken great care that I not trace the sender. The message said that the woman I found carried unapproved adaptations, and that that was the information that the virus was sent to delete." She listened, bright-chipped eyes unmoving. If she knew any of this from Bedevere, she would give no sign. He had learned from her how people valued a virgin ear.

"I have heard that it has happened," she said. "But not here. Neither I, nor any other elder of Scole would countenance it." She fixed Rache with a sharp eye. "I remember that a certain friend of yours made reckless suggestions of that sort."

"I remember it, too," said Rache, briefly.

"I have heard that it happens. But we at Scole paid for a much lesser arrogance in the blood of one of our children, and we will not let it happen here. If that is the reason behind this, then I will summon the inquisitors myself, and if I'd known this before, I would have had other questions for Daven. No matter; they will be asked yet. So, where did this woman come from?"

"Her utilities were Messnier-design, with Messnier olivines, but it was a party from Kense that came for her. Maria of Kense."

"Kense," said Tove, with a hiss on the word. "Grandmother or granddaughter? Old or half-blind?"

"Neither. Young, but with both eyes sound."

"Then it was neither Maria of Kense," Tove said, almost triumphantly. "The younger Maria of Kense took a medusa stripe a year ago. She would not go to the landsmen's hospital, and so is scarred and blind in the right eye. Tell me," she said, leaning forward, "tell me about your meeting with Maria of Kense."

He told her of that strange conversation in the seas over ringsol six, of the woman's insinuations about the blight. It relieved him, somehow, that those insinuations had not come from either the elder of Kense or the elder's granddaughter. It did not relieve him that Tove nodded slightly, as though she had heard it before.

"Do many say this kind of thing?"

"I have heard it before," she said, dismissively, "and taken no account of it. So," tapping her wrinkled hands together, fingertip to fingertip. "Your dead woman was claimed by a party purportedly from Kense. Kense, I suspect, will claim ignorance, whatever the truth of it. Someone wishes you to connect the body, illegal adaptation, and events on ringsol six. But that someone prefers anonymity; why? It would be convenient, in the absence of a body, given Daven's folly, and yours, to seek among pastorals for cause and criminal. You have been used once; would you be used again?"

"No," he said, "not even by you." He rolled to his feet; a clumsy maneuver. "When you are ready to tell me what you know, I will listen. But nothing you have said has persuaded me that I may not ask Daven to step forward and answer for himself at the seas-court."

"Don't posture," she said, tartly. "It does not suit

you." She waited a moment for him to sit. He did not. After a moment she waved a long, gnarled hand toward the seaward door, and he left.

He plunged headlong from the raft into the bright, shallow water of the compound. The depth here was no more than three times his height; he could clearly see the cropped weed and scattering of small, bright fish, chosen for their harmless prettiness. He could hear, from among the outer rafts, the shrieks of children at play. They would be chasing each other between, around, and beneath the rafts, playing hunters and sharks, or sentries and raiders, or scenes from early exploration. Their imaginations always seized on the spectacular and unlikely. The common, prosaic dangers—poisons, stingers and lashes, parasites, storms, human error, and physical limits—there was no drama in those. The most imaginative children could be the most difficult to teach. He thought of Juniper; she had been nearly impossible. She had, he supposed, been impossible, since she had died in the sea. Daven, by contrast . . . Daven had been good in the sea.

He reached Bede's raft, and heaved himself onto the platform, anger making the effort uncommonly easy. Whoever had sent Daven to him would answer for it. They had to their account the deaths of four people, the ruination of a boy's innocence and a man's work. He did not know yet what he would say, but he knew how he would say it. And his words would be spoken again and again, in the retelling of the meeting.

He heard voices from within the main room, through the latticed walls. Courtesy demanded he announce himself, rather than simply go to his room; sound traveled too well. In turning the corner, he found Noelle and Ayna, crouched beside the door, ostensibly sorting shells, in actuality enrapt by the argument ongoing inside. Their father Einar, Bedevere's eldest son, was saying, "He has no right to bring landsman's business here." His dark voice carried clearly, his diction crisp. That had been Rache's gift; as a child Einar had mumbled, and had been sullenly resistant to correction. It had taken Rache long and subtle labor to draw him out.

Bedevere's answer was tired. "Whether we like it or not, if it were not he, it would be another."

"It has nothing to do with us," Einar said. "The people who died—they're landsmen: only one of them had the slightest modification. Adam de Courcey had a notorious prejudice against adaptation. Elisabet Blakeny was an expert in post-terraformed ecologies: her name was all over those development proposals—"

The quiet, dry voice of Rache's mother interrupted. "Then you think there is a different law for pastorals and landsmen?"

He was startled to hear her, though he should have expected it. Though she was more often at sea than not, without exception she attended each seas-court. She had a quietly passionate interest in justice, and would speak for anyone who she thought had been ill heard, whatever the right or wrong of them.

"Landsmen do. *You* know that."

There was a silence. The children, absorbed in their listening, had not noticed Rache. Rache felt ill; he could not bring himself to walk in at that moment.

"Are you referring to the accusations made against me—and this community—over Athene's death?" There was a silence, wherein she must have received some confirmation, for she said, simply, "But I was guilty; we were all guilty." A pause. "The children should have been monitored, those two, especially. But I was a young, orthodox woman, steeped in the distrust of landsmen. Rache and Athene caught it too: we only learned afterward how long she, and eventually she and Rache together, had hidden her illness. We betrayed Athene, as a community." Another pause. Rache wished now that he could see her face. She said, "Indeed, there *is* a different law. The medics on Rossby base were punished far more harshly than any of us. Their careers were ruined. My rehabilitation was more therapy than punishment, and I returned to the life I had led. Nobody intended harm to me."

But they did harm, Rache thought. And some of that harm was to her relationship with her surviving deep-adapted child. Astrid, a nomadic incomer to Scole, had been his first, best teacher in the tropical seas. But she had returned from Rossby withdrawn, uncertain, remorseful. They became distant and wary with each other, each assuming the other's accusation, and first she, and then he, were more and more absent from Scole. Over the past four years, their returns had not coincided.

Rache stepped forward with a thud on the deck. His shadow dropped over the two small girls. They spun around, open-mouthed. A reflex they would have to lose before they went to sea. Rache said, "This is not for you to hear."

Ayna's expression was defiant. "*You* were—" she began, haughtily, and Rache caught them by one arm each and pulled them bodily to their feet. Noelle squeaked. Rache marched them to the edge, and pushed them in. They bobbed to the surface, coughing with outrage. Behind Rache the slatted door slid open and Bedevere and Astrid appeared.

"We *weren't* listening," cried Noelle, ingenuously.

"He *hurt* us." Ayna rubbed her arm, ostentatiously. "He threw us in. I'm *bruised*."

Bedevere said, sourly, "Aren't you a little too old to be throwing girls into the water?" He turned and walked back into the main room, passing Einar. Einar gave Rache a single, contemptuous glance and crouched at the edge of the dock. The children swam to him, whimpering their hurts. He ran his fingers gently down Ayna's arm, letting Noelle hold his other hand. There was nothing pointed or ostentatious about the intimacy; his children always had the best of him.

He had been a lonely, demanding little boy, the middlemost of three born to Bedevere and Keri within four years. There seemed no reason for him to be as he was, except for being a little slow to speak, a little slow to understand, a little slow to appreciate the swift give and take of human interaction. He would never say what he wanted, seek out what he needed, or be satisfied without; he would simply stand yearning, his whole body eloquent of deprivation and accusation. From his fifth year, his yearning was toward Lisel. She was the one he loved, though she had no patience with his clinginess and doleful looks. Rache was the one to undertake him, to teach him how to speak clearly, how to go more easily in among other children, and how to survive the sea.

There was still much of that little boy in the man. He trusted only in the admiration of acquaintances—he could muster a startling charisma—and in the adoration of his children. He released his daughters' hands and bade them swim out to the floats. When he stood and turned to Rache, his eyes were cold. "If you hurt my children again," he said, "I will kill you."

"Einar," Astrid said, quietly.

Einar said, "And leave Daven alone." He turned, and dived from the raft, in a quick, choppy racing dive. It was a primary style, most incongruous with Einar's arch-traditionalism. Rache looked after him, feeling, despite himself, regret. Rache's desertion had inflicted a deep wound. Not merely because of Rache's loss but because ultimately Rache's leaving had led to Lisel's. Einar had been eighteen and deeply, despairingly, in love.

And whatever time may have achieved, in healing that wound, it had allowed the growth of irreconcilable differences. Once accepted into his society, Einar had become its absolute defender; he would not admit the smallest compromise or change.

"I sincerely hope," Astrid said, dryly, "you did not bruise that tiresome child's arm." She did not embrace him, nor he her, but shoulder to shoulder they went into the striped shadows of the main room. Bedevere was stretched out on a hammock. He moved only his eyes as they came in, and Astrid pulled the door closed behind them. Keri sat cross-legged on the floor, stripping down a speargun.

Bedevere said, "There are times I wish I were a childless man."

Rache willed himself to take the remark as innocent, any barb quite unintended. Astrid spoke first. "People get the children they deserve."

"Thank you, Mother. Do you think you deserved Rache and myself, not to mention Apple?"

Rache looked from brother to mother and felt his anger rising. In front of Einar they could speak of

Athene, but in front of him, nothing. He let himself down hard on a sprawl chair, and looked up to find Astrid watching him.

"Are you not afraid," Rache said, grindingly, "like Einar, that this is going to lead to a repetition of forty years ago?"

"Yes," said Bedevere, sitting up. "I am, and so I think we must settle this as much as possible within the boundaries of Scole, *without* involving outsiders at the seas-court."

"To be blunt," Rache said, "nothing I have seen or heard so far has satisfied me that there is a will here *to* settle it."

Astrid said, musingly, "The generation after yours has a special burden. They will be coming into their prime when the decision is made whether or not to terraform Blueheart. If that decision favors terraforming, they will live to be redundant. Einar knows there are plans which could make the seas uninhabitable for decades—"

"Those are not favored—" Rache began.

She continued as though he had not spoken. "Even the most benign plans will change our seas utterly, and end our way of life. He does not want that."

"Nor do I," Rache said.

"Yes, but you think you can have an effect. Einar does not. He fears, as do others, that the outcome is inevitable. The machinery—the survey service, the AOC, the rafttown governments—was designed for one thing—to prepare for terraforming. It does not allow the other option."

"Einar," Rache said, "does not understand as much as he thinks he does."

"He is not the only one who fears the machinery."

She leaned forward and brushed her fingertips along the silky floor, gentle, even motions, back and forth. "I hear things in my travels; I hear people talking, and I understand some of the coded messages along the boomer-relays. You do know, I trust, that not everything which passes through the boomer-relays is recognized as such . . . by the pastoral-liaisons."

"I know that," Rache said, wondering what she intended. Astrid was not a storyteller, never had been; she laid out arguments like mathematical proofs.

"People also talk to me, because I am something of a symbol." Her mouth twisted. "We have long memories, we pastorals—landsmen do not understand that.

"There is a great deal of anger and fear in the seas, now. In a way, again, you are responsible. You slew the illusion that we were an independent people. And you have slain the illusion that life as we live it will go on forever. Because of you and your work, we know more, and trust less, the shape of the future."

He shook his head slightly, not wanting to hear, or bear, those responsibilities. "Do you know anything about illegal adaptation?"

"Yes," she said.

Bedevere started to say something, stopped himself.

"As I said, people who see me as a victim of the landsmen tell me things. They try to use me. I would not let myself be used. I learned a great deal in my rehabilitation, not necessarily what was intended."

"I could imagine," said Bedevere.

"Yes," she said, austerely, "you could imagine. So," to Rache, "could you, I suspect. But neither one of you," she said, deliberately, "has ever asked. I was the first to learn how much we had diverged from the landsmen. They think—or some of them do—that it was simply a matter of body. That adaptives are created anew with each transfected generation. It is not so. Inheritance is cultural. We are an alien culture, here in the seas. I was not ashamed of the things they expected I should be ashamed of. I did not grieve for the things they expected me to grieve."

Rache read on Bedevere's face his own unease. The unease before suffering one had caused, or if not caused, failed to recognize and alleviate. "I think," Rache said, "they are more sophisticated now."

"Yes," she acknowledged. "I agree. We are not as mutually ignorant of each other as we were. That creates its own problems. More people sense the difference. What was I talking about?"

"Illegal adaptation."

"Ah, yes. It happens. I have heard it happens. I have once or twice been approached by people, wanting my involvement." Her reserved expression hardened. "I told them I would have no part of it. So," she cast a glance toward Rache, "there is nothing I can tell, except that it happens." She looked toward the door. Sunlight laced one side of her face and glittered in one eye. "I trust Einar has taken those two home."

Silent Keri spoke. "He encourages them." She looked up from the speargun she was carefully reassembling. "I've seen them on the platform of Tove's raft, when the elders are meeting." Bedevere sighed; Keri and Astrid exchanged identical, female glances.

Astrid said, "Bede says your dead woman might have been an illegal adaptive."

"Yes."

"Trouble for us if it is so." She leaned back on her hands, a sinewy motion. Seeing her, Rache thought she must herself have spent time on land, to build the sinew and the ease of motion. "You should go back to work. Your yellow-striped proposal may be more important than you know. You do not have to be official in the survey service to work on it, do you?"

He did not want to think of his proposal. "The support for development may be withdrawn," he said, briefly.

"You'll have my support," Astrid said. "Mine and others."

"Why?" said Rache, irrationally moved, though he knew they did not have, could not have, the expertise the proposal needed to be acceptable for higher striping.

"Because the Einars need to believe in the alternative."

Keri snapped the last catch into place and handed the reassembled speargun to Astrid; Astrid tossed its weight, stood, and shouldered it. "Thank you. I'll bring you a lava eel." To Rache, "Perquisites of being a matriarch: sparing my aging eyes." Then she smiled at him, a brief, swift-quenched brilliance. Lines radiated from eyes and mouth like a sunburst. "How long has it been since you and I hunted together? We could reach the south hunting grounds by sunset."

"I should wait . . ."

"Do you expect Tove to produce today? It suits her to keep you—and everyone else—in uncertainty. Let Tove be a little uncertain of you, too. Come out hunting with me. Let us see what *we* can scare forth."

NINE

I f we are going after lava eel," Rache said, surfacing beside his mother at the compound barriers, "we should have a third."

"Quite so," said Astrid, amused. As well she might be, given the relative spans of their experience. "I thought of asking Einar to join us."

"Family diplomacy?"

She did not respond to the slight, edgy levity. "Every generation has a few distinctive voices, speaking to, and for the others. Einar is one of those voices. I have heard his name far from Scole."

Rache grunted. "It bodes ill for that generation, then."

"It bodes ill for all of us." She stretched out in the water, kicking her feet idly. "In the seas, we have settled in the belief that the old rule and the young yield. But this is a time of change; the young will have as much voice, if not more, than the old. They must be courted, Rache. Remember, Einar is older than you were when you left the seas. Think of the forces arrayed against you, and think how little you were moved."

"And you think hunting lava eel will reconcile myself and Einar."

"I think," Astrid said, "it may start him thinking differently of you." She looked at him with bright, challenging eyes. "You were close, once."

"I cannot say I have great faith," Rache said, "but we need a third, and you are leader and he is your choice."

She cuffed his cheek with just enough force to make it more than a caress, water spraying his face and the float behind him. Her face was alive with irony and amusement at such traditional deference from him. Without another word, she surface dived and he watched her glide away, underwater, in the direction of Einar's raft.

She swam them hard through the fields and barriers. Rache had forgotten what it was to keep pace with an experienced seawoman, and even Einar, younger and now more seasoned, had little energy left for antagonism. Well clear of the barriers, and the debris, Astrid turned south, surface swimming with the current. She was not, and had never been, a subsailor; she did not have the depth and endurance in the dive which would let her move through current layers. After the first kilometer, Einar, who had been carrying his speargun in his hand, yielded to necessity and strapped it to his back. He would not have kept Astrid's pace, otherwise. That was almost the last detail Rache noted. Then thought dissolved in the endless rhythm of his own stroke, in the paradoxical impression of water streaming by, and of slow, slow progress. He swam with eyes half open, seeing no more than an impression of shaded blues glittering with brightness. The taste of the water, the feel of the water, the vibration of the water through the fine skin on sinuses and ears, all slid over the surface of his mind. He was too experienced in the sea to take more than passing note of the unthreatening, and too experienced a hunter to waste energy and concentration he would need later.

Their destination was immediately south of Scole, between Scole and the next newest seamount on the chain. A wide, ropy old lava flow supported one of Blueheart's largest sessile plant-beds, its grazers, and its predators. Lava eels lived among the broken and newly exposed rocks in the shallows, and preyed upon passersby of almost every species. A primary scientist had once described them as biochemical pirates: instead of digesting the specialized molecules of their prey, the toxins, pigments, and enzymes, they sequestered and used them. And that description, and the innocent glee with which that scientist had expounded on the ingenious biochemical and behavioral adaptations of the lava eel, had been Rache's first true experience of culture shock. He had been prepared for the change in diet, prepared to wear clothing, prepared to be shocked by primary relational mores, and to be patient with their shock with his . . . but he had not been prepared to hear someone making merry with one of his own culture's totems. One's first hunt of a lava eel was a passage into adulthood. There was no more valued, and dangerous prey in the temperate shallows of Blueheart. The mix and effect of their poisons were completely unpredictable. And, by sound and scent, a trapped or wounded lava eel drew others in on the attack. The first stroke had to be the killing stroke.

Astrid slowed as they neared the hunting grounds; Rache and Einar matched her pace, softened their stroke. Patchy free-floating algae drifted across the surface, casting hazy clouds and long lances of sunlight into the depths. They would have to find an area where the sea-floor heaved surface-ward enough to bring it into the light. At least to scout. Lava eels were readiest on the attack at dawn and dusk, when the eyes of their prey were least sensitive. But first . . . Astrid heard the signal first, changing their direction. Attention, Rache knew, not acuity: Astrid's hearing had been augmented for undersea by surgery, and was inferior to his, which was ingrown.

Not for the first time, he regretted not being able to talk to his mother about what had made her decide to request deep adaptation for her younger two children. Ordinary adaptations were done postnatally; the mother need only submit to a gene scan. He and Athene had been conceived and modified *in vitro*, allowing their more extensive adaptation, but meaning that Astrid had to submit to intervention and monitoring. She had, moreover, borne Athene nearly two years after her partner's death, an unnatural birth, in pastoral terms. He had always assumed she had consented because she wanted them to have freedoms and abilities she did not have, and that she had proceeded without further thought and with the hearty approval of the holdfast. A simple-minded assumption, he thought now; little wonder she had never talked about it with him.

They surfaced at the buoy above the mustering place. All hunting grounds near sessile communities had one or several, beneath which were slung emergency equipment, including (controversially) several rafttown-made flares. The water was too shallow to be on the boomer-relay, and no adaptive-made clicker could summon help from as far as help might need to come.

Astrid said, "There's a place I passed on my last hunt that looks as though it might be good, open rock: dense undergrowth close by, and not too deep. We'll need to scout for numbers. You've both been out with me before: you know what I want." Yes, Rache thought, black rock, shallow, clear, relatively well lit. Some idea of how many lava eels were nearby, and a bolt-hole should they trigger a mobbing. Anyone who hunted with Astrid had to be prepared to return home empty-handed when nothing suited her. But anyone who hunted with Astrid knew that, barring utter disaster, they would return home. "Have a look around, make sure you have an idea of what it could have been eating. I'm not going after lava eel which have been eating lasers or trollfish." The fish themselves were too small for their venom to be more than unpleasant, but the dose concentrated in the eel's system was dangerous.

"It's a harder swim home with an empty sack," Einar said, quoting a hunter's adage.

She looked not at him, but at Rache. "Wait until you have swum the hardest swim of all."

"It's big," Astrid said.

Under the yellow light of early sunset they held their final conference, drifting in the slow swell. Below their feet, just barely visible, old black lava heaved out of the thick growth. Low on one side was a cleft, and beneath the cleft the rock was speckled with white. Fragments of bone and scale, castings by the eel within the cleft.

"The bigger they are, the lonelier," Einar said. That was true. Lava eels did not share feeding grounds, and the larger the eel, the larger the territory. They had scouted the formation below, and seen only the one fresh deposit, and the suggestion of three more, but stale and abandoned.

"One thing," said Rache. "I found this." He showed them an arc of cartilage, lined with the spurs of radial teeth, the jaw of a medusa. He lifted it to the sun, showing its translucency, bent it in his fingers, carefully indicating its flexibility. It had not lain there long. "There's ribbongrass and forest vegetation seeded throughout the sessile forest, probably driven in here by the last storm." He did not need to expand. If the eel's latest meal had been medusa, its venom sacs would be charged with the medusa's agonizing poison. Rache would almost rather trollfish.

Astrid looked from one to the other of her companions. "Well?"

Einar looked a challenge at Rache, the slanted sunlight splashing across his face, filling one eye and shadowing the other.

Rache opened his hand, and let the small, sinister finding vanish into the depths. But it was not Einar, but Astrid who smiled at him.

"I'm first spear," she said. "Einar, you're second spear and bag. Rache, you're herd." Spear required reflexes and skill. Herd required subtlety and nerve. Most of the casualties were herd, caught too close to the lair while driving the prey. His life could depend upon her accuracy with the spear, in the dusk, with no warning. He merely nodded, giving her his consent.

He had forgotten, he thought, so much. Not of the process, or of the sensations. Those he remembered, the suspense, shading to sheer terror. But he had forgotten how little he would see, how the final moments of the hunt would be a blue-stained shadowplay. This one, like all the others, they would re-create in words, until they believed they had seen clearly. But in truth, from below, he could not tell her shadow against the sea's pale underskin from the rock's shadow. She held herself so still, so close to the rock. She would feel through her skin the shock of the lava eel's lunge.

Einar he could see, outlined whole against the wrinkled blueness. The light shone slightly through the pale capture sack, which he held ready so that the shot eel might be sealed away before it released any attractants. In his other hand, he balanced his speargun ready, point toward the rock. Rache rather hoped he would not feel prompted to use it. Astrid he trusted in any light, for any cause. Einar he felt less certain of. Seaweed stroked his skin as he sculled his way toward the den, coaxing fish before him, keeping them just uneasy enough to move them higher on the rock than would be their wont, not uneasy enough to scatter. Their shining flanks were mere flickers in the twilight before him. But the eel would see them, as Rache saw Einar, dark against the dusk above . . . He slid beneath them, belly to the rock, peeling them away from shelter. They dithered, sinuous bodies flexing. And with belly to rock, he felt through the rock the thrust of a long, thick bolt of muscle from its lair. He saw it, slanting above him as its jaws closed upon its last meal. He heard the click and rush of the spear, and saw a faint white streak like phosphorescence, and—he would have avowed, a burst of faint white light as the spear embedded itself in the base of that armored, spiny skull.

The spear's striking drove the skull downward toward him. He glimpsed the tail, as it lashed free of the cleft, leaving the eel free and convulsing in the water. He thrust off the rock, rolling outward and aside from its paroxysms, and felt a ragged, spine-combed current brush his thigh. He dived, scraping skin on rock. Astrid loosed a wordless, underwater shout of triumph, and snapped on the light in her hand. Green fluorescence bloomed around her, and Rache had an impression of scattering fish, of a huge, barbed rope, writhing down the rock's edge toward the rippling map of sea-growth. He scrambled and sculled himself clear, and heard over the scraping of the eel's spines on rock the soft clicking of Astrid's tongue.

A moment later, her laughter turned to a shout of warning, as Einar dived to capture the spear and force the head into the bag. Rache saw the eel twist, did not see the spines strike, but Einar suddenly stiffened, and released the spear. Astrid caught it herself, with a desperate plunge, pinning the long, twitching body against the rock. With her free hand, she pointed surfaceward at Rache.

He obeyed. He caught Einar in his arms. All he could do for Astrid was push the floating capture sack toward her. Some small part of his mind reminded him of the orders he had given outside the plexus, and how easy such orders were to give, and how difficult to take. He burst through the surface, into the last of daylight. He pinned Einar against his body with all his strength, forcing his lungs to collapse and expel the water he had inhaled in his shock. Warmth gushed over Rache's shoulder; Einar croaked against his ear. He released the young man and placed his body between Einar and the waves while Einar gasped and coughed up clear froth.

A green glow suddenly bloomed in the water beside him. Astrid surfaced, the lamp riding her hip, flooding them from beneath. Her hands were empty, but the light touched upon the taut belt tether, reaching down to a pale bulk below. She assessed Einar with a glance, seeing, as Rache saw, that the froth was bloodless, colorless, and easing, that he was breathing, moving, not paralyzed, convulsing, or edematous. She caught up his hand and showed it with a pattern of feathery scores, no embedded barbs, just beginning to weal. Rache said, his voice strained, "In my pouch. A tube labeled 'de Courcey-four.' Adam de Courcey made it up for our divers."

Einar did not flinch as she smoothed it on. She held his wrist lightly, feeling his pulse. "Medusa," she said. "As you said."

Einar shuddered and moved slightly against Rache. Not resistance, just a small, exploratory motion, beginning to test the limits of pain. If the eel's last meal had been medusa, the effect of so light a scratch would quickly pass, except in memory. But Rache remembered the one time he had been medusa-stung. For days afterward, the lightest brush by something unseen had awakened a phantom agony.

Astrid nodded. "And I was right about the size. Big bastard." Then she inhaled, and Rache saw the breath shudder in her nostrils. He freed one hand and laid it on her shoulder, and she laid her hand on his, in return, drawing close. Between them, they sheltered Einar from the waves, as darkness fell.

Teal came out of sleep or faint or unconsciousness bowed down before the portal, face bent to the join of console and deck. There was blood drying on the deck, blood crusting her face and hair. Her nose was plugged, but no longer bleeding. Every heartbeat drummed pain against her skull.

She raised the canopy, though she did not seal it. She leaned against the recliner, since the headache seemed less thus, and she could breathe more easily. She dozed, brokenly, until sunset, and then found herself able to lie down; did so, and slept, rocked by the empty, empty sea.

Dawn woke her. She considered the empty sea, watched the changing light on the shifting contours. Her headache had nearly gone. But she was aware of a profound disorientation, of thoughts that stuttered, of perforations, ellipses, amnesias large and small. She had not known how habitually and unconsciously she referred to her cercortex, how much of her memory was now contained therein. And therefore, how much of her *self*. She held onto the edge of the capsule and thrust her attention down into herself, reaching for the internal interface. It was gone. She had been erased. She thought thoughts which would not complete themselves, reached for knowledge that was not there, sensed the outlines of lost memories. She shook with a terror beyond simple terror at being marooned. The emptiness of the sea was nothing compared to the emptinesses within her mind.

Pain brought her back to herself. The pain of her hands beating the edge of the capsule. She pulled her hands against her stomach, doubled over, rocking slightly, against the motion of the sea. The autistic motion was calming. She threaded infant thoughts together. I didn't always have an interface. Other people go their whole lives without. I should remember how to use my mind. I can think without it. Listen to me thinking. She experimented: it might only be the interface. My datastore might be intact. I should be able to restore from backup. She rubbed her fingers over the hard little spur beneath the skin of her shin. Back, forth, back, forth. While she worked, she kept it open, but during coldsleep the skin grew over it. It will hurt to cut it open.

There will be blood. She rocked and rubbed, rocked and let the sea rock her. The sun grew higher, hotter. She slid down into the capsule, trying to escape the glare. The light and the heat followed her. She was hot, and growing intensely thirsty.

She stood up, slid her hands along the capsule cover and slammed it closed, sealing out the sun. She drew a tumbler of water, and drank it in one breath, aware of nothing except the waves of water in mouth and throat. Then she gripped the tumbler in shaking hands and sat grappling with the significance of her own actions. As a child she had learned how to ensure her own comfort and safety. Even without her cercortex she had remembered the cover and the water. If she were to live, she could not let herself be fearful or despairing of her own ragged thoughts.

She tried the capsule's AI. She worked the tactile interface slowly, with many errors. She had to struggle to remember commands she would have flicked from internal memory at will. Even her hands were suddenly clumsy. The sway of the sea taunted her, punishing each unready movement. The AI remained unresponsive.

She breathed, reasoned, promised herself that there could have been no hardware damage, that she could restore from backup, given support. When panic threatened, she rocked, thought small, simple thoughts. She let animal instinct take care of her body, eating and drinking as it urged. Her mind was absorbed in its own evolution.

The capsule AI was unusable as a temporary store. Her backup could be inaccessible: she could not command an upload. She was entirely without computer support. Her assets were very few. Such native wit as remained supple outside her interface. Fresh water in, for all practical purposes, inexhaustible supply, and even should the filtration unit fail, Blueheart's brackish seawater was just drinkable, even by a primary. Food in finite supply. An unsteerable, but unsinkable craft.

And the sealed pouch Rache had pressed upon her. Clumsy-handed, she spread the contents over the recliner. Simple instruments. Maps. Instructions, all in diagrammatic form. She nearly laughed. Had she not known deep spacers and orbit stationers with the same obsessive concern for redundancy, she might have found this most suspicious. But, whatever grudge he held against her, he would not have sabotaged her and at the same time given her the means to save herself. She felt incongruously lighthearted; she had not known until then that she had feared it had been indeed he, whom she had regretted indicting. She found the wafer which included compass and electronic sextant. She sighted it as directed, edge on to the sun, then flat to the sea. It flickered, and displayed two sets of symbols, bright against its olive screen. But she remembered children's games in the women's enclave, games of mapping and searching. She laid the maps out, until she could match the symbols, and bring her fingers together at a point. There, she thought. There. Her spatial sense was independent of her cercortex; she had had it from a young girl. She could look toward the islands which the map showed, and be sure they were there.

Then she turned her attention to the maneuvering of the capsule. When the navigator failed, the craft had hove to, leaving the sails flapping, powerless, in the wind. She sat cross-legged on the recliner, tracing the rigging until she understood it, understood where the wind was trapped, and how the thrust went, and how thrust and direction might be changed. Until she could feel them, intuitively. Until she could remember how the dune-yachts felt under her hand, when she raced Juniper on Berenice.

She drew more water and washed her face and hair, then secured tap, tumbler, bunk, freed the mechanical tiller from its brackets, and climbed carefully out onto the pontoon to fit it in place. It had been far too many years since she had had to manage body, hands, and balance together. She could not tell how many: it seemed she had stored, rather than remembered them. The tiller jerked, the rudder pulled, the swell ground her collarbone against the strut she embraced while working. She slipped off her shoes and let them float away, gripping with bruised feet. Seawater stung where the pontoons abraded. Tiller affixed, rudder freed, she had to release the sheets from their useless clips and scramble back into the capsule, one-handed, the other holding the sheets. She simply sprawled for a long moment, panting with unaccustomed exertion. Then she braced her back against the side, locked the tiller in place, and pulled in the mainsheet. The wind caught and filled the sail; she felt the boat surge forward, and lift; she felt herself borne upward and stared down at white water below her feet. She let go the sheet; the sail snapped it through her hand, the boat slapped flat and water splashed into the capsule. Her heart hammered; perception was bright, sharp, and unreasoning. And somewhere she heard Juniper laugh. She hitched herself up onto the edge of the capsule, ankles hooked beneath the bunk, took sheet and rudder in hand, and trimmed the sail, more carefully this time. When the wind took it, she leaned outward. The boat wheeled as she pulled the rudder with her, the sail went slack; she nearly fell backward, and she had to squirm aboard.

Juniper's teenaged ghost laughed again.

In the following hours she learned what tension she could manage with arm and weight. She learned that the wind was steady and unvarying, but subsurface currents could make merry with one's course-setting. She learned that she no longer had the balance and belly muscles to hold a sail close-quartered, and so she simply let the yacht run with the wind, and steered as the run allowed. She learned to be thankful that she was Berenici, with desert-hardened eyes and skin; even so, her eyes stung and her skin smouldered. She was no longer sure she could reach Grayling itself, but the longer she stayed afloat, the longer she sailed, the more likely she would be to cross paths with a search-craft, a pastoral's raft, or a fellow traveler. The longer she could survive, the more likely that she would survive.

She felt the change in the weather through the change in the sea. She had ceased to perceive the sky, except as a whiteness above the sea, and so she did not understand the growing jerkiness of the waves, the growing perversity of the wind. She thought it was she who was tiring. But when she released the sheets, and slid into the capsule, she found herself thrown against the edge hard enough to wind her. Before her eyes, the pontoons drove so deeply into the flank of a wave that its crest lipped the bottom. She slammed the capsule lid, and through it, looked up at the sky. Overhead was opaque and the color of old ivory, shading to gray. To the north west the sky was dark gray, and the sea nearly black. Unthinkingly, she reached for the net, and stumbled against the void outside, the void inside. She heard herself make a soft sound of panic, as she hung, swaying, between waves. She had been so beset by the calm sea that she could not conceive of anything worse.

Navigation had promised her clear sailing, but that was for the duration of a journey which should have been over. She had downloaded a longer-term weather report, but that was gone. She remembered something in Rache's stiffs about storms, and restraints. She braced herself across the capsule, jammed Rache's stiffs beneath her hips, freeing and replacing them one by one until she found the one she needed. It was terrifying. In extreme conditions, pontoons and mast were designed to break away and disintegrate. The capsule itself would float, ballasted so as always to turn upright. Unless punctured by collision, it was watertight and stormproof. The occupant's protection from being pulped against the inner walls was a cocoon of smart-fiber, wound around the bunk. The fiber contracted against the stresses of a moving body, immobilizing it. Teal rammed the board into its fiche and secured it, with a shudder. That must be a last resort. She cracked the capsule, and wrestled the tiller inboard, spray slapping her face. For the sail, she could do nothing. She braced herself across the capsule, shoulders against one side, feet against the other. The sky outside darkened, the pitch increased. Spray looped and spattered on the capsule. The capsule slid into a trough with a force which nearly buckled her knee, and rose again with such thrust that she heard vertebrae grind. Against the next, or the one after that, she could not hold. She turned her head aside, finding the circle on the pillow where her face needed to be. Smart-fiber could not tell face from feet. Her feet rose on a wave; for an instant she felt they should surely overturn. Then they dropped away, until she was crouching over them and ready to fall on her face. As she tilted backward, she caught the straps above the bunk and heaved herself round, occiput hitting the circle. Two-handed, she pulled upon the emergency lever, and a web of smart-fiber cocooned her from left to right even as the yacht plunged again. Its tensioning drove all the breath from her lungs. The yacht plunged, plunged, and as it struck bottom she felt the quiver of vibrations, magnified by the smart-fiber. The interior light wavered, and strengthened, and, looking up, she saw water and froth stream by as mast and pontoons broke away and the capsule overturned.

She closed her eyes, opened them again at the threat of vertigo. Water and froth, turning and turning. She thought, oddly, that this was what it must be like to be born.

Death, by comparison, should be peaceful.

Stretched out, pinned to a dissecting board, the lava eel measured nearly four meters, and was as thick around as Rache's thigh. Four meters of ropy, rock-textured skin and muscle, its dark, scaleless flanks stained with pigments sequestered from its victims. By the time Rache limped into daylight, the dissection was complete, the eel opened along both spinal planes, relieved of venom sacs, spines and gut. Material Scole did not use would be passed to the planetary survey banks on Rossby. The eel's gut, replete with toxin-binding proteins and inactivators, would be used to synthesize antivenin, and perhaps eventually in the design of venom-resistant adaptations. Astrid and Keri were head to head over the tail, teasing apart fibers. A third woman sat with her back to the door, watching them. The early daylight shone on broad, dark shoulders. It was not until she turned to look up at him that Rache recognized his wife.

He merely stood, flat-footed, until the raft rocked, the wind pushed, and he jarred against the doorway and clung to it. Nobody spoke. She gathered long bare legs beneath her, and stood. He could not lift his eyes. He stared at her feet, her unmistakable feet, long for her height, narrow in the heels, well spread and supple in the toes.

His wife's feet.

One day, eight years after he left to pursue landsman's sciences, landsman's disciplines, he had returned to Scole to find her gone. She had left no message. Save one. She had stripped and dismantled the raft that he and she had lived on. She had given it away, in pieces. On rafts all around him he saw the pieces: a carved strut, a painted shade, a particularly well-shaped ring of fiberkelp. From that, and from the stories, he had known the shape of her last days on Scole.

He had not seen her since.

He heard of her sometimes, a mention, a glancing rumor, enough to confirm that she lived. He had not tried to look for her. She was the one who had left; she had to be the one who returned.

He managed at last to raise his eyes. He had thought that he might come upon her and find her a stranger. But she was still the Lisel he had known. Bareheaded, magenta-skinned, with broad, round shoulders, heavy breasts, full hips. A high-bridged, slightly hooked nose; a long, straight mouth. Her eyelids were thick and heavy, shading dark gray eyes.

She wore a loincloth wound around her hips, a sash across her breasts, a belt of polished shell, with knife hanging from it, bracelets, earrings, and torque of the same dark, polished shell. He had a tactile sense of tearing that drapery from the body he had loved so well.

Loins and face competed for blood; his brain starved. Lisel said, "Tove said you wanted to speak to me."

And he felt the blood recede, and congeal in his heart. He said, "You."

He was dimly aware of Astrid and Keri rising, leaving, their footsteps whispering behind him. Such soft steps to be audible over the rushing of blood in his ears.

He could think of all kinds of stupid things that he could say to her. Why did you leave? It was all my fault. Forgive me. But she had never been the kind of woman to whom a man said stupid things. She never welcomed anything less than his best. That was why he thought she had understood why he left. He wanted to be the best he could be, and lay that at her feet.

He said, again, "You."

"That's right," she said.

"You asked Daven to come to the ringsol."

"Yes." He nearly asked why, but held it behind his teeth, knowing her intolerance of the obvious question. She answered it for him. "I wanted to know what was happening aboard the ringsols."

"And the computer virus?"

"That, I know nothing about," she said.

As though she expected to be believed. "What did you want to know?"

"I wanted to know the state of the knowledge-base."

"So you sent Daven. You could have asked me."

She looked at him in silence.

"You betrayed me," he said. "You betrayed me, and near destroyed everything I have tried to do these twenty-five years."

"And what have you *done*?" she returned. "What have you done with your twenty-five years? After all your grand plans, yours and Juniper's, for the saving of Blueheart; what have you achieved? What have *you* done to make it all worthwhile?"

He remembered the small patch of empty sea, the shade on one raft, the strut on another, fragments of their lives together that she had given away. "You do not know," he said, "because you did not come with me."

"To watch you wanting *her*."

"I wanted *you*."

"If you'd wanted me you would have stayed."

There was a silence like the drawing back of the surf.

"I asked you to come with me," he said.

She said nothing.

He said, bitterly, provoking, "How it must gladden you, then, to see me brought down."

She stepped forward. "You are a stupid man," she whispered, into his face, "if all you think me capable of is jealousy and vindictiveness. There is more to this than you know or have ever known, or ever *will* know. Twenty-five years ago you made your choice, and you deceived yourself that nothing would change when you went away, that you would not change, that *I* would not change, that the seas would not change. You might go and learn and indulge yourself, and become the great leader that she had you dreaming of being. Are we all to wait on your coming? Of course not. When you leave a place behind, you *leave it*. When you leave a person behind, you leave them. Nothing stays as you leave it, Rache. People look at their lives, look at their choices, and all the time, measure them."

"And covet their wrongs," he rasped, "cradling them and nurturing them like children—"

She hit him. Threw him back against the slatted

wall, and leaned against him, her arm a bar across his throat. Over her shoulder he could see the black skin, the pale flesh of the flayed lava eel. He braced his arms, pushed her enough away that he could speak in turn. "I was stupid enough to love you. Stupid enough to take you without knowing your kin . . . stupid enough to let you refuse treatment which might have given us children . . . You never, ever told me where you were from . . ." And then understanding came like a ripple of charge across his scalp.

He said, "Are you yourself . . . an illegal adaptee?"

She pushed herself away from him. He steadied himself, crouched, prepared to move between her and the door. They stared at each other, both breathing hard. "Thinking about it, I thought . . . it would be easy to do, because of the size of the oceans, and all the biomass. Was that what you wanted from ringsol six? The biomass surveys?" She said nothing.

He said, "If you had died out there, like her, would anyone have . . . asked for you?"

She cleared her throat. "Of course not. Out here, I do not exist."

"And so you know . . . so much . . . about not going back. Did you go back then, when you left me?" He did not feel as strong on his feet as he had learned to be. He wondered, fleetingly, whether the lava eel had indeed scored him with its spines. It was not unlike the sudden belated awareness of his back injury. But it was a sensation which seemed to pervade him wholly, body and emotions. "The reason you would not go to the labs about . . . All these years . . . Lisel."

"Don't be maudlin."

He put a hand back, felt the wall and slid down it. He slid, slid, and landed hard, felt floor and walls shiver slightly. He said, "You could have left us. You could have simply thanked us, lied a little, and gone home. I never knew . . ."

She sat down herself, facing him, framed by the striped shimmer of the sea beyond the walls. "If what you are about to say is, 'I never knew you loved me so,' don't be absurd. You knew. If you had not been so certain of me, you would not have left."

He gasped, with sudden painful understanding. "Yes," he said, "I left because I had an anchor. You. But I did not love you . . . any less. Though I haven't . . . given you anything . . . been able to give you anything . . . equal to what you gave me. You could have told me."

She flared, "You are the very last person—"

He flared in turn, "Because you needed it to hold against me? You needed to hold against me that you had given up more than I had, more than I ever could."

"At least admit this," she said. "You left because of her. Juniper Blane Berenice. You deluded yourself, but you did not delude me."

"It was different—"

"Different!" She savaged the word.

"It was," he said, struggling. "You were my anchor. She—she was the wind."

"Ach!" she said, a sound which combined disgust and insurrect amusement.

Angry, he cut himself off, and simply met her stare. "How did you come to be?"

She flipped her hands out, curt, dismissive. "Do you expect me just to tell you? It's a secret kept to death."

"One that's close to disclosure."

"Will you betray us?" she said, a lash in her voice.

"Are you still involved? Do you know where it is still going on . . . ?"

"Oh yes," she said. "It is still going on." Her tone was sly, secret. "But the one thing I would really fear, they cannot do to me. They cannot touch my body. They cannot change me from what I am."

He said, "The penalties—"

"Rache, you think like a landsman, of possessions, and opportunity, of status and the regard of landsmen. I have none of these things; and I do not fear to lose them."

"And your freedom," he said.

"Whatever happens, it is worth it." But even as she spoke, he saw her shudder: she knew Astrid perhaps better than Astrid's son.

"*What* is worth it?"

She shook her head slightly. "Wait."

"Lisel . . ." he said, and stopped, his nerve failing him. He had been so sure he knew the currents and shallows of their marriage. He had them all charted and defined, and known. It had seemed so clear: he was drawn to landsman's disciplines, she was sea-born, sea-alleged, fixed, and unmoving. Knowing this, he could chart his course. But he had charted all unaware of the deep currents, and it had taken them farther apart than he had ever meant them to be.

"I am . . . afraid," he said. "I am afraid we are . . . going to be enemies. We never were, were we?"

She considered a moment. "I nearly hated you, when you left with her. And I surely hated *her*."

Rache shaped a question with his lips.

"Because she knew what she was taking from me," Lisel said, quietly. "She knew, and she took it still."

"I am . . . sorry," Rache said, at last. "I was infatuated."

She let out a little breath, a stillborn comment. Perhaps she wanted more; he readied himself to say more. He could remember what he had felt for Juniper. He had been infatuated; he had been mesmerized; he had been besotted. Lisel spoke before he did, making plain what he had not grasped: "She knew what I was."

"She—"

"I wanted to tell someone. *Had* to tell someone. If you had been there, if you had asked, it would have been you."

"You told Juniper," he said, that sensation of charge gathering on his scalp again.

She said, continuing unwitting, "But you'd stopped talking about it."

And what would Juniper have done with such knowledge? "They control the numbers, the balance, as long as they control the numbers, the balance you will never, never, never . . ."

Was *that* the breakthrough which had so excited her, so distracted her as she swam into those polar seas? Not an artistic inspiration at all, but a grand conspiracy to secure one future for Blueheart. When the numbers were attained, the knowledge gathered, the decision to be made, if adaptives outnumbered primaries . . . He stared into his wife's haughty, secretive face. "How far has this gone? *How many of you are there?*"

A suspended moment, she staring blankly at him. Then she shook herself, and laughed, the laugh merry, unforced, real. "Rache. My poor Rache. What are you thinking? That we might have carried through Juniper's wild scheme?" She reached forward, tapped his face with her fingertips; he felt the edge of her nails. "I hope for your sake you have not spread *that* notion too widely."

He caught her wrist and held it hard. "Why did you send Daven to me? Who was extracting information from the ringsol net?"

She looked him in the eye. "We were concerned about the blight. We were concerned that something was happening—pollution or some perturbation of the ecology—to spread and prolong the blight. Some of us even wondered about sabotage."

"You could have come to me and asked," Rache said in a low voice.

"If it is any consolation to you, Rache, I wish I had. I never would have wished on you, or ringsol six, what happened. In future," she said, "I will ask."

"Will you testify to the inquiry now?"

She leaned against him, lightly but so he could feel her warmth. "If I could have come to Rossby," she said, quietly, "I would have come twenty-five years ago. Rache, now, as then, I am a woman who does not exist."

TEN

Stillness, at last. Beyond the capsule's tired internal light, Teal could see daylight. A daylight scored by dark shards and spars, interwoven by shafts of sunlights. Things ground and creaked against the capsule. Teal hung at an angle, head and right shoulder lowered, cradled by her cocoon. Her weight kept the smart-fiber tensioned.

The storm was over and she was still alive.

Wedged, at what depth she did not know, in packed debris, somewhere on the seas of Blueheart. The air seemed stale, and below her head was a small pool of water, formed to the capsule's contour and rippling slightly with the shocks.

She felt no great fear. Fear had peaked and passed with the discovery of her erasure. Perhaps it was because to her the world inside was the more real. Her contest with the worm in ringsol six had felt like a mortal struggle, while this was a slow progress through unmapped terrain, to an uncertain end.

She turned the thought over in her mind a while. An uncertain end. There was a thing called a will to live; she doubted she had it. A habit of living, perhaps. She had put away all thought of life being a choice, of death being an option. Juniper was always dying, or threatening to die, when thwarted or offended. Teal had never thought of either as being an option: one lived, and then one died. One did not reject life because it was unsatisfactory, unpleasing, even painful. Juniper might; she did not.

But Juniper, who believed in choice, in will, in her own immortality, was dead. Teal, who only had a slack habit of living, was alive, and facing an unaccustomed choice. The choice whether it was worth the effort to free herself, worth the risk to try and reach the surface, to keep seeking help. Slow asphyxiation might be miserable, but it would not be terrifying, or excruciating. And should she reach the surface, should she be rescued, what then? Juniper was dead. She was damaged, perhaps beyond repair. Her specialization had precluded development of any other skills. If she could not repair herself, she would be marooned, unskilled, a person of little professional or economic value. She would have lost what made her worthwhile in the eyes of others.

But she had survived this far, she thought. She had survived an attempt to destroy her brain from within. She had with her own hands sailed her intractable vessel nearly a day on the open ocean. She had outlasted the storm, and come perhaps to land, perhaps only to the edge of one of the floating forests, but a floating mass nevertheless. She was, if nothing else, durable, and if nothing else, she wanted to see how far she could survive, how long she could endure.

Without the violent overturning of the storm, the smart-fiber cocoon had eased a little. Carefully, without shifting her weight, Teal slid her hand up toward the upper edge of the bunk to the manual release. She braced herself to fall against the capsule lid, but did not; release only made the fiber relax to its fullest, so that she found herself hanging in a hammock of limp fabric.

Which was as well, because merely the slump made her gasp. Every muscle had seized.

Grimly, teeth set against unrelievable, unaccustomed pain, she squirmed free of the loosened cocoon and slithered into the pool of water cupped in the capsule's curve. She tasted her wet fingers, and found it brackish. Possibly it was water which she had taken inboard during her sailing. And possibly the capsule was cracked. She looked down at the braided shadows beneath. The sea between them was lustrous, sequinned with bubbles. Bubbles caught, clung, trickled around the transparent curve. Some were as large as her fingertip. She could not be very deep, given such light, such copious broken air.

She reached up beneath the bunk, where she had jammed Rache's stiffs, and leafed through them. She found what she needed: instructions for emergency release of the capsule, emergency rebreather, emergency flare guns. She looked quickly for the last, found it, cradled it in her hands. And laughed. A single snap of laughter, quickly silenced by her own startlement. She could not remember when she had last laughed. A moment later, she drew her knees close, shuddering. She had had the means of rescue all this time. She need never have endured what she had endured. And then, laying her face down on her knees, she thought that the flare could not have saved her. Flare or no flare, she would have been erased. She could not blame herself for her own disorientation or incapability, but this gave her the measure of both. And she knew now how close she had been to death.

Very carefully, she studied the directions for underwater capsule release and rebreather. That done, she resealed the stiffs in their package, and folded them around the flare guns, and pushed them into the waist-band of her trousers, tying her tunic in a bulky, clumsy knot. She held them between thigh and body while she fitted the rebreather and mask. Then she primed the switch and cracked the capsule.

The water which seemed outside so bright welled up tepid, turbid green, a soup of shreds and scraps of seaweed which slid up her trouser cuffs and twined around wrists and ankles. She felt its swift ascent up shins, thighs, stomach and spine, touching breasts and knees, throat, jaw . . . a line of cloudy green moved like a veil upward across her mask. She felt the water creep root by root over her scalp. Her breath was rough and hollow in its confinement. She felt a seepage across her cheek and jerked the straps tighter until it stopped. The little pool of water lay against her skin like a droplet of mercury. All she could smell was sea.

She eased one foot leftward, into the crack between hood and base of capsule. It was the width of her thigh, no more. She explored with her hands. Above her, the two sides met, with no opening. Experimentally, she pressed. Nothing yielded. She turned, feeling the water rolling down her cheeks, wedged shoulders against the capsule, heels against the planking, and tried to straighten. The capsule shuddered, and then she felt the lower half tilt, a motion so uncontrolled and unexpected that she let go, panting. She floated in the turbid water, feeling the opening until she understood, and then she braced herself across the rear of the capsule, forcing the base back and aside until the opening at the rear was shoulder width.

She could feel the shifting pressure from outside, a pressure which pressed and released, pressed and released. She could see dense, twisting shadows closing her exit, and while she held it open, explored them with one free hand, finding them firm. She could not simply slither from the capsule between one pressure and the next. She released her brace—her muscles were beginning to tremble—and felt the capsule close like a shell. Moving by feel, a slight grimace on her face at the slimy lengths winding her fingers, she brought the salvaged tiller from its store.

She held the tiller in place by leaning upon it, one leg hooked around the bunk. With hands and forearms she forced apart the cross-packed, twisted spars which were not wood, dark and solid as they seemed, but flexible and fibrous, a little spongy. They yielded, they deformed to a degree, but they did not hold, and the cavity she had created, like the opening in the shell, did not remain without her pressure. She drifted a moment, bracing rough, slimy columns, the tiller laid across her ribs, and felt the sea press, press, press upon her. There had to be a way to do this.

There was. The idea came shyly forward, and, as with the water and the capsule lid, her hands knew it before her mind. She dragged upon the spars, bending them inward, tearing them and dragging them inside. Those she could not break, she pulled into the gap between capsule cover and base, so that when the gap closed, it would close on them. She had to stop, several times, to breathe, whether because she was herself unfit, or the rebreather unable to support her, but around her the capsule filled with refuse, and a wedge of bent and broken spars packed the angle between cover and base. The sea around her was murky with her rendings. Half blind, she shouldered forward into the cavity she had made. Hand over hand, clearing her way with forearms, elbows, and shoulders, she dragged herself toward the light.

She struggled through into a brilliant Blueheart day, struggled free until she sprawled facedown across the matted growth, shuddering slightly, and shifting away as subsurface forms nudged and gummed at her body. She stared past clinging bubbles, past the cross-laid dense spars of growth, to the dim, submerged bulb of the capsule she had left below her. She could feel the sun already drying hair, back and shoulders, salt drawing her skin. She reached out with her tongue, and touched it to the trace of seawater on her face and mask. It was tart and brackish.

Of the past eighty years, she had been awake for perhaps fifteen, and had aged another three in coldsleep. She had spent them in rooms and corridors, in modules and capsules, engineered to satisfy her physical needs and to keep her, a most valuable commodity, safe. Before that, on Berenice, she had been surrounded by women who wished for her happiness, her comfort, her pleasure in life. Even out on the dunes, she had been watched over, thought about, safe. She was not a rebel, unlike Juniper. That had, she supposed now, been her best expression of affection for the people around her, that she let them cherish her, watch over her, design places to please her and keep her safe. Unlike Juniper, she had never rejected anyone's caretaking. Caretaking measured her value.

She had the beginnings of a new measure now, she thought, gazing down through the water at the trapped and sunken capsule. She had the measure of her own efforts toward her own survival.

Luminous lettering appeared across the mask. The rebreather she wore was manufactured to process water, not air. She had heard, but not heeded, the suck and gasp of its asphyxiation, as it dragged air over its gills.

She was warned it would shut down to avoid damage. It did, but she lay a moment longer, looking down. The mask flashed a warning of deteriorating air quality. She muttered an oblique Berenici obscenity at it, and rolled belly up to the sun. With a soft snick, the mask's air vents opened, and she could breathe the warm, faintly sour air of Blueheart. Juniper, she thought, might have removed the mask then, and let it sink until it snarled. But she, she had at least a little wisdom, since the mask would protect her from sudden immersions.

And she needed it, for when she tried to kneel, she floundered, for the matted growth was neither solid nor buoyant enough to support her weight. She slipped and sank, into a self-created gulf; the mask's slits closed, the rebreather swished into life; ungraciously, she heaved herself out, her heart beating swiftly. Again, body had better wits than mind: she pulled together a packed handful of growth, holding it between arms and body until she mounted it. Straddling and holding with her legs, she looked around her, turning her face first into the wind. A fine drizzle of spray came with it. The edge of the growth was near enough that she should be spattered with the waves' frustration. They rolled in with the wind, high and proud, to be snared by the matted growth, reduced to the slow heaving which it rode, and she rode on it. The growth stretched out before her, a slow-shifting, dimpled, ribbed stretch of water. And leeward of her: leeward of her, within a wide arc of dimpled water, beyond a broad shelf of green sprouting, a cluster of low-roofed rafts floated in their serene enclosure.

No one came at her first flare. The sight of safety made her impatient; she sent up another, thinking it far too pale against the glaring sky. If that went unseen, she thought, she must wait for night. She had formed an impression of pastorals from her studies, that they would align with anyone against the sea. Perhaps that was wrong. If they did not come to a flare at night, she would have to rely upon herself. She had a body-sense of pulling herself downward to the wreck, and a moment later, she thought, Yes, salvage supplies. She doubted she could raise the capsule herself.

From the far side of the rafts, an outrigger canoe came on broad, soundless wake. She followed it with her eyes, as it cut through a flagged channel to her right. She readied a flare should she need it, but it came as surely toward her as though the wind blew it, and stood off in the hard swell beyond the woody growth. There were four paddlers, red-skinned, naked, and as she watched, two dived overboard and surfaced among the ragged outergrowth. They slid, as she had done, belly-down over the matted trunks and spars, moving and going still, moving and going still, and she thought of the motion of lizards in the desert, that same alternation of thoughtless quickness and paralysis. And she watched them come, she went cold and qualmish. Since her tenth year, she had never met anyone of whom she utterly lacked knowledge. Everyone's data was in the net, for the asking. Moreover, what she knew of pastorals resided in the fragments snagged in fleshly memory. She waited, without breathing, as they approached.

Both were women, quite naked but for their belts. Amphibian-like, they raised their faces from the water, blinking at Teal with heavy-lashed eyes. The right eye of the elder was half closed and a curdled, unhealthy white. A thin cord of scar crossed from mid forehead to cheekbone, slashing the eye socket. It looked, to Teal, like an odd, ugly decoration. She had never seen such scarring before in her life. She felt no revulsion, only interest. The woman stared back at her, eye to eyes, resisting. When Teal's gaze did not waver, she spoke. Words Teal could not understand. She had not thought of the possibility. Local language subroutines resided in her cercortex. She said, in the common language of the settled worlds, "Who—are you?"

The woman's lip twisted slightly, and she spoke to the younger woman, who responded, with deference. The scarred woman flicked a hand at Teal, spattering her lightly with seawater. The younger woman said, to Teal, "She is Maria the younger of Kense." Her accent was marked, with peculiar misplaced stresses, but understandable. She was a broad-framed, well-fleshed girl, her skin firm and unmarred. Her face looked narrow for her build, with shy, black eyes and a long, slightly incurved nose.

Teal said, "Teal Blane Berenice." That, at least, was simple.

The younger Maria of Kense placed one hand on the untidy sheaf Teal was riding, and scrambled up, causing their support to bob and sink. Teal moved before she thought, backward and sideways, away from them both, slithering down into the water, limbs tangling with the dense growth. The water closed over her head. She struggled, losing coordination. Her rebreather wheezed on air and froth.

Someone was in the water around her. Not touching her, not pulling on her, but moving aside the spars which trapped her. She surfaced, breath rattling in the confines of the mask. The younger of the two adaptives floated beside her, the sun shining off water like varnish on her face. She essayed a tremulous smile. "She does not talk Basic. Very few people on Kense do." The smile went a little grim. "They're very traditional. I am Athene. Athene of Magellan. Athene Magellan Blueheart. *I* am a citizen of the galaxy."

"Where is here?" she said.

"Kense on Great Diamond. Is that your capsule below us?"

She was waiting, she realized, for her internal stores to render up answers for questions barely formulated. Her interface had been so refined as to be almost anticipatory. She had no idea, now, how to gather the most elementary information. Never mind how to determine the parameters of courtesy and discourtesy. Already, it seemed, she had given offense. "Why did she go?"

The girl hesitated, then looked down, eyelashes shadowing black eyes. "She doesn't like primaries." She lifted her head suddenly, appealing. "But it is the law of the sea that we take you in, treat you well, and make sure that you are returned to your own . . ." She used a word Teal did not understand. "People," she said, finally, a poor approximation. "We won't harm you. Are you hurt? I'm sorry, I should have asked."

"I am, or I was, an expert-voyager. I have been erased."

"Expert-voyager." The girl turned over the words on her tongue. Then her eyes went fierce. "And you are Teal Blane Berenice." She threw a glance over her shoulder, to where the scarred woman waited on the fringe of the floating growth and the boat beyond. "What are you doing here?"

So sudden a change. Teal merely stared at her. The

girl moved agitatedly. "The law of the sea," she muttered, and something in her own language.

"What is it," Teal said, "that I have done?"

"You blamed Rache of Scole," she said. "You were wrong."

She could hardly remember what it was that she had done. The days of her investigation had been days recorded rather than lived. They came back to her in fragments, isolated stills of a continuous stream, herself and others caught in poses, gestures, emotions. She said, "I would have drawn the conclusions the data allowed, no more and no less."

"You were wrong," the girl said, and tossed her head. "But it is the law of the sea that we give you refuge. Follow me." She turned and began to crawl-glide toward the edge, into the increasing swell. Teal balked. The girl halted, and slid around. "Why aren't you coming?"

"You are not friends."

"The law of the sea says—"

"The law of nets says that nobody should do what they did to that underwater place and me."

The girl belly-slid back to her. "You are not normal, are you?"

"My cercortex was erased."

"Cercortex. That's the—implant in you that lets you talk directly to computers. That lets you do what you did to Rache." She nodded slightly, satisfied. "Then you won't be doing it to anyone else. And we keep the law of the sea better than anyone keeps the law of nets. Keeping the law of the sea, helping each other, means that we can count on help when we need it. Who would break that?" She gave Teal a long, narrow look. "Yes," she said, slowly. "If we help you now, you will help us, later."

Her rescuers hauled her aboard like a sack, waited until she had righted herself, and herded her forward until she crouched on hands and knees in the center. Two moved aft of her, one the girl, and two behind. Without a word, they lifted their long paddles; a man's voice was raised in chant, four paddles bit hard into the sea, and the canoe surged forward, biting into a wave and rearing sideways and up, upon its pontoon. Shallow water coursed across Teal's hands and shins. She swayed into the swell. The paddler behind her caught a handful of her clothes, saying something. The girl twisted. "Please stay still," she said. "You are safe." Then she leaned into her stroke again.

They ploughed a short curve toward a second flagged channel, and paddled a switchback course around interlocking barriers. Almost immediately, the swell softened, the spray ceased. On the girl's broad back, the water drew down like a sheet, leaving lines of twinkling drops too small to be shaken free. Beyond the stippled water was a thick mat of green, and on the other side of that, a wide area of clear water, with the rafts at their center. The canoe swung around the rafts to a floating jetty, and nudged into its place among a cluster of others. The lead paddler jumped ashore and secured it. The others followed, except for the girl, who turned with an uncertain smile and faced the crouching Teal. They looked at each other, a moment, aware of gathering audience. Then the girl brushed her fingertips against her own hairless temples, where on Teal the straps for the mask rested, and a moment later, Teal understood; she lifted her hands, unsnapped the catches and lowered the mask from her face. The girl looked toward the adults on the jetty, questioningly. Teal heard someone say her sister's name. Much distorted by the accent, but she knew it still. She turned her face toward the voice, and said, "Teal."

Only when she had spoken did her vision clear. She felt a moment's almost vertigo at the sight of the people gathered there. They were too many to be so strange: quite naked, men and women, hairless, with matte skin dark as raw meat, and pink-stained eyes. The half-blind Maria was not the only one with signs of unmanaged healing. One held a half-gutted fish, dull-scaled and gaping pale flesh like a mouth. Another held a net.

A man stepped level with Teal and held out a hand. He looked to be in early old age, well over a hundred, the muscles in chest and arm sharp-edged beneath thinning skin. After a moment's hesitation, she laid her hand in his, and let herself be pulled in among them. The girl followed, and stood, staring at her feet, looking both shy and stubborn.

The old man said something. The girl lifted her head, a flicker of satisfaction crossing her face. "He asks me to welcome you."

Teal said, "Was it you who called me Juniper?"

The girl translated. The man nodded, said something. The girl said, "You have her face."

"I am her twin. Natural born," she felt moved to add.

More people were still arriving, coming from both directions along the jetty, and climbing out of the water on the far side. Adults came with assurance, confident of their rights, adolescents with a shy stubbornness or defiance like the girl's, children peeked and whispered at a distance, on the jetty or in the water. The old man glanced around, and said something in a low, curt voice which could not have carried—and, with backward glances, the onlookers melted away, adults willingly, adolescents grudgingly, gathering up the children as they went. The eight who remained were old, but for the half-blind Maria and the girl translator.

The old man who was the speaker said something. The girl did not translate, but answered him with a diffident request. He acceded, and Teal caught the glitter of triumph in the girl's eyes as she turned to Teal and said, "Would you like to come with us to the meeting place?"

Teal set her feet. "I need," she said, "to go to Rossby."

Indecision crossed Athene's face. She spoke to the old man. He shook his head. She said, to Teal, "After. Maybe after."

The meeting place was a raft at the heart of the holdfast. On it was a single, large cabin whose walls were slatted, and could be slid aside, in sections or half-sections, to create windows or doors. Most of the upper sections had been removed, so that the wind blew through unhindered. Broad eaves shaded the inside from all but the earliest or latest sun. Teal took a step inside and halted. The center of the floor was hollowed out, and a square of dull, shaded water creased and shifted. The girl beside her said, eyes glinting. "It's meant to suit everyone, those who like to be in the water, and those who like to be outside."

One of the others spoke, and she dipped her head. "They would like you to tell them how it is you came to be here."

"Who," Teal said, "are they?"

The question startled the girl. "The elders. The elders of Kense. Some of them, anyway."

She told them who she was, and what she was. Maria the younger interrupted the explanation, angrily. That, she said, speaking to Athene, was not what they wanted to hear. Athene, her voice flat, translated. Teal explained why she had come to Blueheart, and what she had found when she arrived, how she had intervened in the ringsol six disaster, and become involved in the investigation, and what came of that. Something in what she said softened the girl toward her. She told them how she had set out, and how her journey ended. The report, to her ears, was incomplete and deeply flawed with inaccuracy; so much had gone with her cercortex. But at least she was no longer unthinkingly reaching into the emptiness inside her, and they seemed satisfied; they asked a few questions, and then waved her dismissal, and the girl Athene pulled her quickly outside. She said, not letting Teal's hand go, "I'll take you to the guestraft. That is where I am staying."

"You are not of Kense?"

"Of course not," the girl said, bright-eyed. She glanced over her shoulder at the cabin on the raft. "Can you swim or should I get a canoe?"

They swam, Teal like a dying fish, according to Athene. The guestraft was in the outermost ring of rafts, with beyond it the compound's edge and the floating pier and all their moored craft. Athene pulled herself, and then Teal, from the water, her satisfaction palpable; she had the air of having executed a coup. "Are you hungry? Thirsty? I can get you fresh water."

"I need," Teal said, "to go to Rossby."

"I know; you will, but the elders will decide when. That is the way. They're very traditional here."

"And you," Teal said, after a moment, "are not."

"Of course not. I'm only here because I had whitesickness and needed treatment. When my mother comes back, we'll probably leave." The thought displeased her; she pushed it quickly away. "Tell me what

Rossby's like. I've never been on a rafttown. Tell me what it's like to travel in space. Tell me what other planets are like. Please."

"I have lost memory," Teal said, but Athene pressed her. The girl's knowledge of anything beyond the seas was as fragmentary as her interest was avid. She was not uneducated; she knew how to organize information, and seized upon even the most fragmentary, worrying it into place. They sat in the shade of the guesthouse and ate dried fish and white kelp—Athene ravenously, and Teal politely—and Teal told Athene about the women's enclaves and the sand dunes of Berenice, her apprenticeship on Chara, space travel, coldsleep, Juniper, and every detail of her meeting with Rache of Scole. Despite the water Athene brought her, her voice grew hoarse with speaking; eventually she begged exhaustion, and Athene slung a hammock inside the singleroom cabin for her. The last she saw was Athene sitting sentinel in the doorway, silhouetted against the light.

"The question for us, Rache," Lisel said, "is you." She lay on the apron of the raft, guddling over the side. He sat beside her, legs over the edge. The water braceleted his shins. He stared between the next nearest rafts at, unavoidably, the rafts beyond. They had newly painted blinds lowered against the sun, and the colors were brash and gaudy, blue and gold; they made him think of Juniper. He felt Lisel roll beside him to look up, waiting.

"How so?" he said at last.

"A number of people's liberty depends upon what you do now."

He shook his head slowly, heavily. "It should not."

"Why?"

He turned over in his mind what he might say next. He did not want to anger her in a futile effort to make her understand. She sat up, suddenly, shaking water from her fingers, and swung on her hip, tucking her legs against his thigh, an intimate posture allowed lovers or husband and wife. She touched his near cheek, then slid her fingers beneath his jaw. Her hand was wet, and left a cooling trail. "Talk to me, Rache."

"To what end?" he said, disengaging his head as she tried to draw it around. But, a breath later, as he felt her begin to move away, he could not stop his head from turning. Out here in the sunlight he could see that time and sun had left small squint-lines around her eyes. "Because," he said, "I would rather it depend upon them, than myself. I would rather that they felt an obligation to the people who died in ringsol six. Primaries or no."

"Ah," she said, quite gently. "You ask rather much, you understand."

"Too much," he said, harshly.

"Rache," she said, "if you tell the inquiry what you know, the damage to your relationship with Scole, with pastorals, could this time be irreparable. If you tell them that such as myself exist, the inquiry, the intrusion, will strip all vestige of independence from us. Because of the proximity of stage III, we might never get it back. And, my dear, whatever else you are, whatever else you have become, you are still one of us."

He closed his eyes, feeling ill. The heat beat stunningly upon his head. He said, "Lisel, I am going to have to do something."

"Because you are what you are," she said, almost entirely without mockery. "Of course you are. We knew you would. The question is whether you must serve the truth whatever the cost, or whether you will be content to serve a portion of the truth."

He looked at her. "What have you planned?"

She tucked her feet beneath her, and rose, a hand on his shoulder to steady herself. "Tove is waiting for us."

Tove was not alone.

"Daven," said Rache.

Einar shifted slightly between Rache and his younger brother, and Daven let him. Tove said, "Einar." Einar did not move, watching Rache with fierce eyes. Tove said, again, "Einar. Be seated." Einar glanced at her again and sat at his brother's feet. Daven moved to join him. Tove said, "Daven," and he, obediently, remained standing, exposed, trembling slightly. Astrid, who stood beside and a little behind Tove, reached forward to put a hand on Daven's shoulder, bracing him.

Rache said, "Is it true? Ws it Lisel who told you to come to me on ringsol six?"

Daven glanced at Tove. Rache said, "I don't care what else they have contrived for you to say. Here and now you owe me the truth."

Daven swallowed. "Yes."

"And was she wanting survey data?"

"Yes."

"Did she say why?"

"No."

"Which survey data? The data on the spread of blight, or the data on biomass?"

"He does not know," Lisel said, from Rache's side. "I did not tell him what I wanted."

"I just had to . . . receive the messages and let them do what they were programmed to do."

"You'll simply have to believe me," Lisel said.

"And you, Tove. Do you know about Lisel's origins?"

"Not until quite recently."

"I suspected," Astrid said, quietly. "I suspected almost from the first." Lisel caught her breath slightly. Astrid said, to Rache, "That is why, when I heard about ringsol six, and what Daven had done, and for whom, I came to Tove and suggested that it should not be Lisel, but someone else who must have sent Daven."

"You want us to . . . cut Lisel out of the circuit entirely."

"It is a solution acceptable to us, and, we hope, acceptable to you."

"But who—" he said, his heart contracting painfully in hope, and a beat later, more painfully in realization. "*You?*"

"That was the idea. I already have a record and a certain notoriety. But as we thought about it, we thought it risked compromising you. I am, after all, your birthmother, and not so estranged from you that I could not possibly have colluded with you." She gave him an odd, sad smile. "No, it had to be someone whose relationship with you was known to be difficult, who was known to mistrust primaries, and who could believably have influenced Daven."

Einar got to his feet even as Rache turned his eyes on him. "*I* sent Daven to you. I sent him because I did not believe what the primaries claim about the blight's being natural and innocuous." He closed his mouth hard and raised his jaw, defying all rebuttal.

Rache looked from grandmother, to mother, to

nephews. His mind would not work. Emotion jammed it. But he could no more have named the emotion than he could have voiced a coherent thought.

Einar said, "I know there are risks. But I am willing to face them."

He would, Rache thought, have laughed. Perhaps he should, laugh down Einar's posturing. But he could not find laughter in himself. Their solution was brilliant, desperate and appalling, their expectation that he would collude equally so. He understood so well the shape of this entire visit, Daven's seclusion, the delays, the hunt, the meeting with Lisel. They had driven him as deftly as any quarry.

"Why?" he said. "Why sacrifice yourself?"

"Because there are other people more important than I am."

"Do you want to be a martyr?" Rache said, harshly.

A fierce glare, and then suddenly, dangerously, Einar smiled. "Maybe I do." And Rache realized how greatly he had underestimated Einar, failing to see past an unyielding and facile bigotry. Having no taste for martyrdom himself, he saw no power in it. Juniper would not have been so long in understanding. Einar would protect Lisel and those like her, indict primary justice, and accrue sympathy and the symbolic power of his martyrdom. By the time he was returned to them, the seas would know his innocence.

Rache said, to Astrid, "You approve of his doing this?"

She did not misunderstand, did not take him as simply asking if she approved of the lie, or approved of Einar's placing himself at risk. She knew—and perhaps her example had taught Einar—of the lingering sympathy for her old injustice. She said, "We cannot think of anything better."

He said, starkly, "There's more. You would not—*do* this if there were not more."

Einar said, "Is making a mockery of primary 'justice' not enough?"

"For you, maybe, but not for them."

Einar stepped neatly around Daven, and came up to face Rache. "You think primaries and pastorals can share. I don't believe that the seas will be safe until there are no primaries left on Blueheart. You think that you can use science and law to avert what science and law have planned. I do not. But first we must prevent the decision being made to terraform, and on that we do agree. And," he leaned closer, speaking intently into Rache's face, "to ensure that there is no terraforming, pastorals have to be *free*. If they have any reason to investigate us, any reason to take us in, they will. They will have us all in to the labhosps, and they will not let us go again. They will decide that we need to be rehabilitated in preparation for the day when the seas will be poisoned and uninhabitable—"

Rache shook his head, slowly. He forced words up beneath Einar's spate, a cold upwelling. "If you are taken among them, will you learn anything, or will you just look for more reasons to hate them?"

"If they imprison me for something I have not done, I have every right to hate them."

Rache looked past him, to Astrid. "He will not learn."

Astrid gave her sad smile. "It is not his purpose to learn, but it was not mine, either. He might learn despite himself. Rache, will you do this?"

Einar had stepped back slightly, giving him a clear line of sight. Rache said, tiredly, "If one of you would but tell me why it is so important."

"It is important because, as extremely as Einar puts it, I think he is right. You remember what happened when Athene died." A pause, as of apology. "It would happen again, if Lisel's existence became known. I am not sure . . . that I could bear that, or to watch you suffer what you suffered then."

"I am not fifteen years old."

"No, but you have as much, if not more, to lose. Rache, for Lisel's sake. For mine. Even for Einar and Daven and the world they hope to inherit . . . lie."

He stared at her quiet, age-seamed face. She alone he would have wanted to believe. Nobody else. He knew Tove's wiliness, Daven's weakness, Einar's fanaticism, and Lisel's long secrets. He remembered thinking, just before his first sleep on Bede's raft, how he wished that Scole could hide its secrets. It had hidden them, but poorly. He shook his head, slow, wounded. Wounded, and still not knowing whether by their venality, or his own distrust.

He said, "I still don't know what I'd be lying for." There was a silence, then Astrid took him gently by the arm, turned him around and guided him out of the room.

Outside on the deck, she said, "If there were anything else that I knew, I *would* tell you. I would not let you swim blindly ahead."

He said, "All those years." Pulled himself together quite brutally, and said to her, "I have to be certain there is nothing more."

Astrid dropped to her haunches, at the raft's edge, and dipped her fingertips in the water. "Do you think it possible, or is that hurt and betrayal talking?"

"I—don't know," Rache said. "But believing blindly won't help me find out. She has no right to demand that I simply trust her. Not now."

"I meant what I said for the best," Astrid said, quietly. "And I still believe it would be for the best."

"Except that Einar would use it."

"He would not be the only one telling the story." She laid both palms on her thighs. "And he would be implicated. He was the one who arranged to have the starfish programs prepared and sent."

"Who prepared them?" He had never thought to ask; he had forgotten that Scole's was not the darkest part in all this.

"His name is Karel de Courcey."

"Dear God," said Rache, making his mother stare. The oath was most unusual for him, but most apt to its subject. He lowered himself onto the deck beside her, and rested his brow on the heels of both hands. "Karel de Courcey's father died in the disaster of ringsol six." She murmured brief sympathy. Rache watched pressure-flares swell on his closed eyelids, and turned over leaden layers of thought.

"What are you going to do?" he heard Astrid say, gently.

"I don't want to name Karel de Courcey," he said, half lifting his head. "I don't want to name Einar and I don't want to name Lisel."

"You have a problem."

He straightened, and roused himself to give an ironic smile. "Thank you, Mother." He slid his legs forward and eased himself over the slick, scratchy float into the sea.

"Where are you going?"

He squinted up at her a moment, without speaking. He did not know why; the decision was already made, and he had no hesitation in telling her. But action was easier than thinking, or talking about it. He said, at last,

"Ringsol six. I am going to try and find out what data they were trying to extract. If I can do that, I might know why they wanted it. And then I might know . . . who to accuse."

Karel said, "You *promised*."

"I know," Cybele said. She sat at her basic console, her hand still in its web, an image frozen on the slanted screen before her. "I know I promised. I would like you to release me from my promise." He said nothing; she twisted to look at him, still without freeing her hand— that would have looked too much like capitulation.

He was staring at her, white-faced. He said, "Cybele, don't do this, or you'll regret it."

"What will I regret?" she said, a little coldly. "What do you know that I do not?" She freed her hand, and stood up, facing him. "The investigation is over. It has just been announced. The findings were inconclusive, the salvage supposedly too incomplete to allow forensic analysis. You and I both know that is not so. Teal Blane Berenice *did* such an analysis. Yesterday I spoke to the counselor who was part of the investigation, Rache of Scole's friend. He had already withdrawn. He said conflict of interest, but he was lying; he all but admitted it. He told me truth would be difficult to come by.

"You are aide to Cesar Kamehameha. You live in his pocket; you *told* him what I had told you, about Adam's findings." Pain crossed Karel's face, and left her unmoved; for his talebearing he richly deserved it. "You knew about the illegal adaptives. What else is it that you know that you are not telling me?"

Karel swallowed. "Why are you doing this?"

"The question is, Karel, why aren't you? You are Adam's son. You owe him truth."

Karel swallowed again; she heard his throat rasp. "If the connection with pastorals becomes known, if the illegals become known, then the people working on illegal adaptation will destroy their records and disperse. There's a . . . higher justice working here."

"A higher justice," she mocked. "There's no justice, only self-interest."

Karel whispered, "Cybele, let it go. I do not want to lose you, too."

She said nothing. He touched the back of her fisted hand, with cold, supplicant fingertips. "Adam . . . brought us up with high moral standards," he said. Moved his tongue in his dry mouth. "He did his best for us, but that was because he wanted the best *for* us. He would not want us risking our lives, risking our future careers, in something that is not our struggle. Leave the wrongdoers," he swallowed, "to the law."

"Michael said I should leave justice to God."

"Him, too," Karel said, in a whisper.

Cybele turned away from him, and found herself facing the crystal tower, and the barren, indigo landscape of λ Serpens II. Twin embodiments of all her hopes, all her yearnings. Here, in this room, Adam himself had sat, only a few days before. His untasted cup was still there on the floor, a fine scum on the liquid's surface. She said, "Remember when we decided Adam was an alien. He had no instincts for fatherhood whatsoever. Abra must have known him very well, very deeply, to give him us. Because the only other thing he took as seriously as ourselves was God. You're right, Karel, he did the best for us." Cybele turned. "And the only way I can think to do the best for him is to learn the truth about his death. Maybe then I will decide, as you seem to have decided, that he would approve silence and misdirection, to serve, as you say, a greater good. But I want to know."

"That's arrogance, Cybele," he said, with brittle spirit.

She turned. "Adam didn't rear us humble. I want to know this."

There was a terrible silence. Karel's face was blanched and despairing. She said, "I trusted you with everything I knew." A pause; he shook his head, mutely. "Go back into the past, Karel. Go and hide." She stepped aside, and she watched him fumble his way past her and from the room. λ Serpens II under its daytime sky was the terrain of her heart.

Teal considered the night sea. Dark, wrinkling, the crests catching the pewter light of the moon. Rafts rode low, dark and silent, their silhouettes overlapping, rocking gently against each other. From one or two, lights showed, outside lanterns hung swinging on the eves, or inside lights, shining through the slatted walls.

In darkness, and alone, her fears returned. The longer she remained without activity in the interface synapses, the more likely she would be left with a permanent deficit. She had twice asked Athene when she might be taken to Rossby. The girl had gone and returned with a refusal, and no reason to give. But her open, mobile face told otherwise; either the refusal or the reason made her unhappy. Since darkness, she had avoided Teal, ashamed.

The coming of darkness, marking the passage of

time, had made Teal examine her situation with a stark eye. They could not, or would not, give her the help she needed. Whether their intentions were even more malign, she did not know.

She still had Rache's stiffs, the maps and navigation equipment. She still had her rebreather. Her hands and reflexes remembered something of their old cunning with wind and sail. She was curious as to how far that old cunning and capricious fortune might carry her. Physical death still held little fear for her. It was the threatened loss of all she was, had been, and had done, that drove her on. Rather than that she would swim, she would steal, she would start chartless across the trackless ocean.

She fitted the mask to her face, strapped the mechanism this time across her chest, where it would be immersed when she swam prone. She eased herself forward, over the edge of the raft. Soft, friable threads slid between her bare toes, parted around her ankles; she swallowed hard at the slick, unfamiliar feel of them after the desert, after the long years in artificial environments, drew her feet back, against the slimy base of the raft, and thrust, clumsily, falling forward. The jolt and churning shocked her; for a moment, in the darkness, she did not know which way she must go. Her outthrust foot met soft, enveloping strands; she thrust herself away, and reared through the water's surface, half turned away from the dark bulk of the raft. Reorientated, she dived, a shallow, uncertain depth, and swam slowly toward the jetty and its moored skiffs.

When she reached the jetty, Athene was waiting.

The young pastoral assisted her scrambling climb from the sea with a hand under the armpit, and dropped to her haunches as Teal crouched, breathless and dripping. She did not speak, but after a long moment of palpable impatience, tapped fingertips sharply on Teal's mask, startling the woman, and again until Teal understood that Athene wanted her to take the mask off. She did. Athene said, "I heard you jump in. What are you doing?"

Teal said nothing. What she was doing seemed quite apparent.

Athene said, "We rescued you! We honored you as a guest. You can't repay us by stealing one of our *boats*."

Teal said flatly, "I have asked to go to Rossby. No one will take me. You will not tell me why. Am I being held here? Because of Rache of Scole, or because of the investigation. Does someone wish me vanished?"

"No! We keep the law of the sea." Then she flushed, deeply. "I'm sorry," she said, in a low voice. "You're being kept here because of me. We're waiting for my mother to come back, to decide what to do with you. I won't let you be harmed," she said bravely, defiantly.

"The longer I go without having my cercortex repaired, the more difficult the repair will be; the more I do without my cercortex, the more my brain will accommodate the loss. In the end, I might need more help than I will be able to afford, or anyone will be able to give me, here on Blueheart. Time is as important to me as your boat is to you."

Athene looked miserable. "We don't mean it," she said, in a low voice. "When I first became sick, I couldn't dive. I needed air in my lungs all the time. I swam like a primary. People, people said I was lazy. Or they made fun of me." She glanced up at Teal from beneath her lashes, an incongruous gesture, since she was several centimeters the taller. "I couldn't hunt, I couldn't harvest, I couldn't help repair the barriers; all I could do was stay in the compound with the little children. Then the boomer-relays described this whitesickness. I was turning back into a primary. Some of the elders didn't think I should be taken back to . . . to the place which had worked on me because . . . they said how could these engineers be good if they'd failed with me already. But it was more than that: it was not wanting to be indebted to primaries, and what my mother did when she was younger and who my father is . . ." She trailed off. "My mother took a skiff, and sailed me to the labhosp, and now I'm as good as I was." She drew a deep breath. "I didn't want to tell you all this. I just wanted to tell you I understand."

"Then will you let me go?"

Athene's eyes moved over the gently rocking boats, the dark water between them. "I can't.

Had she been Juniper, Teal thought blackly, she could have charmed anyone into doing her bidding. Had she been fully herself, she could have used her privileged status as expert-voyager—but had she been herself, she could simply have reached for the planet, and requested a skimmer be sent her. She need seldom have asked anything of a human being. She need certainly not have her wishes denied in such an emergency. She gathered her feet beneath her, and stood. "My rebreather," she said flatly, "is my own. My maps are my own. My life is my own. I will take what is my own, and I will go, and you cannot stop me." The girl caught her as she made to step overboard. They swayed precariously, but Athene was by far the stronger; she prevailed.

"You can't go. You don't know anything about the seas."

"You have no right to hold me."

"All right. All right. I'll take you." The words came breathlessly, with neither surrender nor resentment. "I'll take you," she said again, in a tone of wonder, and rising excitement. "I can take you to Grayling, at least. You can go to Rossby from there. Quickly." She caught Teal's wrist and pulled her along the jetty, now as though she were the fugitive and Teal the laggard. "Climb in. I'll get us rigged."

"I think not," said a voice from within one of the boats. A figure rose out of its crouch, balancing carefully. It shook something, and cold fluorescent light splashed over it and them, the jetty planking, the nearest boats, the facets of the water.

"Mother!" Athene said.

There was no mistaking the relationship: they shared the height, the big-boned, solid-fleshed frame, the incurved nose. The woman said, in Basic, "I saw you as I was stowing my gear. I would have called to you, but things became entirely too interesting to interrupt." Then she inhaled deeply, ribs marking her skin, and stepped ashore. Carrying the lantern high, she walked up to Teal and gazed down into Teal's upturned face.

"Teal Blane Berenice, I presume. I am Lisel of Magellan. Lisel Magellan Blueheart, if you will."

Her look was long, and her expression unfathomable.

Athene said, "She needs to go to Rossby."

"Ah yes," said Lisel, "*needs*. I remember how conveniently her sister's wants became needs. Why do you need to go to Rossby, and for that matter, why are you here?"

"She was shipwrecked, Mother," Athene said,

coming up behind Teal. "We rescued her, by the law of the sea."

Lisel turned her head to look at her daughter. Face and tone softened slightly, into a dry, knowing irony. "And you, of course, had to be involved?"

"I speak better Basic than anyone on Kense. You taught me. She needs to get to Rossby because her cercortex has been damaged."

"I heard." Still she looked at Teal with measuring, unfriendly eyes. Athene, at Teal's side, drew breath. "Athene," she said, "a word."

"I know it's important," Athene said. "I just want—"

Lisel pulled her daughter away firmly. Teal heard Athene say, in Basic, "But it was you who told me all about it—"

"So you would understand. Not so you would rush into it. We cannot have that, Athene, you know why—" Then they moved too far along the float, and their voices dropped too low, for Teal to hear. She sat down, feet dangling over the edge, one hand on a boat's tether, the other resting upon the mask which dangled still from her throat. She could find in herself no concern for either the subject or the outcome of the argument. If they took her, she would be glad; if not, she would still go.

Her indifference seemed no more than Lisel expected of her. When Teal felt her again at her side, she was wearing a slightly bitter, knowing smile.

She set the glowlamp down between them, and over her shoulder, waved Athene away. Grudgingly, the teenager moved a few steps further, and stood idling, one knee hooked over a mooring line, rocking gently.

"I have heard from my daughter how you come to

be here. I knew your sister. I knew her very well." When Teal did not speak, Lisel said, "I understand you have been looking for evidence of her."

"Yes."

She drew something from a belt pouch and laid it beside the lamp. It was a double loop of metal, tarnished, pitted, and twisted into an infinity sign, decorated, if that could be the word, with round gray and white stones, and bare, wire-circled mounts. "I looked for her, too. So did others. That is all anyone ever found." Teal lifted the object, turning it over in her fingers, rubbing gently at the lumps. What this had to do with Juniper, she did not understand.

"She wore it. Around her ankle."

And Teal saw. Saw the decorations which Juniper affected when her impulsiveness barred her from wearing glass. Circlets of fine silver and gold, with glass cabochons mounted between wire. This was a travesty. She twisted it, trying to force it back into shape. One of the cabochons sprang free, bounced toward the raft's edge. Teal grabbed at it, missed; it winked once from the water, its eye true, pale blue, and disappeared. Teal moved, and Lisel caught her arm. "It will have passed through the compound netting," she said. "And the water here is deep."

Teal clenched the bracelet in her hand, staring into the water, feeling an aching loss.

Lisel said, "When we knew she was lost at sea, I let it be known that I would welcome any artifacts identifiably hers. We have scavengers whose occupation it is to survey the shores and seabed for natural and manufactured valuables. Four years after her death, this was brought me."

"What happened to her?"

"What," Lisel said, leaning back slightly, "do you already know?"

"She disappeared on her way from Grayling station to one of the holdfasts in the north."

"And Rache of Scole, what did he tell you?"

"That he surmised she had grown reckless in the seas, and been lost."

"Reckless, indeed," Lisel murmured. "Of course, he did not see her in her final days. I think she sought to surprise him. Your sister," Lisel said, slowly, "had undergone the first stages of adaptation." Her eyes were half closed; she watched Teal sideways from beneath her lashes.

"There is no record of that," Teal said.

"Record," Lisel said, "ah yes, you are the expert. You would study the records. No, there was no public record. Your sister was selective of what she placed on public record: only finished work, never drafts. She insisted upon confidentiality. But she had undergone the first stages of adaptation: she carried the oxygen pigments of an adaptive. And she was impatient. Nothing of her equipment was ever found, nothing aside from this bracelet. That, I believe, is because she carried no equipment. She tried to swim, unequipped except for her adaptation, in the polar seas. I could do it. My daughter, even, could do it, but your sister did not have the experience. That is what happened to her, and no search will tell you anything more."

Lisel shook her head slightly. "I think" she said, "she had visions of deep adaptation. She could not have achieved it. There are limits to postnatal adaptation, and further limits to adult adaptation." And then she frowned slightly, as though she had said too much. "Athene says that you need to be returned to a rafttown. I can take you to Grayling myself."

"They would not let me go," Teal said. "But you will."

Lisel smiled. "And you wonder why? Or if I merely want to take you far enough out to put you overboard." She glanced over her shoulder, to where Athene stood in three-quarter profile, toeing the prow of a moored canoe. "She would never forgive me." There was no amusement in her voice. She turned her head back to Teal, decisively. "The right of decision, for reasons you do not need to know, was to be mine, and I have decided that you must be returned. You have an enemy, expert, an enemy who respects neither life nor the law of the sea. I do not want that enemy drawn nearer my daughter. I will place you in the hands of someone I have trusted with my own freedom, if not my life. And in return, if you must give a name to your rescuer, give mine. But forget my daughter's. And forget," she said, more quietly, "your sister. This is all the sea will give back now, now and forever."

ELEVEN

Blueheart's dawn came with a white crystal light, harsh on tired eyes. Cybele braced herself against Karel's console with one hand, the other dragging on the web. It took her far longer than it should have to instruct the windows to darken, and instead of a smoky darkness, they turned purple, staining walls, floor, her pale shaking hands, the air itself with a bruised gloom. She closed her eyes on it, with a shudder. Seven hours' looking, and she still could not find her brother.

His yacht was gone. That she had established within the first hour's search. She had recalled the docks images, had watched him loading and preparing to depart under yesterday's clear evening light. He was wearing his usual sailing clothes, a loose sunproof shirt and trousers, snug tacky-soled boots, gloves, a wide-brimmed white hat. Only the hat made her uneasy, for he wore it square and pulled down, not canted and with folded rim, like the affectation it was. He wore it as though he wanted to hide under it. She watched, over and over, as he hand-rigged his boat, and loaded aboard a rope and a heavy bundle. She watched, and stopped the images, and watched some more, as he raised sail and worked away from the jetty. She watched him sail from camera to camera south around Rossby, and then out of range. She had tracked him along his registered route until just before noon. And then his signal had simply disappeared. His ship's AI was no longer receiving from the navigational net. His emergency beacon was not signaling. He had done something to his navigational linkup, to his tracking identity, to his beacon. He had gone alone, unsafeguarded, into the sea. She searched on, alone, clinging to a fierce, protective silence; such risktaking was criminal. But in protecting him from the law, in raging against the inadequacy of safeguards, the reliance upon navigational nets, linkups, homing devices, she protected herself against a deep and appalling fear.

In the third hour of her search, she thought to look again at Rossby at sunset, and find him there, but the evening sea was littered with tiny ships like new-hatched fry. Somewhere between the fourth and fifth hour, she started to examine them one by one; and toward the end of the fifth she had painstakingly begun to compose a routine which would search for her. But the routine would not execute and she did not know why, and she was so tired.

When the net advised her of a visitor, she opened the door without a thought.

Cesar Kamehameha hesitated upon the threshold. Looked around the lintel, brow wrinkling at the light, saw her sitting upright at the console, said, "May I?" She nodded, jerkily, and he stepped inside. She knew she should free herself from the web, get up, but she did not. She could summon neither will nor energy.

The director of the AOC came over to her, warily, she thought. Listening, and glancing around, peering in the stained illumination. She did not want to try to correct it, and fail before him.

"I have been trying to contact your brother," he said.

"He's not here. I've been looking for him myself."

"Ah. But looking wide indeed." He gestured to the image on her console.

"The last records I can find are of him loading his yacht and sailing out of Bergman bay yesterday evening."

"Ah." Cesar looked almost amused. "You do realize, Cybele, that about an eighth of Rossby is black zone. And Karel is well acquainted with those areas." The black zones were enclaves where the residents had petitioned against standard exposure. Some for reasons quite reputable, others for reasons less so. "I think," Cesar said, "that if your search has failed to turn him up by now, then he has very likely quietly berthed his yacht in one of the black zones, and switched off navigator and homer. This is not the first time."

Cybele said, tightly, "This is not one of those 'a boy does not need his sister looking over his shoulder' homilies, is it?"

"Did you two have an argument?" Cesar said, mildly, but his eyes were watchful.

"Yes," she said, shortly.

"May I ask what about?"

"It was personal."

There was a silence, then Cesar said, "Your father raised you to unite against the world, didn't he?"

Her father. Cybele drew a shaky breath. For most of the past seven hours she had pushed Adam from her consciousness—except when she considered reporting Karel, and thought of Adam's inevitable disapproval—but he must still have lodged there, making loss larger, more imminent, than it had ever been before. She said, "Sometimes we united against him." She drew a deeper breath. "I am sure you are probably right and Karel is just fine." She looked down at her hand. "I am so *angry* at him for doing this to me now. Leaving no message, showing no thought for me. I do not care how inadequate I am in helping him through his grief. I am doing my best." Her words slapped around Karel's walls. She did not want to look at Cesar's face.

But she did when he said, quite gently, "Don't report him, Cybele. Give him a little longer to come back. Or to show some thoughtfulness and send you word."

She was tired; she was angry; she was persuaded. She freed her hand, and carefully turned her chair away from the console.

"Tell me," he said. "How much did you discuss with him of our last conversation?"

"I told him you were going to take care of it."

"And he—"

Cybele hesitated, then said, "He did not believe you would."

"And you?"

She turned to face him. "The investigation is over, isn't it? Findings inconclusive. I know that is not so. I know there were findings."

"I did," he said, "advise you this might happen."

She said, directly, "What is it Karel knows that he would not tell me? Why does he insist that if I look further into this, I will regret it."

He sighed, softly. "You are," he said, "a determined young woman, but I cannot claim that Karel told me otherwise." He left her suddenly, walking over to the window. In the indigo light it seemed as though he swam. He clasped his hands behind his back, and stared through, or at, the window. She could see his reflection in the stained glass; she thought he might be watching hers. "I am sure that to you it seems as though I wield abundant power, but there are situations with which even I cannot contend. This is one." He paused. "How many illegal adaptives do you think are out there? How long," he turned, "do you think this has been going on?"

She said, cautiously, "The woman Rache found was in her late teens, so at least that long."

"And numbers . . . ?"

"A . . . few hundred."

He said, crisply, "There are nearly thirty thousand illegal adaptives on Blueheart."

"How can that many people exist without—?" she said, in disbelief.

"Have you found your brother, whom you know exists?" Cesar said in a barbed tone. Then feathered his hands. "Forgive me: the question was valid. Firstly, they represent under two thousand unreported births or illegal adaptations per year. Secondly, we did not find them because we did not look for them. Most of the illegally adapted are nomadic pastorals. They move with the floating forests. They do not use the nets, do not use power-tools or synthetic materials. To survey algorithms they are merely part of the biomass. The casual pilot, flying over, would not know what he saw. Power seacraft are banned from the forests.

"We are still accustomed to thinking of a non-adapted environment as being contained, of the adaptives as dependents. Nobody ever thought to *count* adaptives. Why should we: we knew the number: we had each and every one entered in the databanks of the AOC." For a moment, she thought he might laugh. "And by the time we discovered that we did not, that there was in fact a substantial sub-population, there were twenty-five thousand extra adaptives, and now there are thirty. In a population of under a quarter of a million."

"But that is—grotesque," Cybele said. "*Why?*"

"The arithmetic of democracy, Cybele. Numbers. When the time comes to decide upon the terraforming of Blueheart, pastorals will choose as their bodies, and as their society, dictates. They want Blueheart, and Blueheart's seas."

She was Blueheart born, but never of Blueheart's seas. She had looked to space for too long. She would rightly be well gone before Blueheart began to be changed. Others would choose, and live with the choice, and she would leave it all behind. With the egotism of the young, she could not see what any of it had to do with her.

Cesar said, "The next stage could be the adoption of permanent marine adaptation, germ line adaptation, the creation of a human subspecies."

She was too much Adam's daughter not to feel dismay at that. "But . . . you *have* to stop them! They should have been stopped years ago." She crossed quickly to him, swimming in the morose light. "I'll make Adam's findings public. Nobody need ever know that the AOC has known—"

He rested his hands on her shoulders and pushed her away from him. She had an unsettling moment of vertigo as he steered her backward, which turned to fright as something caught the back of her knees. She fell backward onto the couch. She looked up at him, unnerved, uneasy, at the way he had overborne her; then she told herself that she was tired. He echoed it, saying, "You are too tired to be thinking clearly, Cybele. If simple disclosure had been the best option, we would have done it years ago."

He waited, until he saw the question on her face. But did not answer it directly. He said, "It's an irony that they had their start from our goodwill. Some thirty-five years ago it was found that pastorals were not returning for follow-up examinations; several died as a result, Rache Scole Blueheart's younger sister among them. Some of us who—rightly, I still believe— found the noncompliance directives repugnant, pushed for pastoral responsibility for adaptation and monitoring. A cohort of pastoral physicians and geneticists was trained. As practitioners, they had access to well-tested material designed to be readily propagated and modified. There was no concern about confidentiality: the Blueheart adaptations were by then public domain, and generally, the penalties for abuse are deterrent enough. But the motivation here is ideological, and there is very little, including death, that deters the ideologically driven. The Blueheart adaptives, the pastorals, resist seeing themselves as a transient subtype. They have created themselves as a society, and now think of themselves as a race. Other adaptations have before them; it is one course of a natural progression, and has not hitherto been serious. But the combination of that, the resentment of the coercive directives, the knowledge being taught pastorals and the fostering of contact between pastorals and medics meant that pastorals had access to gene library material and specialists, and specialists who were impatient with the ratification procedures had access to a compliant population. It might have been a transient phenomenon, but for an additional factor: Juniper Blane Berenice. She appears to have had the idea of systematically accumulating a population to bias the referendum. We were all well aware of her daylight efforts, her artwork and propaganda; we simply did not know about her night activities as well, until somebody traced the pattern of her movements during her last year of life, and realized that she visited most of the northerly centers known to be involved."

"Juniper Blane Berenice was my half sister," Cybele said.

"I know."

Karel, of course.

"And I know you visited Teal Blanc Berenice yourself," Cesar added, and Cybele's face colored. Not that he could see it, standing dark on glowing violet. He said, abruptly, "Far be it from me to complain about your taste in decor, but I wish you would set these windows to a more unobtrusive filter."

She twitched, embarrassed. But stood up, obediently, to go to the console. "I was trying," she mumbled, "to make them smoky." She moved quickly, leaving him, and any attempt at tactful recantation, behind. She cradled her hand, accessed the decor protocols, and gave the windows a translucent, slightly grayish tint. She waited a moment until she had her face under control, then pushed away from the console. He was watching her, without overt sympathy, but as she sat down again, he said, "Have you not had enough of this kind of frustration, Cybele?" His voice was kind.

She held her face stiff until the urge to weep had passed. She said, "If they killed Adam to hide their illegal adaptations, then I don't want to wait. I don't want to be politic. I don't care if there are larger issues in this." She let her declarations stand, without voicing the threat. In truth, she did not know what the threat was, whether she was ready to step out and denounce both the illegal adaptives and their creators, and the AOC's silence. And she did not know whether she wanted him to believe she might, or not.

He regarded her with a weighing air, and then sat down on the couch beside her. "Justice," he said, "will be done. But it must be done in such a way as not to compromise Blueheart's future. However these people were created, they will have a voice. They cannot help the way they were made. If we make disclosure now, that voice will continue . . . unchanged." He was speaking in a low, almost warning tone, watching her carefully. "Your quest for justice, Cybele, laudable as it is, could compromise Blueheart's future as a primary habitat. It could compromise humanity's future unity. If you force a disclosure, or draw attention to the possibility of illegal adaptation, then you may force an ill reckoning."

His face, so close, seemed to waver slightly with her fatigue. He continued, "Adam believed in the divine construction of the human form as it originally evolved on Earth. I do not believe he would have asked for anything if it were to cost future generations of Blueheart their birthright, membership in the human race."

She said, stubbornly, "He will have justice."

"Would their thwarting be justice enough?"

"You have told me you cannot do anything."

Again, he did not answer immediately, but sat considering her, weighing her.

"Had we known twenty years ago, even ten, our situation would have been different. They would have been fewer, and much younger." He shook his head. "It was a high-resolution mapping project over one of the gyres, an ill-regarded project that barely drew support— and there they were, riding the forests, three thousand of them where the census placed only five hundred.

"Legally, their position is ambiguous. The children are untouchable in law. The adults could plead ignorance that they were being unlawfully adapted. The doctors and engineers who adapted them will most certainly be indictable. But even if we could indict the adults, they are there, they are unalterable. They are what they chose to be."

He stared into her face a moment, and said, with quiet authority: "The whole history of the species is marred by our tendency to include and exclude. Us/them. The greatest divisions were between human subtypes, between races. Even now, on Earth, the vestigial subtypes remain. But out here, we are integrated, united. Yes, we may divide temporarily into subtypes, but only to achieve an end. The integrity and unity of the human race must endure. And that, not health, not legality, is the reason for our existence."

She said, quietly, "What have you done?"

"No one else must know about this. No one, *not even Karel.* If they are discovered, or if our countermeasures are discovered, then Blueheart may be lost to primary humanity."

She said, "No one else will know."

He held out his portan. "This," he said. An annotated diagram came into being on the gray screen. He had had it ready for her; he looked not at it, but her.

She said, "What is it?" Part she recognized, human transfection vector; part was entirely foreign to her. "What will it do?"

"It will ensure the failure of the illegal adaptations." He paused, eyes on hers, watching her reaction. "This virus reverses one specific modification of which our illegals appear very fond, excising the inserted cassette. The majority of adaptives are young, not tolerant of inconvenience or restriction. They will start to wonder whether adaptation can achieve everything they hope."

"They *must* detect it."

"No. By the time the virus activates in the human host, it has cleared the seas. By the time the human host feels any effects, even more by the time they seek help, any unintegrated virus has cleared their systems. It is untraceable. It seems merely to be a result of an unforeseen complication, or a . . . flawed conception."

"No," Cybele said, and could find nothing more to say. The guardians of the law powerless against so vast a conspiracy. The guardians of the law taking up the instruments of the conspirators. Illegality answering illegality. Immorality countering immorality.

Cesar said, "This is a prototype, released a few months ago. It is packaged in a common algal virus—and spread through ingestion of plantlife. Unfortunately, it appears to have depressed the normal resistance to painter's blight, with a spread of a form of algae which pastorals avoid. We are investigating solutions, for the next release. But in the meantime, we hear of an outbreak of a new disease. One the pastorals call whitesickness."

She stared at him, and knew her look was wild.

He answered it: "Shall we let them have their way, then?"

Yes, Cybele wanted to say. Yes, anything rather than that.

"We are," Cesar said quietly, "the peacemakers. It is something larger than law. It is possible the species would not have survived without us. We repaired biologically based psychoses, sociopathies, and genetic and degenerative diseases which drained human and social resources. We defined what the human organism could and could not tolerate, and forced societies and industries to respect human biological limits. We engineered the cryogenic adaptions which made coldsleep accessible, and the neuronal compatibility to cercortexes. We made it possible for humanity to coexist and to expand. But even before then the limits and objectives were chosen for us: unity, harmony. We cannot let our discipline be misused to seed divisiveness . . . and perhaps war. Even if it means that we, personally, must be . . ." he spread his hands slightly, and smiled almost wistfully, "damned."

I am more frightened than I have ever been in my life, Cybele thought.

"So you see," he said, again gently, "Adam's justice must wait on greater things."

Her hands were very cold. What would Adam have said to this: ah, but saying was easy. She knew what he would have said about it: that evil could not be used to fight evil. But what would he have done?

Sometimes, in fighting evil, good lacked the strength, and the strong had to choose damnation.

She nodded understanding; words were beyond her.

Rache reached the signal buoy above ringsol six still in daylight. He tried to fold his sail, tried to press the sun-stiffening out of it, and then to crush it by overlaying it and pulling it into his shadow. He stopped only when he felt it tear under his fingers, stopped and drifted above it, face down in the water, eyes closed, cursing himself. The tear in his sail was small enough compared to the tear in heart and hope and self-regard.

He would have said, five days ago, that he knew himself, his family, his world. That he was at ease with his past, and secure in his future. That he had undertaken work commensurate with his beliefs and his abilities. That he accepted his own limits, and those of other people, but that he was a capable, balanced, and trusting man.

And he had misjudged his nephew, an error of judgment which had taken four lives; pursued an arrogant and ill-advised investigation; abandoned that investigation to chase a twenty-year-old wraith; in utter disregard, no, in utter distrust, of the denials of wife and family.

His hand was still snagged in the tear. He opened his eyes, looking at the dark-threaded membrane drifting before them, and carefully, by touch, worked his fingers free.

After twenty-two years how many uncounted pastorals might the seas hold? Enough to shift the balance. They were so far away from Earth, from the tetrad; their nearest neighbor was still in early first stage. The decision must be made within Blueheart, and pastorals might hold the balance.

He had to know.

Not, he thought, for Blueheart's destiny, but for himself. He might think—he could not help himself—of numbers and possibilities, feeling exhilaration and dread. But what he wanted to know, what he had to know, was whether he could trust himself, whether he could trust the others.

And he was driving himself on to a place where he would know one or the other, but not both.

He sculled carefully over the spread surface of the sail. He could not fold it, so he would anchor it to

Blueheart's buoy and leave it. He slid from the fringe of the sail, separated the lines and towed it slowly toward the buoy. Riding swell with the buoy, he looked around, and saw not far away a small single-handed yacht, sail lowered and seemingly empty. He watched it a moment, with a distracted curiosity, then sighed, tethered the sail, and started to pull himself hand over hand down the cable toward ringsol six. A few meters below the surface, he released the cable, and swam free.

The sight was so familiar; he was nearly grateful for his tiredness, his emotional battering, his worries, for they bled away all concerns about an unfriendly reception. Boulle and cable were illuminated; he could see movement in the plexus. He swam for the plexus, and paused above it, resting his palms against the surface. There were fewer people than there should be, and all were suited and wearing rebreathers. But they were working, and he watched someone speak and someone laugh, and saw Oliver in his cage with a beanbag dangling from his long hand. Unseen, he sculled over the curve to his wedge-shaped office, and triggered the lock, to take him in.

When he stepped out of the inner lock, Meredis was waiting for him. He was not whom she was expecting, Rache thought. He had an impression of tension. Her eyes shifted past him, looking for someone else. "What are you doing here?" Her hair was electric, her face haggard. She looked harried.

He said, "I need to consult some survey records."

She blinked away distraction. "Out of the question," she said. "Surely you appreciate that." The words came more smoothly, now. "You're suspended, under investigation, and you left Rossby without leave. Where did you go?"

"Scole," he said, flatly.

"Did you find Daven?"

"Please, Meredis. It could be important."

"Go back to Rossby and ask the investigating committee. You're not cleared personnel here, and you are certainly not cleared personnel on this base. You have no right to be here, your presence is a distraction to me and liable to upset certain members of staff. Your administrative style seems to have created strong personal loyalties, *and* strong opinions about your innocence and your suspension. Intervening in a fistfight between subordinates is a new experience for me, and one I am not avid to repeat."

Rache nearly asked whom, but knew she would not tell him. He said, "I am sorry."

Her eyes flickered upward at some passing shadow. She said, "You'd better go back to Rossby and report what happened at Scole. You know I can't give you access to any part of our system."

He shook his head, understanding. He had been a fool to come here, to try and use old alliances. And worse than a fool: if his conjectures were correct, then ringsol six had already suffered undeservedly through this. No one of good conscience could knowingly draw them in again.

He had the sense that he had never stood upon this deck before. Another man had worked here, and called this place his own. He spread his thick, dark hand and was aware of it as a stranger's hand, a pastoral's hand.

Meredis said, with disguised impatience, "Rache, I'm due for a meeting."

They were waiting outside the sea-lock when he emerged. Primaries, by their build, a man and a woman, in insignia-less diving suits. Nobody he recognized.

Mirrored helmets showed him blue blankness: they had helmet lights off, in defiance of courtesy. They could see him, but he could not see them. Some distance removed, well clear of the ringsol's revealing light, was a summer-sub. The divers watched him away before ducking into the open lock. He knew then how no one below had known he had come and gone. She had made preparations, not for him, but for them.

He surfaced, into a day that seemed not much older. He hung onto the buoy, leadenly contemplating what next to do. He could feel depression growing, parasitic in his gut. He knew he must make himself move, he must find, had to find, somewhere to go, and go there. Rossby seemed inevitable. And still he hung, legs trailing in the water, hip bumping gently against the buoy. With his own hands he was shredding the systems which had sustained him these twenty-five years, profession, relationships, ambitions and illusions. And for what? When he found what he wanted to find, what would he do with it? Would he know? Would he have the capacity?

Motion caught his eye. He was unaware that he had been turning his head from side to side, seeking a way out of the maze of his thoughts. The motion was of someone rising to stand in the formerly empty yacht, the face turned toward him. Primary, given the hair, and the cool color of the bare skin. It stooped, and lifted something. A wave reared up between them and Rache heard a splash. Not the splash of a dive, even the artless dive of a primary, but the splash of a weighty fall into water. Rache grabbed the cable and pulled himself up on the buoy. The small yacht still rode the swell, but its empty mast whipped with the violence of its rolling. No one stood in it. Rache exhaled, and pushed himself off the buoy.

He heard, from somewhere out in the bright haze, the unmistakable sound of primary vocal cords spasming under water. He turned his head toward the sound, surged forward, scanning the underskin.

He stopped, beneath the boat's silhouette. All around it the filmy surface flexed and waved, and sheer brightness flowed into and around and past transparent blue. Nothing disturbed it, no shape, no flurry or spatter, no rising bubbles. Rache cast his eye farther, listening hard, squinting against the haze.

What made him look down, he did not know. But below him, against the murky depths, he glimpsed a white smudge. He piked, and surged downward, fixing upon it. Human features resolved as he swam. An upturned face, spiraling into the depths, mouth stretched wide, eyes staring upward, whites shining. Rache caught a bare shoulder, lost it, caught it again, hard. Now he felt the drag of weights. He gave a staying kick, unsheathing his knife. A rope looped around the body; he cut at it where its coils presented themselves, and pushed them aside as they drifted away. Still the weights took them down. He let go, twisted and dived deep, found in the shadows the rope linking ankles and weight; grabbed it left-handed, and cut it as it pulled him upside down against its prisoner. With a lurch it separated; the tail of the rope rushed away into darkness. He piked in the water, pulled the body to him, and powered them to the surface. The boat silhouette had not moved, merely rocked there on the creased, pleating waters. He surfaced at the stern, hooked the side, and heaved himself out of the water, letting rage propel him.

The boat was empty. Had he truly thought otherwise, he would have seasoned his anger with caution. He heaved the limp body, and then himself over the stern, slithering belly-down onto the deck. He dumped the body—it was a young man—on his stomach, and leaned on his ribs. Seawater gushed from his slack mouth. Rache dug thick fingers beneath his jaw, and found a fast, fragile pulse. Fit young man, good heart. Young *idiot*. He hauled him face up, ungently, hauled him around so that he could breathe into his lungs. Only then did Rache recognize Karel de Courcey. Karel's olive skin was brutally sunburned, his eyes swollen. He lay sprawled obliquely across the base of the boat, one knee up against the side, one leg stretched from the hip, open and exposed. He wore only a pair of swimming briefs, and the shreds of rope with their heavy knots. Wrists, legs and ankles were striped with raw rope-burn, and his fingertips were pulpy. He had fought the ropes he tied so well. Rache swore, crouched, and breathed hard into the young man's mouth, bracing himself against the swell with one hand on the far deck. He was not built for this exercise. Karel gasped, gulped; Rache heaved him onto his side as he began, weakly, to vomit. A slime of seawater spread around his mouth. He stilled, lay breathing with a high whistle. Then his body convulsed again, and this time he clawed himself up the side and looped one arm and shoulder over it, retching. Rache reached past him, to find the first-aid kit. He tissued dry an area of the sunburned skin, and applied an antinausea patch. Beside that, he applied an analgesic. Karel clung to the side in limp silence, then slid down onto the floor, and lay with his face pressed against the side. His breath came in rough whimpers. Rache continued to search through the first-aid kit, finding sunburn lotion, liquid bandage and a waterbottle with a tube. He settled beside Karel, and began to spread lotion on what he could reach of the young man's arm and back, pausing only to cut the ropes and throw them overboard.

After a moment, Karel said, hoarsely, "I can't see."

"Not surprisingly," Rache said. He turned Karel's head to examine the swollen eyes. "I've seen worse; they'll come right in a day or so."

Karel squeezed his eyes shut, tried to open them wide. Rache leaned over him, found the water tank, and read it as nearly full. One-handed, he filled the waterbottle, and pushed the tube between Karel's lips. "Drink. Or I pour it down your throat until you drink or drown."

Dryly, Karel began to sob. Rache shifted around, levered him upright, and rested him against his shoulder. Between sobs, Karel drank. Rache refilled the bottle. Karel drank again; this time, he held the waterbottle himself. He drank a third bottle, with bullying, while Rache covered him with more sunburn treatment, and checked his temperature. He touched the boat's console, center mounted. No response, merely a blank screen. "What did you do to the boat?"

Karel peered at him. "Rache? Rache Scole Blueheart?"

"Yes."

Karel sucked in a soundless, agonized hiss of laughter.

"I get no response from the boat's AI."

"Oh, that. I wiped it. I wiped everything. It, me. I was going to wipe it all out." He retched again, bringing up a little water. Rache took the bottle from his hands, and refilled it, concentrating on the simple task. But his tone was not much more moderate than it would have been without the delay. "Ropes. Weights. And a deleted AI. You couldn't trust yourself."

Karel convulsed. Rache thought with vomiting, and then realized that the man was sobbing, clenched into a tight, agonized huddle on the base of the boat. Rache caught his shoulders and rolled him against his thigh. He spoke loudly, with rough concern. "You sit out here a day or more, getting sunburned, sunblinded, and sunstruck; then you need ropes, weights . . . and then you tear your skin and nails fighting them on the way down . . . And," rather tartly, "you wait to throw yourself overboard until someone's around to catch you. You don't want to die."

"I don't deserve to live," Karel gasped.

Rache grunted. Glanced up at the sky. An hour, perhaps, to sunset. Fibrous cloud covered half the sky, thickening to the north east. Rossby would be riding gray seas by dawn. He shuffled around Karel, locating manual controls, tiller, sheets, finding Karel's clothes: sensible primary sailing-wear. He said, "Come on," and laid hands on the young man, heaving him across the slimy floor to lie against the stern, out of the way. The boat rocked disconcertingly with their motion. Karel said, "What are you doing?"

"Getting us back to Rossby." He slung Karel's clothes over the side, wetting them thoroughly, and plastered them over his torso and legs. He ripped a length off the shirt, re-rinsed it in fresh water, and used it to bandage Karel's eyes. "Now, don't touch that."

"You can't take us back. You've no nav, no control."

"I've sailed more years without than with."

Karel's mouth worked around words which eventually emerged as, "Please, please don't take me home."

Rache considered him and decided there was no argument to be made. He sat with his back against the console, big hands resting on his thighs, waiting.

Karel's movement did not take him by surprise. Karel's speed did. He twisted, reached out blindly, found the side with a seeking hand, and rolled himself half over the side, all before Rache heaved himself out of his crouch. Rache measured his length on the deck, jarring his back, but he managed to pin Karel's inward leg against the side, reach up and use his weight to heave Karel inboard. He rolled across Karel's legs, and lay there, rock-heavy, rock-inert. He had no idea what else to do. Karel fought until he was semi-conscious. Rache raised himself and knelt, looking down at him. He was past anger. Pity was all that was left. He collected Karel's scattered clothes, doused them in fresh water and wrapped the young man in them. He reapplied the sunscreen, and the two patches detached in their struggle. He forced water down Karel's throat. He bandaged his rope-burns. The sun finally set. Arcturus shone low, faintly red, in the north east. He laid uneasy hands on the controls, and began to steer toward Rossby. Karel lay quiet in the stern.

"I killed Adam," Karel said, out of the darkness behind Rache.

Since his final essay at suicide, he had not spoken. When water was forced between his lips, he swallowed. When cold cloths were wrapped around him, he did not throw them off. His temperature had slowly declined to near normal. His words came completely unexpectedly.

It had been some time since Rache could last tend

him. Nearly an hour since he had last seen the stars. He had been concentrating utterly on the close, pitching darkness ahead of them. He was navigating by touch compass and dead-reckoning. This was not a confession he wanted to be hearing, not now. Could the boy not feel how nearly overmatched they were by the waves, even with stabilizers extended? Rache's joints were swollen and hot from the ceaseless effort of shifting his weight as he tacked the yacht.

"I made the virus," said Adam's son, in his hoarse, salt-scoured voice. A gulp, a trace of tears, self-denied. "You all thought it was an adaptive, or someone connected with the illegal adaptations. Everyone else thought that, too. I needn't have worried." He gave that same agonized hiss of a laugh. "Except for my sister. And my conscience."

"I am glad," Rache said, "you have a conscience. Those are rather too rare. Tell me, was it you who sent me a message, saying the woman had been an illegal, and the virus intended to remove all evidence of her, or was it your sister?"

"Me," Karel said faintly. "She doesn't know yet. But oh, God, she'll learn. She won't stop." A small catch in the darkness, like the beginning of sobs.

Rache kept his voice level. "What more can you tell me?"

Karel said, "Do you know about . . . Lisel?"

Rache said, "I saw her on Scole. She denies all knowledge of illegal adaptives."

Karel gave a thready laugh. "Well, she *would*, wouldn't she."

Rache swung around, only realizing how forcibly when the boat heeled with his weight, and Karel, half blind as he was, stiffened and stared fearfully back.

Rache got control of the yacht, and, with more difficulty, himself.

Karel said, shivering, "Someone I knew, recreationally—I'm not a very g-good little boy, you know—wanted someone to design starfish programs. So I did, but I made them so they'd send a copy to me." He was silent for a moment. "It was q-quite diverting, working out who, and then trying to work out why. And then Cyb—Cybele—brought me Adam's fiche, and it all made sense, and I told Cesar. Cesar said—" There was a long silence. "Cesar said . . . it would be a p-pity if the illegal adaptives were discovered at this stage before the AOC investigation was complete. He wanted them all. Everyone who had been involved, especially the scientists."

Blood beat hard in Rache's ears and all the aching places in his body. "Did he instruct you to release a virus?"

"I was such a fool," Karel whispered.

"He made his wishes known," Rache said, for him. "In such a way that he could not be incriminated."

Karel began, quietly, to cry. Rache breathed hard. He could feel his heartbeat like tides across his skin. Adam's ghostly voice breathed warnings about his circulation. He felt ready to detonate, to erupt with anger. All that was allowed him was words. "No decent human being uses another in that way."

"No," Karel said. "It *is* my fault. I did it. I was . . . lazy. I was careless. I was thinking of other things, and I was . . . so pleased with my own abilities. I gave myself over to him. I—" He could not continue.

"In killing yourself you kill one of the two truly valuable things your father left behind him. And let Cesar Kamehameha live on, untouched. Is that the best you can offer?" Karel did not answer. Beneath them the ship heaved and Rache had to bend aching joints against the heave. Over his shoulder he shouted: "What would Adam say?"

"Repentance . . ." Karel said, almost inaudibly. "And restitution."

"I can attest to your repentance," Rache rasped. "And as for restitution . . . we will have to see. I do not know yet what either of us can do about this. But we must do something. Will you agree to do something . . . other than die?"

From the peak of a swell he saw lights, lights against a thin, bluish line on black. Rossby. He said, "Will you?"

"Yes."

Michael opened the door to Rache's pounding, a very human and unprofessional irritation on his face. Irritation cleared as he saw Rache and Karel. His eyes moved quickly up and down Karel, taking in bandaged eyes, sunburn, rope-burn; then shifted to Rache and absorbed the salient points of Rache's appearance: nakedness, pained stance, and expression.

He stepped back, let them enter, stepped forward again with that unexpected quickness as Karel wavered on his feet. Between them, he and Rache helped Karel through into the guest bedroom. Aquaria lined it, but within the aquaria were not living things, but artifacts, adaptive-made, preserved beneath seawater.

Michael said, "Go through into the pool. I'll see to him."

Rache made his way, hand over hand along the walls, down the long, curving slope to the sunken center of the main room. There, the floor slanted down into water, a wide, wedge-shaped pool which filled half the room. With a great effort, Rache waded in knee-deep before he let himself topple forward, exhaling hard. As a last concession, he used his hands on the bottom to turn himself face up beneath the water. He could feel the push and pull of it with the waves outside. Somewhere in the deeper water above his head was a port to the undersea passages of Rossby. He had come and gone that way himself. But with heavy seas outside, it would have been closed. Eyes half lidded, he watched the underskin pleat and interweave the colors from around him. The room had been designed by a former student of Juniper's. She had spared no thought for realism—no attempt at re-creating beach and shore. But she had given great thought to making it beautiful. Blue, gold, and white pebbled tiles beneath the water became mauve, gold, and white on the curved sides and rear of the pool. Alongside were sunken dry areas, furnished for primaries, but readily accessible from the pool. Above the pool's shallow end and the long curving ramp, a window-wall overlooked Michael's dock. Overhead, a mirror-screen, now at rest, reflected room and pool upon itself.

Rache lay, underwater, meditating on blue, gold, and white. In stillness, his joints' throb eased. The blood grew stale in his veins. With his fingertips, he sculled himself surfaceward, until he felt the skin of the water peel away from his face. He breathed, settling in his lungs the reserve he would need to sleep, unsecured, in such still water. He did not think he would sleep; he did not think that Scole, Lisel, or Juniper—or even Karel—would let him; but the thought was diverting.

He heard Michael come into the water, heard the churn of his movements and felt the agitated chop of the water. He opened his eyes. Michael, fully clad, bent and put a hand beneath Rache's head, supporting him, and sat down beside him. Once the ripples of his arrival had abated, he withdrew his hand.

"I kept expecting you to contact me," Michael said, with the touchiness of friendship uncalled on.

Rache said, wearily, "It was one thing after another."

"But *medical* leave, Rache. I was worried."

He had not known about that. "An official fiction," he said, firmly, with a slight smile for his friend's possessiveness. "There's nothing wrong with me." He grunted a laugh at what "nothing" swallowed. "Karel?"

"How much of it is true?"

"He told you—what?"

"That he created and released the virus that crashed the ringsol six net."

"I think that is true."

"I left him sleeping, and I have monitors on him. And I was in touch with Frede." Frede was Michael's partner, a surgeon who worked at medical central on Esquimalt rafttown. It was rare that her image did not appear on one or other screen in Michael's home. Michael said, "She says he will be fine, physically. You did good work on him. Psychologically . . . I think he will recover there, too, with time. He has, as you observed, a strong will to live."

"I will do everything I can to help him," Rache said. "There's been enough waste already."

"He seems to think," Michael said, slowly, "that you mean to go after Cesar Kamehameha." He let the words ebb away on tile and water. "You may not know the investigation into the R-Six disaster has ended, with a finding of inconclusive." He glanced at Rache, for a reaction.

"I did not know," Rache said, "but I am not surprised. I have a great deal to tell you." He began with himself and Daven, returning from Scole. Finding the body. Returning the body to ringsol six. He told the story of a man's complacent progress through an ordinary, absorbing life, quite oblivious to the possibility of alternate stories, of other people's stories.

Michael said, mildly, "Don't be so hard on yourself." But when Rache described the meeting with Lisel, the conclusions he ventured, he lowered his head, face unusually guarded. At the end, he said, "Rache, God knows we are in the habit of being honest with each other; forgive me for being brutally so with you now. If there is one subject on which you are neither rational nor realistic it is Juniper Blane Berenice. *Thousands* of uncounted adaptives. A conspiracy to unbalance the referendum. If it were anyone else's name attached, I do not think *you* would for an instant believe in any of it."

With a sudden thrust of his hands, Rache sculled away, and righted himself. "What is it you refuse to believe: that there could be such a conspiracy, or that the AOC is trying to suppress it?"

Michael half sat, half floated, watching him soberly. He said, "Oh, I have no doubt the AOC is trying to suppress something. Of course, you cannot know: I resigned my part in the investigation before it announced its conclusions. A protest, of course, a rather futile protest, and if I had any illusions that I would remain unblemished, I lost them the following day." He waved a hand toward the door. "I have some small part in that. Cybele came to see me, and I was by no means as careful as I should have been; I was too disturbed. There is a certain plausibility in what Karel says, about the AOC protecting its own investigation. I'll leave them to work out their own damnation. It's you I am concerned about. You seem—

taken with this idea of a conspiracy, and that is not in character."

"I am not taken with it," Rache said. "I am afraid."

Michael half smiled. "You know, in all the years we have known each other, you have never suggested to me that I take transfection myself. Many others have, but not you. I suppose I have made up explanations for you, ranging from the facile . . . that after Athene, you were more aware than most of the risks . . . to the egotistic . . . that you appreciate me as I am, appreciate the differences between us . . ."

Rache said, "Do you need my voice in this discussion?"

"You know me: never know what I think until I hear myself say it . . . I think you were yourself responsible. I might have succumbed to the sense of it, had I not had your counterexample. You have never considered having your adaptations reversed."

Rache eased himself back in the water. This was no digression; this was Michael at work and at play, developing text and theme as artfully as any pastoral storyteller. He had a pastoral's taste for long, complex narrative. But the characters in his stories were neither fictional nor historical; they were living, and needed, Rache thought, a certain thickness of skin. "I am what I am."

"My friend, you are a romantic. You will no doubt take that as an insult at your age, but true romanticism is ageless. You have the romantic's ability to *imbue*. You transfuse your own traits and wishes, and potential into a person, a place, or a thing. Half of what Juniper was to you, you made her, for the sake of the part of you that was starving in Scole. You and your brother are more alike than you will admit. You both wanted a part of a larger world, so he played sacrifice, and you played lovesick fool. Tell me, Rache, is this what you would like to happen? There be enough illegal adaptives in the sea to turn the vote?"

"Not that way," Rache said.

Michel waited a moment, but Rache offered nothing more. "Yes," Michael said, "it would be a great violation of the social contract between nonadapted and adapted humanity."

"It would be dangerous."

"That," Michael said, "is what I meant."

Rache drew a shallow breath, and rolled underwater, sculling along toward the deep end of the pool. The tiles slid into focus as his eyes adjusted to the refractive difference. He grazed the end wall with shoulder and flank, rolled over, pushed off with his feet and glided back to surface beside Michael. He said, "I am not going to let it be."

Michael nodded.

"I need to find Exper' Blane Berenice. If anyone can find evidence among the survey data, she can." He stood upright, water dripping in a ring around him. "She should have reached Grayling base by now. May I use your console?"

There was no message.

Michael, standing clad and dripping beside him, tried to supply innocuous reasons. Rache was having none of them.

"She's an expert-voyager; she does not forget. She's spent more time on orbital stations and ramjets than you and I have lived in still-life."

"Check the registry for her ship and try her locator," Michael said, a slight edge in his voice. He watched the blizzard of symbols across his console with an abstracted expression, monitoring the contact through his internal interface. Before Rache spoke, he said, "That's not possible. Let me." He shouldered Rache aside, and Rache yielded, knowing that ill manners betrayed his friend's true alarm. He watched Michael's mobile face gray and sag slightly. "Rache, there's no pickup on her locator. There's no search been initiated. Ocean rescue has no log of her being in transit."

"*I* filed a log for her."

"I know," he said, "I know. I'm going to search for her locator signal in the stored satellite data. She left, what, noon three days ago . . ."

Rache said, "Karel."

"What?" Michael caught his arm as he turned to go, exerting some force to stay him. "What about Karel?"

"He sabotaged his locator. He wiped his navigator. And he could not have left Rossby waters without filing with ocean rescue, but I will wager that that log was later erased."

Rache started toward the ramp; Michael held him back. "*I'll* go," he said. He moved between Rache and the ramp and braced him by the shoulders. Satisfied, he let Rache go with a light pat, and padded quickly up the ramp. Rache recradled his hand, staring in black dread at the screen.

Michael returned a few minutes later, guiding Karel. He shook his head slightly where the half-blind young man could not see. Karel felt his way to the console, fetching up against Rache. He flinched back, stepped away, but leaned to peer at Rache's face. His eyes were even more swollen, slitted, and as reddened as an adaptive's. Karel said, plaintively, "I didn't do anything to her ship. I didn't even know she was going."

"But you did something to your own," Rache said, in a voice that ground. "And presumably, you kept copies of the virus routines you used. Presumably you had a workshop where you created them."

"Yes, but I deleted them all—" and then he stopped, swayed. "No."

"When," Rache said, already certain of the answer, and ignoring Michael's headshake, "did you delete them?"

"Let me," Karel said, his voice riding high. Rache yielded the chair to him, and stood over him as he fitted a trembling hand into the cradle. Whatever he was doing made Michael's eyes recede in a frown of deep concentration. Rache waited, sick with certainty.

When Karel drew his hand slowly from the cradle, Michael was the one to say, "Well?"

Karel's head drooped forward to touch the console. "I found her record when she left. I found the log you filed. Three point two hours later—just after you are on record as leaving Rossby, administrator—that log was erased. The last navigational contact was immediately followed by a transmission from the net. Why she didn't pick up the anomaly, I don't know. Maybe she just didn't know that was anomalous. I don't know what was in the transmission, but the routing," he lifted a tragic face, "the routing was one of the ones used for the starfish programs going into R-Six, but the gateway—that was one I used to use in the AOC for sending sensitive material." He laid a limp, helpless hand on the console, and thus directed Rache made sense of the image: it was a weather map, dated the day before the day of the storm.

"And you did not delete your virus programs until just before you left Rossby," Rache said, trying to keep the growl out of his voice. "And until you did delete them, Cesar very likely had access to them, and even when you did delete them, he very likely kept copies." Michael put a warning, restraining hand on his shoulder. "*Why! Why Teal?* She wanted nothing more to do with the investigation. She wanted only to retrace her sister's—" And then he stopped, staring past Karel at the map, at the sinister whorl of cloud obscuring Rossby. His eyes moved upward, to the northern hemisphere. The skin on his scalp crawled with the galvanic charge of insight. He said, already knowing the answer: "Is Grayling labhosp on the AOC's suspect list?"

TWELVE

The summoning chime from the console pulled Cybele from a sticky, ominous dream. Blue and green light splashed across the ceiling, and she woke rigid with the conviction that if she moved, she should fall upward with the light. But then she recognized her surroundings, Karel's high window, and the garish lights of Rossby's nightplay. The chime came again; she rolled from the couch and crabbed across to the console. Her skin was tacky with perspiration.

The caller was Karel.

"Karel. Karel, where've you been?" His image was sharp-focused, the background carefully not so. That required some artistry with the imaging algorith. She had an impression of mosaic color, ocher, red, white. None of his acknowledged acquaintances had such subdued taste. One-handed, she brushed in a request for a trace and had it denied. "Where are you?"

Karel dropped his head. His hair was matted, clinging to his scalp. His voice wavered slightly. "I'm safe. I'm fine. I had to tell you. Cyb, I'm so sorry."

"What did you do to your logs?" she said, sharply. "I tried to trace you, but you'd done something to your logs. That's an offense, you know; I nearly reported you!"

He gave a laugh like something breaking. She saw his eyes were swollen, caked with gel, and his skin reddened, cream applied in uneven swirls to face and shoulders. Something had happened. She did not know how to ask what.

"Cesar came looking for you."

He glanced aside, a quick, desperate look at someone beyond the pickup. Beneath sunburn and cream, he paled. "Cyb, what's he told you?"

"This is a public channel, remember. We'll have to find somewhere private, to talk."

"Cybele," he said, desperately, "what's he told you?"

She felt her teeth bare in a desperate grin. "Everything. He's told me everything."

Karel's eyes closed. Tears seeped between the swollen lids and rolled, beadlike, over his skin. "You must hate me," he said, in a whisper.

She shuddered violently, feeling fouled. "How can I hate you when I have insisted on being part of it myself?"

He lowered his head. "You don't know," he said, in a whisper. "She doesn't know. She cannot possibly know. I can't tell her."

A voice murmured, blurred by a filter; Karel shook his head. "I can't."

"What is it, Karel?" Cybele said, sharply. "What else is there?"

Karel looked up, his wet, reddened eyes desperate. "No. Oh God, Cyb, I can't talk about it. Stay away from there. Stay away from *him*." And to someone beyond the frame, "I think I'm going to be—" Rising, he swiped his hand across the pickup, trying to close the channel. His nails were torn, and perspiration filled the creases across the palm. Dark bruises chained his wrist. Another hand, broad and blunt and melanin-stained, reached in to sever contact. She said, "Karel!" but he was gone. The image shifted to an insipid seascape, long horn of beach, with inward-rolling waves. Cybele dashed them away with the side of her hand. "Damn you, Karel! Damn you."

She laid her face on the console. She wanted to weep. Weep for the life that had been not only extinguished, but judged of little worth. Weep for her only brother, and his suffering. Weep for herself, and her futility and befoulment. But she could not. The tears were frozen within her.

What more was there yet to know?

What part had Karel taken in this; what was it he could not tell her? Did he know about Cesar's plan, or was it something else? But what else was there?

Knowledge of good and evil, Adam had said, is God's own gift. Good and evil are God's own creations: angel and serpent. The externalization of evil is psychological and theological cowardice, irresponsibly perpetuated in religious doctrine. The evil in us cannot be exiled. The choice is not between being nor not being evil, it is between doing and not doing evil.

What evil had Karel seen, or been part of? What evil did he accuse in the AOC? Cesar's counterconspiracy, or something else?

The illegals would not wish their existence exposed. They would need the body, and all its records, to vanish.

But so too must the AOC. For the body of a young adult, with such sophisticated adaptations, hinted at an organized scheme, of long duration. Its uncovering had uncovered a corner of the conspiracy, and perhaps would lead to the uncovering of the whole.

Either had cause to wish Adam's data erased.

She had not prayed for years; now, she tried, thinking, God, which is true; God, what shall I do? As ever, she saw only her father's ascetic face. He had always been the intermediary between herself and God; she had never had any intimacy with God of her own. No wonder He would not heed her.

She drew the vial of preserved bone marrow from its niche, and thought of the woman, only a few years younger than herself, who had begun all this. In the pit of her stomach was a hard chill like frozen tears. Cesar had told her what he had to purchase her silence and to prevent her pressing further on her own. He had taken a risk in telling her, but likely not an unwarranted one: he had taken care to explain that the virus had left no trace, but for the disease. Who would believe such an improbable and scurrilous story of her?

Had he told her the truth, for the reasons he said, or had he lied? Was this yet another layer of falsehood over the truth?

She almost wished it were. The truth should not feel so foul. But if she dived deeper, what else should she find? The thing that tormented Karel, had caused him to appear burned and bruised and fearful. She could not imagine any evil her blithe, feckless brother might have intended, but he might have done, or been part of something unintended. And, being Adam's son, he had a conscience. He needed forgiveness, she thought, and she would give it him. Her anger was shrunken after all those hours searching, too shrunken to thaw that burden of frozen tears.

She turned the vial in her fingers, a relic of a young woman. Like this young woman, she was alone in her crisis. Unlike her, she would survive. Cesar had taken her fiche, and scoured her system for all copies, but he had not taken away her memory. She could remember the searches of the unapproved database she had conducted, looking for similarities to the woman's adaptations. She laid her hand in the web. At her shoulder she felt a sudden sense of presence. She said, aloud, "Do you approve?" There was no answer; she felt no approval, but neither did she feel disapproval. She said, "You should approve."

And there, she thought, some while later, *there*. She had remarked upon this proposal, to Adam. Remarked upon, but no more, because the contributors' names meant nothing to her; and she had not mentioned them to Adam. Had she done so, she thought bleakly, perhaps everything would have been different. The name was Meredis Lopez Blueheart, former director of Grayling labhosp, newly appointed vice-director of ringsol six; Dr. Meredis Lopez, who had induced the crash-hib from which Adam had never recovered. Yes, Cybele thought, she would find Meredis Lopez, and hear her rendering of the truth.

The summersub was cramped for a man of Rache's bulk. The skin on his forehead crept with the near-touch of the casing. He concentrated on the screen, placed awkwardly low and close for his far-sighted eyes. He was scanning the satellite data for signs of a small boat, a capsule, even wreckage. He would not entrust it to any recognition algorithm. He steered without reference to navigation control, though he had done as the law required and submitted destination and route. He felt vindicated in slapping away the mindless instruments of human treachery. He could not bring himself to think of all the treacheries, and the traitors themselves. He was not going to think of anything beyond the simple task of finding Teal Blane Berenice, if she still lived, or some evidence of her if she did not. It was a task he understood, one he could do, one that would not twist and sully him to do. Everything else, he told himself, was beyond him, and tried not to know that that was wish more than truth.

The docks on Grayling base were an internal platform, like those on Rossby, but unlike Rossby, the subs were secured in berths rather than removed for storage. Thus as Rache rode the lift to the gangway, he could see the others berthed in the row of platforms alongside. Including four gray-painted, virus-emblemed subs whose like he had recently seen moored outside ringsol six.

And a single sub in the black-trimmed blue of the survey service.

He walked along the gangway, each heavy step reverberating slightly, until he looked down on the spine of the sub, on the decal and identifier code. He recognized the code. But he had known he would.

She had not had the wit to instruct the system to keep her whereabouts confidential. Reception directed him to a waiting room in the research suite, an enclosed alcove surrounded by filmed screens. The chairs were all too small; he was obliged to stand. Reception would advise her she had a visitor; he did not offer his name. He did not know what he would say to her.

Through the filmed screen he glimpsed ocher and green, adaptive red, a crest of red hair. He heard the voice say, confidently and impatiently, "It has to be there. Repeat the correlation. Look for evidence of later transfections: fast-heal treatments. I'll be back with you shortly." When she rounded the screen with her brisk, driven stride he was standing directly in her path. She stopped so swiftly the two people dogging her steps collided with her. A man and a woman, of height, weight and proportions like those he had passed outside the airlock.

"Meredis," Rache said.

"I left Chandar in charge," she said, sharply, as the door slid closed behind them. "You approve of Chandar . . . Premier diver, knows procedure. Knows the staff."

"Is this," he ground out, "official?"

"Of course not. Is your visit official?" She lowered her voice slightly. "Rache, this was an emergency. An emergency, a newly appointed director . . ." She gave him a wry smile, inviting him to sympathize. He did not respond.

She had steered him into an office; he supposed one that might have been hers. He accepted the chair she offered him, broad, black and high, suited to his physique. She sat down opposite to him, in a similar chair. She said, "I do apologize for . . . my brusqueness down on R-Six. I felt . . . beset from all sides." Her face belied the easy words: her color was poor, her eyes undermarked and puffy.

"Meredis," he said, grittily, "ringsol six is where you should be."

"Ringsol six is where we both should be," she said. "Did you go back to R-Six after I left? Is that why you're here, because of me?"

"Teal Blane Berenice left to sail to this station four days ago. I expected a message from her to say she had arrived. When none came, I made inquiries. Her required logs have been tampered with, post departure. Her ship's locator is undetectable. Have you seen anything of her?"

"Not personally . . ." Her eyes unfocused as she queried the net. "No, she's not been on station. Why . . . would she want to visit Grayling?"

"Juniper disappeared just after leaving Grayling, twenty-five years ago."

Her shoulders eased down slightly from their tense squaring. "This is ocean rescue's job, Rache. Or something for the boomer-relay. Of course, if you want to look around, speak to those of our clients who have just arrived, please, feel free, but stay out of the treatment and laboratory areas—for your own comfort." She gave a bright, tense smile. "You would overexcite some of our students. We don't do embryos here, only postnatal transfection."

"Yes," Rache said. "I have heard. Meredis, what is the nature of your emergency?"

"Surely you have other things to worry about than the internal upheavals of a labhosp—"

"I have heard," Rache said, iron in his tone, "that not all the work here is done according to AOC guidelines." Her face settled into disbelief. She did it boldly and well. He continued, "The woman Daven and I brought back to the ringsol was illegally adapted. Adam de Courcey sequenced the genome. He took his findings to his daughter, Cybele de Courcey, who works for the AOC. The AOC knows. The AOC is investigating."

"That is their job."

"I also know," he said, "that it was on account of that woman that the virus was introduced into the ringsol six net."

"By whom?" Meredis said. "Who introduced the virus?"

"On Scole, I learned that my wife, Lisel, is an illegal adaptee. I learned that illegal adaptation is happening to this day. And I learned enough to suspect that Grayling base is involved."

"Suspect, maybe, but not prove."

He said nothing.

"And you have told me that your wife is an illegal adaptee."

"If you are honest, then that was a mistake," Rache said. "If you are not, then it was not."

"She . . . mentioned Grayling?" The question was a probe. She watched him closely for a response. He had none to give.

There was a silence. Then she pushed her shoulders back against the chair, saying uningratiatingly, "You can't prove anything. You can't use anything I tell you, without the proper legal forms."

Rache said nothing. He did not yet know what he would do. He was bleakly amused both that she would take refuge in law and that she would presume he would be bound by it.

She studied him a moment, and then those square, expressive shoulders resettled, as though resigning a burden. "You're right. If you've been talking to Lisel, you probably already know it."

She looked levelly at him, without defiance.

"For the past eighteen years, I've worked on pastoral and nomadic newborns, just five or six a year, for whom no records exist."

"That carries considerable risk for you," Rache said, neutrally.

"I had it in me to be one of the best engineers of my generation," she said, in a quiet voice. "Eight of my designs for human adaptation were red-striped by the

AOC. They're still in the databanks. None of them was given final approval. Too radical for a planet so late in stage II."

Her gaze shifted to the tall, faceted window, and the clearing slate and blue-glazed sky. Then back to him. "I thought of going offworld. I might have qualified for λ Serpens II, but all my life I have had sun, open air, open seas. I did not want to leave it all. I was approached. By," a slight pause, "an adaptive colleague. This person knew my work. They offered me the opportunity to execute my designs. Introduction to others, who shared my frustration, and to adaptives who wanted to be independent of the official machinery. It was not just self-gratification!" she half cried in response to something in Rache's face. "There were ways to make the adaptations more effective, the vectors more efficient. Our work is subject to peer-criticism as rigorous as any AOC review. Poor workmanship would betray not only our clients, but ourselves. We *knew* what the AOC would do to us, should we be caught. But it was *worth* it, to be able to do what we had trained to do as we knew we *could* do it." Color and head high, she said, "I would have been ashamed to do any less."

She continued, more subduedly, "Lately . . . there have been failures: clients presenting with apparent reversion to non-adapted type, an aberrant mosaicism. We are doing everything possible to find out where the problem arises. It could have happened with approved adaptations; it *has* happened with approved adaptations . . ."

"But unlike approved adaptations, who may go wherever they have need," Rache said, "those people must make their way to you."

"That is why Grayling base is in these waters. Despite the risk." Three words too many; from his face she knew it, and fell silent. He reminded himself that a defensive interviewee was an unreliable interviewee. "So, your former colleagues insisted you come back and assist them."

"I had to," she said, shortly. "I had worked on some of those clients." She leaned forward, spread her hands in appeal. "Rache, I've told you this because whatever you ultimately decide to do, I need you to give me time, time to put right what's going wrong here. We've done good work: I'll argue before any panel of peers that we've done good work. And I can't walk away from it."

"Why did you give up your directorship here? It cannot have been an easy decision, or one readily accepted by your colleagues."

She gave a huffy laugh. "Oh, no."

"Then why leave after all these years? Were you afraid of discovery?"

Precisely, buying thinking time, she lowered herself back into her chair, and steepled her fingers. She stared into the wedge of her hands. "Was it," he said, "this problem?" He put contempt into his voice, goading her.

She said, quietly, "No."

The quiet told him that her difficulty was of another order entirely. He said, "What did your colleagues want to do that you could not agree with?"

"Can you not guess?"

"I am not a geneticist; I have no idea," putting a certain dryness into his tone, "what constitutes excess."

She looked at him coolly, with raised brows. "This from the author of the proposal which seriously advocates preserving Blueheart as an aquatic habitat. Do you not realize the ramifications of your own proposal?"

"I have been made to realize them since," he said, with some rue. Then his breath caught; his lungs, losing rhythm, compressed, and he had to struggle a moment to regain speaking air. "Germ-line adaptation."

She gave a single nod.

"And over that, you resigned?"

"That was my sticking point."

"Was it doing it illegally, or doing it at all?"

She laid her hands palm down on her chair arms and got to her feet. "You do have a talent for asking hard questions." He did not watch her as she paced past and round behind him. "Doing it illegally," she said, at last.

He felt her watching him and wondered if that were true. "But," he said, to the empty chair, "you never thought of reporting."

"I have colleagues here. Friends here. Lovers here. I could not do that to them. And of course," circling to sit and look him in the face, with a faintly knowing smile, "there were selfish motives, too. I have been twenty years an illegal. I would be lucky to escape with rehabilitation; more likely I'd get some kind of aversion conditioning which would make me *unable* ever to use these skills again. So," with only a suggestion of defiance, "what are you going to do about us?"

"How many illegal adaptees are there in the seas?"

"How many?" She searched his face, looking for the reason for the question. "I'm not sure I should answer that."

He looked at her with blank anger before he realized that she meant he might thereby deduce how many of her colleagues were involved. He said, in a low rumble, "I do not think you know. I do not think anyone knows. Have you ever met Juniper Blane Berenice?"

"Never in person. She was a public personality when I was young." She frowned slightly. "But where's the connection?"

She would not believe him, not knowing Juniper. He simply shook his head.

"So," she said, quietly. "What are you going to do?"

He heard an assurance underpinning her tone. She thought he would be silent, on account of Lisel, and those like her. Athene, to her, was a case-history, a cautionary tale. She would argue her competence, and her convictions, and expect him to respect them, for his people's sake. As though her thoughts coursed parallel to his, she said, "It's important that we get this problem of the reversions resolved. You must, if nothing else, give us time for that."

He thought, wearily, that she had read him right, if for the wrong reasons. He did not want to be the one to bring down the investigators upon them. Because of Juniper, because of Lisel and those like her, and most of all because he had done it once before, and once was enough in any lifetime.

But simply to leave, simply to let her be, was unthinkable.

He said, "This has to stop."

The door clicked discreetly and slid aside. Cybele de Courcey stepped through.

Meredis said, "Excuse me, but we are busy."

Cybele de Courcey smiled. "I think you both might want to hear what I have to say." She took a few more steps inward. Her coppery eyes were feverishly bright. "But first, I want to tell you that I have left messages stating where I have come, and why. If I do not return, they will be released to the net, the AOC, and the survey and developmental directorships." She looked from one to the other. "My father died in your hands. You could not expect me to come to you without some safe-guard."

"Adam was already dying," Meredis said. "Nothing I nor anyone else could have done would have saved him."

"Adam had evidence which could have proven your involvement in illegal adaptation."

"I *beg* your pardon."

She thrust at the woman a vial of red gel. "That's preserved bone marrow from the body he found. You might recognize the alternations in the genome. The AOC-approved database does not."

"Ah," said Meredis, and took the tube, holding it not quite securely in hands that were, nevertheless, quite steady. "Ah."

"I found proposals in the unapproved database which were obviously precursors. They were submitted in your name."

"Ah," said Meredis. She turned the vial in her fingers, looking down at it for a long moment. "It never occurred to me that she could be one of mine. But it should have; it should have. Thank you," she said to Cybele, stressing the words.

"I do not think," Cybele said, "you have any reason to thank me."

Meredis laid the vial down on the ridged edge of the console and sat back, face calm, but tense. "What do you want?"

"Tell me who was responsible for the virus which destroyed ringsol six."

"I don't know. I would tell you if I could."

"I want that person," Cybele said. "The rest of you

can work out your salvation or damnation as God allows, but I want that person."

"Then as God is my witness," Meredis said, "I do not know. I was there on ringsol six, and I want them, too."

Cybele's coppery eyes targeted Rache. Their sockets were dark-printed, and her layered hair was unwashed, capped around her skull. This was the sister whose retribution Karel had feared more than his own conscience, and almost more than death. Rache had almost understood, remembering his own half-delirious impression of her. But now he resented the young man's dramatics. Had he even told her he was safe?

But when he did not speak, neither did she. She placed herself between him and Meredis, facing Meredis and speaking to her alone.

"Did it ever occur to you to wonder about *their* intentions in letting you work on them? Did you ever think of how many there might be, in accumulation? Enough, perhaps, that *they* will decide for Blueheart's future. And what will they choose? What else but that Blueheart never be terraformed, and that they themselves become the permanent, dominant human subtype. *That* is what they plan; that is what they have used you for!"

"You are imagining things," Meredis said.

"Am I? Do you really know how many people are involved in illegal adaptation? Do you go up to each other at conferences, and introduce yourselves? You've been kept apart: kept in little cells, each believing yours is a unique position . . ."

"I've heard enough."

"You took an oath, you took several oaths, stipulating how you would use your knowledge for the good of humani—"

Meredis stood up. "When the proper authority calls me to account for what I have done, then account for it I shall. I am sorry that Adam died; I had no part in his death, and indeed, I tried very hard to save him. And I sympathize with your disturbance. But none of that obliges me to listen to your abuse and fabulations."

Cybele said harshly, "Thirty thousand! There are thirty thousand of them." She swung on Rache, with an outstretched arm. "Ask *him* if you do not believe me."

Meredis looked at Rache. "That was what you were asking me."

Cybele said, "It was your lover's plan."

"Juniper was full of plans," he said, before he realized that showing unthinking certainty about *which* lover might be a mistake. He leaned his head back against the chair. "I think," he said, quietly, "we need to look at the cumulative high-resolution survey data."

"The data you came looking for on R-Six," Meredis said.

The wallscreen shimmered blue-white into image. A map of Blueheart, as primaries regarded it, depth-marked, the shallows pale blue, the abysses indigo. Meredis said, "Population, per hundred, as indicated on planetary records." Points, pink as Arcturus, sprayed across the blue, following the volcanic arcs, the sea-mounts, the ridges, the drowned highlands of prehistoric continents. A handful scattered across the darker blues, the indigos. "Nearly a quarter million." A pause: "Population . . . as indicated by high-resolution biomass survey." Suddenly the deep indigos were pearled. There was a silence. Meredis said, in a whisper, "Dear God."

Rache found himself getting to his feet without deciding to do so. Having risen, he did not know what else to do. Dryland motion required too much effort for thoughtlessness. He sat down.

Meredis said, "Almost thirty thousand more."

He pushed the chair around, thinking to look at her. But when he saw her looking at him, he stopped himself in the turn. He said, hoarsely, "The survey data . . . may I?" A narrowing of Meredis's eyes, and a cradle offered itself up from the chair arm. The display projected upon the wall, for them both to watch his transaction. He imported his translator from his planet domain: that, at least, he could not be denied. The great wallscreen made him vertiginous; he diminished the display until he could concentrate. The information was there, the information and confirmation he had been seeking. And would have found, he thought, ego defending itself. Would, eventually, have found.

Meredis said, quietly, "Did you know about this, Rache?"

"Since ringsol six, I have had . . . intimations."

"Only since ringsol six. I find that difficult to believe."

Rache shook his head. He remembered that he had found Juniper's defense of Blueheart inexplicable. When they argued, he was the progressive, she the reactionary. He did not want to listen to her stridency. He did not want to hear ill of the new world he was entering. He maintained a necessary, stubborn obliviousness.

Part of it, he knew now, was an ancestral grudge. Juniper was Berenici, and Berenice adaptives had resisted their own extinction for some decades. But, technologically dependent, and in a hostile environment, they had been vulnerable. Twelve generations on, their granddaughter raged in their voice and schemed to revenge their lost cause.

A larger part was new love. Juniper was a sensual-ist, and the seas spoke in a sensualist's language. Juniper gloried in swimming, in sailing, in skin-paint, in the brilliant days and gaudy nights aboard the rafttown. Juniper delighted in expeditions into Blueheart's floating forests and northerly reefs, in listening to his accounts of the bizarre, sometimes perilous natives. Juniper had found her personal paradise.

And the largest part he could only call the creator's imperative. In the penultimate year of her life, her work had been crude, dilatory, dictatorial. She was tired of the art of artificial reality. Art depended upon uncertainty, and too much was known and foreordained. At the end of that year she laid down her tools, withdrew from the net, took to the seas.

And the next time he saw her she was incandescent with excitement and triumph. She had conceived, was working on, her masterpiece. She had found a new medium to manipulate.

He thought, the sea was wiser than I, in taking her.

His hands hurt. He had closed his fists, hard, and it was the sight of those closed fists which had prevented either witness from interrupting his thoughts.

He said, "She was wrong."

"She has given you what you wanted," Meredis said.

"No," he said.

As though he had not spoken, Cybele said, "We'll find a way to prevent it. A legal way."

"They are citizens of Blueheart, all of them," Meredis said.

He lifted his head at her tone, looked at her, saw that eyes and mouth were tight. "So," he said, "it was not the illegality you objected to, after all."

Green eyes shifted sideways, in recall. Her mouth twisted as she remembered. He supposed that she would have some complex rationalization that reconciled her own lawlessness with this orthodoxy. He said, "It does not matter. I would not want it this way, either."

"And you claim you did not know."

"No," he said. "I did not know." Explanation, he thought, served no purpose. She was no readier to listen to his than he to Meredis's.

"But you have a wife who is illegal and a—" Meredis checked herself, and regarded him oddly.

He said again, "It does not matter."

He brought back the map. Pale pink on shades of blue. He could not see the seas that he knew. He reached into the net and drew out the seas as he knew them, marbled with the browns, greens, blue-greens of their living selves. The peopling made sense then.

He saw Juniper as he had not seen her for years, painted skin iridescent under the sun, poised—no, posed—on the edge of the dock. She had understood the sea better than he knew. She had understood what the sea might hide, and cradle, and reveal. What might she have intended for this revelation? Sooner; later; never, perhaps. Perhaps she could have achieved her displayed intent, and persuaded the citizens of Blueheart to preserve Blueheart unchanged. Perhaps the hidden others were simply Blueheart's safeguard against extraplanetary influence. Perhaps, he thought, she had no such coherent design, but had simply inspired others to enflesh an outlaw impulse. Year by year, the numbers so modified would have been quite small: a little over a thousand, each year. But over twenty-three years, unchecked. Did all the Meredises think themselves unique?

But thirty thousand. Ten percent of a planetary population nearing effective population and preparation, nearing the decision to terraform. A very particular ten percent, who had gone wider and deeper, further from the shores of their origins, than even pastorals. Now he understood why his wife had sometimes seemed no less strange than the outworlder primary, Juniper.

How had Juniper planned to use that thirty thousand, if indeed she had planned *for* them? She would not have had the patience for twenty-five years' waiting. Perhaps she merely planned to subvert the system, to corrupt all the Meredises she could touch. Artist and consummate manipulator, she understood the egotism, the resentment, the achievement denied. She was fluent in all dialects of temptation. He knew.

Cybele blurted, stammering slightly, "I will not let them profit from my father's death." Rache, surfacing, could not tell whether she had spoken in response to something Meredis had said, or out of her own exigencies. Yet Meredis answered her as though they had been having a conversation. "Only a few might be involved."

Cybele said, "Adam would. Adam would have been." She sought words to convey all that Adam would have been. Rache thought of the small, fragile, irascible man he had known; and of the old, solitary mind he had sensed, and felt again the regret for the loss. He wanted to know what Adam would have been.

Cybele said, "Rache, I want to know who killed my father."

He swung his chair to face her. The pallor, the bruised eyes, the close-clinging hair. He thought: No, child, you do not. Not until you are much further along in your mourning than this. Not, indeed, until you are further along in life. Not, if there were any mercy in the world, ever.

"Please," she said.

He said, "It was not pastorals, that I promise."

She was silent a moment, then said, "I shall ruin you. I shall ruin all of you."

"You will ruin yourself," said Meredis. "You have disclosed highly confidential material."

"It cannot be concealed," Rache said. "I will not conceal it." Cybele's eyes widened. Meredis merely sighed. Rache said, to Cybele, "There have been too many victims already. That girl in the seas. Adam. Elisabet. Micah. Ainsleigh." Karel, he added silently. Cybele herself. Daven. Oliver. Himself.

Meredis said, "Sweet Christ and all the saints, Rache: have you any idea what kind of reaction . . ."

He remembered Michael, that reasonable man: a great violation of the social contract . . . And, with an upsurge of the anger he had not felt then, Rache thought: an imposed contract. We were given no say. But that was Juniper speaking, he told himself, not he. He was merely an administrator, author of a proposal which might, in twenty years, become a contender for development. If, in those twenty years, he and his could persuade the Adams and the Cesars, the Cybeles and, it seemed, the Meredises, that permanent adaptation did not present an offense to God, a dangerous fissioning of the human race, a violation of the millennial plan of settlement. If, in those years, he could persuade the Toves, Einars, and Lisels that primary culture, technophilic culture, was valuable, worth studying and preserving, and that pastoralism had to become more supple if the future were to accommodate all. Juniper had never understood the need to listen and wait for people. Had she been so much beloved that she was so certain of forgiveness? Was she so sure of success?

He could feel his heart laboring beneath a burden not of body but of spirit. He thought, why did she give me no warning? Leave me no mention? But what could I have done then? What can I do now?

Meredis said suddenly, "Ah." In his peripheral vision, colors flickered and changed. The green-tinged map changed suddenly to the open docks; a small sailboat close-hauled on the shining sea. The image expanded, and corrected for backlight, and there on the screen Teal Blane Berenice held tiller and sheet, while Lisel leaned over the bow, face in the spray. Barefoot, unsmiling, ragged-cuffed, Teal was Juniper's image incarnate. And Lisel—Lisel simply looked like herself.

Rache thought, What else can I do but gather it into my hands, though I hardly know how? But it was Juniper's, at least in part. It is Lisel's, at least in part. He caught his breath, and released it, as though for a very deep dive. He thought: And it is *mine*.

THIRTEEN

Cesar Kamehameha's image said, "What have you done?"

"Nothing," Cybele said, "of which I am ashamed."

She saw that he was breathing quickly, in anger or effort. She watched his eyes shift past her, taking in her surroundings, the office, and shift back to her, demanding. "I'm alone," she said. When Cesar's summons arrived, she had been going with Rache and Meredis to meet the arriving yacht. She said, "You have been tracking me."

The director of the AOC settled himself in his chair, framed by blue-lit aquaria. His breathing steadied, but his voice was still hard. "What have you done?"

Rache Scole Blueheart had turned in the doorway, his ill-clad bulk filling it. "He cannot know who said what. He need not know it was you told us, and not I you." She had stared back, a little shocked at his perceptiveness, wondering why he should extend protection. She could find no reason, except that he understood both her position and her fear.

But she would not take his protection. She would not lie; she was not ashamed. It was they, with their lethal secrets, who should be ashamed.

She said, "I found a proposal in the unapproved database. It was a draft of the adaptations in the body of the illegal woman. Meredis Lopez was the author. I told her the numbers. I told her what the pastorals were doing. I told her about Juniper Blane Berenice."

"So." For a moment he seemed unmoved. And then, with utter contempt, "You self-indulgent little fool."

She caught her breath, feeling his judgment strike home in stomach and diaphragm. She said, "He was there. Rache of Scole. Meredis was so smug, and so ignorant. She would not believe—"

His voice overbore hers. "Are you one of those righteous abominations who would ruin us in the name of God? Who find humanity so ugly that you would gladly see us destroy each other, so God may start anew. There is nothing better," Cesar said harshly. "We are God's best creation; every part of us is God's creation." He looked out of his frame a moment, away from her. Spoke quietly. "Will it gratify you to see them turn on each other?" Looked back at her, bitter-eyed. "Will you enjoy watching the testimonies, the confessions, the denunciations? It will consume Blueheart; it will scar us for a generation. It will split colleagues and families and friendships. The cost in grief, in mistrust, in broken relationships and work left incomplete will be immeasurable. It will end careers and ruin reputations, and leave gifted people branded for the remainder of their lives. I could have saved us all that." He caught himself, on the raw arrogance of that last. He considered qualification, or retraction, and then, with a setting of his face, let it lie as truth. He said, quietly, "It is a flawed society, a flawed profession, but it is our own."

She thought, shakily, You are not so different from Meredis. Your true regret is that it will not be done *your* way.

Cesar said, "You do not understand, do you?" He spoke with quiet distaste. "I trust you will not be made to, by this. You may need the lesson, but Blueheart does not need the teaching of it."

"I only told the truth," she said, in a high voice.

"And do you expect to be rewarded for it?" he returned, leaned slightly toward the screen. "My poor child, I believe you do." She heard slight, mocking wonder, and colored. "But *why* did you tell the truth? Because you objected to Meredis Lopez's smugness. You told the truth out of malice, my dear, not out of any nobility of purpose." She could not find the breath to protest; he could see her too clearly.

"You have forced my hand. Meredis Lopez will be suspended, and as soon as we have secured Grayling records, her colleagues will join her. I want you to leave there, immediately. I do not want you speaking to any of them; not one word. I should have you charged and dismissed for violation of confidentiality." He caught himself, before he spoke the next words. There was a silence; he did not speak, and she could not. She had been naïve, or worse than naïve. She had not believed that power could accrue without honor. For all that she denied her childhood faith, its moral structure still skewed her eye. She said, at last, numb-lipped, "If that is what you feel you must do, then do it."

"Ah, you have a taste for martyrdom, then," Cesar said. He shook his head slightly. "Another self-indulgence. Tell me, Cybele, which is the greater sin, theirs or mine?"

She looked at the smooth, dark-shaded face. Adam could have told him, would have told him: yours, because you have misused your power. But Adam had, at the last, strayed, in turning what he knew to his own ends, in offering it to her for hers. That had been, if not merely selfish, a morally ambiguous deed. He had seemed tired, she remembered. She had not seen it then, not been able to see it since, through the brilliant distortion of grief.

He leaned forward slightly again. "They have broken planetary law, adaptation law, and God's law. They have done it to preempt the decision-making process, to give their existence a legitimacy which they could not obtain any other way. They have been quite ruthless in defense of their secrets." He smiled, watchful-eyed. "I admire you, Cybele, for being willing to confront them, knowing what they are capable of doing. Or was that, too, a searching for martyrdom?"

"No," she said. "I'm not looking for any kind of martyrdom." She paused, but there was nothing to be gained in denying her convictions. Let him mock her, if he would. "I am looking to do what is right."

"And are you so certain of what that is?"

"I try to be. I hope . . . to be." Her voice sounded thin to her ears. She thought of Adam, sitting in her dingy quarters on the last night of his life. She could not imagine he would have brought the material to her had he known even a portion of what she now knew. He would not have endangered her, any more than she would have endangered him. But he had been tired. She knew his tiredness now, in her own muscles and bones, in her own heart and soul. She could not imagine Adam uncertain as to the right, but she could imagine Adam measuring the fragility of right against the great crushing weight of human venality—self-interest, self-deception, convenience, inertia—as she measured it now. Perhaps he had given up hope for the greater good, and settled for a very small, selfish gain, their reconciliation. He was, whatever he tried to do and be, no more than a man.

And she had never loved him more, knowing that. She remembered her childish image of her soul, a small light cradled in both hands. And it seemed to her that Adam's soul might also be cradled in her hands. She turned them up, looked down at them, but the light in the office was very bright, and they were empty. He had gone to his God tired and with the mark of selfishness on him. She would never forgive his killers that.

She said, quietly, "They must be stopped."

She lifted her eyes, found him watching her, olivine eyes unreadable. An arrogant, amoral, ruthless man, yet the one with both the conviction, and the instruments to do what must be done when the knowing of truth, even the telling of truth, was not enough.

She drew breath to speak, but could not find in her the words that must be spoken. But he saw her capitulation, and she saw him relax, an unremarked rigidity going out of him.

"Come back to Rossby," he said. "I have work for you to do."

The mooring rope, flung hard at Rache, unraveled in flight, the hardbound end flicking his chest as he caught it. He crouched, straining joints and ill-fitting seams, and lashed the skiff to the dock; he took his time. When he looked up, Teal was on the dock, but Lisel still stood in the boat, watching him. He trod level with her, and held out his hand. Her hand closed on his wrist, his on hers, and he pulled her up onto the jetty. He did not let her go. She tugged, once, sharply, before letting her wrist remain tethered.

He said, "Was it too much to just once let me be right?"

The textured eyes searched his face.

Rache said, "High-resolution survey data confirms that the records underestimate the population of Blueheart's seas by nearly thirty thousand persons."

Lisel said, in a light, brittle tone, "Rache, I have never heard such—"

He released her wrist, caught her shoulders, shook her; her freed hand snatched up her knife, and held it up between them, point uppermost and level with their lips. He said, "Lisel, no more lies."

"At last," she said, quietly. She put her other hand on his chest, fisted it, catching a thin pleat of the fabric; she smiled slightly at its inadequacy, but, nevertheless, drew him in. "I never wanted to lie to you," she murmured. "Come find me." She flicked the tip of the knife neatly along his inner wrist, parting nothing but the skin. Despite himself, he twitched, his grip slackening; she hit the water in her second stride, laid out in a running dive, and two heartbeats later was a swift warm shadow in the ocher murk. Rache stood, flat-footed, indecisive, resistant. She offered him a chance to plunge after her, in pursuit. But not from generosity, he thought, but from a kind of contempt at his split loyalties. Hers had never been so well proven. He turned up his wrist, and looked at the black line etched there.

Meredis said, sarcastically, "Nicely done."

He lifted his eyes, glad of the innate inscrutability of his heavy features. Teal Blane Berenice, in her ragged clothing, watched him with a peculiar, wide-eyed stare, quite different from her earlier abstraction. Her tunic front carried a long tongue of rusty stain, her tunic sleeves were spattered, though she showed no sign of injury.

She said, "She says I should show you this." She offered him a twisted loop of heavy wire, curved around four opaque stones. But when he went to take it for a closer look, she would not let go. Awkwardly, worried now, he fingered it. "I am sorry. I don't understand."

"Is it not," she said, "Juniper's?"

"Juniper's?" He looked again at the ruined thing she held, not recognizing it, not understanding. "I don't know," he said. "Teal, are you all right?"

She tilted her head slightly, squinting at him, the gesture eerily reminiscent of Juniper. "No. I was erased, through the net." She drew the metal and glass away from him, against her chest. "I need protection." She turned to Meredis. "She says I can trust you."

"Of course," said Meredis, a little dryly, with a glance at Rache.

"No gross neurological damage," Meredis reported. On the office viewscreen, Teal Blane Berenice slept in a diagnostic bed. Her nearer palm was upturned, coral-pink and pearled with blisters; the ruined ornament lay beside it, where it had slipped free. Scanners and transducers circled her head on spindly arms. "I thought head bleed for sure, though I wondered at her being on her feet and talking. And, judging by the download from the physio-chip, she's lucky something didn't rupture. And I can tell you this, there's nothing wrong with her autonomic implants." She folded her arms, looked at Rache. "Somehow I have the feeling you're not surprised."

"No," Rache said, grittily.

"Well?"

"Virus."

"On an expert-voyager? On *the* expert-voyager who interactively destroyed an active virus in our net."

"Not," Rache said, "while partially disabled."

"By a simple malfunction of a low-level autonomic implant," Meredis supplied. Yes, Rache thought, and may it not come to her who, besides herself, might find it "simple"; who would have the expertise and bent to employ it so strategically. Rather than let her develop her thinking on the subject, he said, "But there's no injury."

"Not gross, but . . ." she said, frowning, both at him, and with the effort of reviewing a download. "There's damage to the tissue-cercortex interface. That can be restored; we've all had to build up an interface after the implantation. But a high-level interface—an expert's interface—comes with years of use and training; and it is that interface, and the internal programs, which gives her her unique competence. If the interface is not restored within a certain tolerance, her cercortex programming will be useless. There are therapies for refining an interface using the programming as a template, but we do not have the expertise to work on someone at her level. The alternative is reprogramming her cercortex, but whether she could, given such a handicap . . ."

"This," Rache summarized grimly, "may have ruined her."

"As an expert-voyager," Meredis said, "it may, though she'll regain some function. I have not investigated her occupational insurance. She worked on η Boötes IV where there are much more damaging viruses than this one: viruses deliberately designed to foul the interface. There are viruses which can actually induce neurodegeneration, simply by overstimulation of certain cell populations—" Rache raised a hand, staying the tide. Meredis looked back at the image of her patient. "If that insurance is still in effect, she may be covered. But it is more likely to have been in effect for only the period of employment, or for conditions resulting from that employment. And I very much doubt she could afford both passage to η Boötes IV, and the treatment." She sighed, and then turned toward Rache. Blinked a moment, focusing upon him with close, undivided attention. "There is always the chance of, if it can be proven, a criminal suit. If this could have anything to do with ringsol six, I should be obliged to report it to the investigation." She paused, watching him for a reaction. "It would benefit her more than anyone."

He looked at the woman on the bed, at her upturned hand and the crumpled jewelry. He still did not recognize it as Juniper's. He thought of how she had stepped into the room, and how for an irrational moment, he had thought her Juniper, come back from the sea. But from that moment on, she had distinguished herself to him, in all her brusque integrity.

He felt a deep sense of failure, for all he knew it misplaced. He had not thought, when he sent her out on it four days ago, that she would have enemies other than the sea. That her likeness to Juniper, her pursuit of Juniper, and her part in the ringsol six investigation, could be such a threat to civilized men. He had learned better since, for both of them.

"I would rather," he said, "you did not, just yet."

"I thought you might," Meredis said, with a twist to her lips.

Rache said, harshly, "I am not leaving her here." He snapped a broad hand out, indicating Grayling.

She bit her lip. "Do you think it had to do with ringsol six, and—all of this?"

"I am sure of it. That is why I do not want her survival publicized."

"Then, if nothing appears in the neuro workup, I can neutralize the sedative and she can be transferred. Judging from what I've seen so far, she may not satisfy competency requirements. Given what you have just said, I don't think you're appropriate to act as guardian, either."

"I have," Rache said, "an alternative. If you will give me a channel to Rossby."

When he returned to the office, Meredis was sitting in one of the large chairs, contemplating the depths of a glass. A second glass and a decanter sat on the flat chair arm. Meredis looked up, and watched him cross the room to her. Her face was disinterested, pale and diminished beneath the blazing hair. She lifted the second glass and handed it to him. It was a pale turquoise like sea water, with, embedded in it, a swirl of tiny silver, gold and black-striped fish, chasing the bubbles and the minute opacities. Rache turned it in his hands, moved to curiosity more by the flaws than the design.

Meredis said, "They're hand-blown. An ancient craft, not to be practiced underwater. Here."

She had the decanter poised. He offered the glass without comment.

She filled his, then her own. The liquid was yellow, pale green in the glasses, and stung the nose. He took one sip for courtesy's sake, and stood over her, holding the glass in both hands. Meredis said, head lowered, "Sit down. You aren't the company I'd have chosen, but then I never thought I'd get to choose either the moment or the company. And, who knows, someone who's been there already might understand." She drank, and looked past his left hip, at nothing that he could see. "Sit down," she said again. He did. She said, "I've often thought about this moment. I've known it happen to other people. But I've often wondered how I should meet it. I decided," she said, "a long, long time ago, that I wanted to meet it with style." She toasted him, with a raised glass, and then drank off a quarter steadily, swallowing the last mouthful with a wince. "And no, Rache," she said, rough-throated, "I am not drinking on duty. As of four minutes ago, I was formally notified of my suspension, pending investigation of my activities on Grayling." She took another few mouthfuls, and refilled the glass. "Perhaps you will be relieved to hear it. You never did trust me with your precious ringsol six." She was, Rache thought, plainly one of those to whom intoxicants meant immediate license. She had hardly drunk enough to be physically affected. He hoped she would find his stolid face ungratifying. She swirled her glass, looking down into it. "I have been summoned to appear before an inquiry at the AOC, by no less august a personage than Cesar Kamehameha himself. My net access has been disabled, and even now, the Grayling archives are being searched for evidence."

"And will they find it?"

"Destroying records would be unethical," Meredis said, precisely. "Destroying records would mean delay in any treatment administered to those people. The colleagues I worked with all agreed that whatever happened, we would not destroy records. Aren't we vir-virtuous? However, that now means that anyone we worked on on Grayling will shortly be known to the AOC. Ev-veryone." A silence. She looked for something she did not find. "Ah," she said, half amused, half irritated, and drank again.

"You are not going to . . . advise your colleagues."

"They'll know soon enough. When the AOC decides to move, they move quickly. Presently we'll receive notice of impending lockout from our systems, invoking weeping and wailing and gnashing of gums. I wonder how extensive this purge is going to be. I wonder whether he will take us all, all." She shook her head, a little wonderingly. "Thirty thousand. Tell me, Rache, last time I'm going to ask, last wish, so to speak, of the condemned . . . tell me the truth, Rache; tell me you knew."

"I did not know," Rache said. "Juniper did not tell me. Lisel did not tell me. I was busy doing other things."

"Do I believe that?" Meredis said, rhetorically. She leaned back in her chair, slantwise, one long leg thrown over the other. "Your friend's on his way by hydrofoil. Not that his being your friend is any recommendation, but I know his partner; she's a good surgeon with a fair working knowledge of cybernetics, and the contacts to ensure Exper' Blane Berenice has the best help available on Blueheart. And she has principles. I trust her; you trust him; it's the best we can do, between us."

Yes, Rache thought, but it is not Frede I meant to have, not Frede who must make reparation. His conversation with Karel had been brief, somewhat harsh, but satisfactory. If anyone could restore Teal, Karel would. Others might commit time, expertise, pride. Karel would commit his soul.

"So," Meredis said, "what're you going to do now?" She waved a hand, and the screen lit with the map, beaded pink and blue. "'Bout that?" She squinted slightly at it. "Hell of a joke on the AOC," she said, and looked up to see if he shared the joke.

"I don't know what I'm going to do," he said. His euphoria was gone; his sense of possession seemed like a possession—by Juniper's spirit. But he was himself again, and measuring the price, to ringsol six, to Juniper's sister, and to people yet unknown.

"I'll tell you this," she said, and took a pull from her glass, "if you let the person who killed ringsol six escape, you're not the man I thought you were, and you're not the man your people on ringsol six think you are. You have people loyal to you there, people who were willing to risk their careers and break their knuckles protesting your suspension. They deserve better of you than betrayal. No matter what higher," there was a stinging mockery on the word, "causes you might espouse."

"I will not let that happen," he said.

"And if you listen, you can hear the wings of the Fury. Cybele de Courcey is a dangerous person; beware, Rache, that she does not light on you." She waved a languid hand, dismissing him. "Now, I think you should leave. In a few minutes the lamentations will begin, and if you can't appreciate an excellent brandy, I know one of several people who will. I wish I'd been able to follow your noble example and write letters of confession, but I don't have your style. Who knows, with me gone, they might be obliged to reinstate you at ringsol six. Goodbye, Rache. It's perhaps peculiarly apt that it should end this way. Remember me to Lisel. And to Athene."

Jolted, uncomprehending, he stared at her. Then

quietly gathered himself and got to his feet, and set the glass down beside the decanter at her left hand. He avoided her eyes, and the quizzical, slightly blurred smile that followed him.

In the doorway, he turned back, unable to resist looking for confirmation, or even explanation, of that name. She was not looking at him. She had turned her head into her hand so it was covering her eyes, the blazing hair caught and tangled in her fingers. Her other hand, holding the glass, knocked against her knee. Spilled brandy made dark streaks on her trouser leg.

Rache let her be.

He stood on Grayling docks, watching the hydrofoil dwindle in the blazing sea. He could do no more for Teal than he had done; she was in the care of one of the few other people on Blueheart whom he trusted, and he could think of no better sanctuary above the seas than the black zone of Lovelock cove. Lisel's yacht was still here, rigging slack, boom swinging dockward with the wind. He stared at it for a long time, until the sea was quite empty. Then he untied the mooring rope, and walked it along to the corner of the jetty, and retied it with a release knot. He pushed the boom aside and climbed stiffly aboard. He secured the boom, released the mooring rope, took sheets and tiller in hand, and steered outward from Grayling in a wide, slow arc, scanning the sparkling water around him.

He did not hear her, for she did not speak, and the sound of the water falling away from her body was covered by the wind. He felt her, through the boat, the sudden thrust of a weight on the stern. When he jerked around, she was heaving herself over the stern, already straight-armed and swinging a long bare leg inboard. She shifted a hand to his thigh for balance, without invitation or apology. She had, he realized, been waiting beneath the dock, or beneath the boat itself, and had ridden with him, clinging to stern or keel. Far simpler and needing less effort than waiting at sea for him to find her. That was Lisel. She slid into place beside him, taking sheets and tiller; he shuffled forward and sat, hunched, on the center seam.

"Took you long enough," she said.

"I had to make arrangements for Teal."

"She all right?"

"Maybe, maybe not."

"Unnerving," she said, looking over his head. "The resemblance."

"They are not much alike, underneath." He did not want to talk about Juniper, and her schemes, and Teal, and her injury.

She brought her eyes down. The intense sun lightened them, highlighting their minor colors, the brown and green. "If you leave me for her, Rache, this time I may kill you."

"How could I leave you?" he said, flatly. "We are not together."

"We could be, now. Now you know about me what you have always wanted."

He resented her tone, frivolous, diversionary, trailing a lure and expecting him to snap and swallow. He resented the lure, something once so precious to them both. And he resented that, after seventeen years, he was obliged to meet her not merely as Lisel, but as faction-leader and force in her own right. They had complications enough in themselves, without Blueheart.

Childish, he told himself. He was not a boy of eighteen. And she: he looked up at her; she was leaning outboard, balancing the wind, lips drawn back in a grin of exertion and strain, toes hooked beneath the ropes, taut muscles making long, smooth lines between her skin. The years had marked her, leaving the skin on breasts and belly a little pouched, and a puckered, pink-centered scar on her nearer forearm. But she seemed so little changed, the same handsome, hawk-featured, intransigent Lisel. He might not be that boy, but he could remember what it was to be that boy.

She glanced down at him, aware of his scrutiny. Without warning she pulled hard on the mainsail and let him scramble as the skiff heeled, while she rode high in the air, back arched, head back. He pulled himself up on the side, his heart beating faster, and their trim settled. She laughed at him, sun and water lacquering her face. Again without planning, he passed the jib rope from one hand to the other, caught the nape of her neck with his free hand, pulled her toward him, and kissed her, lip to lip, tooth to tooth. She released mainsheet and tiller, and in the instant before they capsized, caught his face in both her hands, holding the kiss as they plunged.

He broke free first, broke free in a sudden incomprehensible panic, and thrust himself upward toward the light, surfacing between the skiff and its spread sail. He caught the mast, and dangled, gasping. Lisel burst into air beside him, near enough to strike, and for a moment, he thought she would. His heart was thundering; he felt the pulse in the palm gripping the mast.

"Having second thoughts?" she said, with angry humor.

He shook his head, not wanting to examine what

had come on him as he plunged and tumbled in foaming water. But knowing he must. And in a moment, he knew. The plunge, the tumble, the foaming water, had swept him back through those long seconds of being borne inboard on flooded ringsol six. The panic, unreleased then, bubbled forth, in this harmless, fraught situation. Where it was as useless as before. He said, "A flashback, from ringsol six."

"Ah," she said, guarded.

"I was swept inboard through a jammed sea-lock," he said, annoyed at himself, at her, at the situation. "Besides, you could have just slapped my face. You didn't have to capsize us."

"I didn't want to slap your damned face," Lisel said, and dived. He felt her smooth body brush his leg, the puff of thrust seawater. He saw her slide out of sight beneath the skiff, and a moment later he heard her shout at him to fling her the ropes and get himself into position.

They righted the skiff. After all, they had done this many times before, and in similar circumstances. He could see the thought lighting her changeable eyes as she heaved herself aboard a second time, unassisted. Before gathering the ropes, she slid forward in the half-flooded boat, and brushed her lips to his. And drew back, before he could respond. Side by side, they bailed seawater from the bilge. The seawater was turbid, a thin ocher green. He looked back along their course; Grayling was but a gray dash on the horizon. He had not known they had come so far.

Lisel said; she had been watching him move: "You didn't tell me you'd been hurt."

"I cracked a couple of vertebrae."

"You shouldn't body-surf," she said. "You're the wrong shape."

"Lisel," he said. She slid a hand around him, and felt with her fingers up and down his spine. Up and down, and up and down; he envisioned his spine diagrammed with all its knotted ganglia and spreading nerves—the doctors had shown him such when they outlined his treatment—and Lisel plucked each like a harpstring as she passed it over. He breathed a groan, and turned his face into her shoulder. Her nipple rested against his collarbone, like a warm, slightly rough stone. His awareness contracted to three points, her moving fingers, her hard nipple, his warming groin. He muttered, "I hate sex in a boat."

"So do I," she said, into his ear. "But you didn't like my solution." She dabbled with a tongue, and a fourth point kindled in his fogged mind. "What are you going to do about it?"

They righted the yacht, again, and wallowed in the bilgewater, sated and irritable, poised, Rache realized, to quarrel. The release of the simple, animal tension exposed the greater. Submission to one inevitability cleared the way for the other. He watched the long, seasoned, supple body and wished it were occupied by a mind which suited it, or rather, suited his mind as her body suited his. She, he suspected, was wishing the same. He rested his face in the water and stared at his underwater shadow on the bottom of the boat, shapeless and wavering as it was. But knowing that she was illegal, suspecting that she had been part of this from the beginning, explained so much. Explained nearly everything except the time she had chosen to leave.

He lifted his face from the water, and wedged his

elbows on the seat so he could settle his chin on his folded arms. Her hand still rested on his back, where the healed bones twinged slightly, gratified by the attention. Or protesting the exertion. Ah well. He said, "Not many people must have known the scale. Otherwise the secret would never have kept all these years."

."Yes," she said.

"But you knew, you knew from the beginning."

She rolled on her side, a dangerous spark in her eyes. "Are you asking how I could collude with Juniper? Or," she paused, touched her toe lightly to his instep and traced it kneeward, "vexed that you did not have exclusive possession?" She smiled at him, very sweetly, and leaned over to kiss him, eyes open, watching his expression as he moved from one thought to the other. She said, against his lips, "That was my only revenge." She eased back slightly and looked him steadily in the eye. "But extremely satisfying it was. It had all the best ingredients: carnal gratification, victory, humiliation, and dissatisfaction. The wrong kind of pleasure, and the right kind of pain. Oh," she said, smiling faintly, "being your secret rival was a little bit sick, but very good."

He said, quietly, "You do not know me very well, if you think—" and then his intended denial sank untraced. He could imagine the gratification, humiliation, and pain that Lisel had invited. He had invited them himself. Juniper was a cruelly accomplished lover; he had learned to stand away from that part of her. The center of their relationship was his learning, her learning, what they thought Blueheart should become. But Lisel, entering that relationship bent on sexual revenge . . . he shook himself; it turned into a shudder. He had no right, to ask for the assurance he wanted.

And she knew he wanted. She smiled faintly, and

slid a hand gently up from his forehead and over his head. "Don't look so tragic. I survived, and it was all so long ago." And then, with her old caustic humor, "At least, I presume that is what it is, and not regret at being left out."

He made a sound which was half choke and half laugh. "The analogy that comes to mind," he said, eventually, "comes more from nuclear physics than biology."

"Your education," she said, with a small frown.

"Your ignorance," he said, in the same tone.

"I knew you very well," she said, a little later. She was settled on his chest, arms folded, her face too near for a comfortable focus. He lay on his back, with his head propped on the bench, head outlined with a frill of small, shifting waves. "I think you rather liked having done me wrong. It gave you a sense of power, during a time when you had cast yourself adrift. It also gave you and Scole some agreed-upon sin. I think you would have been appalled to have me trespassing on your secured domain. And then there was Juniper, who would, I am sure, have twisted us into all kinds of interesting configurations. I am quite surprised that she never told you."

"She . . . hinted. I never understood."

"Oh, happy innocent," she said.

"And I don't think she could have told me outright. Her . . . aesthetics of personal relationships were always Berenici."

Lisel snorted lightly. "Your education."

"Your ignorance."

She lifted her head, braced her forearms on his chest, nearly submerging him. She stared down, intently. "I want you to understand: Juniper was my only revenge. All the rest of it—was necessity. Because of who and what I was."

"Even your leaving."

"That most of all," she said; seemed about to say more; then shook her head.

He said, harshly, "I spoke to you. I explained to you. I was willing to come back to you. You gave me no word, no explanation, no *hope* of ever seeing you again."

"I had my reasons."

"You kept everything that was important about you back from me."

"Only my origins."

He had to resist his own urge to press the argument, to ride on on that old, familiar gyre, to return the argument to the present. "The plan was to secure the numbers for the decision."

"Yes," she said. "That was the plan."

"It was ill conceived." She said nothing. He opened his eyes, squinting against the glare. The sun shone matte off her drying forehead and the long curved nose. There was little expression in her face. He said, "It could not have succeeded."

She pushed off him. "Have we done badly?"

"Yes," he said, grit in his throat, "I think you have." He set his teeth against saying anything more and heaved himself over on his face. This was not what he meant to say. Not what he had meant to do. He was letting old knowledge, old lust, old abandonment intrude upon the present. Since ringsol six he had been a stew of bathos.

He felt her move beside him, saw her long, folded legs beneath the water, and the rhythmic churning of the shadows as she began to bail. He nodded slightly, resting face down, the intense sun drying the skin on his back. Presently he would right himself and assist her.

How much, he thought, he could still tell about her. The rhythm was crisp, not idle; he could see the tension in her legs and be aware of the effort she was making not to jostle him, even in their close confines. He wondered, for the first time, whether she had a partner who could know these things as well as he. The wondering hurt, and brought him to the surface before he planned. He pulled himself upright with a hand on the side, rocking the boat, and reached out dumbly for the second bailer.

"Why," she said, "have we done badly?"

He flung water into the ocean in a glittering arc. It pitted the waves briefly and was gone. He said, "Because the AOC knows, and will do whatever they must to stop you. Dismantling laboratories is the least of it. Because you could never have achieved the numbers you needed before you were detected. Because the greater you were in number, the greater threat you would represent to the moderates. The greater you were in number, the fewer primaries would support you and what you wanted." He felt a great upwelling of bitterness, at the destruction of the future he had worked toward so long. Carelessly destroyed, by the two secretive, reckless women he had loved. He turned his head away, so that she could not see what he felt. "You have lost us Blueheart."

"You think so," she said, behind him.

"I think so."

She was silent so long that he finally looked at her, though he did not know what he hoped to see. She was waiting for him, textured eyes glittering in the sunlight. "Then," she said, "shall we find out?"

FOURTEEN

I n Cesar Kamehameha's office, Blueheart turned, suspended between door and console. Through its holographic translucency, Rache saw the director standing, watching him. But in coming to meet him, he walked around the image, leaving it mounted in the air, turning slowly, its reflection shining faintly in the faces of the aquaria.

The image, Rache saw, was not the traditional cobalt and indigo geological map, but the biomap, and the fine marbling of greens, browns, and gray-blues moved slowly, with the currents they represented. It was the sea he knew.

Cesar said, "If you mind, I will turn it off."

Rache steadied himself. "No. It seems . . . fitting, given the reason I am here."

"Indeed." Cesar let his eye travel the length and breadth of Rache's frame, a tacit commentary on his attire, the blue and black uniform of the survey service. "What may I do for you?"

"I need to arrange an amnesty."

"Indeed," Cesar said, and smiled. "Direct as ever. One question, before we go into further detail: do you want this on record, or off?"

He had anticipated this question, and how to answer it; still, he felt a fleeting apprehension, as at the start of a hunt. And this man was as dangerous as any lava eel. "Off," he said.

Cesar commented silently with a raised eyebrow, but said nothing except, "There are now no active recording circuits within this office. For the purposes of nulling of our contribution to all distance recordings, voice samples must be supplied. Please identify yourself."

"Rache of Scole. Rache Scole Blueheart."

Another raised eyebrow, but subtler. "Cesar Kamehameha, director of the AOC." He spread small hands. "We are now as private as law and protocol can ensure." He led Rache around the curve of the projected world, to his desk and console. Side by side behind the desk sat two chairs, one light-framed, uncoupled from the console, and the other broad, wide-armed. He waited until Rache sat down, and then sat down himself. "Amnesty. Amnesty for whom?"

"For the illegal adaptives."

A slight smile. "For which ones?"

"For them all."

Cesar's lips parted. "Indeed."

Rache leaned forward, bracing elbows on black-clad thighs. "I want . . . to arrange an amnesty for the people who were modified without AOC knowledge or guidance, so that they can be quietly integrated into the records over the next ten or fifteen years. That should allow the development deliberations to continue as planned, with the added virtue of our now being able to contact and influence people of whose existence we were previously unaware."

Cesar folded his hands and considered them. "That is an extraordinary proposition."

"This is an extraordinary situation."

"Indeed," Cesar said, and looked over his shoulder

at the projected planet turning with exquisite slowness beside them. "Have you taken this to anyone else?"

"Not yet."

"Not yet," Cesar echoed quietly. "Tell me, Rache, what would we gain by it? Given that it would require the overturning of centuries of law, law upheld across the settled worlds."

"Time," Rache said, "for an orderly decision as to how to develop Blueheart."

"By the government and institutions of Blueheart compromising itself."

Rache eased himself slightly straighter. Cesar's tone was cool, curious, civil; that of a master engaged in debate with an advanced student. Rache said, "It is a question of what you consider the highest form of government."

Cesar heard the change in tone. He said, "Have you become their spokesman?"

Rache smiled faintly; he had been waiting for this question. "In this, I am acting for myself, and my own faith in the institutions charged with determining Blueheart's future."

"Ah. So what do you consider the highest purpose of government?"

"In this: to ensure orderly progress. Government provides a structure."

"And law."

"No," Rache said, quietly. "In this, only structure."

"You place them beyond the law?"

"I think," Rache said, "the law will not be adequate in this case. It will not serve peace, and it will not serve justice."

A silence. "I see." But what he saw, he did not elaborate. "So, you are not a spokesman."

"No. The bird that flies before the storm, maybe, if Blueheart had such." He had reached a moment of decision, upon which depended . . . everything. The best analogy he could find was the choice between the surface and the depths. He was a deep adaptive: he dived. "In a few hours, the first of them will start coming ashore."

"The illegals?" said Cesar, showing surprise.

"All pastorals."

Cesar got abruptly to his feet, his face darkening. He walked the few quick strides to the aquarium wall, and stood facing it. "And what do they think that will accomplish?" He turned quickly, resolutely, to face Rache.

"It would be," Rache said plainly, "a show of strength, and of solidarity."

Several beats passed. "And you'd use this to persuade me toward amnesty?"

"If I cannot otherwise persuade you, yes."

"You're no politician, Rache."

Rache said, "Lying is a waste of breath."

Once more in possession of himself, Cesar returned to the chair and sat down. "There will be no amnesty." There was no indulgency or pedagogy in him now. He engaged with Rache as an equal, and an adversary. "It would serve neither Blueheart's present, or Blueheart's future."

"Then what will serve Blueheart's present and Blueheart's future?" Rache said. He felt a subtle delight in being able to challenge this powerful man. And a moment later, recalled Einar's mistake in the hunt, and thought, careful, *careful*, you cannot indulge yourself. "What will you do?" he said.

"We will ask them," Cesar said, "to consent to

reversal of their illegal adaptations. Afterward, they may be re-adapted, legally, and may go about their lives as they please."

"You would make that a condition of amnesty?" Rache said, striving to keep expression from his voice.

"Could I in good conscience let them live with unapproved, inadequately monitored adaptations? We have Grayling's records; they commendably resisted the temptation to destroy incriminating material. Others will be less scrupulous, leaving their clients with no record of what procedures they have been subjected to. You yourself know the dangers of inadequate monitoring."

"They will not agree."

A subtle smile. "They might. I understand from Grayling's records that their adaptation failure rate has been uncommonly high. It was a matter of some vexation to their gifted, and arrogant, former director."

"She mentioned it, yes."

Cesar nodded. "And I'm sure you appreciate the work involved in analyzing, reversing, and re-adapting thirty thousand people. It will set back, quite considerably, the work on new adaptations."

It was a moment before Rache understood what Cesar said, what Cesar intended. He heard the blood in his ears, like the song of distant lava, undersea. He said, "I now know the origin and purpose of the virus which destroyed the ringsol six net. I know why it was sent and who caused it to be sent."

Cesar sat very still for two heartbeats, and then gestured toward Rache's clothing. "And yet, in a statement made but an hour ago, you denied that your visit to Scole had elicited any further information."

"Understand me, I am not trying to bargain with

you." His voice had taken on a different strength, a strength of despair. He had little hope, now, of securing the amnesty. Perhaps, as Michael had warned, he never had. He reached now for something else, for definition, for everything made plain between them. "I want you to know that I know what you are. My people . . ." He saw the change of expression in Cesar's eyes, and only then realized what he had said; but perhaps that, too, should be made plain. "Have a powerful enemy, and a ruthless one, in you. I know that the destruction of the ringsol six net happened as a result of your wish to suppress Adam's finding on the dead woman. I suspect, but cannot prove, that you authored an assault by virus on Exper' Blane Berenice, and I surmise that you would have done so to prevent her pursuing either her investigation into ringsol six, or Juniper's late activities."

"I apologize," Cesar said, exquisitely poised. "You are more politician than I thought. Your statement to the inquiry was a masterpiece of elision."

"I would not destroy a young man without being able to prove charges against the one who used him."

"And," Cesar said, "you would have implicated your own." He shook his head slightly. "Karel de Courcey is, by any definition, a criminal."

Rache drew a hard, angry breath, feeling anger and oxygen as a shock of tingling through his skin. "He was a young, innocent man."

"Innocent? Spend a little time in the black zones of Rossby. It would prove you are not the sophisticate you think you are."

Rache breathed out, hard. He could not lose his temper. "I am not here," he said, on the barest possible breath, "to defend Karel de Courcey. I do not want to see him punished, yes, because I think he has been, and will be, punished enough. If that is wrong, so be it."

"But you are still proud of yourself," Cesar interpolated, unprovoked.

"Proud?" Rache brought his head up. "I have been appallingly oblivious to things I might have realized years ago. As you say, I am likely twenty years too late. No, I am not proud. I am desperate. I am desperate enough that I will collude with you in obstructing the investigation of ringsol six. I will let no one else know about your actions. I will betray four of my people—and Teal Blane Berenice—for the sake of thirty thousand others."

Cesar said, softly, "And the other quarter of a million on Blueheart: have you forgotten them?"

Rache was silent, his breath held. His impulse was to deny; Cesar's question had shown him something he did not want to see and should not show. Instead, he said sadly, "Yes."

The master manipulator had not expected truth. He did not know, for that moment, how to use it. Then he shook his head. "But I have not." He stood up, turned away, walked over to one of the aquaria, and stroked a hand gently against the back of the glass. A pair of pale lilac fish, Terran and unknown to Rache, followed its shadow. He could see the barest sketch of a reflection of Cesar's face. "I did not forget the quarter million others. Nor do I forget the hundred billion in the settled worlds. Your people, Rache, have brought themselves to this, as I," he said, quietly, "have brought myself to where I stand. But, unlike you, I do not believe in saving people from themselves." He turned. "To grant them amnesty would be to countenance what they have done. To grant them amnesty would be to permit them to continue toward a divided future for mankind. We have evidence that on Grayling station, at least, development work was underway for germline adaptation. I promise you, that evidence and all other will be declared, and if you choose to make charges against me, concerning ringsol six, or any other matter, I will fight you in each and every way I can. I will destroy you, if I must, to save Blueheart."

Rache got to his feet, both large hands on the top of Cesar's console. "You are fulfilling your own prophecy, treating us already as outcasts from the human race." He subdued his temper, tried to subdue his breathing, afraid he had lost as much as he had gained in this terrible honesty. "Please," he said, frankly pleading. "What you have done, you have done because you are afraid of the consequences of this conspiracy, of these numbers. So am I. Give me time."

"For what?" Cesar said. He moved soundlessly to face Rache across the console, his thin, fragile, olive-skinned fingers spread at the console's base, reflecting Rache's. "Why should I give you time when I know how you mean to make it serve you? I know where your loyalties lie, Rache, and they are not with humanity, but with your own." He gestured, over his shoulder, to the lit, softly humming aquaria. "I love the seas and the things in the seas as I do because I know they must pass, because I know I have only a little time to love them, and because I love humanity more. All down history, humanity has changed its environment, its traits, even parts of itself. Oftentimes, simply as an exercise of power, but also for simple survival, because we cannot live within that environment, or survive those traits, or cohabit with those other parts of ourselves. So I say to you, Rache of Scole, there will be no amnesty."

"What else did you expect?" Michael said.

They sat in the tiled inner cove in Lovelock, side by side on a hard tiled ledge. Rache's bones ached for the sea. Michael scowled at the floor, not seeing the delicately graded colors.

"I hoped," Rache said, "for some time. It was not reasonable, I know."

"Cesar Kamehameha already is beyond reason. His is not the work of a civilized man, and he knows it. Ironic," he shook his head slightly, "given that he believes genetic manipulation was the saving of us, morally and socially, and that evil was merely a flaw in the genes. I pity him, Rache," Michael said, sounding slightly surprised. "Even seeing his handiwork, I pity him; or rather, especially seeing his handiwork, I pity him. From where he has gone, there is no returning." He paused. "What will you do now?"

Rache eased upright against the tiled wall. He looked over the quiet pool; the water was clear as crystal, clearer than any seas, and utterly still. He said, "In a few hours, Lisel said, they will start coming ashore."

"That is not wise."

And that was the lesser part of it, Rache thought. "The AOC is already moving against Grayling."

"One labhosp, and that as much because of what Cybele made known to them as because of what they are doing. Were I the AOC, and wishing this to go no further, I would offer amnesty in return for silence, or cooperation, to Meredis Lopez and her colleagues. How strongly did you argue against this?"

"I argued against them coming ashore," Rache said.

Michael nodded, abstractly, responding to some internal dialogue. "Do you think the holdfast might still persuade them otherwise?"

"I sent a message to Scole, to Emerald Ridge, telling them what was about to happen, asking them to try and contain it. But if they cannot . . . if they will not, I told them that they should not let the illegals come alone."

He watched Michael appreciate what he had said, what it meant, in blood, bone, and rebellious spirit, theirs and his own. "Dear God," Michael breathed, "have you utterly lost your mind?"

Perhaps he had, Rache thought. The view was different from the open seas. He remembered that, when she said, "We shall come ashore," he had had something of the same sensations as he had had being thrown inboard on ringsol six. History had the same inexorability as the sea.

"Talk to me, Rache," Michael said, in a low, tense voice.

Michael would have no patience with "perhaps," Rache thought. There was nothing of perhaps in what Rache had done. He said, "I thought that the holdfast and nomadic pastorals might dissuade them—"

"You knew better than that."

"I thought they would be too vulnerable if they came alone."

"Vulnerable," Michael said, looking at his upturned hands, as though the word had fallen into them. "Dear God."

"Had I been able to secure an amnesty . . ." Rache said.

Michael brought his head up, speaking to the air before him. "Would they have taken it?" The words rang from the tiles. "I think not."

Rache was silent. Michael stood up again, and paced away, bare feet slapping softly on wet tiles. He swung back. "It's an assault on the sensibilities and convictions of your supporters, never mind your opponents."

"I hoped you could help me make it less so."

"Why should I?" Michael said. "There is nothing about this I can approve. This is pure provocation, pure confrontation, and it has nothing to do with the amnesty. It has to do with conspiracy, secrecy, manipulation and criminality." He took a few paces away, his quickness and lightfootedness as always a surprise in a man of his size, and turned. "It provokes *me*, and I am a pastoral liaison, and a supporter of non-development. Imagine how it will provoke those who are neither. It frightens *me*, who knows your people well, and sympathizes and supports. Imagine what it will do to people who have difficulty with human adaptation, who have great financial, political, and emotional investment in the terraforming of Blueheart. Imagine what it would do to you if thirty thousand Indi primaries arrived by dropship tomorrow." He sat down with a jolt that made Rache's spine twinge in sympathy, and put his head into his hands.

Rache sat beside him, in silence. He had known what Michael might say. That did not mean, he thought, that Cesar was right. Blood did not make a brother, or likeness in body, family. He could not believe that in choosing their altered form, his people would be outcasts of humanity.

Michael lifted his head. "I would rather not help you," he said. "I think you have lost your judgment, that you have let yourself be drawn into this, whether because of Juniper, or Lisel, or because of a wish to retaliate against Cesar Kamehameha and the AOC. Think what will happen if you provoke them!"

"I have thought," Rache said, huskily. "And I am afraid for the illegals, for all of us, if they come ashore alone. We have to ask for the mercy of the people of Blueheart. Will you help us?"

"I have no choice." Michael looked at him with a kind of wondering anger. "I cannot simply watch disaster happen. Tempting," and there was a slight mitigation of tone, recognition that he was no more noble than any other, "as it would be to give myself the chance to say 'I told you so.' I fear that this will be a disaster despite our best efforts. I am going to contact my fellow liaisons. And I warn you, we are going to use every means of persuasion possible to discourage pastorals from doing this." He said it flatly, the tone of a man already feeling the inexorable thrust of history.

"I understand," Rache said, quietly. "And I . . . thank you."

"I do not want your thanks," Michael said, grimly, rising.

Unremarked, the seas rose.

Unremarked, at first, because always pastorals came and pastorals went from the rafttowns and island settlements. They came to bring their newborns and young children for adaptation and monitoring, to trade specimens and knowledge for such necessities as the sea did not provide. They came to initiate their young into their obligations to their primary neighbors. And they left, usually, as promptly as obligation and need permitted.

Nobody noticed, at first, that they were not leaving. That the modest areas of the docks reserved for pastoral visitors were becoming well populated, then crowded, and then, within a single day, spreading beyond their bounds. The jetties reserved for pastoral craft were moored three deep. The craft moored were not the small one- or two-person dinghies or canoes, but the wide, ocean-going pontooned canoes and masted tainu. They came, not as single trading parties of adults and youths, not as small groups of parents and infants, but as entire families, entire holdfasts, with compound-bound children, teenagers, adults, and elders. Instead of sleeping in the berths, or in hammocks in the open air, they pitched brightly colored tents, or unloaded squares of slatted walling, and constructed low huts. They slung nets and buoys around their jetties, creating a compound for their children.

Around them the greater life of Rossby continued, lived and broadcast, unaware of the beginnings of revolution. Except for a few.

Cesar said, "You see."

She said, "I see."

That was all. He looked down over her shoulder at the image of the pastoral gathering, and his olivine eyes were unreadable. "What," she said, after a moment, "will you do now?"

"It depends. Upon who emerges as their leader. Upon what they want first. Upon how much they can be shown to have transgressed the law. There are certain things which cannot be done to citizens merely upon suspicion of criminal activity. We cannot, for instance, obtain blood or tissue samples from any of them without permission. And were I they, I would not give permission. Tell me, Cybele," he made a fingerflick gesture toward the screen, "which there are legal and which illegal?"

She looked at the screen, at the crowded, industrious red bodies. Pastoral adaptives, of all ages, all types: tiny children on uncertain legs; haughty, striding youths; pregnant women, careful moving; stooped, scrawny elders. Red-skinned, raw in the sun, or melanin-enhanced and slightly dusty with residual salt; most were lean, with barely a softening of subcutaneous fat, while a few were deep adaptives, thick-bodied, their faces heavy and secretive. Most were naked, but for equipment belts and ornamentation, anklets, bracelets, torcs, rings and beaded strands threaded through pierced ears, noses, navels. They looked, Cybele thought, like the gathering of some ancient primitive tribe. But they were here, in her place.

She had always been aware of adaptives; one could not be otherwise, on the raft cities of Blueheart. Members of her family hall on Minaret had taken adaptation, for the purposes of work or pleasure, safeguards against equipment failure. It did not make them . . . alien. She did not know when she had become aware of the pastorals, of the people for whom adaptation was more than convenience, who sought its limits. Karel, she remembered, had been very aware: he was the one who had regaled Adam with statistics, how long they could stay submerged, how deep they could dive, how many weeks they could swim, fasting, across the open seas. In those days he had been spirited and ingenious in his arguments.

And she herself . . . she had known of pastorals, but

they had been merely a distant backdrop to her private concerns. She would be offworld, she thought, before the decision was made, and the slow dismantling of their civilization began; she would have no part in it.

Fool that she was, she thought bitterly, *fool* that she was. Adam's death was on these people's hands, all those centuries of life, experience, travel, exacting goodness, and demanding love . . . taken away, in a moment, in the passing of a wave. A wave that Rache of Scole had survived, and she came close to hating him merely for surviving what Adam had not.

"We have the records."

"Ah, but even legals come in only when they must. Many legals were last visual idented as very young children. Given both founder effect and adaptive interventions, there is a certain convergence of genotype and therefore phenotype. Could you be certain of identifying, say, one particular sixty-year-old adult from an age-enhanced image of a four-year-old?"

"I would not know," Cybele said. "Until I tried."

He leaned forward slightly; she thought for a moment he was going to touch her. "I am not mocking you, Cybele. The whole gathering appears to have chosen to shelter the illegals within its body. It is a brazen move, which means that we cannot, for the moment, touch any of them."

"But by sheltering them they show themselves in collusion."

"With their existence, not with their creation. You see the distinction; it is their creation which is illegal. The question is," his eyes veiled to her, he watched the screen, "who planned this? What do they intend by it? When we know these things, the way ahead will be clearer."

On the screen, a cluster of children were swirling about a uniformed Rache, giggling and staring. A man came and gathered up one of the smallest, a little girl. Something in his expression, the slightly irritated patience, reminded her of Adam. The little girl spoke, peering appealingly from beneath her lashes, and the man's face cleared; they shared a smile of pure complicity. Oh, she remembered that, she thought, how she remembered that. If Cesar spoke, she did not hear him, deaf to anything but longing. She remembered having what they had between them. And they and their conspiracy had taken it, and any chance of regaining it, from her.

She said, "You do not have to look at the adults. We have images of the children, the legally adapted children. Eliminate those. Any children who do not appear in our records are illegals. Identify their caretakers . . ." she pointed at the screen, "and prosecute them, for abuse of the children in their care."

When the slow eye of history blinked and shifted, Teal knew it.

She was immersed in the Blueheart net, manipulating a fugue of processes and uplinks, while diagnostics tracked the faults, the fumblings, the blebbings, and shreddings of her interface.

It was as she had feared: the hypertension which might have killed her had sheared synapses between brain and cercortex, damaged cells trapped between tissue and implants. The programming she had pulled from backup addressed synapses, employed circuits, which no longer existed. On Blueheart, there were nei-

ther the facilities nor the expertise to remodel her physical interface to suit her programming. Her sole recourse
was to redesign her programming to accommodate the
changes. She and Karel could do that, she was certain.
But how, or what, she would be at the end, she did not
know; whether she could, in her new configuration, re-
create the integration and the unique programming
which had comprised her mastery, she could not tell.

She had come to hope, for Karel's sake, that they
would succeed. Even without Michael's guidance, she
understood that he looked to the task as redemption.
She would have argued against his culpability, but
Michael said no, let him help. And he was helping,
though not in the way he thought, and not in the way
she would have expected. His need helped her, not his
expertise. He was imaginative and sure, an extremely
promising designer, but his need burned brighter than
any ability. He drove her onward, harder than she
would have driven herself.

All the time she had been lost at sea, she had been
desperate to find a place, find help, to begin the salvage of her ruined interface, capacities, life. Now,
with the task begun, she hesitated. She found herself
thinking of the taste and glitter of the sea, of the heave
of the yacht beneath her thighs and the pull of the
ropes in her hands, of an open, avidly curious young
girl. No matter what happened to her cercortex, those
memories would remain clear and complete. She had
made discoveries during her days of deprivation,
about herself, her sister, the world around her. She did
not know what she wanted to do with the discoveries,
but she knew she did not want to lose them. She did
not want to be exiled again to the inner world. Karel
thought the recalcitrance with which he struggled was

the recalcitrance of the interface. It was not: it was Teal's own.

So it was with near gladness that she recognized the sudden flux of attention in Rossby's net, the reassignment of channels to monitoring the docks, the abrupt increase in messages subject-labeled "adaptation," the shift in message currents toward docks security, adaptive liaisons, the AOC. The outer world and its concerns demanded attention, and she was pleased to answer. She terminated and detached her contacts, hearing Karel's mutter of protest and dismay. She opened her eyes—on Michael's tiled floor, screen-paneled booth—and turned to face Karel's concerned argument.

She said, "It has begun." As they watched, one by one, like tiles falling, all the screens shifted to show the docks. Docks not merely on Rossby alpha, but on the other Rossby rafttowns, on Messnier, on the rafttowns which rode the equatorial currents and the polar currents, and on the island and polar bases. Karel's eyes blurred as he reached into the net again. She did not join him; through her own eyes she watched the pastorals gathering, staking claim to the docks with their bodies, canoes and tents. She got to her feet, and padded up the ramp to find Michael, savoring the smooth articulation of hips, knees, ankles as she walked. The tiles felt like nuggets beneath her bare feet, a not unpleasant sensation. On her hands she wore light gloves, protection for her tender palms and fingers. She felt a deep, contented animal tiredness, the tiredness of danger past and sanctuary found. She had not been so aware of her body for many years.

Michael was sitting at the console in the main room, his back to the window overlooking the tiled bay. The bank of screens which rose above the console showed an array of faces, and a map of Blueheart's seas, beaded with points of light. Michael was saying, his voice strained, "Whatever happens, we should work to keep our lines of contact open . . ." He caught sight of Teal. She walked up to him, a slow, even step, absorbed in the motion. "Just a minute," Michael said, to the soundless others.

Teal said, "You asked us to tell you when Rossby noticed. Rossby has noticed."

"Ah, God," Michael said, quietly. "Thank you, Teal." He turned back to the screens. Eight faces, Teal saw, men and women both, adaptive and primary. Michael said, aloud, "This is it, my friends. You might want to go back down onto the docks now . . . I don't know what it will achieve, yet, but good luck." One or two would have argued, but Michael drew the sound-piece from his ear, visibly, deliberately, and, like the others, they waved good-bye, if with poorer grace. Michael lowered his head, shook it slightly. "Monitor," he said, aloud. "Image-search protocol. Person, current: Rache Scole Blueheart. He's probably in green zone of Rossby docks."

Teal envisioned the algorithms as they searched the multiplicity of incoming images for the face and form of Rache Scole Blueheart. Almost, she slid into the net to watch. She felt the urge as something nearly palpable, and to resist it she laid a finger lightly on the map of Blueheart and said, "What is this color?"

Michael blinked at her, and then studied her closely for a moment, a penetrating, professional look. She simply waited. "Color," he echoed. "That's blue. A rather pure blue, if I am any judge. The darker bands are nearer navy."

"Blue," she said. "Navy."

The center screen abruptly yielded up an image of Rache standing on Rossby docks, bulky, durable, and misplaced in his blue and black. Michael said, "Communications, uplink with audio implant, Rache of Scole. Open channel . . . Rache."

On screen, Rache blinked. "Michael. They've noticed. Over." Rache nodded slightly, impassive, and Michael leaned back. "And good luck," he added, for no one's ears but his own.

Midday sun shone hard on Rache's bare head. He wished that, like primaries, and most lines of adaptive, he could sweat to cool. Or dive into the sea, as the younger ones were doing, a constant swirl of plunging and splashing and scrambling. His uniform was hot. He wished for some other banner besides this, but could think of nothing more appropriate. He longed to be cool and obscure, rather than overheated, light-headed with fatigue, and highly conspicuous.

Out at the mouth of the bay, a double-hulled canoe slowed its stroke, making its dainty way inward like a grazing laser on the lava. The sternpost supported an ornate, circular emblem in black, but Rache did not need that emblem to know it. He and Athene had taken their earliest open sea voyages in that tainu, and had fought for their first stroke with the paddles.

He could, he thought—he should, probably—let them come to him, here on Rossby docks. Particularly if Lisel were with them, as he thought she should be, or she would have been here already. He smiled, a little grimly, at the gamesmanship. He knew her too well to think she would make anything easy for him.

His feet took him step by step to the edge of the docks. The milling children parted before him, circled him, whispering and looking strangely at his uniform. Most of them should have seen such a uniform before, even if not worn by a man so obviously an adaptive. Some never would have. He could not tell, from their covert stares and whispering, which had, and which had not, which were pastoral, and which illegal.

He should draw comfort from that. He had intended it. Unless the AOC could be certain that a given individual was an illegal, they could not petition for genetic analysis without consent. The company of ninety thousand fellows was less shelter than the seas, but it was shelter nevertheless.

And now, he thought, and now . . .

Most recent extrapolations placed critical population at just about three hundred and fifty thousand. This based upon the current demographics, and upon the relative contributions of each subpopulation to the data and skills bases. For the true determinant was the accumulation of the critical knowledge and skills for implementation.

Cesar had accused him of failing to recognize a vital ramification of his proposal—permanent adaptation. It was the lesser omission. The greater was that he had not understood this: that if the choice were *not* to implement terraforming, then they already had the knowledge and skills at hand. They knew, and were, everything they needed to prosper to Blueheart. And so the hour of decision could be any hour they chose.

And ironically, he thought, he never would have pressed through to the realization had Cesar not denied the illegals amnesty. Necessity might be the mother of inspiration, but sheer desperation hung high in the family tree.

His implant suddenly spoke in Michael's voice. A curt message, with no well-wishing. He nodded acknowledgment. Light glinted from a shifting lens, low in one of the walls, and Rache thought fleetingly of Juniper, and what she might have made of these days. And then he thought of Rossby's laws and protocols, its grading of domains according to allowable surveillance—and he stepped to the edge of the docks and dived, fully clad, into the sea.

He swam through the long, inclined shadows of the moored boats, and surfaced through the unimpeded column of light. The sea, so near Rossby with its filters and processors, was translucent, faintly luminous. He surface-swam toward the double-hulled vessel, arriving to leeward and in its narrow shadow. Hands reached down for him, hauled him aboard, Lisel's hands among them. She caught a fistful of blue fabric at his waist and leaned close. "What's this? Afraid the mere sight of me might make you disgrace yourself?" Her voice was tight, brittle; she searched his eyes as though trying, by intensity alone, to isolate them

Einar, gripping his oar with both hands, turned his face from Rossby to Rache, his eyes full of sunlight and triumph.

From the cabin on the platform between the hulls, Tove stepped lightly across the line of shadow and sunlight. She wore a wrap of red and gold, wound slantwise from her left shoulder, leaving her right bare, and again around her waist. Shell badges secured it, thin almost to translucency, their original form marred by chips. She said, "Well met, Rache."

"Tove."

To Astrid at the helm she said, "Hold us here." To Rache, "Come with me," and he did, with Lisel a half step behind. She half turned at the cabin door and said, to Lisel, "Him. Not you." He glanced behind, saw Lisel's wry, sour expression. She tugged once more on his wet sleeve, and toed the door closed between them. A high window let a solid shaft of light in. Beneath the light, he could see the edge of a slingseat, its shadow, floor. Nothing reflected or diffused the light. Everything else seemed in darkness. He saw Tove's bare feet step through it, ruby red. He heard her say, "Rache, this is madness."

He waited for his eyes to adjust, for the difference between light and darkness to soften, and the room and her form to complete itself before him. The sky beyond the window was colorless with its brilliance.

Tove said, "Have you nothing to say to me?"

He was just beginning to see her, seated very upright on the sling. He could see nothing of her expression. He said, with mild, deliberate surprise, "Of course it is madness, but what else could we do?"

She snorted laughter, and tossed her head; he saw a glint of a facet of her cheek. "Another fifty years and you might be able to dissemble before me, not now. You do not think it madness, or you would never have proposed it. Sit down!" She gestured to the far side of the column of sunlight, where he could just see the outline of a second sling like hers. He sat.

She said, "You should not have done so. We owe Lisel's kind nothing. We most certainly do not owe them our protection. They have violated the principles under which we were given freedom of the seas. We will not be put at risk to defend them. Do you understand that?"

He understood, all too well. She continued, "The elders of Emerald Ridge are agreed. The holdfasts of Emerald Ridge will not join this uprising of yours. Let the AOC settle with the lawbreakers."

He could discern her face more clearly now, the aged, subtle matriarch of Scole. She reminded him of no one other than Cesar Kamehameha, and he was certain that neither words nor face revealed her true intentions.

He wondered what those might be. She had never shown him, by word or deed, what she thought Blueheart's future should be. She upheld Scole as her one concern, her one cause, and yet her knowledge of primary culture was unmatched along the Emerald Ridge. Not a season went by when she did not visit one of the rafttowns on its passage. She had never condemned his choice of career; her condemnation was for his personal failings and infidelities.

She said, answering his silence, "This motion that the AOC might forcibly reverse the illegals" adaptations is a shibboleth. Their powers are mighty, but they are finite, and they cannot circumvent the requirement for consent of people in their right mind. But that is between the illegals and the AOC. We will not permit the AOC to use the illegals as an instrument to justify the withholding of legal adaptation from ourselves."

He thought of Einar's eyes, full of sunlight and triumph. Einar understood what stood to be gained here, and how it might be thwarted. And thwarted, he would not have looked upon Rossby, or Rache, with triumph.

If Tove had opposed this, she had been overborne. Or rather, had sensed the pull of an irresistible current, and turned to swim at its head. She would have him plead; she would have him explain his mind, his thinking, his hopes; she would have him grateful for the mitigation of an opposition that never existed.

"I appreciate everything you have said," he told her. He gathered himself, and stood. "I swam out here, rather than waiting for you to dock, because I had just been advised that our gathering had been noted and would presently be questioned. I wanted to talk to you in privacy, and advise those who do not know about it about rafttown conventions for monitoring. But it seems there is no need." He started toward the door, not briskly, giving her time; but she did not take it, she did not even move; and so he had to be the one to yield, and turn, and say in a tone as devoid of anger as he could make it, "You want me to appeal to you for help."

Her face, half lit, flickered between anger and amusement. She said, "But your pride will not let you." She gestured, regally, "Sit down," and leaned back to watch him. After a moment, knowing that he needed her, he came back, and sat. "If you want to know what I am doing, and why, you could simply ask."

"And you will make me ask," she said, with a trace of hauteur.

"Einar's face tells me that our people are coming. He watches Rossby as Astrid watches an eel's den."

The sunlight caught the back of one age-sculpted hand as it moved in her lap. "Forgive me, Rache. Old habits."

Old habits, he thought. The habits of an old, subtle intellect for whom simplicity, honesty, pragmatism were too unchallenging. She affected to despise Juniper, yet they were much alike. Tove would have enjoyed the enclaves of Berenice, or the esoteric rapacities of New Boots. Tove, he thought, with a needling of his own amusement, should have been in that office with Cesar Kamehameha.

He said, "When did you learn that there were so many illegals?"

She tilted her head slightly, listening to what he assumed and what he would not ask. "It was in good conscience that I tried to persuade you to name Einar in Lisel's place."

"In good conscience?"

"In fair ignorance then," she said, with a muted flare at the challenge, "but the good of Scole. For the good of Lisel, too, since that coincided with Scole, and I cannot imagine you would reproach me for that. I thought she was one of few, not one of many." The hand shifted in and out of sunlight; the yellow on the wrap flared. "I did not lie to you."

He could not discern how genuine was her agitation. He thought it genuine, but superficial. "You feel events moving beyond your control? So do I."

"You might tell me the truth yourself," she said, piqued. "You knew what Juniper envisioned."

"Yes," he said. "But I never believed she might succeed."

She laid both hands palm down on her thighs. The left shone like blood coral. "Do you want," she said, "my help?" She would not ask if he needed it, he thought; it would never occur to her that anyone might not.

"That depends on the price I must pay."

A soft snort of laughter. "A small price. I want to know your plan for your revolution. Oh yes, it is your revolution; though Lisel congratulates herself for having deceived us all, and Einar cherishes his purity of heart, they are both ignorant of the other half of our world. They do not think it," she dripped the word like acid, "matters. But you have the knowledge that this will need."

"There isn't . . . exactly a plan," Rache said, after a moment, feeling a sudden chill at her emphasis of his position. He was not ready for this, not ready at all. Again he had the sense of water striking his back, hurling him ahead of it.

"Then make one," Tove of Scole said sharply. "Or others will, without your knowledge or consent. They have in the past."

"I know," he said. There was a silence.

"It came to me," Rache said, "that the decision to preserve Blueheart as it is need wait upon nothing and no one. We do not need to wait for knowledge or numbers. We have the knowledge; we have the numbers."

"Ah," said Tove. A soft, unguarded sound, almost wondering. But she granted him no more than that, and he could not see her face.

"Beyond that," he said, "I do not know. I have an idea who would support us, and who would not. I have an idea what should be discussed. I thought, in twenty, thirty years, we would have a design for the conservative development of Blueheart which could be a contender. I thought, in twenty, thirty years, I would be well enough placed in survey to have a certain influence. That," he said, quietly, "was what I educated myself for. I did not educate myself for revolution."

"But revolution is what you have," Tove said. "And there will be those with other ideas as to how it is made."

"Yourself?"

"I am old," she said, and he shifted his weight forward, preparing to rise. She leaned forward, as he did, turning her face into the light. Her expression was unreadable, cross-hatched with her years, but her illuminated eye was bright.

He held it. "May I presume upon your support, as elder of Scole?"

"No," she said. "No, you may not."

Rache nodded, and started to stand.

"When I said I was old," Tove said, arresting him,

"I was not being evasive. I am old. I have seen the glories of the seas, and the golden age of adaptation on Blueheart. I expected that these things would pass as I did, but I expected that passing would be graceful." And that, Rache thought, was as near as she might come to confession of what she feared, the passing of her own day. In the seas, she was a power, by authority of years, experience and character. Beyond the seas she was simply another citizen, and less than most, uneducated, unskilled, lacking implants. Being pastoral, being Tove, she had chosen the one over the other. He was the least able to judge her, since he had chosen otherwise and knew the price. But that did not prevent him wishing that she had been able to find it in herself to support him.

She said, "Be not so hasty," clearly seeing enough of his expression to tell his thought. "I have made no decisions. Yours is an infant revolution, and you, for all your years, an infant in revolution." She leaned back, so shadow draped her face, and spoke out of it. "I will not offer you my support until I understand what you would do with it."

He almost smiled, at how nearly he had pitied her her dread of eclipse, and how little she was entitled to pity. He said, quietly, "I understand."

FIFTEEN

I am Lisel of Magellan," Lisel said. "It was my message brought you here, and it is time that you knew the story behind that message . . ."

She stood on a bench in the middle of the docks. Above her head, glass eyes, cameras tracked her. Through the press of their people, Rache could see the uppermost portion of the dockside screen, and on it, her face. On dock screens and room screens throughout Blueheart, her image would be speaking, to the expectant and the curious.

He glanced over his shoulder, up at her. She looked far more calm than he felt, a tall, hook-nosed adaptive woman in middle years, declaring the start of a revolution.

"Though I stand before you here," Lisel said, "I do not exist. My birth was never registered, my genome never made part of a databank, my adaptation never recorded. My exact origins are irrelevant—shadowy, somewhat grubby, and for many years a shame and a burden to me. I left Magellan against the wishes of my kind, seeking a place and a measure of legitimacy. Through misadventure I came to Scole, where, all unknowing, they took me in. I married Rache of Scole, and our life was as full and fraught as any partnership can be when one partner has a vision and the other such a secret."

He heard her swallow, above the silence from the crowd. Near his feet, bright-eyed, crouched the children, legals and illegals mingling. The members of Scole holdfast stood in a wedge, to his right, elders to the fore. Somewhere toward the back, he knew, was Michael.

Lisel said, "There were not many like me in my generation, not enough to change a world. Certainly we never imagined we might; we were as inward-looking a little band as ever lived to ignore the future." She shook her head slightly, ruefully. "When I started on my wanderings, it was out of a need as selfish as the need which created me. I should never have come to rest, never have married, certainly not a man of the settled holdfast of Scole, which had its own tragedies, and I should never have met the offworlder Juniper Blane Berenice. But I did, and because of that, and what ensued, between myself, Juniper, and my husband, I let slip the secrecy surrounding my origins for the first and only time before now. I told Juniper Blane Berenice, the offworlder, that I did not exist. I told her in order to enlist her pity for me, orphan in the world, so that she would cease to entice my husband away from the holdfast, from the seas, where of course," a brief, slurred pause, "I could not follow."

She drew a deep breath. "I, in my pride, preferred to believe it was her doing, and not his; and I, in my anger, never told him why I could not come with him and why he should not leave me . . . and so Rache followed his own path, to his own end . . . But that is his story, which he himself might tell. I did not know until after she died how Juniper had used my confession, how she had traced others involved in unapproved adaptation, and inspired them in their disaffection. She seeded conspiracy across the seas, and many of you are the issue of that conspiracy. For, you see, it was Juniper's belief that Blueheart's terraforming was foreordained, no matter that we are said to have a choice. Centuries of planning, practice, and ideology could not be defied, not by keeping to laws designed to serve that same planning, practice, and ideology. The constitution of the seed population would be controlled, not by us, but by the plan. And so it was Juniper's intent that the population be found to be . . . skewed, when the decision came to be made." A ripple, like the ruffle of a squall on waters. Lisel shivered a little with the uncontrollable mirth of suspense; her face alight with it, she said, "Hear me out. *Please.*"

"Juniper's plan should have run another thirty years. In thirty years our majority would have been unassailable. But another young wanderer was less fortunate than I was: her dead body was found drifting in the seas, and what happened after has brought us to realize that our secret can no longer be kept."

Einar, standing close to the front of the gathering, sent Rache a black stare.

"There are those among you to whom our existence should be no revelation. To the others," Rache felt the barest touch, like a slight current, on his shoulder, "I hope you will forgive us for presuming upon your support, presuming that you, like ourselves, believe that what we have done here in the seas of Blueheart is not insignificant, and should not be evanescent. That we are neither insignificant, nor evanescent. Juniper started this, and we have continued it, because we believe in Blueheart, the waterworld, with its own unique ecosystem and its own unique cultures, floating and aquatic both. We are forty light years from Earth: why *should* we be bound by the plans, the traditions of a society so old, so alien and so far removed?" She stopped, trying to catch her breath. Rache glanced up at her, and she smiled fleetingly and unseeingly down at him, and rested her hand on his shoulder. He could feel her trembling. "I have very little more to say. It is up to you now. To you all, pastoral and primary. For you all to decide."

"What is there to decide?" A woman shouldered to the front of the congregation, her face bitter and marked forehead and eye with a disfiguring, blinding scar. Maria the younger of Kense, Rache thought, if Tove's description served. She turned her head in quick jerks so that her good eye might move from one to the other. "We have lost. We are still too few, and too many of those are still children. You have gained nothing by summoning us here. You have," straight at Rache, "betrayed us."

"It is you," said a voice from the right, "who have betrayed us." The speaker was Neils, elder of Scole and Tove's one-time partner. Though some years her younger, he looked the elder; his voice was an old man's voice. "You thought to use us to shield you from the law. You thought to smear us and drag us down with you. Even now, you hide behind us." He raised his voice, wavering, imperious. "Show yourselves! Show yourselves to us!"

"No!" cried Einar. "You cannot offer up your own kind to the AOC."

"If our survival demands it we will," Tove said. "That is the law of the sea."

There was a roar of affirmation and derision. Tove stood proud against it all. Rache clambered up onto the plinth beside Lisel and turned to face them all. His appearance opened a momentary silence. Into it, he said, "There was something Juniper failed to realize."

Someone shouted, "There's a great deal Juniper

failed to realize." There were shouts of agreement, and angry laughter. Rache folded his arms, and waited them out. He could see faces in the backward ranks, faces he knew, faces he did not know, in all their individual expression of excitement, anger, apprehension, and doubt. Very few wore Tove's mask of proud self-containment. Behind the rearmost, he could even see Michael, who, returning Rache's look, shook his head slightly, his face grim. Beside him stood the seven members of the boatyard partnership, their tracheal implants glinting in the sun. On the docks screen, behind them all, he saw himself, large and obdurate in survey blues and blacks, the sun shining on his head. He understood why Lisel had trembled.

He waited until they had subsided to a low, restless muttering. It would not last; he felt the charge of their mood with his skin. He laid out each word with the force of a knell. "Juniper failed to see that this one choice has no set hour. If we choose to go on as we are, we already *have* what we need to build our future. We already are who we need to be. The choice is not thirty years beyond us; it is now." He brought both hands up before him, upturned to fill with sunlight or air. "This very day we may elect to keep Blueheart . . . unchanged."

There was a sudden, reverberating silence.

"That changes nothing," Maria of Kense said. "We are still too few to prevail in the vote."

Rache drew breath to speak, but Lisel slid her hand around his wrist, and said, in an unyielding voice, "Those who do not want to be part of this may go."

He looked at her, in dismay at the implicit ultimatum, the frank demand for unearned trust. She stared straight ahead, granite in her profile. The gathering rippled, shifted, began to fragment into smaller huddles.

People began to gather up their belongings, not looking toward the duo on the plinth.

Maria said, loudly, "First I would like to hear how it was that you, Rache of Scole, betrayed us."

"I did not betray you."

"You stand before us in *that* uniform, and say that. It was you who found the wanderer, you who took her back to ringsol six, you whose subordinate surveyed the genome—oh, yes, we know about that, now, though we took her from your hands as quickly as we could."

"Rache!" Daven cried out in a high voice, breaking forward from the party from Scole. "Rache knew nothing about it." He looked at Rache, turned, sweeping the people around him with a pleading gaze. "I give you my word. I was *there*."

Rache heard Tove say, "Daven, *enough*."

Daven looked, not at her, but at Rache, his face raw with appeal. Rache nodded to him: I forgive you. But Daven did not see, for at that moment, Einar moved, distracting them all as he shouldered his way toward his brother. He pulled him toward the front, and turned them both to face the gathering, one arm around Daven's shoulders.

Einar swept his gaze across the gathering, and fixed upon one withdrawing group, from one of Kense's satellites on Great Diamond. "Josen. Anthonia." A young man and woman stopped, and looked back at him. "Is this your wish, or your elders'?" Einar said, with knowing warmth in his voice. "What do you think you will accomplish by this?" An older woman pulled at the young woman's arm; she tugged it free, face still turned toward Einar, expectant.

"Yes," Einar said, "we are all young, those of us of the generation of Juniper's . . . seeding. Our elders have known long, unchanging lives in the unchanging seas. *They* say, obey the law, make no trouble. Why not: they will be gone before our world is destroyed. Do not condemn them; they knew nothing else. But do not let them deny us the chance to change what we all thought had to be. Young as we are, our voices are as important as any elder's. And what happens now is *more* important to us than to the elders, for it is *our* present and *our* future which is being decided." He turned, and held up a hand to Lisel. She looked at it, looked at him, and took it. Einar said, clearly, "*I* and my brother stand with you and yours, Lisel of Magellan, whether I know them by name or not."

"Thank you," said Lisel, in a quiet voice. Even to Rache, her expression was unreadable. Einar went to speak again; she tightened her hand hard on his. He frowned at her, and pulled free. Will met will, and Einar held his peace. Lisel said, "Those of you who wish to go, should go now."

The gathering shifted, rippled, bled in slow lines toward the docks, but did not crumble. Einar stepped suddenly into the crowd, reaching out to the nearest departing member. He did not argue, merely gave greetings and acknowledgment, touching hands to hands, hands to shoulders, exchanging the occasional light embrace, asking the same quiet question, "Is this *your* wish?" He did not, Rache noticed, wave to anyone who hailed him from a distance; he kept his head lowered, his attention exclusively upon those who were nearest. He drew them to him, and greeted them warmly when they came. The ripples centered now on him. The cracks in the gathering closed; some who had gathered up their goods now set them down again. The young, not many, but few, broke from their elders, letting themselves be folded into the gathering.

They had lost, Rache reckoned, perhaps a tenth of their numbers, but few turned to see the canoes pulling away, the boats raising sail. He smiled in simple appreciation of what he was watching and said, to Lisel, "He knew, didn't he?"

Her mouth twisted, a little wryly. "He was always quicker on the uptake than you, m'dear. And more widely traveled— where it matters. He worked it out for himself some years ago."

And that, Rache thought, was why he was so willing to offer himself up to justice in Lisel's stead. "He knows your people?"

"Some of us, yes."

From within the crowd, surrounded by laughing, touching youth, Einar looked back, his face luminous and triumphant. Rache met his eye and nodded approval, and for the first time in years, Einar smiled back.

To him, Rache said, "The nub of it is that we will not stand alone in this." With a small effort, he remembered that the two of them were not alone, and widened his address. "We are not the only ones who love Blueheart's seas, and believe they should be," a pause, while he considered the neutral, scientist's word, and rejected it, "cherished. Look around you . . ." He gestured at the long-fingered, boat-adorned docks, at the buildings with balconies wide open to the seas. "Is this the work of people who have no love of the sea? If there will ever be a time to ask them to show their love of the sea, of Blueheart, it is now. Before the expectation of change becomes a habit, and the expectation of loss, familiar.

"We are not," he said, "alone in loving this world."

Across the gathering, he caught, and held, Michael's eye. "We are not alone in loving the seas. With the support of those aboard the rafttowns who also love the seas, and who see no need to live in any other way than they do, we will have the numbers; we will prevail." At Michael's side, two shipyarders raised their fists in silent approval. He said, "Shall I tell you my," a tiny hesitation, and again he rejected the scientific term, "vision for Blueheart's future?"

The docks were in afternoon shadow before he had done speaking, and they, questioning him. Their mood, as they scattered to attend to their own needs—food gathering, childcare, boat maintenance—was a mixture of skepticism and anticipation. Rache clambered down from the bench, looked at it, and sat down; he felt utterly drained. He would sit for a moment, he decided, and then he must make his own declaration of revolution. All this had been but prologue. He heard Einar's voice from nearby, and looked up, saw Einar talking with Daven and some of the other younger members of Scole, his face luminous still. Rache thought of the shy, sullen, stammering little boy whose care he had undertaken, all those years ago. He had not done badly, then, and he had been rewarded now. He got to his feet, and walked, limping a little, toward Einar, and Einar left his company to meet him halfway.

"Thank you," said Rache, quietly.

The luminosity faded from Einar's face, but went unreplaced by any of the usual expressions. Einar simply looked at him. "I didn't do it for you."

"I know." He would have said how much he was

impressed, how greatly moved, by what he had seen. But Einar seldom granted anyone the right to praise him; and if Rache had had that right once, he had forfeited it years ago.

"How is your hand?" he said, part parental concern, and part cowardice. Einar glanced at it; the scoring was barely visible on the red skin.

"You could have protected us," Einar said. "Why didn't you?"

There was little hostility, and only faint accusation in the voice. Perhaps, Rache thought, after all these years, he has finally accepted what I am doing. I owe him the truth, now. "Will you come aboard the tainu with me?"

Einar read this as prevarication; he reared back slightly. Rache said, a little desperately, "If we speak here," a forceful thrust of the hand downward, expressing all his pent-up urgency, "anyone can listen in. If we speak there," he indicated the tainu, "they cannot."

Einar glanced from docks to the tainu with a slight smile. "Indeed."

To have explained the intricacies of privacy law, and the algorithms enforcing it, would have been pointless. "Einar," said Rache, "please."

Lisel said quietly, from behind them, "Go with him, Einar. The three of us need to talk." She had come up unnoticed by either of them. Rache sent her a grateful look, over Einar's shoulder. There was a moment's suspended silence, then Einar walked quickly to the docks edge and swung himself lightly aboard the tainu, and up onto the center platform. Rache followed; he knew by a vibration in the boards that Lisel had come after.

"All we needed," Einar said, turning, "was ten more years. In ten years we would have been set to breed true." Rache took a moment to grasp what he meant, and in that moment, Einar continued, "As long as we must be adapted each generation anew, our existence will remain conditional."

Rache turned his hands palm-upward, and considered them: broad, stub-fingered and dark red, the hands of a man as profoundly adapted for the sea as any human living. He said, quietly, "I agree." As he voiced that agreement, he could not but wonder how those hands might be reshaped when their shape was no longer limited by the human germline. And by whom, for whom. Might the exquisite monstrosities of Juniper's "Transformations" yet be given flesh? They might live to be cursed, he and Einar both, by their mutant descendants. He might live to know that Cesar and Adam had had the right of it, that neither law or goodwill could preserve what should have been left to God. "I cannot regret," he said, "that you did not have your ten years."

Lisel dipped her head, the thoughtfulness on her face suggesting she had followed his thought.

Einar drew a sharp breath, Rache knew to accuse. Rache said, with muted force, "I had no power to protect you. The AOC was already preparing its case against you. They already knew. A high-resolution survey some years ago showed a discrepancy between reported and observed populations."

"We will not be safe," Einar said, deliberately, "until the last of them is gone." He caught his breath slightly at the intensity of Rache's gaze. Caught his breath, caught himself at it; resentment hardened in his face. "As long as pastorals must be remade with each generation, our existence remains conditional. And as long as primaries remain on Blueheart, *Blueheart*'s existence—the seas' existence—remains conditional. Bluehcart will not be ours until everyone living on Blueheart is committed to Blueheart, and to the seas. Until everyone living on Blueheart is an adaptive, and the primaries are gone."

Rache turned on Lisel. He knew now why she had insisted that they talk, he and Einar, he and she. "You think this too?"

Anger flickered in her face at the tone. "Yes and no."

"Many people agree with me," Einar said, a little coldly. In a barely unspoken subtext Rache heard, I don't need you. He turned, and walked away from them, treading out his distress and perturbation in slow, heavy steps along the length of the platform. He found the idea hideously compelling. It was, as Einar said, the way to ensure Blueheart's unconditional preservation. And it was too much akin to Cesar Kamehameha's bleak, cerebral bigotry.

He spoke with his back to them. "You would find the cost of that safety too high."

"It's a price worth paying."

Rache turned, and measured the distance between them with despair.

Lisel looked from one to the other. "Without primaries," she said, quietly, "there is a great deal else we would have to do and learn. We would have to preserve the expertise, the knowledge, of both primaries and adaptives."

"I don't—" Einar started, but she continued over him.

"We are not primitives. The thousands of years of knowledge and experience contained in the nets are our heritage as much as the primaries'. We are citizens of the settled worlds; would you surrender that citizenship for your children? I would not."

"We don't need—"

"Enough, Einar," Lisel said, temper showing. "I am telling you that you do. I have years of experience—which you do *not* have—of the life that the seas alone can offer, and I am telling you it is not enough. It is not enough for me, and it would not be enough for you. I did not live as I have lived, do," an eyeflicker of a glance toward Rache, "what I have done, without the hopes that one day I too could bring my life whole to the surface. I may be a pastoral, but I am also a member of the human race." She drew a harsh breath. "As are you." More temperately, but without the least conciliation, she continued, "You have it in you to be a leader worth following, for all your youth. And you have it in you to be a leader not worth following, but one whom people will nevertheless follow, to their regret. You have much to learn. And there," she snapped a hand at Rache, "stands someone who might teach you, should you give him a chance. Yes, he is a flawed man, with a flawed vision, but he has still done more than most of us. And if you envision a future without primaries, then I suggest you study Rache, because Rache *is* what pastorals will be, when pastorals must be all things to Blueheart." She leaned over and tapped the underside of Rache's chin, eyes sparkling with anger spiced with humor. "Close your mouth, m'dear. Try and look intelligent." He brought his hand up, unthinkingly, but she allowed him to do no more than brush her hand with his fingertips before she moved away. She had other matters in mind.

Einar looked as stunned as he. Lisel continued, "You need his knowledge of development protocols, and the support of his allies among the primaries. He needs your knowledge of the seas, and the support of your—and my—allies among pastorals. So acknowledge this," a sharp glance at Rache, "the both of you, and get on with it. You have very little time." She turned, and vaulted onto the docks, leaving them together, looking at each other.

Rache lowered himself carefully onto the deck, his feet trailing above the water, their reflection a slightly warmer patch of shadow on shadow. He waited. After a moment, Einar sat beside him. Rache said, "We must pull lightly on any line that draws upon permanent human adaptation. Do you understand why?"

"I left the child compound some years ago."

Rache consigned tact to the deeps. "*Has* your hand done hurting yet?"

"Yes," Einar said, starting to rise.

"I am not done with you," Rache said, with a force that caused heads to turn dockside. Einar's eyes widened; he stopped with one leg drawn up. "You rushed that eel. You put your life at risk, and you put Astrid's life at risk when I had to leave her to get you to the surface. And all for a moment or two. You may have left the child compound, but you have not learned some simple lessons of the hunt. I have been working twenty-five years toward this day. I, better than anyone else on this or any other docks, know this quarry. I know what we can, and cannot, do. And we *cannot* press the issue of permanent human adaptation, not now. We cannot flaunt before our supporters, never mind our opponents, that in ten years we would have essayed permanent human adaptation. What we have done here is audacious and indefensible enough. The fundamental argument here concerns Blueheart. We are laying claim to Blueheart, to Blueheart's seas, to a particular future for Blueheart. Let the rest of it," he heard the undertone of pleading in his tone, "unfold with time."

"You," Einar said, "may be laying claim to Blueheart's future. We are laying claim to our future." He stood, his head turned seaward. From the prow of the incoming Scole outrigger, Noelle and Ayna waved wildly, shouting his name. The timing, Rache thought, a little bitterly, was fortuitous. "Their future," said Einar, triumphantly, and, without giving Rache the chance to answer, dived from the platform clear over the far side of the tainu, vanishing between the tainu and the next moored boat, with a splash as fine as a reed falling in water.

Rache, his expression somber, got up to go and declare his part of the revolution.

"You cannot do this," said the representative of the development directorate, a little faintly.

Rache said, "I can, and I will."

He watched the man on the screen try to gather himself. He did not blame him. This was a common, dockside public access booth, such as were situated on all districts and levels, and he a mere middle administrator, distinguished from a hundred others only by disgrace and controversy. A most unlikely source of challenge to the millennial plan. But Sven Osthorpe Blueheart had a reputation for flexibility and suppleness of wit, and while his eyes were light gray, and his hair salted black, he had the ruddy skin of an adaptive; his sport was distance swimming.

Rache had spoken of the primaries who loved the seas; here he would find out whether primaries could love the seas enough.

"This is a highly improper use of the mechanism."

Shock, Rache supposed, would elicit the baser bureaucratic reflexes. He said, patiently, "Any citizen can submit a request for planetwide discussion and referendum on a matter that impacts Blueheart as a whole; I have studied the procedures and criteria. I am in a position to follow the procedures, and I believe I can satisfy the criteria. This is of sufficient significance, and I believe there is sufficient interest."

By Teal's reckoning, fully fifty percent of access requests in the past few hours had drawn upon material directly related to adaptation, development, and the people most involved. How much personal communication concerned it, she could not tell. But she thought that the idea of keeping Blueheart unchanged was attracting intense excitement, if not yet well-reasoned support. That, Rache thought, was almost more than he had hoped for.

He said, "I intend therefore to make a formal request that the possibility of leaving Blueheart unmodified be discussed immediately, and I thought to do the development directorate the courtesy of advising them beforehand."

"None of the proposals under development are sufficiently well advanced to give guidance—"

"None of the proposals under development," Rache said, "are relevant."

There was a ringing silence. The man leaned forward slightly. "You really mean this," he said, in an ordinary voice.

"Yes."

"You are suggesting that we scrap all the development proposals—" Was that a little twang of glee in his rendering of "scrap"? "Yours included, and proceed . . ." He lifted his hands slightly from the null panels on his console, and let them settle again, his face reflecting dissatisfaction with all the ways he might finish that sentence.

"We already know," Rache said, more persuasively, "almost everything we need to know about Blueheart. We have the technology, and the expertise that we need to thrive: we have the planetary surveys, experience in habitat design, experience in adaptation. Numbers are irrelevant. We do not need to ensure sufficient skilled labor force, or to insure against casualties during terraforming. We have already proven that we can prosper here, in an unaltered environment. Why should terraforming be obligatory?" He caught his breath, feeling a warning tingling in his skin. "What I am asking for is the opening of public discussion of the possibility of preserving Blueheart as it is, a waterworld."

The representative shook his head slightly. "It behoves us, I suppose, to wonder what fresh audacities you might conceive of should you be denied."

His phrasing might be arch, but his tone and expression were grave. Rache said, "If by you, you mean the illegals, I cannot defend what they have done."

A slight smile. "But you will still use what they have done to your own ends." A statement, Rache thought, not a goad, and appreciative, if not approving.

"I will defend what they *are*," he said. "And yes, they and I have common goals."

"So your loyalties are to pastorals?"

"My loyalties are to Blueheart, and to all the inhabitants of Blueheart. Made to choose," since he could see the question already in the other's eyes, "made to choose . . . it would depend upon who was making me choose, and what the choice was. I regard it as my obligation to resist extremes. Moderation begets a certain inconsistency."

"The AOC's concern," the representative said, "is that you—or if not yourself, the pastoral isolationists— intend to continue on to germline adaptation."

"That is a possibility which will have to be discussed."

"But not one you have made explicit either in your own development proposal or in this request for a decision on Blueheart's future." The sentence came almost as an extension of his own; the representative had been prepared. "In fact, you are phrasing your request entirely in terms of terraforming or not terraforming."

"It is," Rache said, "the matter we are in a position to decide." The representative watched him with steady eyes. Rache was glad he did not sweat as primaries did, or he would, oceans' worth.

"I suspect the separation of the two may prove intractable." A slight pause, considering not what to say, but whether to say it. "You may find that there are those who might support Blueheart, but cannot find it in themselves to support pastorals, given your people's apparent indifference to settlement—"

"You will find," Rache said, grit in his voice, "if you examine the attributions in the survey databanks, that that is not so. Much of the detailed biological and ecological understanding has come from the observations of pastorals living in the seas."

"—and their illegal actions," Sven Osthorpe finished, as though uninterrupted.

"I appreciate that," said Rache, and tempered his tone with an effort. "But even if we fail, now, the possibility of leaving Blueheart as it is will have become a serious contender, and *I* contend that it will become an increasingly attractive one as the costs of terraforming are explored."

"Tell me this, Rache: why did you not come forward before? Why now, when numbers, as you say, are irrelevant? Why not twenty years ago, when Juniper Blane Berenice had such support . . . in her legitimate cause?"

"It took this," Rache said, "to make me think of it."

"A pity. I have never myself liked the idea of terraforming an established ecology. But I think you will find your case fatally contaminated." He paused, showing contained regret—and reproach, Rache thought—and then spoke with professional mien. "If the request passes through the appropriate stages, and is tabled as a matter of planetary concern, then I cannot see but that the development directorate must view it as seriously as one of its own. We will be obligated to make available all the information we would have made available during the planned deliberations—on the understanding, of course, that it is some thirty years shy of completion. And I suspect we shall confine ourselves merely to comment upon the development proposal for the planet and population, and leave all matters of adaptation and demographics to the AOC." He paused. "I shall try and impress it upon my fellow representatives and directors that a strict neutrality in so irregular and controversial a matter would be to our advantage. Particularly since I suspect the issue will be with us for another thirty years." A longer pause. "And, like yourself, what I myself would choose will depend upon who is making me choose, and what the choice is."

"I heard," said the director of survey, a few minutes later. A response of characteristic brevity. She was a small, round woman with rosewood-hued skin, a fortuitous blending of inborn pigmentation and adaptation, and, despite her age, eyes as blue as the summer seas. Appearance belied temperament; she was austere, economical of words, promises, and demonstrations. She only took one bite, but she had a bite like a lava eel.

She said, "I do not believe in reproaches after the fact. They serve no purpose. But I resent having to watch a man of your ability ruin himself."

"Ruining myself is not my intention."

"That makes it worse. The policy and obligations of the survey service are specified in our founding charter. We will serve, as we were intended to serve, as a resource, whatever our private convictions. We cannot dictate your convictions, or the use to which you put your education and experience. But you may not call upon survey resources to prosecute this insurrection of yours. As of now, you have only the rights of access of any private citizen. I understand you visited ringsol six two days ago. Such visits must cease."

Ringsol six, Rache thought. Inextricably entangled with the present, and already belonging to the remote past. Had he not been director of R6, he would not stand as he stood now. But then, had he not swum out to mourn Athene, he would never have found Lisel before she died and disintegrated in the sea. Destiny was a matter of place, and timing.

She was watching him, closely, her intense eyes unblinking. She was herself adapted; she had worked closely with adaptives and pastorals; his face would keep no secrets from her.

"You've been a damn fool."

"In many ways," he said, though he knew he and she would not agree in which. "May I ask . . . how they are doing?"

"Not well. Meredis Lopez was not your fault, but coming so soon after the disaster and you, it gutted them. Chandar's a good scientist, and we're reluctant to give him less than a fair chance as director, but we don't know if he has what ringsol six needs. He has eight or nine loyals working their hearts out for him, and we're holding the transfers for as long as we can."

If he thought he had felt her bite before, he had been greatly mistaken. He gathered himself and asked, "Will there be charges laid?"

He saw a flicker of unease cross her face. "The inquiry failed to turn up any consistent findings."

"Impossible," Rache said, before he thought, and saw her start slightly at the force of the assertion.

"Indeed," she said, "and what do you know?"

Rache made himself pause. Made himself think through that flicker of unease, and the anger which had answered it, an emotional interaction swifter than analysis. He said, "Was the investigation compromised by other interests?" He gave her no longer than a ready answer would have needed. "The AOC, perhaps?"

"Go on."

"The AOC was as concerned as the illegals that the young woman I found not be identified as an illegal adaptee."

"We were asked not to embarrass the AOC," she said, watching him.

Rache drew a deep breath. "Then the AOC owes you a courtesy," he said, his voice harsher than he meant. He gripped the chair arms, beneath the console. "I asked Cesar Kamehameha for amnesty for the illegals. Prosecution will create more conflict than it would serve justice. He refused."

"And you want me," she said, evenly, "to call in our

debt. Do you believe that the AOC could be sufficiently 'embarrassed' by the outcome of the inquiry that they would grant that amnesty?"

Rache hesitated, and lost his chance at the lie. She had asked him about the realities, and the realities were, no. Neither Karel de Courcey nor Teal could give a rigorous and unblemished testimony. Neither could touch Cesar, much less damage him, and they risked too much doing so.

"I see," she said, at last. "Then no, Rache."

And now, he thought, for the last. He requested uplink to the director of the AOC, and leaned back, trying for an illusion of unshakeable confidence. But when the screen shifted, it was Cybele de Courcey who looked out of the screen.

For a moment, neither spoke, each similarly taken aback. Then she leaned forward slightly, bracketing the console with her arms, conspiratorial, he thought, or possessive. He saw behind her the flat plane of glass, the fish like set jewels.

He said, "I thought to speak with the director."

"He is involved in a meeting. I have instructions to screen his contacts."

She looked desperately tired, haggard-faced, and bruised around the eyes. He caught himself before he expressed an inappropriate concern, but she saw the thought, and her eyes hardened. "What do you want?"

He said, "I thought to advise him that I was initiating the formal process to have the decision made on nonterraforming." She said nothing. "I have submitted a request that discussion and referendum on the matter be considered. I have little doubt that the necessary interest will be shown."

"You cannot win," Cybele said, flatly.

"You do not know that," Rache said, "any more than do I."

"The AOC," Cybele said, "is about to announce a complete moratorium on human adaptation, until the investigations are complete. And I—I have just begun compiling a list of people known to be genetic parents or caretakers of illegally adapted children. Those on that list will be charged with abuse of the children in their care."

She had spoken quickly, and when she stopped, she was breathing fast and shallowly, color like an unhealthy rash across her cheekbones.

"Should you be telling me this?"

She reared back slightly; whatever she had expected it was not such a question, in so mild a tone. "There's nothing you can do about it."

That might be so, but while Cesar Kamehameha might know that, he would not wish Rache to have the chance to do anything about it, even to prepare himself. She would surely suffer were Cesar to learn that she had given Rache this chance. Tove would have mocked his absurd tenderheartedness toward the young. But they were not anyone's young; they were Adam de Courcey's, and he knew her haggard young face would haunt him. "It may cause trouble for you."

A brilliant bitterness lit her eyes. "That's my concern. And God's." And she was gone. On a red background, the tri-dimensional caduceus-helix hung in space, the ancient symbol of medicine mated with that of the genetic engineers.

He thought about her while he completed his submission to planetary arbitration. Of what she had said, what she had done, and that extraordinary flash in her eyes as she spoke of her God. Michael would have understood far better than he. For himself, he wondered whether Cesar Kamahameha understood what he harbored.

He paused a moment before he dispatched his submission, looking for uncertainty in himself. Trepidation he found, but no uncertainty, even at the thought of losing the future to Einar and his extremists. The lack unsettled him. He remembered one other such time: when he left Scole with Juniper. He had gone without uncertainty, without remorse, without seeing anything but Juniper, and the future. He had certainly never foreseen what would come of it. And had he foreseen, would he have done otherwise?

He heard a quiet, synthesized voice say, "Submission received and acknowledged." He looked down, at his right hand, which now rested on the touchscreen over the dispatch icon, broad, red, passive. He did not know when in his reverie it had moved.

"So?" said Lisel, as he came out of the booth. She was slouching against the door to the next booth, tall, red-skinned, daunting; he rather suspected that that booth had gone unused as long as she stood against it. The far wall was paneled with screens, the length of it, showing scenes of the pastoral shantytowns on the docks. She returned a passerby's glance with a scowl, and said in a low voice, "Everyone knows who we are, but nobody speaks."

"Rafttown etiquette," Rache said. "It's extremely impolite to approach in person someone you know about, but have never made personal contact with." She looked skeptical. He said, "It is a way of managing the fact that so much of ourselves goes into public domain. It limits imposition."

She grunted, and let the subject be. "Have you done it?"

"I have."

He steered her outside by the nearest door, onto a broad promenade which overlooked the end of the docks. She shaded her eyes against the setting sun, and leaned forward to study the gathering. Late sunlight gilded her, warm gold on dark, warm skin, highlighting head, arms, breasts. He did not hear what she said next, and not because it was taken by the breeze. She repeated it, with a sharp, mock-irritable nudge. "I *said*, 'What next?'"

Below them, the pastorals were beginning to settle for the night, as best they could. The earliest arrivals had complained of nights disturbed by the lights playing upon their tents, by the omnipresent music, by the murmurs of curious passersby. They were accustomed to the immense, spangled darkness over the ocean, which would be brushed aside only a little by the fluorors, and to the murmurous quiet of the sea. They were accustomed to the faces and habits of family and raft or holdfast kin, and such visitors as had been welcomed and introduced. They were not patient with his explanations of the whys of rafttown life. He would have to see if he could do something about the lights.

"My submission will be posted, and if enough people indicate that they think it is worthy of discussion at this point, then it will be formally entered—"

"And Blueheart will be preserved?" Lisel said.

"No," he said, hiding impatience. He had explained this before, to her, to Tove, to Einar, to others. "Acceptance of the submission opens discussion and *starts* the process toward decision."

"You said yourself, we know what we need to know. What is there to discuss?"

"As far as I am concerned, nothing."

She tilted her head slightly. "I'm annoying you."

"You're wearing me out, arguing about what you understand and I can't change."

She turned her head, looking grimly up, into the eye of a camera. "Isn't there anywhere we can be alone? I'm worn out with arguing with you, too."

"Yes," he said, and understood something of what had brought the flash to Cybele's eyes, pure anger at the terms of service, whether to God or humankind. "But I . . . we can't. Things . . . are going to start happening quickly now."

They returned to the docks in time to walk into a quarrel. At its white heart were Einar, and Ayna's mother, Aile; she standing with Ayna pressed to her, saying, ". . . I never fooled myself that you were faithful. I did think you had a certain amount of cleverness. You were certainly clever enough in getting me to forgive you getting my cousin pregnant before *I* even gave birth."

"It has nothing to do with you . . ."

Lisel was staring across at the trio with an expression of sour enlightenment. Catching his eye, she lifted her hand to her chin and pointed, a small, secretive movement. He did not see, at first; he was too busy being relieved that she did not resent his rejection. He recognized Noelle, and Noelle's mother, Tris, Ayna's cousin. He saw Tove, looking on with disdainful irritation. But then Tove had always prided herself in having done with one partner before taking up with another; she had said so to Rache. Einar had never had such restraint; he clung to whatever he had, and grasped at whatever he could have. In love, he behaved with the greed of a starving man. Something, some sense of satiety, of sufficiency, had always been missing; that, neither Rache nor Lisel had been able to give him.

It seemed to Rache that memory shaped an image, of Einar as a small child, a little boy of perhaps four, perched alertly in a woman's arms, watching his elders round-eyed. But the mother was not Keri, not Lisel, not anyone he knew, and he could still hear Einar's adult voice. He looked from the child to the man, and back to the child, confirming that they were together in time and reality. And then he looked again at the mother, recognizing her an illegal, come with the most recent arrivals. She was very young, and as proud as Tove, her expression an assertion of immunity. She would never stand where Aile stood, shout as Aile shouted; she would never need to; he would never leave her.

Einar's face was dark with humiliation. He knew as well as did the listeners that this was jealousy speaking, but a jealousy as agile and chameleonlike as an illusionfish, which would feint, and feint again, and would not be trapped. Aile, for one of the few times in their life, had the verbal advantage. She was saying, ". . . consider your daughter, whom you purport to love . . ." And Ayna, thus cued, turned dewy eyes up to her father. Her small face was angry and excited; the tears in her eyes quite real.

Lisel breathed in Rache's ear, "If he'd just give in . . ."

"He won't," Rache murmured back. "Did you know?"

"I've not been long back in these waters. I'd have expected it, though, knowing Einar." Her voice was a little bleak. "It's not the women he loves, Rache, it's the children; they're the ones whose love he trusts."

Bedevere was whispering urgently to Tove, appealing, Rache thought, her intervention; unusual from Bedevere. It was Rache, and Lisel, who had defended Einar in the past, while Bede and Keri regarded their difficult son from an uneasy remove. But that past, their past, was long ago.

Tove lifted her head from their conference and looked past the quarreling couple, directly at him. *"Enough!"* she said, forcefully. "This is unseemly before kin, never mind outcomers. And we have larger concerns to occupy us. Bedevere tells me that the AOC have stopped *all* adaptations. They are moving against the illegals' centers, and they are intending to prosecute those they can identify as caretakers of illegally adapted children for child abuse."

"They have just announced it," said Bedevere, impassively.

Aile caught Einar's arm. "Ask your father how it is to be the child of someone charged with abuse!"

He jerked away, and his eye caught Rache's. "You," he shouted. "You said we'd be safe if we all came together."

There was a shift in the gathering, an opening out around Einar, who strode forward, his color still high, to confront them. "It's not *his* fault," Aile said, making a last bid for Einar's attention, which went unheeded. The people who had been grouped around her moved to encircle Rache, Lisel, and Einar, leaving her behind. Tears shone suddenly in her eyes. Ayna squirmed free, evading Aile's reach, darted up to her half-brother, snatched at his foot—Rache did not see what she did, but the child squealed—and squirmed away through the crowd. Noelle scrambled after.

Rache said, "I never promised you safety. I wanted

us to be taken seriously, and we have been."

"You're saying this is good?" Einar said, with bright incredulity.

Tris caught Aile's arm, pointing after their children, speaking urgently. Aile shook her head, her face downcast. Tris let go her arm, threw it down, her face sharp with contempt.

"I think," Rache said, choosing his words carefully, aware of where he stood and who might be listening, "that the AOC may find their right to decide how adaptation is to be used, for whom, and for what purpose, is called into question." He saw Tris walking quickly toward the exit through which the children had gone, and looked around for Astrid, thinking she should not go alone . . .

"So, this is about your political ambitions."

Rache turned on the man who had spoken, a cousin his own age from Scole. "This is about Blueheart's future. This is about preserving the seas as they are, and preserving ourselves as we choose to be."

Einar slipped between them, and laid a hand lightly on the other's shoulder. Rache glanced back at the exit; Tris was already gone, bravely into the gaudy, unknown night. Aile stood with slumped shoulders, deep shame on her face. Painfully, Rache shook off the distractions and turned his attention back to the argument.

"We're not helpless," Einar was saying. The other pulled away, his face showing what he thought of Einar's impertinence, or the conspiracy. Einar drew back his hand, his face guarded, then he slanted a slow, triumphant look toward Rache. "We have our own resources. We have people among us who have the knowledge to adapt our own, and whom we can trust. *Let* the AOC withhold its services: *we* do not need them."

On Lisel's face, Rache saw his own dismay. He should have taken them aboard, where they were not being monitored, every word. He had thought an open deliberation would earn them more support, or more understanding, at least, than retirement. He had misjudged. He saw the knowing glance that Einar gave him, and knew that Einar at least had not forgotten Rache's explanation. His word had been as deliberate as Rache's. He was bent on confrontation, whether with Rache, or with the unseen authorities aboard Rossby.

"I think not."

Bedevere's voice. Bedevere who had stood silently on the periphery, watching and letting no one, except maybe Keri, know his mind. "I, at least, will not do this."

Across Einar's face moved shock, betrayal, defensive cynicism. Bedevere said quietly, "You do not know what you ask."

"Did I ever?" Einar returned, as quietly.

Bede flinched, and Einar smiled slightly; and Bede straightened, looking his son in the eye. Slow-kindling anger lit him from within. "You would be well advised not to promise what is *not* yours to offer." He shifted his eyes from his son to, briefly, Rache, and then moved them slowly across the gathering.

"*I* am one of those experts to whom Einar refers, and I tell you now, I will *not* be involved in any aspect of unauthorized adaptation. I urge those of you who have been so adapted to present yourself for monitoring. And I will argue, with whatever influence and authority I have, against any punishment." Rache glanced over faces; they were guarded, with the beginnings of resentment. They had been promised too much, given too little. Bede saw it too, he mitigated his tone. "I should say who I am. I am Bedevere of Scole, and I had a sister, Athene. Athene died of an undetected defect in her adaptation—which was authorized but had been poorly followed up—and my mother Astrid was charged as some of you have been charged, with failing in her responsibility to her child. But the guilt was not hers alone. None among her fellows and elders had encouraged her to keep the necessary appointments. Why upset the children, they said; why put them in an environment so unfamiliar, so frightening?" He paused, visibly gathering himself, though Rache thought he did not so much search for words as try to hold them back. A man who prided himself on his fairness and reason moved to anger. Immersed in his own mourning, angry at and rejected by his own kin, Rache had never thought that Bedevere, too, might have deeply felt Athene's death. Deeply enough that he would let it guide his life. Bedevere said, "Adaptation is not something to be lightly undertaken. There are risks; even with careful monitoring there are unforseen side effects. But that is not the heart of it."

He spoke more slowly, thinking out each phrase. "The heart of it is this. Your bodies are not counters on a scale. Your bodies are not political tokens. You might say," and there was for the first time the edge of the arrogance which Rache well knew, "that you might do as you please with your own bodies. I say you may not. Your bodies are *not* purely yours; they are your children's, and your children's children's; they are your holdfast's, or your tribe's; they are Blueheart's, as well. You cannot use the manipulation of the human form to serve the ends of the moment. Juniper Blane Berenice was wrong to use you so, you are wrong to use yourselves so, and the AOC is wrong to meet you on your terms."

"So you think we should throw ourselves on the mercy of the AOC?" Einar said, bitterly.

There was a silence, as son looked at father, father at son, across a narrow space and years of friction, misunderstanding, and disappointment. Bedevere said, "Yes, I do." He glanced at Astrid, who was standing, like him, on the docks edge. She did not welcome the attention. She looked awkward, resentful, though she tried to hide both; and when she shook her head, she did so grudgingly.

She would not have spoken, but Einar said, "Astrid knows," and she brought her head up with a flash of black eyes.

"Be still, and let your elders speak." Having spoken, she set her stance more firmly, and said, "It would be unwise to throw yourselves on the mercy of an authority you have so resoundingly challenged." Fierce, hunter's eyes shifted from one to the other; Rache wondered, for the first time, if he himself was capable of that look. "You yourselves chose to swim this gyre. You cannot blame its force, or its ending, on Rache."

"It was not our choice," someone said.

"You think not?" Astrid said. She had reached back to clench her hand on the stock of her speargun, and the strap, hanging loose across her chest, trembled barely perceptibly. But there was no tremor whatsoever in her voice. "We have all challenged authority. We have lived as we pleased, in defiance of our part in the settlement plan. But, until now, it has not mattered. We have not mattered. Our defiance changed nothing. In a hundred years, we will no longer exist. Our culture, our traditions, our history, our skills . . . our creation, will be eradicated." She paused; her hand slid from the stock of the speargun. Rache realized he had not drawn breath since she had begun to speak. He did not breathe now.

"If we do nothing," Astrid said, "we are doomed. No matter how obedient we are, no matter how law-abiding we are, we are doomed. If we lose, the AOC will have no mercy on us. Why should they: we have declared ourselves their enemies, simply by insisting upon our right to exist and to have children like our-selves. Faintheartedness has no place here."

"So what do we do?" said someone.

Rache said, "I have submitted a request that a development plan for Blueheart that does not involve terraforming be considered. It is the first step toward the preservation of the seas, as we know them. What we must do, each and every one of us, is register our inter-est in that deliberation. All that that requires is twenty-five percent of the population, and we have the numbers for that. I realize that there are many of you who know little about popular decision-making; you need only ask myself, or one of the pastoral-liaisons." He paused, at the sounds of a struggle and raised voices on the docks edge.

The crowd heaved, knotted, and split, to show a furious Maria of Kense being forced inward by three others. Daven, on her left, started to speak, but she pitched her weight against him, throwing him off bal-ance, and pulling free. "I can speak for myself," she said. Flung her head back, breathing harshly for a moment, the cords of her neck standing out. The medusa scar across her blinded eye flared red. "I see no purpose," she said, "in letting others swim into the same trap."

Daven burst out, "She was going out to the boomer-relay, to tell everyone else not to come."

Rache heard a ripple pass through the gathering, as

of agreement. It would take only one, he realized, with dismay; one from any of the docks, one who might already have left, unimpeded, or even encouraged.

"It's no trap," Lisel said. "It is what we need to do."

"*What* . . . deliver ourselves to the AOC, or wait until they come to take us? They will not look for us in the seas . . ."

"No," Astrid said. "They will not. They will not need to: they will have achieved everything they wished; they will have rendered our numbers irrelevant if we do not stay to be counted. We have come as far as we can on our own terms. We have made our choice; we already know that we can live with the seas. The primaries have not. This development proposal is how they will learn, and decide. We must submit to their way, *honor* it, even. *We must stay.* We must be numbered, each and every one of us. If we leave, if the proposal goes unsupported, then we fail the future to serve ourselves."

"They are charging us with child abuse!" said the mother of Einar's son.

Astrid looked steadily at her. "You will survive. Rehabilitation was the making of me, though in ways unintended. And you will be far from alone, given your numbers. *I* was alone. So do not bleat to me about your fears of punishment. This is a hunt, and there is danger in it. But there is also a great prize to be had."

"Isn't she splendid?" Lisel breathed in Rache's ear.

Rache nodded, and said, "Any charges laid against you will not affect your voting status. You can still support the proposal."

Einar stooped suddenly, and lifted his son into his arms. He slid one hand behind the woman's back, and guided her forward. Her face showed her struggle with uncertainty and pride; he presumed only on the pride. His voice carried, clear and confident. "Show us what we must do."

"In a moment," Rache said. To Maria of Kense, "It is only fair that people come warned of the risks. Would you send such a message? Tell them why we need them, need their numbers, and tell them also the measures taken against us." She gave him a scowling nod, jerked her right arm free and thrust her way back toward the edge of the docks. A spotlight caught her as she dived, lighting her emerald green on a shining sea, and then the pastorals closed about him.

"Wise," murmured Lisel. Rache nodded again. His appeal and granting of leave would be spread through the seas, if not by her, then by others. She nudged him gently, and said, "You do have your moments. So, show us."

Teal tracked the children. Two small, bareskinned fugitives, flitting from corner to corner and shadow to shadow, rapidly outdistancing the woman behind them. One child led, the other followed. The one leading was the child who had snared Teal's attention with her small cruelty, something sharper, brighter, than the adult dramatics before it. Those, she had seen too often to trust. But the child, the child was a primer of emotion, and one Teal thought she once upon a time might have read, or written. She let lapse the other channels she had been monitoring, her therapy; she eased away from her surveys of law and protocol, her obligation. And through the cameras, she followed the children.

They moved as though accustomed to hiding,

between the lights, using corners. They crouched; they scurried; their wide, dark, furtive eyes widened and fixed at still wonders and sudden movements. Drawing closer, closer, Teal could see, within their narrow chests, their hearts beat. In the diffuse light outside the spotlights, their skin was warm and dark. Each rib showed as a glossy curve as it moved. Their shifting, trembling eyes held shaven spotlights.

She remembered the ruins beyond the edge of the enclave, ruins from the first years of settlement, and as old as time. They were hers by day, under the sun's exposition, devoid of mysteries; she studied them with an archaeologist's eyes. And Juniper's by night, when shadow made the simplest step uncertain, and the barest sound monstrous. Day by day, she uncovered them, probing the planetary net for an accounting. Night by night, Juniper reburied them, each night's story contradicting the last. These children were like Juniper, night children. Or the one leading was. The follower was more hesitant, more questioning. And as Teal had Juniper, the lagging child's resistance fired the leader on.

It was as though she watched herself and Juniper. She was quite aware of what she saw, and the memories which came were imprecise, indistinct; she could have put neither words nor images to them. But what she had, what the sight of the children evoked, was an impression. A whisper of sand in the wind, a coarseness of rock against her ankle, the fold of veils crossing her face. The words, the images, she could have recalled: she had been implanted so young, and stored so much. But the feelings, the impressions she had thought lost, until now. Passing from camera to camera, she followed the children into the labyrinth.

They kept outside, to the promenades. They

watched, through windows, the long screens which showed their elders filing to declare themselves. While the minority who would not declare themselves struck their tents, packed their canoes and yachts, and struck out across the dappled bay, for the darkened sea. They were mesmerized, and would have watched longer, but that they were seen. With a flashing of dark red legs, they ran, turned the corner, and in a fumbled transition between cameras, she lost them.

She found them again, on an open ramp off the main concourse, which wound in slow, converging angulations, all the way to the top of a pyramidal block. They had gone far enough to realize they had left behind the sea; they were hanging onto the railing, looking over; their toes curled over the edge, seeking the water below. The leader hesitated; the lagger reasoned, obedient, childish reason. The leader twitched, stiffened, her whole body caught by impulse. Teal remembered, remembered standing beside that impulse. Remembered the electric energy and the twinge of fear. She knew, before the lagging child did, that the other was not going back. And if not to go back, she must go up, then up, up! She ran for the high corner, and hung onto the edge of the railing, panting, looking back with a smile which dared. The second started up, still complaining, wheedling. The first ducked out of sight. Teal split her vision, watching the first hiding, panting, waiting; the second wavering and then cracking, running up toward the corner, crying out, "Ayna, Ayna." But by the time she had reached the corner, Ayna was gone, rounding the next corner, bouncing hips off the wide silver railing.

The lagging child stopped. Sat down, squatting with her back against the wall. She stared straight ahead, aware, Teal was certain, of the small, round head which peered around at her. I'm not going any further. Oh, Noelle . . . No, I'm not. Then I'm going all the way to the top, *alone*. Disappear with a flounce. Knowing, of course, knowing all the time, that this is but a ritual, that her partner, her mirror, her other half, must come.

At the summit, quarrels forgotten, they looked around in wonder. Higher than they had ever been, they gazed up at the inner towers of Rossby, out at the light-daubed bays, down at the docks, across at walkways and balconies, long windows, and screens. They ran from corner to corner, along edge and edge, bathed their hands in the railing lights, threw handfuls of air seaward with all their strength. Would have climbed upon the railings, but for the net's spoken warning; the ethereal voice froze them, huge-eyed. They turned at the laughter of a quartet of primary children who had come upon them unseen.

The children ran as outlaws, and Teal followed, her awareness shifting effortlessly from camera to camera overhead. She watched the antagonism, like lines of flame, between Ayna and the eldest of the primaries, a boy named Ingmar. They were a little too much alike, in their bragging, in their swagger, in their need for followers. Their exploits grew wilder, their eyes brighter: he had been to γ Serpens IV, on a terraforming survey mission; *she* had sailed, with her grandmother Astrid, up to the Northern seas; *his* father was a representative of the development directorate; *her* father and her uncle were leaders of the pastorals who would keep Blueheart a waterworld. They stood face to face, on a walkway lit with luminous globes, the black-haired boy, and the red-faced, smaller girl: Blueheart would never stay a water-world. Blueheart *would*. People *weren't* meant to live in the seas. People were, and could, and did; she could do everything he could do, and more. She was so stupid she didn't know about the warning systems; he was so stupid he did not know about the seas.

The other children drew away a little, together, daunted by the struggle, afraid to be drawn in, reluctant to move away.

She'd prove it to him, she would.

Would she?

He turned, and the rest followed, and Teal followed them, sensing something familiar, dangerous. A fossil feeling, rank as the living.

They stopped on the mouth of a narrow canal. He pointed along it, but stayed her as she would have moved around the corner, indicating the cameras, laughing at her. She set hands on hips, and faced him. The other three primaries watched, silently.

He said, Swim that.

It's dangerous, one of the others said.

She won't get past the sensors, he said. She can't go that deep, or stay down that long; it's too complicated for her. He leaned over to her, talking in a conspiratorial voice, pointing out where she must swim, and where dive. She listened, her head tilted slightly, her small mouth firm. He asked her if she had understood; she said, yes. He smiled, a little superiorly. She pulled away from him, pulled away from Noelle, who, at the last moment, reached for her, and dived neatly into the water. Teal split her screen, and scanned for the public channels carrying the underwater surveillance.

She rattled through the images, framed the swimming child, closing upon the wilful, intelligent face so unlike and yet so reminiscent of Juniper. She wove through the water, diving and surfacing, bellying along the bottom, skimming beneath the surface so nearly that her shoulders rippled its underside. Along the walkway, the other children moved with her. There was, Teal noticed, no ornamental vegetation along the channel bottom; it did not run between the great platforms supporting Rossby, but across one of them. She watched Ayna scull against the wall, sliding around in a slow arc beneath an eye, sought the eye's ident, and did not find it. She reviewed what she had seen, and found a pattern to Ayna's swimming, one which evaded a series of mounted underwater cameras, cameras which were identified as part of the underwater traffic control and safety. She recognized the codes: she had seen their like on interstellar ships, vacuum colonies, settlement domes . . . And on the screen, Ayna suddenly stopped, and hovered in the water, uncertain. Above the water, the children froze in horror, and then hung over the railing, screaming down at her. Beyond them, Teal saw a slow wave, and a hulking shadow.

She was not aware of putting words to her realization. Words would have been far too slow. A single image came and went in a millisecond, of the child being borne down upon by the blind mechanical. She plunged into the net, ripping ruthlessly through to the navigation control, abandoning all discretion and courtesy. She found the input circuit, nearly bypassed it for the control algorithm, in all the arrogance of an accomplishment which was no longer hers to claim. She could no longer be sure she could analyze and alert the algorithm at source. She dragged the image of the child from the public camera, thrust it into the information stream, followed it down, as the witless slow algorithm finished a surveillance cycle and began afresh; and then the outputs changed, the alarms were sent—she could have designed far better, she thought. She had no idea how much time had passed in the world outside. She followed the alarms, up through overrides and rechecks—and she saw in horror that the system identified the origin codes of her image and disallowed it as public input. She jammed the image back into the input stream, stripping it of public codes, saw it admitted; and then everything lit red from outside, and the system closed her channels, thrust her out.

To look at blankness where the public underwater channel had been, and the faces of children white with shock. Powerful lights shone directly down into the water. Showed the long flank of the submarine as it lay obliquely across the channel. Showed the swirl of hands and faces within its windows. Showed, from behind the sub's distal fin, the slow blooming, deep in the water, of a darkness whose hue Teal could name with her guts, her heart, her blood.

SIXTEEN

In morning sunlight, before the eyes of their world, Scole holdfast prepared its dead child for the sea, wrapping her in weeds harvested from the ornamental grottos of Rossby. There had been no undoing what childish mischief, childish ignorance, and gross metal had done; Ayna had been crushed into oblivion between the sub's fin and the canal walls, and like Adam, no medicine known to Blueheart could restore her as herself.

Since she was so very young, regeneration was an option, an option rejected by her father, her grandmother, and the elders of Scole. She was dead; she could not be brought back; she would be given to the sea.

Rache had argued for her, aware that Aile was too devastated to reason, and Einar gripped with a revulsion against all things primary. But he had argued alone, alienating his kin. Lisel had kept silent, and Rache had fallen silent when he found that his own arguments ceased to make sense, even to him. There was no way back from this.

So Ayna lay on the docks, her crushed body restored to some semblance of the shape, if not the color, of life, and they shrouded her with the most muted of the brightly colored transgenics from Rossby's gardens. Einar, kneeling, looked up at Astrid, who stood with her hands full of fresh-cut dripping strands. "You said,

'Wait until you have swum the hardest swim of all.' Do you remember? When we went out for lava eel." His tone was lucent with pain; it hurt Rache to hear.

Astrid crouched and laid her hands over Einar's. "Oh, my dear," she said. "I remember." She closed her hands gently on his. "I would never have wished this on you."

"You said, 'Wait until'. You never said, 'If.'"

Astrid looked into his face for a long moment, and wordlessly shook her head. It was what she had said. She had never allowed that Einar would be spared. She put into his hands the weeds which would cover his daughter's face, and slid her hands beneath the child's head, sparing him the pulped feel of it. Her expression was hollow, emptied of emotion, as she let him bind her hands to Ayna's head. Bind and bind, with slow, stunned movements, until she laid her burden down, freed her hands, with a little struggle, and held his again until they were still.

Bedevere and Keri stepped forward with the ropes, and began to tie a net around the shrouded body. They worked around their son, and Bedevere's mother, not touching either.

Tove stood at Ayna's feet, watching the preparations with an austere, exacting eye. It was she who had ruled Rossby's weeds suitable, despite their unnatural colors, she who had insisted that they wrap her here, she who deemed that they should do exactly as their tradition demanded, be exactly what they were. Ayna was their child and would be sea-gifted as she deserved, no matter how barbaric primary sensibilities deemed it. She was one of the few who remembered the cameras. Everyone else was drawn into themselves with grief. And all along Rossby docks, the screens were blanked.

Bedevere and Keri tied the last knot, coiled the long tow cables and laid them down beside Einar and Astrid. They looked up at Tove, and Tove nodded satisfaction. She said, "Einar, it is time."

Einar did not raise his eyes. He was not looking at his daughter's shrouded face, or at Astrid's hand, but into some other, better place. And Rache saw, with sudden dread, that if there were such a place, he might never come back. He stepped forward; and Einar, recognizing the step, or glimpsing the alien blue and black, looked up suddenly with hatred in his eyes. "*You* cannot come," he said.

Rache, scalded by the hatred, could not reply.

Tove said, after a long, deliberate silence, "He is still of Scole, Einar. He is your father's brother. I say he comes." She looked at Rache, letting him appreciate her largesse. "But he comes as a man of Scole."

His wits dulled with fatigue and grief, Rache did not grasp what she meant. They were all watching him, some, he saw, mistaking his incomprehension for refusal, and already in their minds turning from him. Tove had no mercy in her; if he did not understand, it was a judgment on him. It was Bedevere who cued him with a slight, subtle motion, reaching one hand across to the other to pluck at a phantom cuff on his own naked wrist. And Rache remembered the uniform. There was some reason, he thought, that he had worn it, maybe should wear it still. He saw Bede's eyes darken, as Bede, too, thought he hesitated. He looked down at the pastel weave of Ayna's shroud, and his thoughts and heart were empty. He waited for his hands to move, as they had moved to send the message. But they did not. It seemed to take a supreme act of will, and strength, to raise his arms, pull the vest over his head, and the pants down over his hips. They watched him, with flat, grieving, and hostile eyes, until he stood naked, an offering to the sea.

"How can you stand this?" Karel de Courcey breathed.

On the screen, Rache stepped heavily away from his discarded uniform, his thick body looking raw beneath the noonday sun. The haughty old woman standing at the dead child's feet gestured, and her father took her head, the sinewy woman her shoulders, and two others her hips and feet. Teal did not answer Karel; it was not the time. Instead, prompted by some ancient impulse, she got to her feet and stood while they laid Ayna on the centerboard of the tainu and climbed, one by one, into position. When the members of Scole holdfast had boarded, the others did likewise, until the docks were empty of people. Their tents still stood, rippling slightly in the breeze. The tainu cast off; the paddles bit; it sheered away from the docks. Others spread out behind it, flanking it, tainu, outriggers, sea-kayaks, rigged boats powered by oar. Bare backs moved in their labor like waves. The wind rippled Ayna's shroud. On the docks, Rache's uniform sleeve flipped, a feeble gesture for attention. Teal remained standing until the flotilla had passed beyond the barriers. Then she sat down, and remembered Karel's question.

He had not risen; he was sitting beside her, knees drawn to chest, watching the screen with a sickly fascination. She felt a little irritation: this was not his tragedy. "What is there to stand?"

"You were there. You could . . . You couldn't . . . you didn't . . ." He could not finish his thought, though she believed she knew what it was. He held her in an awe which she found oppressive, arising as it did from remorse rather than respect. He treated her like someone too fragile to be crossed, rather than too vital. She did not care for the distinction.

"Save her," she extrapolated, a little curtly, and saw him cringe. She said, "I did everything that was within my power to save her."

"You were *watching*!" he said, he accused. "You watched her all the way. You saw her dive into that canal."

She thought about him, about them, about the tone he used. She had an idea, but she did not trust it. Nevertheless, she extended herself, into his thoughts. "You think I should torment myself with my failures?" And in her own voice, "To what purpose? I was not responsible. I am nearly as ignorant as she was of Rossby." Her informational download had gone with her cercortex.

He snatched back his hands. "I think," he said, quite precisely, nearly spitting, "you have a dead soul."

That hurt, surprisingly keenly, even though she was not sure what exactly he meant. She knew better than to ask him, or to uplink immediately and explore possible meanings. Which left her nothing else but silence; and almost immediately he said, stricken, "I'm sorry. *Sorry.*" He clutched at her hands, and she let him, though she did not return his grip. She sought a way to explain herself which was not redundant, but he knew what she was.

He blurted, "If you hadn't been erased, you might have saved her."

The logic was opaque. She stared at him, without regard for his discomfort, puzzling it out. It did not fit, until she reminded herself what she knew of him and his excruciatingly tender conscience. He meant that if he had not created his erasure routines and left them for Cesar Kamehameha to use, then Teal might have saved Ayna. Was it youth or religiosity or temperament which made him so self-centered? She said, "The emergency evasion algorithm in the sub was not designed for such confines. The system relied upon the underwater monitoring to ensure the canal was clear of obstacles. When the emergency evasion algorithm was given priority over the steering algorithm, the submarine went out of control and collided extensively with walls and base. That resulted in her death." Fact, she saw, was not what he needed. But it was all she had. She turned to face him, directly. "I have analyzed," she said, "a number of disasters arising from system failure. There is nothing to do in these cases but learn, and use what one has learned. If you think it is painful to feel the burden of the unforeseen, think what it is to feel the burden of repeated disaster."

He swallowed. "I hear you," he said, huskily. "But don't you feel—anything?"

The question slid, humbly, into Teal's heart, and despite herself, she remembered the color of that cloud in the water. She felt a shaft of phantasm pain, so keen as to make her gasp. She measured what she felt now against what she would have felt had she been able to save the child, and realized that the distance was vast. For half her life, record had substituted for memory, preserving it painlessly, perfectly. What she did not wish to remember, she erased. But this, this would be with her always. "Yes," she said, huskily. "I feel." And turned away from him, toward the screen, clearing away the subdued and empty sea with a thought.

"I'm sorry," he said.

She lifted her eyes, but kept her profile to him. "Why? I do not wish to be what I was before. And before, I would not have felt."

After a while, she heard him leave. She paused in her work, reminding herself that the house's system was monitoring him, and would warn her if he tried to do himself harm. And then she remembered how the monitoring algorithms had failed Ayna.

She found him sitting in the tiled bay, trailing a hand in the water, his face morose. He looked up, a startled, guilty expression on his face. She walked over, and sat down beside him. The water was most diverting; unlike the sea, its ripples were subtle, simple. They sat side by side, watching the wavelets he made.

He said, "She was such a little girl."

"Yes."

"They could have brought her back."

She said nothing. Their reasons for not doing so needed no explanation, not by her.

Karel said, "It's all coming apart."

She touched the net, glancing over the polling algorithms she, Karel, and Michael had assembled to sample opinion. "Not so," she said. "It is still uncertain."

He shook his head. She drew breath to argue, and then forbore. His judgment might be the truer. He was Blueheart-born, and he had sensitivities she lacked.

"You could do something."

"About what?"

"About all of this. About Blueheart. The pastorals." A slight pause. "Juniper was your sister."

"You think," she said, slowly, "I have some obligation to intervene simply because my sister was the author of this. Or I have some power to intervene because I am my sister's twin. Would my intervention not be as reprehensible as hers?"

He said nothing. She took the moment to dip into the news-streams and the infostreams. What she perceived troubled her. People who had expressed their support for Rache had withdrawn it. Their argument, that Ayna's needless death indicated the need for integration of pastorals. The AOC list was continuing to lengthen, though no offensive had yet come of it. Rache's proposal was undergoing scrutiny befitting of a full development proposal, and being judged quite unequal to it. She was not sensitive to language, but several of Michael's algorithms were, and they showed the language of argument was hardening, moving toward rhetoric.

She stood, and went over to the console in the tiled bay. She had almost forgotten he was there when he spoke from behind her. "What are you doing?"

It should have been apparent from a parallel query, and a little reasoning on his part. He had certainly visited Juniper's gallery often enough. "Unfinished work," Teal said. "She released it to me."

"You're adding unfinished work to her gallery?"

"*I* could not finish it."

There was a slightly pained silence. "If she had not finished, would she want it shown?"

"That does not matter," Teal said. She felt him tense at her shoulder, and waited for what he might next say, but he did not speak. She turned in her chair, to face him with the plain, ungiving gaze she used upon the obtuse and the obstructive. "I cannot finish it, as she would have finished it. I could not even have begun it, as she began it. This is the best I can do: to put her thinking before the people who want to know what her mind and thinking was then, when she did what she did."

But that was not the truth entire. She was giving them Juniper, Juniper's unfinished work, so as to be spared giving them herself. She could have told them what she knew about Juniper, and what she believed Juniper might have meant, but she had grown averse to accounting for Juniper. Let Juniper account for herself, in the drafts, sketches, and scraps preserved from her last years. But of course, she did not. She would not. Juniper had preserved very little of her own thought, her internal life. She was the director, standing beyond the frame, and they all the players, trapped within. Teal said, "Most of her personal records were erased upon her death, by prior request."

"I didn't know she had kept personal records."

"The request was challenged on the basis that as an artist her personal records should be retained as part of Blueheart's cultural heritage. The challenge failed."

"Do you think this will help?" He pointed at the screen, a lush montage in green and blue.

"That, I do not know."

"You disapprove of what she did," he said, and there was no question in his voice. He had the reputation of flightiness; he had alluded to it himself, and certainly his deeds had been irresponsible where not unlawful. But flightiness and irresponsibility now clung in tatters to a fragile, steely morality. His "disapprove" had a force beyond mere priggishness.

"I dislike lawlessness," she said.

He said, quite pitifully, "I have a sister, too."

"We have met."

"What did you think of her?"

She had thought little, because she knew little. A scented and veiled stranger, who made claims on her; Rache's Fury; and keeper, willingly or unwillingly, of

Karel's conscience. The last she understood better than she liked.

She said, "I think you should take back from her what is yours. No matter how much she wants it, or you want her."

Karel flushed beneath his olive skin. Teal studied him, thinking it a revealing response; and then it occurred to her he might have misconstrued. "You want her to think well of you," she said, starkly. "You fear her wrath. But even more, you fear her distance. You give her parts of yourself that you should not. Common genetic endowment is simply a tendency. Juniper and I committed the same error. We assigned it a spiritual significance. Biology is simply biology. We would have been no more, or less, related in the flesh had we been separated at birth. You feel no such ties to me, nor I to you, despite our sharing a mother. Difference and sameness carry the same weight." She stopped, somewhat startled at herself. She could not remember when she had last spoken words so free and precise.

"I'm going to have to tell her," Karel said, sounding stifled. "I can't leave Cybele to be part of all *this*, without knowing what Cesar Kamehameha *is*." He choked. "She'll never forgive me."

Teal wondered what healing thing Michael might have found to say. "I think," she said, at last, "she should appreciate that you have spared her from . . . evil." The last word was one she rarely used, and she rendered it a little uncertainly, unsure of its resonances. She was not given to trying others' language. But Karel's face eased; she had somehow said the right thing.

"I thought I'd ask you to do it, at first." His eyes were shiny. "But I won't even ask. It's something I have to do, I alone."

"I should remain in Lovelock," she said, "if I were you." She turned to look at him at last, to give her statement weight. "Cesar Kamehameha is dangerous, and it is best he not know exactly where you are."

"Or you," he said, pacing quickly across the room, once, and back. "I'll ask her to meet me at *Albatross* on the docks." He gulped. "Quickly, quickly now, before my courage fails me!"

Cybele stood, looking out of the windows at Rockport bay, beyond the docks of the AOC. She was several minutes beyond bearing the sight of the screens, but she feared the image of that small body, wrapped in its weeds, would remain indelible on her inner eye. As would the excruciating grief of the child's father. Fatherless daughter; daughterless father. Whether above or below the sea, pain was pain, grief was grief, death was death. She stared, unblinking, at the sea, as her eyes grew dry. When she closed her eyes she would see them still, child and father, and must recognize them for her own kin.

Behind her, in the room soft-lit by aquaria, Cesar Kamehameha sat at his console, working. She could hear his quiet movements, the occasional murmured word. He was composing a statement for public release. She had watched his grave expression lighten with anticipation as he studied the commentary on the death.

She said without turning, "Even this, you will use."

The movements ceased, but he did not speak. She felt his eyes on her back. She would not have turned, but she blinked, involuntarily, and saw within the red shadow of her lids the outline of a small body; and she turned hard. His face was still, his eyes watchful.

"Yes," he said. "I will. So that no more children should die." But he made no move toward the touchboard, only laid his hand beside it, considering her. "Your feelings are commendable, Cybele," he said, eventually. "I shall try to respect them."

Respect, she thought, as in value. Or respect, as in danger.

A motion caught her eye, three iridescent indigo fish unsettled by artificial day, vibrating with indecision in a corner of the aquarium. And she saw him and herself within glass, an uneasy cohabitation of incompatible species. They had nothing in common. She knew he had curtailed the ringsol six investigation, to conceal the illegals' existence. He had loosed an illegal virus on them. He would now loose a legal onslaught, exposing their crimes and motives, and stripping credibility from their arguments against terraforming. There was nothing he would not use, for this good cause. What would Adam have made of him, this pitiless champion of right? Must one be good, Cybele thought, to serve good? Or can good be served by evil? And Karel, what had Karel known of this? All of it? Was it that he was too strong, or too weak, to walk among shadows?

She said, "Will you still be wanting your list?"

"Certainly," he said. "The need now is to bring them in, to make sure they have suffered no ill-effects from their illegal adaptations. Whether we put your list to legal use will depend upon them."

"Those who come in will be granted amnesty," Cybele said. "And those who do not, will not."

Cesar merely nodded.

"And the virus?"

There was a silence. "What virus?" Cesar said, the two words spoken quietly but with emphasis. A simple sloughing of his own deeds, like a shed skin. With realization of his meaning came relief, gratitude, and a profound envy. Relief and gratitude that she no longer need be part of it. And profound envy that he could so simply go on, leave behind what he had done, while she grappled with it still, and might do so forever. Could he, as his question implied, forget?

Or would he simply conceal from her if he were going on? He had erred once, in telling her why Adam's death must go uninvestigated. He thought that, like him, she would measure virtue by effectiveness.

She had no measure, that was it. While Adam lived, even through their estrangement, she had had a measure, *his* measure. With his death, in such a way, for so unclear a reason, she had lost her measure, lost all certainty.

She need not ask. She need never know. She need only choose to believe what he was implying. Her palms hurt with the cutting of her fingernails. She said, "Was there any use in it after all?"

He laid his hands down on either side of the console. Small, smooth olive hands, like a child's. "We were at war, Cybele. A moral or legal war, but a war nonetheless. A war for survival. I did not enjoy the things I had to do. I did them because I believe someone had to do them. But I am glad not to have to do them again." He paused. "They have made their bid for permanence, and though they may not know it yet, they have lost." He turned his hand palm up on the console and considered it, its contours and olive tint. "We have all measured the human cost of letting them live in such ignorance." He looked at her, without apology. "The body of that child speaks more eloquently than days of persuasion."

"So everyone blames her for not knowing, and not those others for goading her into it. *They* knew."

"It is no good to expect people to be better than they are," Cesar said, simply.

He was so very calm, she thought. Repellently calm. And yet his repellent calm, and use of this tragedy would achieve what his virus could not, and should not have. Blueheart would realign with the millennial plan.

"What now?" she said.

On the screens, the wide arrow of canoes and sailboats sped for the barriers and the open sea beyond. The docks, moments ago so crowded, had only empty tents and shelters, in a ragged formation with gaps, and a discarded uniform. On all the docks, all across Blueheart, the gatherings bled slowly into the sea. Cesar said, "They will find that the rifts that Rache of Scole has opened do not close. There will be those to whom he, and the illegals, are heroes. They will want to continue his case, and they will listen to him when he says they must learn primary customs, primary ways, because he will. So they will come, and they will learn, and if we are careful with them—more careful than we have ever been—they will become part of our future. And there will be those who believe he was a villain and a failure. They will disappear back into the seas, try to be what they were before, and quietly wither away in their bitterness."

"I am not sure," Cybele said, a soft rasp on her words, "that it will be as quiet as that."

"I would like it to be," Cesar said. "But no." He closed the fist he was contemplating. "The AOC will, I think, be fully justified in restricting new adaptations while those who were adapted without AOC monitoring are fully investigated. Given the lack of cooperation we have received, that will take quite some time. By then, we shall have persuaded the directorates that the more extreme adaptations are no longer necessary. And by then, we shall have the beginnings of a strategy for reeducating and reassimilating the pastorals into the cultural mainstream. Throughout Earth history it has been done, though usually with overt or covert brutality. The accomplishment will be in doing it so there are no enduring scars; I think it is possible. They are the descendants of adventurers; they have no lack of boldness and imagination themselves. The creation of a new world is no mean adventure. It only remains to enlist them." He paused, and said, quietly, "You think the cost has been high. It is far, far lower than it might have been."

She shook her head slightly. Adam, she thought, would have told her where she erred, precisely, why she felt as she did, why victory crumbled rotten in her hands. Perhaps, she thought, it was because of her impurity of motives. She had acted against the pastorals because of what they had taken from her, not because she believed they should be acted against.

A moment longer, watching her, then he turned back to his console. "Cybele, I cannot claim, as the old often do before the young, that once I was just like you. When you visit Earth you may understand why that might be. Or perhaps not. But I will tell you this: there will come a day when you, too, have to serve right in a way your conscience might not approve. And do not say it will never happen. You are the kind of person to whom it will. You will not confine yourself to small things." He laid a deliberate hand upon the touchscreen and refreshed the image.

She said, aloud, to herself, "I do not regret what I have done. I regret only why." The words sounded thin and hollow. The sunlight, against which she would not close her eyes, could not warm her. She leaned her head against the window, looking down at the edge of the pier and the walkway, and let her vision blur. When night came, she thought, she would answer Karel's message. She would persuade him to go with her to Minaret. They would walk in the sloping shallows of the children's beaches, and remember a time of certainty, and faith.

Dusk found Rache sitting on the edge of the Rossby barrier around Lovelock bay, his feet trailing down a long, steep slope to the water. The retiring citizens of Lovelock bay were not given to play with lights, and the surface of the bay had the same thin patina of last daylight as the open sea; only near the jetties did the lights fan over the water. To his left, Manhattan bay was as garishly lit as ever, the sea iridescent and opaque, the yachts waltzing and promenading. And further to his left, the incurving barrier showed beaded with red, very dark to eyes whose pigments had been blueshifted for the depths. He, too, might readily pass by one of Rossby's warnings.

Water dried slowly, on and around him, giving him a slight chill. Red light spilled from behind him, spilled over him, down the slope onto the water.

The wind eddied over the barriers, warm, fleet, and rank. Above him, unbroken by the barrier, it continued on its long, long course, arcing with the turn of the world. It would pass, he thought, nearby to the place where they had left Ayna.

There had been bitter words about that. Einar had wanted them to return to the forests nearest Scole. Others had insisted that tradition, and commonsense, said that it did not matter where she was released: the seas would bear and scatter her as they would.

They had gone, in the end, further than they might, but not to Scole, moored their boats where the sea grew still, and filed into the woven shadows of the forest, drawing their burden. He had never known so slow and endless a swim. In the end Einar had had to be forced to let his daughter go. He had wound his wrists in the ropes, binding her to him. Wound his wrists, and at the last, his neck, so that Astrid had been compelled to cut him free, in defiance of all custom. She had struggled with him, amid the soft, twining leaves, while the others retrieved the severed rope and drew Ayna's corpse away, beyond his sight, beyond his reach.

And after that, there had been very little talk between them. The sea had for generations devoured foolish, unwitting children. There were those to whom this was another such devouring, not ordinary, certainly no less than heartbreaking, but understandable; and there were those to whom this was quite different, something fundamentally offensive, alien, appalling. And they had nothing to say, each to the other, which would not be bitter. Some—Aile, Tris, and Noelle among them—had returned to Scole. Others had come back here, to finish what they had left unfinished.

But they would need time, he thought, to find the strength to swim this gyre they had set themselves. As would he. He dreaded what he would find, on the nets, among the pastorals, from the pastoral-liaisons. In Ayna's needless death, in the pastorals' mourning rites, in what they said among themselves, the primaries

would perceive, as never before, the gulf between their
cultures. And he had scarcely had time to begin to shift
the weight of their perceptions from its center on themselves. To themselves, they were still the norm.

He did not see Einar until Einar broke the surface
before his feet. Rache saw the dark flash of recognition
in his eyes, and then he threw hands and speargun onto
the slope with a great surge of water, and heaved himself
up. His eyes were crimson. In the red light, he looked as
though he had been flayed. He climbed the slope, blinking seawater from his eyes, as Rache got to his feet,
slowly, feeling every pound of his weight.

"Why didn't you come back with us?" he said.

"I wasn't ready."

Einar made a sound of derision, and stalked away
from Rache, along the flat of the barrier, eclipsing the
lights in his passage. Rache simply stood, leaden-footed,
leaden-boned. Einar whirled, as at a phantom footstep;
stood rigid a moment, looking across the distance
between them with an expression Rache could not read,
and then came back.

"Are you giving up?"

"No," Rache said.

"Why not?"

"Because it's important that I keep going. All I need
is a little time."

"All I need is my daughter."

The words came flat, lay on the deck between them
like dead things. Rache said, "I know."

"I blame you," Einar said. "If you had not brought
us here, she would be alive."

"If that is all I can do for you, then I accept your
blame."

The tone was wrong, he knew even as he spoke.

There was neither generosity nor grace in it, only weariness. He saw the red blaze of hatred in Einar's face. He heard the snick, and the swish, and the thud as the spear hit him, in his left side just below the ribs. For that moment, he felt no pain, though the impact pushed him back a step. He brought a hand up to the spear, in the first unthinking impulse to yank it out. His fingers would not close on the shaft. He folded his left leg and dropped to a sitting position. It was his last deliberate act. Landing, he toppled sideways, the hand he would have put out unresponsive. The spear-shaft caught; the tip ground deeper. He tried to open his mouth to scream. He tried to draw breath to scream. He could do neither. He could not breathe. Venom, he thought. And a small, irrational part of him was furious at the carelessness of it: nobody carried a venom-packed spear into a holdfast, even a hostile one.

Einar dropped to his knees beside him, repeating his name, in a hoarse whisper. Through the agony, he felt Einar's touch, on the skin around the spear, on the pulses in throat, wrist, and temples. Those would communicate life, if not awareness. Unable to breathe, unable to move, only dive endurance kept him conscious, and would do so until he suffocated or bled to death. "You shouldn't have said that," Einar whispered. "You shouldn't have said that. I told you I would kill you if you hurt them."

Rache's eyes were drying. Einar's form was a red blur, lit and shadowed red, kneeling with his hands pressed to the slope: "You shouldn't have left. You should have stayed in Scole. None of this would have happened then." He rocked, weight shifting from hand to hand. Something fell, winking briefly bright, past Rache's eyes onto the deck. Einar said, "I didn't want to do this. I didn't. I loved you once." His teeth chattered, a sound unnerving and sinister; he closed his mouth and was silent. In the great distance, beside his hand, the sea snapped at the barrier's edge. Rache felt the throb of waves on the windward side through the platform on which he lay. Einar said, "I can't . . . have killed you." He felt again for Rache's pulse, and Rache heard him sigh. His voice came fainter and more distant as he straightened and turned his head. "There's a boat out there. Primaries." He stopped, tasting the word. "I'll get . . . them." Through filmed eyes, Rache saw the dark shape thin and recede. Einar's dive was nearly soundless. Then he was alone, but for the faint voice of the sea and the tearing beat of his own heart.

When Cybele arrived at the jetty beside *Albatross*, he was not there.

Lovelock was dark, only single, spaced globes illuminating walkways and jetty, and quiet, with but a few people passing. She had not come here before; she knew it to be a quiet, somewhat eccentric neighborhood, whose members had chosen black-zoning largely because of a liking for privacy and quiet. Several pastoral-liaisons worked out of Lovelock, due to its peripheral location and lack of surveillance.

She crouched beside the moored *Albatross*, and ran her fingers lightly along the coarse rope. The boat was empty, its gear neatly stowed. Beyond it, the sea was black, and far beyond it, the lights studded along the barrier cast long reflections, like red teeth. She thought she could feel the movement of the water beneath the jetty, but it may only have been tiredness. Her exhaustion was almost hallucinatory; she had the sense that, without warning, reality would tilt and slide gently sideways. It was not unpleasant; she almost looked forward to having an alternative to this painful present.

"Cyb—" She lifted her head. She had not heard him approach. Perhaps she had slipped out of the world for a moment. He was standing, a little way away. In the dull blush of a corner light, she saw someone—a woman—step back around the corner and out of sight. He cast a desperate glance backward, saw the absence, and turned back to her. The whites of his eyes showed. When she stood, he stepped forward as though to clutch at her; without thinking, she recoiled, lifting her hands. He stopped.

She said, a little hoarsely, "Don't. I'm very tired, and I've been very worried about you."

"You didn't come when I asked," he said. "I've been sick waiting."

"You said, don't tell Cesar. I was at the AOC. I couldn't leave."

"That wasn't the reason," he said, gasped. "You were angry with me. You were punishing me."

"I had work to do," she said, flatly.

"For him?" his voice going high. "Oh, Cybele."

There was a silence. She felt an oppressive weight of onus resting upon her. "You wanted to speak to me."

"Yes," he got out, and suddenly leaped sideways, onto *Albatross*, landing with a great thud, making her start and the yacht rock wildly. "Let's get away. Well away."

After a moment, slowly, she climbed aboard, jerking away from his reaching hand. "I don't need help." She sat quietly as he rigged *Albatross*, his frantic movements making the boat sway and bang the jetty; fatigue and motion left her a little nauseous. He pushed them off and the sail caught the odd, twisting breeze, and they slid smoothly away from the jetty, into the darkness. Karel lit a single blue light at the tip of the mast; she thought to ask that he quench it, but forbore. Who might be watching; who could? The eccentrics of Lovelock bay guarded their privacy. She said, "Where have you been staying?"

Karel swallowed. "With Michael. The counselor."

"Ah. But that was a woman with you."

"Teal Blane Berenice. It's—what I have to tell you. It's—complicated."

Just within the barrier he said, "Stop," and the yacht hove to and folded its sail. The barrier was a huge, dark shadow, pointed with red lights; the teeth on the water had narrowed and shortened, into fangs. She could hear the hollow waves striking on the far side, feel the way the wind snagged and eddied down on them. Karel knelt in the stern, watching her with huge eyes.

She said, "Did you know?"

He swallowed. "Did I know what?"

"What Cesar was doing about the illegal adaptives?"

"Oh Cyb," he said, and laid his face in his hands.

She had never thought that there would come a time when she would envy him his easy tears, rather than resent them.

But he was not crying; when she did not speak, he sat upright, drawn-faced and dry-eyed. "I have something terrible to tell you."

She said, "Don't," thinking he was alluding to what her challenge to Meredis had wrought: the rising of the adaptives, the millennial plan endangered.

He burst out, half rising, "Listen to me! I sent the virus into ringsol six. I helped kill Adam."

She turned her face into the wind, and let it blind her. Out on the barrier, something thudded faintly, a large fish, she thought, leaping to its death on the platform. She pictured it, twisting on its side, gulping air in senseless panic. Dying, out of its element and never knowing how.

"It was not meant to happen that way," he cried. "It was because of their upgrade, because of their experimentation. The tutor virus modified the worm; it took out the limiters. The worm deleted everything—it wasn't meant to be that way. It was supposed to delete the information about the *woman*.

"Tell me you hate me," he gasped. "Tell me you'll never forgive me. Tell me now and get it over with."

"You," she said.

He thrust out his wrists at her, showing the faint traces of the marks on them. "I tried to kill myself. I tied weights to myself and I jumped overboard. I sank and I sank and I sank." He scrambled to his feet. "I'll do it again," he said, wildly, and swung one leg overboard. She flung herself at him, catching him around the waist. They fell, together, side by side.

She slapped at him with all her strength. He shied away, and she rolled onto her knees and followed the blow with a second. It was as though the first blow had jarred loose a lifetime of restraint. Her hands disconnected from her head and thought; she could feel the breath, see the blur of their passage, feel the jolt as they connected, but they did not seem to be hers. She closed her eyes, abandoning herself to the vortex, uncaring whether she struck him, or the planking, or the mast, only that she strike and strike, and strike again. And when he caught her arms, and pinned her on her back, leaning on her with all his weight, that was gratifying, too, that was connection, that was struggle, that was force and counterforce. His arms were shaking when the vortex whirled away into the darkness. She said, hoarsely, "You never thought I had it in me."

"Oh Cybele." He laid his head on her breast, his breath sobbing. She stared past the weaving mast at the luminous blue of the night sky. The stars were hidden by light, moisture, and maybe some high clouds. She said, quietly, "I understand."

"You—understand," he said, lifting his head.

"Oh yes," she said. "I understand."

He pushed himself off her, drawing back. "I don't want your forgiveness. I don't deserve it. I can't take it. I don't want it." His pitch rose, in denial, in panic.

"I didn't," she said sharply, "say I forgave. God will have to forgive you. And Adam, if he achieves his after-life. God will have to forgive us both."

"I don't deserve—"

She reared up, and felt the vortex gathering around her. "Do you think you're the only one who has *sinned*. You have no idea what has happened to *me*. You never thought to ask. You were so full of yourself and your sin and your suffering." She doubled over, and then spirit, pride, and individuality rebelled: that was something *he* would do, one of his self-dramatizing poses. She jerked herself upright, muscles in back and belly quivering. "Go on, Karel, *ask* me what I have done. If you care. If you *dare*."

"Cybele," he said, in a tiny voice.

"Ask me, damn you."

He swallowed. "What have you done?"

She said, "Cesar never told you the real reason he

did not want it known about the illegal adaptives. He does not care about legalities. He means to make sure the illegal adaptations fail, that those people de-adapt. He released a virus into the food supply that will reverse characteristic illegal modifications; it causes something the pastorals call whitesickness."

Karel made a small sound which was not quite a word.

"He's *had* me, too, you see. Had me with him, believing him . . . all this time he's known, he's been the one, and he's been . . ." she gasped a breath, "dangling me, trailing me, *using me.* Suggesting that you were not reliable, that I was too close, oppressing you—I would have looked harder for you but for him—" He put out his hand; she pushed it away; he caught her, clear-eyed, anguished, and she let him hold her, finding a dim and distant comfort in the touch of her brother sinner's hand. She said, "Suggesting that I was overwrought with grief for Adam. Yet all the time . . . reminding me of what Adam would have thought right, Adam would have thought wrong, about all this. He did not know Adam at all. He did not know me. He called me stupid, self-indulgent, a little fool. But I am none of these things."

"He t-told you this. About the adaptives."

"He had to stop me questioning Adam's death. I think he counted on me not knowing, never knowing, what had really happened. I think he counted on me hating too much to look right or left. I think he counted on me feeling—too *fouled* to—deserve Adam. And I would, I did, and if you hadn't told me I would have gone back to him," she said, in a sick voice. "I had nobody else. Adam and you gone, and no justice. Karel, you have saved my soul."

Karel started to cry. "Don't," she said, tiredly, and he, "I can't help it. I thought you would hate me."

She said, more sharply, "Don't!" and turned her face away from him.

And found herself looking at a red hand hooked over the yacht's sill, at the curve of a bare, red head. She leaped up with a shout; the hand unclenched, the head sank. She threw herself forward, nearly falling, but the water was jet black, depthless. She leaned on her hands, staring down, shuddering slightly, Karel at her side saying, "What is it? What did you see?"

Rache was semiconscious, lying in a thick, internal twilight, when he felt himself draw breath. That was the way it was: mind had withdrawn from body. He supposed he was dying, not least because both pain and fear had grown remote. But quite suddenly, his diaphragm released, and he breathed. The spear sawed beneath his ribs, and he sobbed, soundlessly. He tried to raise a hand, to steady it. Could not. Gasped in another breath, despite the agony. He had no choice. His blood was stale and polluted, running navy through his arteries, through his darkening brain and starving heart. He panted, trying to keep his breathing shallow and the pain coming in short strokes. His skin stung. He could not close his eyes, the lids were sealed open. He had no tears, wept, or bled, dry. But not yet dead. He breathed. His fingertips twitched. He crept his right hand up to his face. He pushed one eyelid down; the other scraped shut alongside. His head pounded; he could see sparks and white jagged lines against darkness. He brought his left hand up, and felt clumsily around the spear-shaft, through the crusted, sticky mess of blood. He slid his palm around a vast stretch of salt-dusted skin and found the hard nodule of the barbed tip beneath the skin. He wanted that abomination out of his body. He could not remember, at that moment, how it had come to be there. But he wanted it out. He needed help, but he would not ask for help with that thing in him. It represented failure, betrayal, hatred; he did not remember why and he did not care; he knew it was so. He closed his fist on the shaft. There was a switch, he knew, which would release the barbs, but releasing them would leave them inside him. To break the shaft took him three tries. He laid the shaft carefully beside him. Then he drew his knife and trapped the ragged broken end of the spear beside the hilt and, giving himself no time to think, pulled the flat of the knife against his body, driving the barbed tip of the spear clear of his back. In a transcendent state beyond pain, he reached back, gripped the gory shaft, and pulled it free. He carefully laid it down beside the remainder of the shaft, close enough to smell the powerful, dark, metallic scent of it. With that scent in his nostrils, he blacked out.

He reached out in his rousing clumsiness to push away the stink of human blood, and lacerated his hand on the barbs. He had pitched from his transcendence into mortal pain; he shook with cold, feeling the ooze of thick blood downward through the crusts and clots on belly and back. He rolled over, looking out over the sea's dark, moving skin. A point of blue light winked above it; he could just see the fine, moving line of the bare mast. The voices came to him again, whispering across the water. Against the lights of Lovelock bay, a fragmentary silhouette formed, a yacht, sails down, rocking gently and at rest.

Karel said, "What do you suppose they might have heard?"

She had not thought of that; she did not wish to. She sat huddled in the center of the yacht, seeing in the red light of the barrier long red fingers, reaching out.

Karel crouched before her. "What are we going to do?"

"We?"

"You and I. About Cesar. About—Adam. About the adaptives."

All entangled, and inextricable. She found that she was holding her hands with fingers apart as though they were snarled in the vile, sticky strands of conspiracy. Karel, as agent for Cesar Kamehameha, had loosed the virus which had killed Adam. She, as agent for Cesar Kamehameha, had colluded in the concealment of the counter-conspiracy, the obscuring of truth, the harassment of the pastorals.

"I can turn myself in," Karel said, shakily.

Everything she had done had been done in service not of her own ends, but of others'.

"Let it play itself to its end," she said.

"But we surely cannot stand by and—"

"Are either you or I fit to serve truth? Have either of us the clarity of sight to know what it is?"

Karel said, humbly, "We may not be, but we are the only ones there are." He drew a deep breath. "Cyb, you must not go back to the AOC. Cesar is dangerous. He almost killed Teal," he swallowed, "with routines I used to—get away from the navigation and surveillance at sea." He glanced at her, a hangdog reflex. "He's done her lasting damage—her tissue-cercortex interface. She may never be able to work again. She's being so brave . . . She sailed herself, without navigator, or control or guidance, to Kense. He mustn't know she's still alive. Not until we have some way of proving—"

"You won't prove anything against him," Cybele said.

"It's so strange," Karel said. "She almost doesn't—mind him. It's as though what's happening to her is separate from him; she shows no anger. I've been trying to find some evidence of what he did to her, but—He knew, Cyb," Karel said, in a different voice, turning his head away. "He knew—I said to him—that I thought I should kill myself. I suppose I wanted him to—do something to help, say it was his fault, something. *Adam* would have."

"Adam would have never done anything like this."

"No," Karel said, faintly. "He would hate us, now."

"He would forgive us," Cybele said.

"That might be worse," a tremor in his voice. "Oh God, Cybele, he'll be so ashamed of us."

She said, very softly, "Karel, Adam's dead."

"I *know* that," he cried, shocked at her cruelty. And she realized that indeed he did know, that he spoke now of Adam in the afterlife. He, for all his surface worldliness, believed that Adam lived on, elsewhere. She felt deeply shamed. She said, "I'm sorry, Karel. I—misunderstood."

There was a silence. Karel said, "It was Rache who saved me. Rache of Scole. I was over ringsol six. So was he. He was—furious at me. He can be—quite frightening. But he's a good man, Cybele. He doesn't deserve what's happening to him. That little girl's death. Teal tried to save her, Cyb. But she couldn't. She just wasn't able. She couldn't alert the system and get into the sub's controls in time. Because of the damage. We have to do something with what we know, Cyb. You and I. Adam would say it is our moral duty."

"He would," Cybele said. Another long silence. She spoke without meaning to, in a whisper. "But Karel, I'm so tired."

"Here," he said, and took her in his arms, resting her head against his shoulder. "I'll take you back to Michael's. We'll think about what to do then."

Through his shoulder, she could hear his heart beating. Whatever else she thought of Rache of Scole, she owed him that, that still-beating heart. It was no small debt. She felt cold at the thought of Karel throwing himself weighted into the ocean. And cold with fury at the thought of Cesar, *knowing*.

She heard Karel gasp. The boat jolted; then rocked; she twisted around to see a thick red arm locked over the stern, hand fisted. In a frightened, protective fury, she hauled an oar from its stowage, with a loud, viscous rattling, and said, "Whoever you are, get off our boat." There was no answer, she lifted the oar high, meaning to drive it down on the unseen head; with a lunge, Karel caught it, two-handed, and for a moment, she struggled with him.

"Cyb, don't!" They stared at each other, the oar a bar between them, and she saw wide fright in his eyes. He drew the oar down, touched her face lightly, and glanced sternward, to where the arm had not moved. "Let me," he said. He crawled sternward, and very carefully, peered over and down. "Good God!" The hand groped at air; then the arm unlocked, and Karel said, again, "God!" and nearly overbalanced, grappling overboard. Taking a weight, he slid further down into the stern with a broken thud of knees and hip and an audible grunt. "Cyb, get a light—"

The light showed Rache of Scole, tethered by Karel's hands, turning in the water like a dying fish to show the wounds on back and belly.

SEVENTEEN

"A spear," said the woman on the screen. "Yes . . . I see." She looked out at their worried faces, with a quick, sweet smile. "No problem," she said, "truly."

Soft-filtered sunlight slanted over her shoulders, and caught feathering strands of hair, turning their brown transparent and golden. She leaned with hip resting against a console, one hand laid atop it, the other deep in her clinical jacket. She wore flowing slacks, brown drizzled with auburn and gold. Her face was thoughtful, patrician, and plain.

Of course, where she was, on Esquimalt rafftown on the far side of Blueheart, was in daylight. But Teal, watching with an experienced eye, suspected that she would always appear soft-lit by sunlight, whatever the weather. "A remarkable interface," she said.

Michael said, tightly, "You flatter us here in the outback."

He stood square before the imaging wall, in his dryland receiving room. Behind him, on a blue and green couch, Cybele and Karel sat side by side. Hair and clothing of both were soaked. Unable to lift Rache over the side, they had supported him in the water while the skiff towed all three to Lovelock's emergency medical facility. It was an automated facility, and Michael, with Karel's help, had bypassed the usual call schedule to involve his partner, who had the necessary expertise, and much desired discretion. It was her relational interface which faced them; the surgeon herself was already linked with Lovelock's equipment.

Teal said, "You are perhaps overfamiliar with it."

The simulacrum of Michael's partner smiled. "Are you suggesting I neglect him?"

Such things could be a sensitive issue, Teal knew. She had not intended innuendo, and in the past, she would simply not have answered. Now she said, "I know neither of you well. I can offer no opinion."

"Ah," Frede's image said. She lifted a hand to brush back a vagrant strand of hair. Gold studs twinkled on her wrist, the attachment points for near and remote surgical waldoes.

"About Rache, what Frede is already doing—" Indeed a sophisticated interface, Teal thought, able to adjust for their understanding and qualify its own illusion, "is repair the intestinal tears and clean him out. That should take an hour or so. He'll be on his feet in a day." Teal eased her projection back from the communications uplink. The input was indistinguishable from any other transmission; all the interesting computations, the processing of the construct, were happening at the other end. She sought the medical uplink, which was not difficult, given the number of channels it occupied, and their activity. Michael touched her arm, then took it firmly, recalling her.

The construct was watching her. "Exper' Blane Berenice, I would rather you did not move in any further. There is a risk that you might perturb one of my connections. With potentially serious consequences.' She tilted her head slightly, "watching" Teal. "And given what has happened to ringsol six and to you yourself, I would rather my watchdogs were not distracted by a friendly prowler."

"I understand," Teal said, flatly.

"I am not implying," the construct added, "that your insertions were clumsy." She smiled. "I detected it because I was," a flick of the eyes toward Michael, "forewarned. Had I had any chance to prepare, I should have quite liked your advice. In fact, if we can agree an exchange of professional courtesies, this might go a little way toward reconciling my superiors for this little episode of moonlighting." Her eyes crinkled mischievously toward Michael, who slowly smiled back. "But I'll leave it to Frede to ask the questions she wants answered. She was just concerned that I should reassure you that Rache will, barring the unforeseen, be fine. She would have me add, I am sure: Michael, take care of yourself." There was no smile now; she brushed lightly at her cheek, as at the thought or memory of a tear. "To have to do this for Rache is difficult enough. To have to do it for you—aside from unprofessional—it would be well nigh impossible."

"Understood," Michael said, soberly. "I'll take care. Ask Frede to have a word with me when she's done."

The image faded into a scene of an underground grotto, with undulating seaweed and diffusely slanting sunlight. Michael sighed, and turned away. Caught Teal's eye, and smiled a little ruefully. "I did ask her to place her highest level of security on this."

Teal nodded. In her prime, all of three days ago, she could have come and gone undetected, forewarning notwithstanding.

Michael said, watching her face, "I am so sorry you have been caught up in this."

Teal shrugged, awkwardly. "I too. But it seems—inevitable. Given that Juniper came, and I. It is what happened. Destiny, if you will. I want only to complete the repairs on myself and . . ."

"And?" Michael murmured.

"And discharge what obligations remain," she said, a little angrily.

"Would you stay a while?" Without waiting for an answer, he went back and crouched down before Cybele and Karel, and spoke quietly to them. Teal did not listen. She turned her attention inward, initiating a diagnostic routine. When the routine ended, Cybele and Karel were gone, and Michael was sitting beside the paired wet impressions on the couch, his head resting in his hands. She walked over to him and sat down, letting her weight announce herself. He looked up. "Better?"

"Still below fifty percent."

"Destiny, you said."

She shook her head tightly. Words were no use to her.

"You're not much given to reflecting upon your place in the universe," he said, leaning back. "Your lack of social graces gives quite the wrong impression of you, arrogance, instead of a profound humility. I have known deeply religious people striving for decades if not centuries to efface themselves so."

"It is not a philosophy," Teal said, "merely learned discipline."

"I think it's more than that," he said, mildly. "None of them ever loved anyone or anything enough to give up not only life, but self for them."

She looked at his face, parsing its form as she had parsed the motion of the sea. His face became shapes, textures, hues, to her. It made the silence pass, and it told him she meant that so. She knew what he meant. But it was not a knowledge to be discussed with him or anyone else.

He said, "I am here, if you need anyone to talk to."

"Was that why you asked me to stay?"

"No. Asking you to stay was purest self-interest. I need someone to talk to. I am no use at pure thought. I have to say what I think to know what I think. A characteristic which perplexes Frede." He tilted his head, and remarked parenthetically, "I shall have to make sure you meet her. Rache is very good for me in that regard: he's of an oral tradition—the man's memory astounds me, even after all those years. It's something I don't think most primaries realized: how much cultural divergence there has been between primaries and pastorals. They—the pastorals—were quite ruthless in discarding what of our culture did not serve them in the seas, and quite deliberate in what they kept. They had the entire database of human experience to choose from. That's where the government by elders came from. Most early human societies, pre-literate human societies, gave elders the place they merited as repositories of knowledge. Attributed status to wisdom and experience. The development of means of memory storage removed authority, the authority of knowledge, from elders and ultimately from individuals, and placed it in external structures. In databases and sunstreams, in governments and protocols. The pastorals have moved away from all that." He shook his head slightly. "We should have foreseen maybe that they would cease to regard our laws as pertaining to them."

"Oversimplification," Teal said. "It is not simply pastorals and primaries. There was collusion between pastorals and primaries. There was complicity among primaries. And there was ignorance among pastorals."

"Ignorance," Michael murmured, head lowered. "Oh my God, ignorance. I can still see that child's head."

"Yes," Teal said.

"It is not as though I have never seen violent death. Not as though I do not know what people feel and say and even do to each other . . . I thought for a little while that, terrible as it was, that child's death might bring about a resolution, but . . . ah, God." He lifted his head, eyes focused on the space before him. "And now this."

After a moment, Teal rose, and left him, with purpose in mind.

Cybele and Karel, dry-clothed, stood at her shoulder as she enhanced the underwater image. Lovelock might be black-zoned, but the black-zoning ended at the water's edge. Beneath, surveillance continued, against underwater hazards. Blue ribbons dissolved behind Rache as he swam, warmth shed from his body. Underwater, he iridesced. They watched him heave himself up into oblivion. Teal skimmed through the intervening moments. They watched the second swimmer rise from below, and tread water, beheaded by darkness. Teal displayed a collage of images of his face. He was immediately recognizable.

Karel said, "That's Einar. Rache's nephew. You think he—"

"He was the only one there," Teal said.

They watched Einar dive back into the water. He swam swiftly away from the barrier, so swiftly that the heat-ribbons were dark blue, swirled and shredded with the turbulence. He surfaced abruptly, and drifted headless in the water, an orange opalescence fringed with yellow, green, blue. Cybele leaned forward. "He's not reached the docks so quickly, surely."

Teal said, "No," adjusted the image; and then the breath went out of Cybele in a soft hiss, as she saw the long rocking shadow in the water. "My God," she breathed.

Karel said, "What is it?"

"Remember that someone was there, listening," she said, "to us on *Albatross*."

"Him?" Karel said, in a whisper.

Einar dived, in coils of colors, diving deep, and passing swiftly beyond the camera's range. Teal leafed through images, records, and summarized. "He went to the rest of them, on the docks. He gathered some, and they have moved beyond the barriers, out to sea."

Cybele seemed not to have heard; her answer, when it came, was to Karel alone. "Him."

"Cybele."

Some time late in the night, in the inner cove. She did not turn to look at Michael when he settled himself down beside her, not close enough to impose an intimacy. Not close enough to entitle her to protest. Her lips parted; she breathed out a sigh.

"Sometimes it helps to talk."

She closed her mouth, and tightened it.

"And if you cannot talk to man, talk to God. Pray."

She turned her head to look at him. The marked side of his face was toward her, the tattoo like an obscure, divine circuitry. "What have I to say to God?

Ask for forgiveness? Or an account of himself? Or a right resolution to this?"

"There may not," he said, "be any right resolution to this."

"Cesar said something like that," she said.

"And you said?"

"I said he did not believe in rightness."

"I don't think," Michael said, quietly, "I deserve that."

She lowered her head slightly, looking at the distinct dryland pattern. "No," she said. "You are trying to help. You helped Karel. Thank you for that."

And mercifully, or perhaps wisely, he said nothing about her helping Karel, too, by forgiving, or by helping herself.

"What do you think would be a right resolution to this?"

She lifted her eyes, past the water, and up, realized what she was doing as she saw the clear ceiling, with the clear dark blue dawn overhead. She caught herself, and stared at the patterned far wall. Michael said, "Yes, why not look up. If only for the most primitive reason: to look for the dawn." Beneath his calm, she heard his weariness. For the first time she looked at him, and saw his tiredness, the drabness of his color, the tension around his eyes. He returned her look with a smile that thanked her for her attention; she flushed slightly.

"I don't know," she said. "I don't know what I think would be a right resolution for this." His eyes were steady on her face. She hesitated, and then said, with an edge of anger that he was forcing her to this, "I don't want to think about what might be a right resolution to this. Sometimes I think that God took my father's life to punish him for giving me those samples, for inviting me to use them for my own ends. Or maybe He took Adam's life to punish me for the use I made of them."

"And that," Michael said, gently, "makes the outcome so important to you: that it brings with it Adam's redemption."

She shivered slightly. The tiles before her shimmered and blurred and she closed her eyes. "I am afraid of what else God may take from me. I do not want this responsibility. I am afraid, and I am *angry*. I want to withhold my service from Him."

There was a silence, in which the last word still rang.

"God is accustomed to that," Michael said. "He is most patient."

"I *can't*," she said in a low voice, "though it makes me just like Cesar, I *can't* accept permanent human adaptation."

"Yet we have already made changes," Michael said, contemplatively. "All the early re-engineering of disease-causing alleles. Then the optimization of behavioral traits. The coldsleep engineering. The cognitive and other enhancements. All of these are permanent, germline adaptations. They create inequalities, between those who have them and those who have not. They lead to different experiences. How are the Blueheart adaptives different from all those?"

Cybele, eyes closed, thought that the quiet voice might be Adam's, delicately picking at the fabric of creation. Except that Adam left no holes, no unanswered questions. He moved from strand to strand, answer to answer. She waited for Michael to answer himself, but he did not. She opened her eyes. He sat beside her, a tired, worried man, with big soft hands upturned on his thighs. He looked as uncertain and ambivalent as herself. If this were a professional façade, she had never known one better. He could indeed talk her own language, as, at their first meeting, he had claimed. She found that she was inclining a little toward him. She eased herself upright as unobtrusively as she could.

"Cybele," he said, "the Emerald Ridge branch of the boomer-relay is very active. We have no idea, as yet, what is being sent, but it is near certain that it has to do with what Einar overheard."

She said, flatly, "He had no right to repeat a conversation held in private domain."

"Private domain refers to monitoring, not human hearing. But I do agree: by listening to a private conversation, Einar violated pastoral etiquette as well; it was an act of deliberate disrespect. Because of the way pastorals live . . . but that's not entirely pertinent here. What remains is the situation we have before us: you have made allegations against the Director of the AOC, quite serious allegations—"

"They are the truth," Cybele said starkly. "He told me himself."

"Where?" Michael said.

"Karel's—" She understood. "Ah." Karel's room, unlike the AOC, was private domain. There was no record of their conversation; she had not thought to make one, and if Cesar had thought, he had announced no such intention. There was only her memory, and Cesar's; her word against Cesar's. And human belief following human prejudice and convenience. The pastoral radicals all too willing to believe, and the primary establishment to disbelieve. She twisted to face Michael. "I will testify under disinhibitors. Karel too. Cesar was responsible for ringsol six. If we can seize the AOC files, *his* files; get proof enough to compel *him* to testify—"

Michael's face was still, withdrawn. "We will," he said quietly, "only condemn Karel. Cesar was very, very careful never to ask, never explicitly to suggest that Karel do what he did. In law there is no basis for seizure of internal files or forced questioning under disinhibitors."

He drew a slow breath, holding her eyes. "Cybele, I am going to suggest to you something which you will find repugnant. But I think I must suggest it, and I believe, very strongly, that I must try and convince you. I am going to suggest that you recant. That you put on public record a version of your conversation with Karel, which you and I will prepare together, which will satisfy two conditions: it will sound plausibly like the conversation which Einar overheard; but it will contain no direct accusation against Cesar or the AOC. As a first thought: it might be a rumor you were discussing. Even a rejected strategy. We can refine it. But to limit the damage, we must do it quickly."

Cybele caught his wrists, sliding off the chair into a half-kneeling position before him. "You cannot do this," she whispered up into his face. Her grip was hard enough to make haloes around her fingertips in his dusky skin.

He said, "It is repugnant; it is terrible, but listen: you have no proof. You cannot use it to bring Cesar down."

"I will *get* proof. There must be a sample—of tissue, of water—"

"And what of the pastorals? What of Einar? You understand grief, Cybele. You lost a father, he lost a daughter; I think he is half out of his mind with grief—

witness what he has done to Rache. I dread to think
what he might do now."

She remembered the dark red lights of the barrier,
the red hand on the stern of the *Albatross*, the faint dull
thud she had thought was a fish grounding on the barrier. She had a sense that she was swinging over a pit.
She said, in a ghastly whisper, "Cesar will go free."

"Not forever," he said, nearly as softly. His head
bent so close to hers that their temples nearly touched.
Her grip on his wrists had loosened, but not released.
"Only for a little while. Only for long enough for the situation to calm."

"Only for long enough for Cesar to obliterate all
evidence." She let go of him. "I will not do this," she
said, in a low voice. "Listen to me," she said, harshly as
he started to speak. "Have I less right in this because of
my losses, would you have me believe that? That I am
fragile in my spirit and unsteady in my mind because I
have lost my father and so nearly lost my brother. That
I cannot be *trusted* to make choices uncontaminated by
feeling. Sometimes feeling is your only guide in darkness. I am in darkness now. We are all in darkness now."

Waking felt like surfacing from a deep dive. Layers of
shadow rolling back, until suddenly, the light. It had
been a deep dive, deep enough that his thoughts were
murky. He tried to draw a deep breath, to purge his system of stagnant gases. There was a rock lodged beneath
his ribs.

"Easy, Rache," Michael's voice said. "Easy."

"Easy for you," Rache mumbled. "What about
ringsol six?"

There was a silence. "The disorientation will pass," a woman's voice said quietly, in the background. She sounded familiar. Rache turned his head, seeing Michael, and behind him, a screen with a woman's image. Michael smiled, but did not move. The woman nudged hair behind her ear with a thumb. He knew the gesture. Frede.

Michael said, slowly, "Karel and Cybele brought you in from the barrier. Frede operated on you. You had a spear hole right through you."

He remembered that the water had been cold, and hard to move in. Not warm and pliant as he thought, as he knew, it should be.

Michael said, "And we know it was Einar."

His body flinched in visceral recall of the impact. He gasped, as the rock ground in his guts. Michael said, "I'm sorry, I'm not giving you time, but we could have a situation. In fact, we almost certainly have a situation, on hand."

Rache closed his eyes. Spare me, he thought. But Michael was saying, "Stay with me, Rache. We're going to need you. Einar went to *Albatross*—where Karel and Cybele were. We suspect he overheard something which sent him off. And if he did overhear what we think he has, there's no telling what's likely to happen next. Are you with me?"

"What has he heard?" Rache said, with an effort.

"To put it simply, that the upper echelons of the AOC, Cesar Kamehameha, and possibly a few others, have released a virus designed to sabotage the illegal adaptations."

Rache stared at him. Michael leaned forward again, studying his eyes. "Frede," he said.

"There's nothing I can do. *You* might give him time."

"I haven't time to give him," Michael said, sharply. "There's been a flurry of messages outgoing from Rossby relays. The codes are neither known nor on record, and it should not take long to decode them, but for now we do not know exactly what is being said."

"The AOC released viruses . . ." Rache said, making little sense of the words.

"That is what Cybele de Courcey says. Is she reliable? I am having the greatest difficulty deciding whether she is or not." He sat down beside Rache, sat down, got up, paced. "I pride myself on my judgment of people; I pride myself on having the imagination to appreciate diverse viewpoints, worldviews alien and antagonistic to my own. But I cannot imagine myself into the mind of Cybele de Courcey. With the greatest of conviction she accuses the Director of the AOC of an atrocity."

"What atrocity?" Rache got out.

"According to Cybele—rather than risk contending with the numbers that existed by the time the AOC discovered the extent of the illegal adaptation, Cesar decided to eradicate the problem by ensuring that the illegal adaptations failed. So he has prepared and released viruses which would cause a reversion to humantype. Evidently, they used painter algae as a vector."

Painter algae. Rache grasped at a thought, and like water in a closing fist, it eluded him. He released an explosive breath. "Do you believe her?"

"That is what I am trying to tell you: I do not know. I believe that she believes it. Or if she does not believe it, if she has come into this as an *agent provocateur*, then she has been extraordinarily clumsy and extraordinarily fortunate to have her confession come by chance to such ears. If she has that cunning, then I am sorely mistaken in her, and in my own perceptions. But is she reliable, that I cannot tell. She is a young woman under great stress. Her father is dead, her brother was in part responsible for that death, and she has found herself in collusion with the man who arranged it." He spread his hands, the hands looking big and helpless, and then he closed them and pulled them in. "But it hardly matters at the moment whether she is reliable, or whether we believe her. She told Karel about this, in an open boat, and Einar overheard. Einar believes the AOC conspired to destroy the illegal adaptives, and what will come of that, I do not know."

"And if," Rache said with an effort, "she is right?"

"She can offer no proof. Without proof, she has no credibility, going up against the director of the AOC."

"Proof," said Rache, a painful sound. "I had no proof of what Juniper and Lisel had done. You did not believe me. My feelings for Juniper were distorting my judgment." He coughed, and felt his side clench. "You have feelings, investments, which distort your judgment."

"I know," Michael said, simply. "I know."

"Michael." Frede's voice was very quiet. She was looking to one side. "Michael, I think you were right about the little time."

Her image suddenly stood against a scene caught by one of the docks cameras. Red, brown, black, bare bodies were heaving themselves from the water. The water on their bare backs and hairless heads shone like varnish under the lights. The spearguns which should have lain across those backs were in their hands. They climbed from the water and moved inward, clearing the way for the next arrivals. They kept moving, crossing the wide dock platform, converging upon wide doors emblazoned with the symbol of cupped hands and double helix, the emblem of the AOC. They did not run, they did not seem to hurry, but they moved as swiftly and unstoppably as a riptide. For a moment, they washed against the closed door, until a man shouldered his way through the press, keyed open the door, and stood back while it opened. It was Bedevere.

Rache tried to sit and grunted aloud with the pain. Without taking his eyes from the screen, Michael moved around to support him, shoulder behind Rache's shoulder, arm across Rache's back. The pain did not abate, but Rache set his teeth, and reached across to grip Michael's other shoulder, bracing himself.

Cybele's image appeared, a minute inset, no more than a smudge of white face and wide, dark eyes. "Michael . . ." she said, voice little more than a whisper.

"I *see*," said Michael.

The view shifted inside. The pastorals diverged, spreading through the open receiving area, backing the handful of night workers away from their workstations at spearpoint. A phalanx moved swiftly across to the central liftshaft, to be thwarted by an emergency lockup—someone had activated the contagion-alert. The screen split to show the upper levels, people rising from their datastations, emerging from their laboratories—the camera coverage was incomplete, certain areas too highly rated for penetration—someone must have worked swiftly to secure access even to the low-rated areas. Rache and Michael watched as Einar left the closed liftshaft and crossed to a cluster of cornered staff. They watched as he held his speargun to the temple of a gray-faced man. Bede strode across the wide hall and struck the weapon aside with his hands.

Cesar Kamehameha's image appeared, inset on the screen, multiplied and miniaturized on screens and consoles in the AOC. He spoke. Bedevere raised both hands as the pastorals rumbled, turning toward the largest screen. Kamehameha watched a moment without speaking, then he gestured sharply, and disappeared. A moment later the interior images vanished.

Cybele's tiny image looked round sharply. "What's happened?"

Teal appeared and said, "He has challenged the news privilege override, on the grounds that it may inflame the situation."

"He doesn't," Rache gasped out, "understand. They're not acting for the cameras." He was shuddering with reaction and the effort to remain upright. Michael pushed him flat. He caught Michael's wrist. "It's not the cameras they care about. It's the AOC. Cesar. Get him *out* of there."

"They're evacuating the upper levels now," Frede said. "The pastorals are demanding release of the liftshaft . . . There's a warning gone out to all adaptation and medical facilities; we've gone on alert . . ." she glanced up with a wry smile, "adapting whatever protocols we find. Invasion by outraged clients is not something we have planned for. They're not responding to attempts to contact them."

"They won't," Michael said. "They're pastorals. Teal—give me faces. Who's there?" Faces spattered across the screen, forming a montage. Rache raised himself enough to see Bede, Einar, Daven. Bedevere looked grim; Daven bewildered. Einar's expression frightened him.

Michael said, tersely, "Any parting wisdom for me, Rache?"

Frede made a small sound of dismay, instantly

restrained. Michael heard, but he did not turn. His voice was gentle to both lover and friend. "They need a negotiator. Someone who knows pastorals, knows those people."

Rache tried to sit up, paid the price. "Wait. Tove's not there. Nor Lisel. Elders may not be involved," he said, in three shallow breaths.

Michael looked at him thoughtfully, and then turned to the screen. "You think it's Einar and a faction. That's useful to know. Cybele . . . any further thoughts on what we talked about?"

There was a silence. He held her eyes. The young woman's face grew to fill a quarter of the screen. "No," she said, very pale. "Never."

Cybele de Courcey said, "You have to help us."

On the screen, Cesar Kamehameha denied the allegations made against him. Cybele de Courcey, he said, was a young woman disturbed in mind by the sudden death of her father. The failure of the unlawful adaptations should not be blamed on the AOC, but on those responsible for those adaptations; the whitesickness was simply wild type reversion of an unstable genome. He regretted the action the pastorals had taken, and would do everything in his power to achieve a peaceful solution satisfactory to all. His small-featured face was grave, ageless, authoritative.

Teal was aware that Cybele was shivering with loathing and anger. Karel had eased behind Teal's chair, shrinking away from his sister's emotion. Or from the sight of the director of the AOC. For herself, Teal simply wished to look. To study the man responsible for her near-death and perhaps permanent impairment. She felt interest, curiosity, but neither fear nor hate. He had acted upon her, and thereby created a connection between them. Not as profound as the connection between Juniper and herself, but of the same nature.

On the second third of the screen, a party of pastorals, led by three whom Cybele had identified from her perusal of AOC personnel files as trained specialists, moved from lab to lab, workstation to work-station. One was Rache's elder brother, Bedevere.

Karel said, in a hushed voice, "They're trying to find proof."

"They won't find anything. The files will be hidden and locked. But they'll be somewhere." To Teal, "You could find them."

"Cyb," Karel said, appalled. "You can't ask her to do that."

Cybele gave him a hard look. "Shall I ask you?"

Karel swallowed. "Better me than Teal. I'm already implicated."

"Wait," said Teal. She closed her eyes, feeling their tension behind her. She had not, for many years, shared the common urgency about time. It did not move for her as it moved for others. Sometimes she caught sight of her reflection, and was surprised to see the mature woman who returned her gaze. Yet in this, the tempo would be set by others' impulses and urgencies; she might have to act soon, to act at all. The question was whether she could. And whether she would. For the third time in that hour, she executed an internal diagnostic. And when she knew the result, she knew what she would do. She heard Karel hiss, at Cybele, "Do you have any idea what the penalties are for an expert-voyager who is indited of any information offense?"

Teal opened her eyes and turned her chair to face them. "Yes," she said, "I do." She paused. "And I think it likely futile: material as incendiary as you suggest exists should be kept in internal store, where it would be inaccessible to us without a degree of assault unjustifiable under any circumstances." She shivered, a brief spasm of muscles. "But I have attained fifty-seven percent efficiency, sufficient, I think, with your help, to try the other. And even if that fails, I think it behooves us to penetrate as deeply as we can into the net, so we may be forewarned of any countermoves."

Cybele simply nodded. Karel said, shakily, "But why?"

"I have my reasons."

Karel drew a deep breath. "That's not good enough. I *won't* be responsible—"

"You *weren't*," Cybele said. "Cesar was."

Teal and Karel ignored her, the seated woman holding the eyes of the standing young man. Teal considered him, one of her long, thorough takings in, indifferent to the object's unease. She had come to know him, and to like him. He could be a fine man, if she and Michael and Rache could bring him through this undamaged. He could, if he applied himself, match her expertise. Or maybe not; he lacked her indifference to world and flesh. The indifference which she wanted no more.

There seemed no better way to renounce that indifference, to burn her former life to ashes, than this.

Karel said, "You're coming back. You might still come all the way back. Don't give it up for this."

She shook her head, slightly, impatiently. She had learned not to offer reasons to people who wanted her to act otherwise; they were merely fuel for argument or manipulation. So she would not explain that it was the possibility of coming back, rather than the fear that she would not, which made her choose this. She would never again become what loving Juniper, wanting Juniper's love, had made her. She would choose exile to the living world, no matter how slow, and lonely, and awkward she was in it.

She said, simply, "This is not your decision. It is mine."

EIGHTEEN

Cybele de Courcey said, "Must I recant?"

Behind her, on the screen, Michael stood in the center floor of the reception level of the AOC. A long finger of early sunlight lay across his feet, broken frequently by the shadows of new arrivals and the pastoral sentries left on the docks. Pastorals sat and stood in a large arc around him, and for the moment, nobody was speaking. They had progressed to impasse. Einar's followers would not leave until they were certain no virus remained to be used against them. The authorities would not acknowledge that such a virus existed or might exist.

But Michael did not look particularly downcast, Rache thought. He had settled to doing what he did best, muddling along the jagged margins of conflict, vague, verbose, inquisitive, apologetic, and unrelenting. Within the first hour he had persuaded the pastorals to free the trapped AOC staff, working on their unease in the presence of primaries. And in return, he had maneuvered the authorities into public commitment to negotiation over intervention. He might not subscribe to any of the self-justifying accounts he had heard, but he gave every sign of sincere attention.

Cybele said, "He suggested that we make up a story which would make it seem as though Einar had misunderstood . . ."

Rache rolled his head to look at the young woman sitting beside him, but as far away as the postsurgical suite would allow. She was staring at the screen, working her hands one in the other. He cleared his throat. "It wouldn't make any difference. Not now."

She turned her head. Her hair was flat and ragged, and the thin underskin on her eyes bruised. "But before?"

Rache grunted. He pitied her her conscience and her situation, but found himself uncomfortable with her, for her discomfort with him. She had not had time to resolve her prejudices against adaptives before finding herself forcibly allied with them. He should challenge her, he thought. For his own cause's protection, if nothing else. He should know how far he could rely upon this ally, with her fine mind and her truly frightening courage. And he should challenge her because she was young, and had not yet learned how to use that fine mind and courage to make choices and follow them.

He resented her. His strength was limited, and dedicated elsewhere. He *had* to get back onto his feet, recover his wits, plunge into the conflict; he could not find a resolution from afar, nor could he stand many more hours as an impotent witness. He said, brusquely, "How far before? This began long before you were even conceived, or conceived *of*. You cannot even claim sins of the father, because neither of your parents are Blueheart-born. And if you want to argue the doctrine of original sin, argue it with Michael, not me."

She turned her head away, showing him the thin contour of a cheek. Her throat moved as she swallowed. She said, "I did it for the wrong reasons. Out of vindictiveness, not justice. It was my idea to identify the children and go after the parents. I was angry at what they had taken from me. But it was not them."

He drew up his left knee, trying to ease the dull knot in his side. She heard the rustle of bedcovers, started, turned quickly. And flushed unevenly when she realized her overreaction. Rache said, curiously, "How'd you come to work for the AOC, feeling as you do about adaptives?"

She blinked, then, understanding, flushed again. "I needed to fund my own enhancements. I wanted to join space exploration, and they wouldn't have me without. The AOC paid well." She closed her lips on further confession. No doubt she did not care to be as self-interested, inconsistent, and impure as other mortals. Well, she was young. And since he had started this, he thought, he might as well continue.

He brushed the bedside console with a thick fingertip, muting display sound. She was watching him, tensely. He said, "Do you mind? Since neither one of us can do more than watch." She shook her head.

He said, "You do not agree with human adaptation?"

After a moment of not quite looking at him, "I don't know."

"Or you are not comfortable with its," his right hand swept the air above his body, "results. You would prefer that all change be internal."

Rebellion kindled briefly in her eyes, and then her ever-vigilant conscience reminded her where she was, with whom, and why. "Yes. Maybe."

"Have you known many adaptives?"

"I had friends who underwent adaptations. I met adaptees in my orientation to the AOC."

"And what has become of those friends?"

Her lips tightened, and she turned her head away. "We were all busy. And I . . . didn't want to spend credit on social activity."

He let a moment elapse, and shifted subject. "Leaving Blueheart has never occurred to me."

Her thin-skinned face was eloquent of incredulity at the very mention that he might have thought of doing as she did. He laughed, no more than a breath, and said, more astringently than he felt, "Even a zygotic adaptee can be unadapted to some extent. I'm a man, not a fish."

She had courage, he thought. And pride. She had never once in the conversation argued, qualified, or tried to make excuses. Now she looked him in the eye and said, "But you never wanted to leave Blueheart."

"No."

"I never wanted to stay."

"Because of the adaptations?"

She thought about that. "No," she said at last. "Because I wanted to be out there. At the edge of things. Adam used to say he listened for God. I'm not sure what I'll be listening for. But there'll be something."

"You've put that at risk, making the accusation you have."

"I did not make it," she said, bitterly. "Einar overheard."

"But you could have recanted."

She tipped her head back, staring at the ceiling. Her jaw was very sharp, her neck very thin. "Yes," she said, in that strained position.

"It is that," Rache said, "which makes me believe you."

She turned to stare at him, offended. What a righteous innocent she was, doubting that someone could distrust her word. He said, "You could have found no better way to discredit pastorals than to incite an uprising with rumors of conspiracy."

Her mouth opened. Rache continued, "But if you meant to do that, you should have denied your story before the situation stabilized. So what I want to ask you now is, do you understand what may happen if the AOC, or Cesar Kamehameha at least, is discredited?" Assuming, he amended silently, that we can do better in the way of proof or argument than we have. Which was by no means certain, and might depend upon you.

She said, "You do not have the numbers, and now you never will."

"Ah," said Rache. "But are you so very certain?" She looked at him and gave him no answer. He eased himself fractionally more upright. He had learned to project presence while sitting, but having come hale into his middle years, he could not escape a sense of diminution when lying down. He said, "Blueheart's ecology is unique and precious. Even without raw numbers, there are many who would rather preserve Blueheart as it is. And of them, some think that, having moved so far into space, we should accept the change that new environments . . . invite." He paused a moment, gathering his thoughts, giving her time, should she choose to answer. She merely watched him with untelling copper eyes. "Cesar," the skin around the eyes flinched at the name, "accused me of failing to think through the consequences of my development proposal. A charge to which I plead guilty. I am not sure I have thought through it now. But having seen what I have seen, I accept those consequences. I embrace the prospect of a future for Blueheart adaptives as a human subspecies, a race. But a *human* subspecies, heirs to all human tradition, and not merely pastoral tradition."

"Einar," she said, starkly, "wants rid of primaries."

Einar, thought Rache. He had avoided thinking about Einar. He did so now, with pain. Einar had fired upon him in the extremity of anger and grief. He had roused the pastorals in outrage, divided the pastorals against themselves. For all their sakes, including Einar's own, Rache could not let him continue in such a catastrophic course. But Einar—Einar took things so hard. To stop him might be to destroy him.

"Michael said you and he were close, once." He could not tell, from her neutral tone, the reason for the question, or the importance of his answer.

"We had no children," Rache said. "Lisel and I. Einar was difficult, not unloved, but not liked. He never took anything lightly, never forgave anything, seemed in a perpetual quarrel with the world. We gave him attention, settled him down somewhat. He took my leaving as an unforgivable betrayal, to him, and to Lisel." His voice was very tired, not by the past, but by what he saw before him.

She turned her head toward the screen, interest satisfied, or lost. "What are you going to do about that?"

"If there is proof," Rache said, "proof of what Cesar Kamehameha tried to do to my—to the pastorals—then I *want* that proof."

She had not missed what he had almost said. Her coin-colored eyes were unrevealing. "I have no proof."

"Would you," he said, "help me find that proof?"

Her face very still, she nodded. "I want Cesar Kamehameha," she said, with cold authority, and absolute understanding of what she was saying. "I want him brought down. For the ignoblest of reasons."

"You realize," he said, "what it may mean, how it may shift the balance of opinion again, and give myself—ourselves—a chance to defend our position, our actions, and our plans."

"Why are you insisting on telling me this?" she said.

He never had a chance to answer. The silent screen changed. Frede's image—her real image, with dusk behind her—appeared; her lips moved silently, until he keyed the controls. "Rache, you're about to have a visitor. Cesar Kamehameha's on his way across. He's at the border of Manhattan and Lovelock already."

"We must resolve this situation," Cesar Kamehameha said.

Rache said, "Yes."

The chair in which Cesar sat would hardly have cooled of Cybele's warmth. If he had passed the young woman on leaving, he gave no sign. Cesar had drawn the chair around, and closer, and sat now beside the bed, level with Rache's raised knee. There was no sign of defensiveness or strain in voice or posture. His hands, folded on his lap, were still.

Cesar said, as though in answer to Rache's brevity, "Let this go on record if you wish. I do not mind."

It did not come into Rache's mind to refuse; he would have asked for a recording himself. Recording was accomplished by a touch. Rache laid his hand down at his side, gathering himself.

Cesar said, "I understand you have undergone surgery."

"Yes," said Rache, knowing that Cesar should not have been able to determine why. But then, Cesar should not have been able to locate him in Lovelock's black zone.

"Some consequence of your earlier injuries, I surmise." Rache neither confirmed nor denied the supposition. Cesar assessed him. "But not serious."

"No."

"As I say," Cesar said, easily—trying, Rache thought, to cast Rache's unforthcomingness into relief, "we must resolve this situation. I came to you, because I trust you have enough influence to have an effect." His eyes were dark, steady, olivine green. He glanced briefly down toward where the covers hid Rache's wound. "Am I wrong?"

"My physical condition," Rache said, "has prevented me from taking an active part. Not that I could have done better than Michael so far."

"So far," Cesar said. "I do not think he will be able to resolve this impasse."

"Not," Rache said, the first engagement, "without assurances given the pastorals that what has happened will not happen again."

"What is *said* to have happened," Cesar said. "Those allegations are unfounded."

"The whitesickness," said Rache.

"Unstable transfection."

"Not . . . satisfactory," said Rache. Settle down, he told himself. Settle down. This will not be easy. He fought despair, the sense that the man's fortifications were impregnable. Cesar had, after all, suggested the recording.

"I suggest," Cesar said, in a very quiet voice, "that it should be. Your people have not served themselves or you well in this. Not in the public domain. Their volatility—"

Rache jammed an elbow behind him and forced himself more upright. "Their *anger*!" he grunted.

"There are acceptable forums for 'anger.' Public violence is not one. They are being watched, you know that. They are making a spectacle of atavistic behavior, this *angry* minority. When you bid for permanence, this is what will be remembered and replayed. This." He waved his hand; the wallscreen lit. On it, Einar angled his speargun toward the gray-faced primary's temple. Rache closed his eyes. He said, "They have every right to be angry."

"Such demonstrations place them more at risk than anyone else." He heard a rustle as Cesar moved, and opened his eyes to find that the Director had leaned forward, elbows on knees, palms comfortably upturned. "There are statutes, you see, statutes which can be invoked to contain dangerous maladaptations. They are very old, having been created at a time when the mental effects of adaptation could be unpredictable. But they have never been revoked." He turned his head, toward the silenced wallscreen where Einar was backing medical staff away from their consoles with drawn speargun.

Rache swallowed nausea, and did what he knew he must: drew the console to him, fitted a hand into the cradle, and searched the legal databanks for the pertinent statutes. They were there, as Cesar had said. He said, despairingly, "They are not dangerous maladaptations. You know that. I know that."

Cesar tilted his head slightly, his expression worldly and tolerant, allowing that Rache would see the irrelevance. Rache pushed the console and web away. "What do you want?"

"Advise your people that there was no truth in those allegations made against myself and the AOC."

"Cybele—"

"What price will you pay for believing Cybele de Courcey?"

Rache shifted slightly, trying to ease the pressure in his belly. Absurd to concern himself with the indignity of vomiting in front of his adversary. Or maybe not absurd, maybe the concern was strategically sound. Cesar had certainly seized upon every other advantage.

And the danger of it, Rache thought, is that I do believe in his conscience. He would sacrifice himself willingly for the future of Blueheart and the integrity of the human species. He would sacrifice himself, and any number of individuals: I have seen him do so. But he will not ally himself with chaos. He will stop—somewhere. I am surer of my adversary than my allies. After the rage, the grief, the hatred, and the violence, some serene conviction is so calming. I must remember that the rage, the hatred, have cause, and conflict within them, and can be changed. Just give me time, and strength.

But as Cesar warned and he knew, he had neither.

He said, "There will be no more sabotage of the unauthorized adaptations."

Cesar sat unmoving, not acknowledging that Rache had spoken. Rache said, harshly, "Will you continue in your undermining of unauthorized adaptations?"

"All adaptations will be logged and monitored by the AOC according to usual procedure. Appropriate treatment will be given those people whose adaptations are unsuitable or inadequate for their lifestyle."

"You will not be part of the review panel."

"I am the Director of the AOC."

"Exempt yourself," said Rache.

Cesar smiled slightly, and bowed his acknowledgment. No, satisfaction. Rache wiped his face with a hand. And that was only a small concession won, and one it seemed Cesar had allowed for; it hardly incriminated him to yield to pastoral whim.

He thought, If, *if* I can persuade them to make themselves part of public record, then they should be safe from that at least. Cesar could not do them harm knowing that they were monitored.

He said, "And the legal case against the parents. I would like them issued amnesty."

"I doubt that is possible."

Rache said, "Then arrange that the sentences be suspended. There must be some clause which would allow that . . . mercy. It is not as though punishment serves as deterrent. The situation is unique; it will never happen again." Cesar said nothing, merely watching him with secretive, olivine-colored eyes. Rache said, "If you want peace, you cannot send them for rehabilitation. They would not stand for it. And it is purely political: to disgrace and disenfranchise them." He checked himself, knowing he did so too late.

Cesar tugged lightly at his fingers, as though checking the fit of his skin. "Rache," he said, mildly, "you speak as though you have a tenable negotiating position. You cannot claim there has been no violation of adaptation law. Those occupying the AOC are in violation of numerous other laws. You are a man of conscience and conviction, yet your best efforts have failed to prevent violence, bloodshed, and death."

"That cannot . . ." Rache said raggedly, "be laid to me."

"I have told you the options."

"Yes," Rache said, "you have." Tempted as he was to try again to sit, he resisted. If he must do this propped on pillows, so be it. "You could have held it in reserve, until you needed it, but you did not; you made sure I knew it; you made sure to frighten me. Why, if my position is so impotent, need you frighten me? You are not given to bullying. I think you need me more than you would have me know. I think Cybele's allegations threaten you more than you care to admit."

"Allegations—" Cesar started, and snapped his teeth closed. The surge of triumph Rache had felt when he started to speak went cold, watery, foul in the pit of his stomach. So *close*. Whatever Cesar had almost said might have been what they *needed*. Rache could see it in his eyes, in the hard muscle closing his jaw.

"Or I," Rache finished, lamely, "threaten you more than you care to admit."

For an instant he saw the arrogance behind the olivine eyes, the arrogance of a century-old earthborn, master and idealogue. The arrogance that dismissed him, dismissed all his people, as a transient artifact of progress. And then the arrogance was gone, and Cesar dipped his head slightly, humbly, as though to take upon himself some of the reproach of Rache's ill nature and ill judgment. There could, Rache thought, with sick appreciation, have been no response more damning.

Cesar lifted his head, his face composed. "I think," he said, "you are still suffering from your misadventure, and that the recording of this session would do you an injustice. I freely consent to its erasure."

"I do not so consent," said Rache, forcefully. "I want it on record that I have asked you these things. I want it on record that you have refused to answer. I will not be alone in facing the judgment of history."

"The judgment of history," Cesar murmured. "I think you may find that the judgment of history is less kind to you than you seem to think. History may judge

your insistence on amnesty, for instance, to be somewhat self-serving."

Rache felt his teeth bare. "Indeed it is," he said. "I
do not want these people prevented from supporting the
preservation of Blueheart."

Cesar leaned back slightly. "Meredis Lopez was
amazed at your ignorance. Somehow, I am not. When I
go back to the AOC, it will be to add your name to the
list of indictable parents of illegally adapted children.
Your wife bore a daughter, some seven months after her
disappearance. The child was adapted, illegally, by
Meredis Lopez. Her gene read appears in the records
secured from Grayling station. A simple comparison
with yours was sufficient." He paused. "Her name, I
believe, is Athene."

"Holy God," Karel breathed, watching the tableau on
the screen. "It's a bloodbath." Rache had half turned
away from Cesar, one hand lifting to shield his face.

"You said it," said Frede, her voice tight with anger.
"I want him out of there, now. If he won't go, I'm going
to need a volunteer to put him out."

Even Teal could feel the stiffening of the brother
and sister on either side of her. "I will. I do not fear
him."

That, Frede's headshake said, was perhaps a little
too explicit, a little too accurate, for gentleness. Karel
looked ready to deny his fear; Cybele simply looked
angry. But Cesar went without argument, his face showing neither remorse nor gratification. Rache lay back,
eyes closed, head moving unconsciously back and forth.
His color was, even to Teal's eyes, ghastly. Frede said,

"The rest of you, eyes out. I'll let you know if I need on-site help." Rache's image disappeared; hers yielded to the sunlit, serene countenance of the construct, who said, "Let's have some consistency here," and a moment later was regarding them with that same serenity from Frede's rain-shadowed, untidy office. "Fear not, my friends," she said, "Rache's tough. And Cesar's made some tactical blunders."

"But there is no proof," Cybele said, blackly. "And he admitted nothing."

"Can he really have the adaptives ruled dangerous?" Karel said. "Does such a law exist?"

"It exists," Cybele said, bitterly.

"Please stand aside a moment," Teal said, and waited until they had moved beyond station pickup before she opened a channel to the public station on Rossby docks. "I am Teal Blane Berenice," she said, to the adaptive-liaison there. "I need to speak with Lisel of Magellan."

Suspicious looks, from both sides of the screen. She ignored her half siblings, and said, to the liaison, "She will talk to me." He disappeared. Teal stared at distant figures, and the shining sea, until Lisel slid into view, wary.

"You said," Teal said, without preamble, "that I had an enemy. You did not want that enemy drawn near your daughter. I regret that that enemy now knows, through Grayling station records, of your daughter's existence."

Lisel laid both hands upon the screen, red palms like starfish, and leaned close, as toward a window. "Teal, where in all the eight quarters of the seas is Rache? Does he know what's going on here, what Einar's done?"

Teal wondered whether Rache would wish the truth told his wife, including that Rache had also learned of Athene's existence, and how. She remembered the sight of Rache's devastated face, and said, only, "He knows. He will be with you when he is able."

"Is able? Something's happened to him. When Einar—" She caught herself, recoiling from the thought. "Einar came back in such a strange mood. I almost feared . . . Teal, is this true, what Einar said about the AOC . . . ?"

"I do not know," Teal said. "But if it can be proven, we, and Rache, will do so."

Lisel looked intently at her. "Tell him I want to see him. I want to be sure he is all right. Einar—I was afraid Einar had done him harm. And we need him; tell him that. Whatever anyone might say, we need him. We are as ignorant as any of our children in this. But thank you, thank you for your warning. Athene is as safe as any of our children can be. An indulgence, I know, that I protect mine, while others . . ." For a moment, tears glimmered in her eyes, and then she contained herself, drew her hands down and stood back from the screen. "Thank you for your warning. Tell Rache to come as soon as he can." She glanced over her shoulder, and slid out of frame. Teal closed the circuit.

"You did not tell her," Karel said.

"No." She did not explain, because she could not have justified what she had done. Lisel could not have known what use Cesar might make of Rache's ignorance. And yet, she thought deeply, wordlessly, that Lisel did not deserve to know about Rache's wound.

"You knew about Rache's daughter?" Cybele said.

"I met her. When I was marooned. She was good to me. Lisel asked that I not endanger her by drawing attention to her. That Athene is *his* daughter, I did not know until now." She looked from one to the other; they seemed to expect more, and on reflection, she found more. "Lisel had brought her to Grayling. She had the whitesickness."

There was a silence. "She *had* the virus," Cybele said, on a breath.

"It won't still be in her cells," Karel said, "or they'd have found it at Grayling."

Heat slowly mounted in Cybele's pale face. "Yes, but she's had it, and we haven't spoken to anyone who has. There may be something she knows that can help us: contacts, location. Teal, where did you meet her? Is she nearby? You said you were on Kense: did you meet her on Kense?"

Karel said, "What makes you think she will help us?" They looked at him; he flushed slightly. "Not to malign her, but she's Lisel's daughter, pure illegal; who's to say she won't be set to follow Einar."

As one, they turned to Teal. Asking, Teal realized, for her judgment. "She knows of the rafttowns. She would have brought me. I think . . ." venturing into unfamiliar terrain, "her father is an ideal to her."

"I hope she likes the reality," Karel said. He and Cybele were leaning forward in identical poses, expectant.

A moment, then Teal understood. She said, quite forcibly, "I cannot countenance anything which puts her at risk."

Karel said, prestissimo, "Wherever she is, she's at risk, and if she knows anything it would help us, and all we have to do is contact her. If I go out on *Albatross* now, I'll be at the boomer-relay in—"

"You don't have to do that," Frede's construct said.

"I can tell you how to send a message from where you are." She smiled slightly at their expressions. "Do you think Michael slogs all the way out to the boomer-relay?" She paused, enough to let them appreciate that the comfort-loving liaison would in all likelihood not, and then said, with much less levity, "But I'd give some thought to the composition. You cannot be telling everyone in and out of the seas who you are, who you want, and what you want."

Karel said, dubiously, "We could encode it."

The construct said, "I was thinking more in terms of using something that Athene would recognize as coming from Teal. An allusion to shared experience." They looked, expectantly, at Teal, who had nothing to say. Encoding was straightforward, allusion something beyond her.

The construct said, "Why not tell us what happened between yourself and Athene. We can work from there."

Teal stood up, walked away from them, making movement speak for her. She had said what she thought, but they were not listening. She would not place at risk that large-hearted, inquisitive child on Kense. She would not draw Athene, in all her innocence, to this place of conspiracy and silent assassination. She waited, staring out the window at Lovelock's sunlit bay, and the hazy silhouette of Manhattan docks.

Karel said, "You won't do it." There was something in his voice that sounded like Juniper, thwarted. She said, a little sharply, "I will not put her at risk." And then, because she thought it was something he might understand, "Without her, I might not be here."

But that was not why Athene was too important to risk in this, she thought, as Karel shriveled. Her life had been an abstraction to her, was in a sense, still. Athene had simply accepted her, in all her strangeness, her dissociation, her irrationality; and that, she thought, even in this, valued company, was rare and more precious to her than life.

She walked back to her place before the console and sat down. The construct said, "I can't criticize you for that, though it would be extremely helpful to have a personal account of the whitesickness."

"What," Cybele said, "do you suggest we do?" Her voice was brittle.

Teal considered Frede's image. Sophisticated as it was, the construct, like all its kind, would have the obligatory legal-ethical underlay to its programming. Though its sympathies might be seemingly engaged, and it be willing to offer its skills and knowledge to their ends, it lacked the latitude of its original. They could not involve it in any lawbreaking. They would not even discuss their activities before it with impunity. Should its underlay oblige it to report their actions, there would be no negotiation.

She said, "Please withdraw all monitoring. Advise us if either Frede or Rache needs our assistance."

"Of course. Please call me if you need further information or assistance." With a slight smile—and a natural-looking gesture toward her console—she withdrew, her image replaced by a sunlit shore, on which waves were breaking. Teal blanked the screen, and laid her hands down side by side on the console. "I have reconsidered attempting incursion into the AOC files at this time. System access on all levels appears to be under high-security surveillance. I do find it curious that the system was not simply locked against incursion."

"Do you?" Cybele said, still sounding brittle.

"Might this not be the way to learn your adversaries"
real abilities?"

Teal acknowledged the likelihood by not dissenting.
"That also suggests to me that the AOC has no concern
as to the accessibility of incriminating material."

"What do you think we should do?"

"It depends," Teal said, "what you wish to
achieve." She found Cybele's silver-toned reflection in
the blanked screen.

Karel said, "Cyb, I'm willing to testify."

"He'll destroy you."

"He's already failed once," Karel said, with barely a
waver in his voice.

Cybele leaned between Teal and the console. "Find
me evidence," she said. "Evidence that will blemish this
immaculate façade of his. It was eight years ago he
learned of the illegal adaptives. Eight years ago he might
have been less circumspect about what he did. Find me
the references he searched. Find me the people he contacted." She crouched down beside Teal, balancing on
her fingertips. "There was a high-resolution survey: I
can tell you which one. Find Cesar's access, eight years
ago. That will tell you when to begin."

It had a certain elegance to it, Teal thought; she gave
it the accolade of a nod, before turning to her work. She
was vaguely aware of them taking their positions on
either side of her, and Karel giving Cybele some instructions before linking to her. He had grown deft at interpreting her difficulties and supplying subroutines
revised for her impaired interface even as they worked.

Some little time later they received an alert of an
incoming message. Teal would have disregarded it, all
her concentration being absorbed in refining a plethora
of data, in extracting a pattern. Karel shook her—a

most novel experience for a former expert—until she looked at the screen, which now displayed a static image of Frede's construct, posed in her tidy, sunlit office. Teal frowned at Karel, and signaled her receptiveness. The construct became animate; she smiled, with a very human self-satisfaction. "My original suggested I monitor pastoral activities in public domain, in case anything of interest should arise. I think, given the subject of our earlier discussion, you should see this." Her image dwindled to a screen-edge sliver, beside views of one of the barriers, one from a distance, showing the figure rising on it as a dark comma, and one enhanced, so that the figure stood revealed. Brilliant water ran from Athene's red skin, and pooled around her feet. Her head was up, her eyes wide, staring dockward; their discolored whites glittering in their shadowed sockets. She hardly breathed. Every sense was alert, fully extended to her surroundings. In one hand, she held a speargun.

The construct said, smugly, "The resemblance is unmistakable, I thought."

"Is that Athene?" Karel said.

Teal got to her feet. "Yes. It is," answering both.

The construct anticipated her: "There's no need to go out. Michael's abode is fully equipped with beacons and whatnot. If you give me leave, I will signal her in."

"I give you leave," said Teal, a little tightly. "But do it circumspectly."

She went out onto the jetty. She did not inquire how Frede planned to signal her in, or respond when the construct advised her that Athene was on her way in. Inside, Karel and Cybele could track her underwater. She concentrated her attention on the distant, empty barrier, and the sparkling water between.

The girl surfaced at the very end of the jetty, saw

Teal, and the tension released in her frame with a great shudder. She slung her speargun from hand to back, before she heaved herself out of the water. Teal went to meet her. Two-handed, she reached out in greeting. Teal said, taking the hands, "You should not have come."

Athene blinked water from her eyes, and shivered again, and said, "I had to."

From the door, Karel said, "Teal, shouldn't we go indoors? In case."

Athene hesitated, looking past her at him. Teal said, "It is best you come," and Athene came. But on the threshold, seeing the primaries, she balked in mid-step. Teal said, "They are trustworthy." Karel flinched, and Cybele's lips twisted. Athene, seeing, looked at her wide-eyed, her narrow nostrils flaring. Teal sought for something better. "This is my half brother, Karel. And my half sister, Cybele. Karel, Cybele, Athene of Magellan. Rache's daughter." Athene finished her step, and dipped into a motion half bow, half curtsey. Karel blushed, sophisticate that he was, at the long, unself-conscious nakedness of her. She wore only a trove of ornate woven bands on wrists, neck, waist, and ankles; even the strap of her speargun was decorative and new. Cybele stood straight, with a look neither welcoming nor unwelcoming. Teal had a sense that she had done something right, understood something important; with her simple introduction, she had invited a connection to form, through her. It warred with her worldless, fretful anxiety. This child was not Juniper, this she knew, but she had had no one since on whom to practice concern.

She said, "We sent no message. Why have you come?"

Athene's face opened in a wide, nervous smile.

"Were you going to send for me?" she said. "Is my father here? I have to speak to him."

Cybele gave Teal a wary sideways glance. "Since you are here, we'd like to ask you some questions."

Athene's face closed, between one breath and the next. Her shoulders tensed, showing their power. "Not before I talk to my father."

"This is important—"

"I want to talk to my *father*," Athene said, to Teal.

Karel said, diffidently, "It might help him."

Athene looked at him, on the verge of a question; then she turned her black, intent gaze back to Teal: the elder, the authority.

Teal said, "I was not going to send for you. I was not going to put you at risk."

Athene said stubbornly, "If you will not tell me where he is, then I will go somewhere else and ask."

Michael might have been able to negotiate; Teal did not know how. And it was not Athene's request she wished to negotiate, but Athene's very presence. She said, "I will take you." And then paused, with an unexpected, unpleasant thought. "But I should ask you to leave your speargun here. Rache was wounded last night, by someone he trusted well."

Athene stared at him, her lips parted. Then quickly, as though she feared contamination or implication, she slipped the strap of the speargun from her shoulder and the knife from her sheath, and laid them side by side, on the floor beside the door. Karel said, sounding pained, "Teal, *tell* her he's all right."

He was right; she should have. But she thought what he said should have sufficed until she saw Athene looking at her, in appeal. She said, "He is not well. But he has had good care, and it will show in time. I think," she said, after a moment, reluctantly, "he will be better for seeing you." It felt a false promise, for all she trusted it would be so. She could not fathom Rache's rich, moody spirit, truer than Juniper's, broader than her own.

She walked Athene along the docks to the medical facility in silence. She uplinked to Frede and advised her of their arrival. At the door, she said, "I will wait." Frede opened the door, and Athene entered, without a word.

NINETEEN

Rache heard the door open and close, felt the probe and curl of a draught. Someone came into the room on soundless feet. He waited for Frede to speak to them, or for them. She had not asked him if he wanted to see anyone; had she, he would have refused. He did not want to open his eyes. The thought of readmitting the world nauseated him. He could not, he thought, stand much more of its treachery and hurt. Lisel had had a daughter. And that, too, she had kept from him. So he learned of his daughter even as he learned of his abject impotence to save her and his kind.

A strange voice said, "Rache of Scole?" A young voice, a female voice, but deeper than most, speaking with the soft slur of the northern waters. Only a lifetime's habit of courtesy and gentleness toward the young prevented him from ordering her away unseen. He sighed, heavily, and opened his eyes. The room seemed very bright; he had been quite some time not looking around him. Squinting, he saw a figure, standing with that tense, slightly slouched posture of the young; he drew breath for a familiar greeting. Then his vision cleared, and he held it: he had never seen her before in his life.

At least, he thought, she did not look threatening. Tense, expectant, but not hostile. He considered her, and she him. She had arrayed herself for this meeting, too;

arms, wrists, waist, and neck wound with woven bands, wide and narrow, inlaid or plain. The widest a collar around her throat, so that she held her head high, and a little stiffly. He took pity on her. "I am Rache of Scole. What might I do for you?"

"I am," a quick breath, "Athene of Magellan."

The name gave him a small shock, and sharpened his attention, made him look past the youth and the ornamentation, and see what had made him almost greet her. She was younger than he had at first thought, her height, and broad-shouldered frame deceptive, and her long face, and curving nose giving her the look of maturity. As Lisel's did.

As Lisel's did. Now he could see Lisel's height, and broad-shouldered frame; Lisel's full breasts and hips, and posture and presence.

Her eyes were very dark, nearly black, like Astrid's, his sister Athene's . . . his own.

He felt lightheaded, alarmingly so. It was not unpleasant, but self-possession was suddenly desperately important. He did not want to be embarrassed by his weakness or delusions. He wished they had met anywhere but here. He saw her swallow against the bright woven band around her throat. He understood her adornment. She had come into this room feeling as he felt now, the utter necessity to be at her best, her finest. He was moved. Sparing her the need, he took a clumsy plunge into the heart of it. "Should I—hope to know you better. Athene?"

"Oh yes!" she said.

Wordless, he put out a hand, both hands. As to clean water after swimming through foul. He had not thought he would ever be clean, after that filthy, futile scene with Cesar. He should have been terrified to find her here, at the grim wall of the storm. But she looked so like Lisel, despite her name, and Lisel was a dauntless survivor. So he simply held out his hands. She stepped in to seize both, smiling like sunlight. He smiled back. He did not want to speak or her to speak. Speech would merely complicate things. With her mother it always had.

"Does Lisel know you are here?" he said, at last.

She tossed her head, irritated. "No. I wanted to do it for myself and," in a rush, "I knew you would argue. Because of her hiding me."

Rache grunted a laugh. How well it seemed she knew them, never having seen them together.

"She had to hide me," Athene said, intensely. "But she told me everything—about the illegals, about Blueheart, about you . . . who you were, what you did. She had stopped expecting to have children; she said she hadn't thought it through properly; she says that she realized she was lucky it hadn't arisen before. Because she knew you would never have let me be adapted illegally. And you would not have, would you?" she challenged. "Not after—the other Athene. And as soon as they compared my genotyping with the database, they'd have known she was an illegal. She *had* to leave. But she does love you."

Rache closed his eyes. "Love," he said, "has never been one of our wants." He gathered himself, opened his eyes. "Don't you *ever* feel you have to explain or apologize for her. Not to me." The wide, black eyes watched him, longing to be convinced. He said, with some difficulty, "Besides, if she has told you everything, she must have told you I was also in love with someone else. I left the sea with Juniper, in part because of her." Still she watched him, wanting something more. He wondered what that might be, and if it might be given as simply as a few words. He said, "And yet, there was scarcely a day went by when I did not have something I wanted to tell her."

She smiled. "And I have something I want to tell you. I know I'm only young," apologizing for the presumption of intruding on her elders' affairs. "But I've been listening to the messages, about this virus and the lack of *proof* and how landsmen won't do anything without *proof*, and what they're saying we should do. And it frightens me." She brought up her head, rejecting the childishness of the statement, and said with authority. "That's why I came to you, because I didn't *trust* the others, what they would do with proof if they had it. It could make them act even worse."

"What would you do with proof if you had it?" he said.

"I'd make them leave us alone," she said promptly. "We are not so many that we have the majority. We are not so many that we will threaten the decision. But we are enough that we will make people think about Blueheart staying a waterworld. And we have chosen what we are and we have a right to remain as we choose." Releasing one hand, she reached for a stool and pulled it toward herself. She perched on it, squirming at its feel beneath her buttocks and twining and untwining her long legs around its legs. "Some people say that they could make us be changed back, because the adaptations were illegally done."

"That will not happen," Rache said, flatly. "It has been a fundamental principle, from the very earliest years of human engineering, that adaptations can neither be made nor reversed without a competent subject's permission." He could not, he thought, accept that arcane, barbarous law with which Cesar had threatened him. He would *not* let it threaten his daughter. He said, "And it has also been an equally long-held principle that political dissent is not a sign of mental incompetence."

She watched him intently. "And what about them accusing the people who've had their children illegally adapted of abuse?"

Rache's hand tightened. "They would have to prove harm, Athene. All those legal moves are harassment. They are meant to distract, and to intimidate."

"Suppose they could prove harm. Suppose they could prove that the adaptations were no good. That they reversed of themselves, broke down."

"You mean the whitesickness?" She did not nod, merely watched him, her eyes like liquid obsidian. And he suddenly saw that this young daughter of his was testing him. Had been from his indulgent and, he now appreciated, impertinent, question as to what she would do. For what was to be determined here was not what she would do, but what he would do. Whether he was to be trusted, as others were not. He felt his hand shake in hers, and her eyes widened.

"Athene," he said, "*do* you think you have proof?"

She straightened, sliding her hand from his. "Yes."

Unheld, his hand was heavier than he thought. He jarred it gracelessly on the edge of the bed. "Will you tell me?"

"What will you do with it?"

"I can bring a man to justice who needs bringing to justice. I can prove that pastorals were as much sinned against as sinning." He tried to ease himself higher on the backrest; a mistake. "If you want to see what I would do with it, call up my development proposal. That contains my best thought, all my best thought."

He did not want to plead his weakness, but though the delight persisted, the excitement was wearing off.

But she was not done. Hands fisted on the edge of the stool, on either side of her thighs, she hunched and nearly glared at him. Glared with all the force of her indecision. "Can you? I mean, are you *strong* enough. Teal told me you were wounded by someone you trusted."

"I don't know whether I'm strong enough to influence either side," Rache said frankly. "From a pastoral perspective, I am only in early middle age, and in the survey service, I am a middle-ranking administrator. I haven't the authority to face down, say, Maria of Kense, or Cesar Kamehameha." Nor the skill, he thought. "My competence as an implementer of other people's policies is acknowledged. But my loyalties are suspect. I have espoused reintegration to pastorals and non-development to primaries. But I have . . . some uncommon assets. I have lived on both sides of the divide. When pastorals accuse me of being primary, and primaries look askance at my pastoral habits, they are recognizing not a failing, Athene, but a success. I *chose* to live in, and be of, both worlds. And I am. I have tried to make a strength of it, and I believe I have. And my other assets are the people I know. I know all the people who are at the heart of this. I knew Juniper. I know Lisel. I know Bede, Astrid, Tove . . . and I have, I have the help of good and talented people: Michael, Frede, Teal Blane Berenice, Cybele, and Karel—yourself, I hope." He hoped, too, he did not sound as faded as he felt. He raised his hand, to what end he did not know, and let it fall.

She said, in a small, tight voice, "And the person who tried to kill you?"

"That lies between him and me," Rache said.

He let the silence expand. He could not believe she could offer the proof that no one else had. No matter what unrealistic part of him wanted to hope she could. But he wanted her to trust him, to regard him well enough to offer.

She said, "I've had the whitesickness myself." She slid from the stool, and stood at the bedside, hands by her sides, looking down at him. Her face was very serious, determined that he be worthy of her trust. "I've had this virus. That is why Mother and I were in these waters, because we rode down to Grayling while I was sick and being cured. *I'm* the proof."

"Athene—" he said, and she, "You don't see it! I've had the virus. If it isn't still in me, it will be in the samples that Dr. Lopez took from me!"

"Don't you think," Meredis Lopez's image said, "that was the first thing any of us *checked* when we heard about the allegations?"

He had reached her, with effort, and persistence, on a floating platform in the southern polar seas. She had family there, who had taken her in, sheltered her, sheltered themselves. They were equipped to: Keyes platform had been privately built by a self-selected community; its black-zoning was even more stringent than Lovelock's. He had used up all his privileges and drawn upon Michael's—as investigator of the R6 disaster—to overrule their interface's polite denials of contact.

Meredis did not belong in the room in which she sat. It was austere, ordered, discreetly decorated and accoutred; he had the impression of gray and piped silver. With her ruddy skin, flaming hair and scarlet shirt, she looked as ill placed in it as a reef fish in a tank, and as cheerful.

"That's not possible," Athene said, from his shoulder—he had carefully narrowed and aligned the pickup so that she should not see where he was. "I was *sick*."

"Athene . . ." Meredis's eyes sought the edge of the frame. "Rache, let me see her . . ." He pushed the console and pickup around so that it faced his angry daughter. Meredis, he realized, had a genuine affection for the girl. "Athene, do you remember when I explained why my treatments would not make you better immediately?"

"Because of the time the virus took to spread and make blood cells with the new pigments," she said, a little grudgingly. But she reached out and held the console delicately between both broad, ruddy hands.

"It would be the same thing here. The virus would take time to affect you. By the time you, or anyone, began losing the ability to dive, it could have been tens of days after you were infected, and by then the virus would be *gone*. There is no virus left in your system, or in the system of anyone who has the disease." Athene looked both sullen and stricken. Meredis's voice said, "But thank you, my dear. It was an honest effort."

"But it wasn't enough." She shoved the console around to face Rache, without regard for Rache's careful alignment; he tilted it up quickly, but not before Meredis's eyes had widened.

She leaned forward, peering at the screen. "Where are you? Are you ill?"

He gazed stubbornly back at her. "What can you tell me about what I might be looking for? Can you give me a timeframe—when Athene might have been infected?"

She slumped forward, bracing forearms on thighs. Her rumpled scarlet shirt slid off one shoulder, and she pushed it irritably back. "Depends on the design of the virus, depends very much on the design. Lisel brought her in three months ago, but said she had been impaired for nearly a month before that. By the time I saw her, she had less than twenty percent adaptive oxygen transport and storage, and her stem cell population had almost entirely reverted. If he were using a standard form of virus, I would say she had been infected two to three months before. But if there'd been active virus, in Athene or any of the others, we would have found it."

"And in people who were infected, but show no symptoms?"

She shrugged, and straightened slightly. "Maybe. But only if we looked. And we can't. The AOC has our records, our personnel files, our samples. I haven't been in contact with any of my colleagues. A condition of my being 'released' to come here." She gave him an unhappy smile, and said in a low, strained voice, "In one way it's such a relief to hear there might have been . . . something. In another . . . we'll never prove it. We'll have something else that we have to deny." She shook her head, sharply. "Hell, listen to me, who's still standing. Rache, about your niece, I am so sorry. So very sorry."

"So am I," he said.

"I'm glad you two have finally met. But for God's sake, look after her."

Rache gave a strained smile. "I'll try."

Athene was standing with her back to him, shoulders slumped. "Athene," he said. "Come back to me. It's all right."

"It is not all right," she said, swinging around. "I was so sure. I put you through all that because I was so sure that what I had was important, and I kept you talking and talking, making you answer my questions." He had forgotten how a sixteen-year-old did remorse, heaping anguish upon anguish until you writhed to hear it—but would turn on you in fury should you presume to suggest that it was anything less than dire, the vilest crime you'd ever heard. Rache simply closed his eyes until she noticed, and said in a small voice, "Rache?"

"It was a fine thought," Rache said. "It might have been right. That it was not is not your—" And the idea bloomed suddenly in his mind. He pulled himself half upright, not feeling the clenching in his side, and yanked the console toward him. Athene stepped forward, and he held up his hand, staying her. "Cybele de Courcey," he said, and stared hard at the screen until the young primary's image appeared. She still looked heartbreakingly tired, skin sallow, ocher rings around her eyes. "Cybele, tell me again what Cesar said about the virus and the algae. Tell me exactly. The algae was the carrier, to make sure it was distributed, yes. And it was painter algae, to ensure it would be ingested."

"Yes." A silence. "But it made the algae less viable, more susceptible to blight. So it didn't get as widespread, or last as long as he wanted." She waited, with a certain distracted resignation. Behind her, he could hear Karel talking, and Teal's terse, low answers.

"But when?" Rache murmured. "*When?* is the question."

Athene said, from his side, "You think it could still be there, in the algae. But why there if not in us?"

Rache smiled, delighted by his daughter's swiftness. "Oh, not in today's algae." He paused, watching the shifting of expression on Cybele's fine-boned, thin-skinned primary's face. Concentration to bewilderment, to the beginning of understanding and hope. He did not torment her further. "One of the studies I was working on involved the painter algae blight. There are extensive samples of algae from all areas and the whole of last year stored in ringsol six, and the central sample banks."

A flush rose in Cybele's sallow face. "Please, *quickly*," she said, and clasped her hands before her in an unthinking gesture of prayer. "Before anyone else thinks of it. Before *he* thinks of it."

He might, Rache thought, already have. If that were what he feared of Rache, and not merely Rache's ability to moderate and unite the pastorals.

"Wait," he said. "Wait." He cradled his hand clumsily, establishing the interface which would let him recall sample information stored in his own cercortex. "As you suggest, we may have but one chance. Though I do think that if he tries to interfere with banked ecological samples, he will have no small amount of explaining to do. But it would be best if we did not risk his being able to do so. He has already persuaded the survey service to truncate its investigation of ringsol six." He scrolled swiftly through records of surveys made by himself, by others, by automata. He could feel his pulse in his wound. "Athene," he said, "tell me where you swam six months ago. Exactly now."

"These," he said, moments later. "These are my best guess, based upon what Meredis has said about the timing of the whitesickness, where Athene has been, and the distribution of the blight . . ." Cybele was staring at him with eyes as blank as scales; she neither could, nor cared to, check his reasoning. He paused, made himself recalculate dates, regions, accounts, before he submitted them to her. His hands were clumsy on the console. Athene was leaning close, fascinated. "These are the samples you should ask to examine from the stores of ringsol six. They're all from areas where Athene was swimming around the time she contracted the virus. They'll all have duplicates in the central stores, so your work can be verified. Do you know what you are looking for?"

"Yes."

"I have no authority to access anything on ringsol six. You'll have to approach Chandar—he's acting director. What you tell him, I'll have to leave up to your judgment. He's never struck me as being perturbed by adaptation, even the possibility of permanent adaptation, but a great deal has happened since we last spoke—"

She gave him a hunter's smile. "Leave it to me."

Frede said, "Rache, I think you should see this."

Rache had been giving Athene her first instruction on the use of the planetary net. Lisel had done nothing to quench Athene's avid interest in the world he had chosen. He rather resented the interruption.

Frede's image leaned against the back of the chair, arms folded, face grave and eyes warm.

"After he left you, Cesar Kamehameha went directly to Rossby docks. He boarded Scole's tainu and conferred with the elders of Scole and Emerald Ridge. Since they were in yellow zone, and he is who he is, we have no access to what was said. But I think we might draw our own conclusions." She placed on the screen an image of Cesar stepping from tainu to docks, his face sliding into resolution. Behind him, the pastorals remained seated and very still, watching him walk away. He looked neither right nor left, moving with a gliding, assured stride. Frede said, "A little later, the Scole tainu cast off, and now I think there is little doubt as to where they are heading." The screen changed, showing the tainu gliding with slow strokes across the cleared water toward the AOC's docks. On the docks, a handful of the younger pastorals waited, uneasy.

Tove stepped, queenlike, from tainu to docks, inclined her head in acknowledgment, and entered the doors. The other elders followed, and lastly Lisel, Astrid, and Keri. Michael was the one to greet them, leaving a ring of young pastorals. He looked, Rache thought, as though he found it a genuine pleasure that they were there.

Tove said: "I have come to speak to our young. Can you grant us privacy?" She gestured to the air.

"No," Michael said. "I can't."

She gave him a look which challenged, have you tried? but Michael withstood it.

Tove said, "A pity." She turned to Einar. "I have come to tell you that it is over," she said.

There was a silence; her eyes moved over the faces around her, measuring her authority. "You must leave here, now. If you do not, you may bring extinction down on us, not in some indefinite tomorrow, but today."

Bede said, quietly, "That is not good enough, Tove."

He was just senior enough to argue with her. "For nearly thirty years I have served the AOC, kept the oaths and code unbroken. I will not leave until I am certain that they have kept their oaths to me, as an adaptive."

"And what," Tove said, "have you found?"

"Nothing," Bedevere said. "But whatever else my son may be, he is no liar. If he says there is something to be found, I believe him."

Einar drew breath, with a glance at his father. Tove said, before he could speak, "Then you are the one to confirm for us all. There is a law, a very ancient law, from the troubled earliest days of genetic engineering. According to that law, a human variant which proves itself dangerous is exempt from all considerations and rights, including the right to bodily integrity and self-determination."

"I have not heard of such a law," Bede said, after a moment's silence.

Tove gestured him to the nearest workstation. Michael's expression was suddenly grim, and sickened. He said, "I have. Dear God, I had forgotten all about it. But they cannot apply it in this case . . ."

"I am told they can, and will," Tove said.

Bedevere leaned over the workstation. Rache had never seen his brother working in his primary environment before, and he was taken by the quickness and lightness of Bede's touchstrokes. Then suddenly Bede's hand closed, thudding against the screen, not violence, but a loss of balance. He steadied himself, ashen despite his adaptive color.

Einar thrust his way to Bedevere's side, scanned the display. His face darkened, suffused with blood. "They cannot do this!" he said.

"You know as little of primaries as the daughter we have just given to the sea."

Einar jerked; his spear hand flinched; Rache's gut

knotted; and Bedevere caught Einar's wrist and pinned it beneath the console. Unseen, but Tove knew what she had almost drawn. Unmoved, she said, "How can you say what they can and cannot do?"

Athene said, "It was him. He hurt you."

He realized that his hand was pressing his side.

Frede said calmly, "Rache? Are you doing all right?"

On the screen Tove said, "Why should they bother with illegal viruses when law allows them to do whatever they will with us?" And in her voice was a profound bitterness. "If we allow them to rule us dangerous, then we have lost even the time we would have had between now and the final decision."

Rache said, "Frede, I need to get over there."

"Teal, I'm afraid I need your help again," Rache's voice said from behind her. With hardly a thought, she pinned up his image on one of her screens. He leaned against the doorjamb, holding his side. He was wearing a red and gold kimono made for a leaner, less ruddy man.

Athene started past him, and paused. "I *am* going with you," she said, in a low voice, continuing an argument.

There was, Teal thought, a fair resemblance between them, despite their markedly different adaptations, and lifelong separation. She interrupted the mutual glaring down. "Whatever you need, ask quickly. I used a rather conspicuous decoy to ensure Cybele and Karel's departure went unobserved, and I am not as adept at concealment now as before." While she spoke, and he, a civil man, looked at her, Athene slipped away, through the door, onto the docks. Teal visualized her as she set to rigging Michael's skiff. Rache sighed.

He made his way across to her, and laid a hand on the screen. Leaned upon the screen; she saw the reflection of the surface shift with the weight he applied. But he was, she reasoned, an adult, and responsible for knowing his own limits. He said, "They got well away?"

She offered him a montage of unedited images of the summersub, now clear of the barriers, churning through the murky sea toward ringsol six. Rache breathed out. "I've managed," Teal said, "to dub the image prior to any storage. Even when my tampering is found and disabled, they will not be able to recover an unedited image."

He raised his hairless brows, in appreciation of the depth of her penetration. "Should you not come off-line now? You have no idea how—aggressive the net defenses might be."

She did not answer, merely laid her hands side by side on the console and watched his image, waiting for him to tell her what he wanted. He tilted his head, the creases around his eyes deepening somewhat, though he did not smile. "Athene . . . and I are going to the AOC. We'll take Michael's skiff; I can't swim that distance. I'd rather we . . . not be intercepted."

"You realize you will be visible all the way across Manhattan bay; I cannot alter that."

"I realize. We'll do our best, but if there's anything you can add . . ." She nodded. He offered a hand; she at last turned to take it, hold it, let it go, as she had done so short a time ago when she undertook ringsol six. "Thank you, Teal," he said. "And I am sorry it came to this. Take care of yourself. Don't resist." He smiled, with an edge to it. "For better or worse, it will be over soon."

She breathed out quietly when she was at last alone. Her part was nearly over, the culmination upon her. From the moment she had moved beyond the legal and ethical limits of her profession, she had known it must come to this.

She allowed herself a long, realtime moment to consider what she and Karel had built between them, the multiplicity of hidden reporting and monitoring subroutines, the layers of analytic and decision-making protocols, ordering, refining, selecting information for upward passage. The final interface bridging the damaged tissue-cercortex junction was simplicity itself. And that simplicity, she thought, was the essence of mastery. For it gave her a new point of balance between the virtual and the real world. Her pride in her commitment and endurance in uplink had been misplaced. That was not the ultimate achievement. This was. This—she stroked the interface lightly—this was the culmination of a career, the expression of a lifetime's experience. Two lifetimes, the one she had lived before Blueheart, and the one she had lived since. She could not have done it without the first, and she would not have done it without the second.

Ah, but she was probably deluded. There is no such thing as a finished creation; there would surely be something beyond her simplified uplink. Something she would never, herself, see.

For her transgressions there was only one sentence, and that immutable by any local clemency. She was a member of an interplanetary guild, and she had broken its oath and half its codes of conduct. Her cercortex would be purged and disabled. She would be reduced to zero order interface, for the rest of her life. And the rest of her life would be spent on Blueheart; she would never again have the intellectual value or simple financial assets for starflight. She wondered whether Rache understood what would be exacted of her. Probably not. Probably he thought that, like his, her fate would depend upon the outcome of this crisis. Cybele would think the loss equally the price of failure, and the price of success.

And Juniper . . . She would like to have thought that Juniper would have understood, but she did not know. She did not know who would have met her, here on Blueheart. But, she acknowledged, had the Juniper she knew been alive, then she would likely never have done any of the things she had done. They violated those old polarities which were the price of Juniper's love. She had stepped from the tower in which she had closed herself, and laid her claim to the world. She should thank Cesar Kamehameha, for his hard teaching: without it she would have feared too much the world outside the tower. She had seen a small part of the life that awaited her, and seen its worth even through her loss. Whatever form retribution assumed, it could not deprive her of her third lifetime.

When they came for her, they would find her waiting. They would have evidence of everything she had done, and an understanding of everything she might have done, and they would still find her waiting. She offered herself, for the last time, as proxy for Juniper, scapegoat for Juniper's offenses, the other of the twinned scheming outworlders who intruded upon Blueheart's destiny. She did not know whether she would be accepted. She was not skilled in popular manipulation. But regardless of what she achieved or failed to achieve, she had determined on this end. Like Juniper, she was neither moral nor principled. Unlike Juniper, she would finish what she had begun.

On the monitors she could see the skiff at full sail, and in the inset, Rache huddled beside the console, sun shining on his lowered head. Athene leaned outboard, sheets and tiller in hand. She was making the best speed she could, for the skiff's rig and keel, but they were visible, and drawing attention: a Rossby security hovercraft had rounded the barriers and was inbound. Several yachts, sportsmen or thrillseekers, were converging to bar their passage. She saw Athene's mouth tighten, and saw her pull hard on the sheets. Rache moved painfully to adjust the trim. She recalled the reconstruction she and Karel had made of her own assault, brought up the implantation and erasure routines, made quick, predetermined adjustments, and squirted them off. Both system and deployed alerts signaled "connection threatened," followed within a half second by "disconnection imminent." The last thing Teal saw before the monitors blanked was the straight, fine line of the skiff's wake, as all around it, yachts pitched, wallowed, circled, and the hovercraft ditched, raising a great bowl of water.

It would not be long now. She settled herself back to wait. The blanked screens showed her the face of an olive-skinned, black-haired woman, with tranquil eyes. Once a shared face, now hers alone.

She did not know what she did, Rache counseled himself, though he felt the insult in his sea-bred bones. He had not thought she would sabotage the navigation systems of boats under sail; he would not have bade her do that. He fought the urge not to look, for had he seen anyone in true distress, a lifetime's training would have turned him back. Athene did, in wonderment and unholy glee. "They're all aback," she reported. He did look around, at sails gone slack and swinging booms, and their cursing crews. Though several were rigging as fast as they could for manual sailing, not a one among them could match Athene, barehanded. And so it proved. All they could do was curse him as far as their voices would carry. They sailed into the AOC docks on the breath of their curses.

They were no more than just in time. The pastorals were already on the docks, though nobody had yet stepped into a boat. Someone pointed, and thin across the water, he heard his name spoken. Lisel pushed out of the crowd, Tove and Bedevere at her back. He looked for Einar, and found him on the periphery. He must have had time to see Rache coming, to appreciate and compose himself, but the emotions still moved over his face like waves, coming and passing and coming again. All across the bay Rache had had only two thoughts, that he must find a way to hold on until Cybele found their proof, and that he must find a way to punish and pardon Einar. He did not move as Athene tacked the skiff into dock. He had his foot on the mooring rope, an infelicity he had not committed since childhood. Athene blushed for him, and tried to free it subtly. She threw it to Lisel, who received it impassively, but with a glare at Rache that promised a reckoning. Mother and daughter straddled boat and dock, with the intent of handing him ashore. He was glad of the help; it was with an effort that he shouldered out of the kimono and got to his feet. He heard indrawn breaths at the sight of the closed, scabbed wounds.

On the dock, he took the few steps necessary to

bring him face to face with Einar. Einar's lips moved, but nothing came out. Or nothing that Rache heard. Figures and shapes seemed translucent, their colors washed pale, their surfaces worn thin by the sea. He said, "Your speargun, please." It came into his hand, even the wrist tether sliding easily free of Einar's wrist. He almost wished Einar had resisted. He might have found something to say. He was standing so close to Rache now, his forehead was nearly resting against Rache's right arm. Rache held the speargun in his left hand, second spear downpointed, the strap entwined in fingers and wrist.

Einar whispered, "I'm sorry."

"I know," Rache said. "But sorry though you may be . . . you carry weapons to feed and defend yourself. You were given them when you proved yourself able and responsible. But you turned those weapons on a man of your own holdfast. Out of grief, I allow, and I myself, I, Rache, hold none of it against you. But I, Rache of Scole, Rache of Blueheart, cannot permit you to carry weapons until you have proven yourself again able and responsible." He took a heavy step back, praying he had the strength for this, bent over, holding the speargun aslant with tip embedded. Lifted his right foot and drove the heel down hard, with all his weight upon it, breaking the mounted spear and its support. Staggering, he dropped the broken weapon. "Pick it up," he said hoarsely.

Einar did, going down on one knee to lift it, and cradle it between his hands. He looked up; in Rache's vision his face wavered like a fish in bright waters, oval, pale, blank.

"When I judge you fit to carry weapons again, you will have the choice of my own," Rache said. "And I give you my word, what justice can be done for your daughter will be done, as I would do for my own." He did not move, more because he did not trust himself to do so than from any desire to sustain the moment.

Einar, putting his own interpretation on Rache's stillness, drew his knives and offered them hilt-first to Rache. His face had the wrecked tranquility of the first dawn after a hurricane.

Rache said, "Keep those. I'll not be sending you back to the compound." Einar lifted his eyes, full of tears. Rache said, harshly and utterly without forethought, "And Gods, boy, will you believe I did love you." He reached down and heaved Einar to his feet, and caught him in an embrace. He felt Einar stiffen, and begin to tremble, and he had to let him go, because neither of them had the strength to sustain two. "I forgive you," he said, gruffly. "And I'll wait for you to forgive me." Then he turned away, because he had not much left, and what he had was going to have to carry him through.

His eyes sought his brother. "Bedevere of Scole, do you accept my judgment on your son?" His brother looked worse than he himself surely could. With his lighter pigment-load, his skin was tinged gray, taut across the temples. Trapped between professional and family loyalties, unable to decide whom to believe, watching his brother accuse his son of an act of savagery, Bedevere was suffering. But Rache needed an answer, and he needed it now. The judgment he had passed on Einar was not the judgment of a wronged kinsman, but the judgment of an elder. He needed them all to accept that judgment.

Bede said, "I accept."

Keri, her eyes clear, but sad, said, "I also accept."

He sought Tove, knowing that herein lay the true test. And she knew it. She had an amused, wary expression on her face, both of which masked her true feelings. She said, at last, "I would have seen you elder of Scole before I died, had you not turned away from it."

"I never turned away from it," he said, hoarsely, understanding that here was another who felt his defection as a wound to heart and pride. Dear life, had any other man such impossible kin? "I did it in the way that I had to do it."

"And now," she said, "we stand on the brink of disaster."

"Would you have that on my account?" he said, tightly.

"No," she said. "You have done your best." She glanced at Einar. "Passing well, in places." In other circumstances, that would have been high praise, grudgingly given as ever.

Rache said, "It is not disaster yet."

Bedevere said, "Without proof . . ." He spread his hands, bereft of words. His eyes shifted from Einar to the broken speargun in his hands. He looked broken, and Rache, who had chafed at his poise and superiority, grieved for him.

He said, "There will be proof. That is why I have come, to say there will be proof."

Einar's face lit like a flare, a brief ascent, and a swift plunge. Rache said, "If I say more, I risk the seekers of that proof. But will you wait with me, here?"

Michael shouldered through the throng. "Rache!" Looked him up and down, questions coming and being ruthlessly rejected. He cut to the essence. "What are you playing at?"

He put a hand on Michael's shoulder, less out of familiarity than to steady himself. "Not at, *for*."

For everything, he meant, and whether Michael

took his meaning, he did not know. "What the hell do you mean 'proof'?"

Rache looked him in the eye. "I mean precisely what I say." He shifted his eyes, to look past Michael at Lisel, at Tove, at Astrid, and Bedevere. "In a little while," he said, "I expect to be able to confirm that there was a virus released to cause the whitesickness and undermine the unauthorized adaptations."

Michael scanned his face. "If you don't get it," he said, in a low voice, "you know what the AOC is prepared to do."

He tightened his hand on Michael's shoulder. "One of these days," he said, "I am going to show you how to hunt lava eel."

Michael lowered his head a moment. The allusion told him of the risk, the uncertainties, the danger, still attendant on Rache's venture. "With friends like these . . ." he muttered. And then looked up, with challenge and decision in his eye.

"You look like you could do to sit down," he said, and turned Rache toward the door. As though it were simply a matter of seeking shade and a comfortable chair. But Michael knew, and Rache knew, that when he went through the door, they would either follow him, to whatever chancy end, or not. Behind him, he could hear nothing but the sea, and the sound of moored boats rubbing against each other and the docks. It was not until the cold shadow fell over him that he heard the sounds of feet, whispering after.

TWENTY

"**R**emember, we can trust no one," Cybele said, and reached to key the canopy. It swung up, and sister and brother levered themselves from the cramped confines of the summersub, and stepped over onto the gangway.

Chandar, acting director of ringsol six, waited. "Cybele de Courcey," he said, and with more warmth, "Karel." Karel stretched a hand around Cybele's back; Chandar shook it, then Cybele's. "What may I do for you?"

She had never met the man, knew him only by reputation. Ostensibly he supported terraforming, had development proposals under consideration, but whether his support was from an ideologue's conviction or a scientist's romance with the possible, she did not know. And nor did Karel, who had met him in his rare visits to ringsol six. Karel had argued in favor of honesty. Cybele trusted no one, now. The cynicism of youth had been flayed away, leaving only an enduring bitterness. She had seen the self-servingness of the great and the petty. Cesar's lies were not only preferred, but defended, against her truth.

She said, "Karel and I have come for the last of our father's possessions." She pitched her voice high, a little plaintive, the sorrowing daughter.

She could see that he did not quite believe her. But

conventionality, or compassion, kept him from challenging her. He said, "If you had contacted us, we could have sent them on to you."

"I could not," she said.

He was silent a moment, looking from her to Karel, and then said quietly, "If you think there may be something to support your accusations against the AOC, we have already looked."

She heard Karel draw breath, and turned her shoulder into him. Not a subtle movement, and not unmissed. Nobody spoke for a moment. Then Chandar said, "I will show you to his quarters, and to medical. There was, of course, some water damage."

His name was still on the door: Adam de Courcey. It did not open. She stood before it, her throat tight, until Chandar reached past her and keyed in a code. The door slid open; she smelled the faint rankness of the sea, and overlaid, the slight smell of cinnamon. Adam had learned scents from Abra; she could see, from here, the scent-pot in a recess beside the bed. For a moment, she forgot her purpose. She must step into the room. But she must step into the room without expectation. The scent was misleading; nothing else remained.

She stepped across the threshold into the empty room, and very carefully looked around, at every wall, in every corner. There were no shadows on the walls, no afterimage of a reaching arm, a turning head.

She heard Chandar say quietly to Karel, "Why are you really here?"

She turned, tensing. The director and her brother were framed in the doorway. Chandar's hand on Karel's forearm, Karel's head lowered. She took a step toward them, not knowing how to intervene, but bent on doing so. Karel said, "We're trying to find proof. As you said."

He lifted his head, looking not at Chandar but at Cybele, telling her with his eyes that he knew what he was doing.

Chandar gave a twisted smile. "Thank you." He gave Karel a light push into the room. "One thing, though, to satisfy the legalities. You'll be on passive surveillance. No eye, no ear, no record, just a low-res positional-monitoring. You can go from here to medical, and from there either to the plexus or the docks. But if you go anywhere else without clearance from me, the surveillance will automatically upgrade to active, eye, ear, and record. You can access Adam's personal console, but if you make any attempt to access the main system, we'll know and stop you. I'm sure you understand why."

It was an allusion only to the virus, not to Karel's guilt. But Karel flushed deeply and miserably, and turned away from Chandar. Cybele saw the perplexity in Chandar's eyes and said, calmly, "Thank you for the advisory."

Chandar gave her the barest smile. "If the situation surfaceside changes, and we have to upgrade to a red alert, everywhere will go on active monitoring. There will be an announcement beforehand. I will be on the plexus. The communications hail is standard."

He reached out to key the door, and said, with mild irony in his tone, "Good luck."

The door closed. Karel, his face still mottled with shame, turned on her. "We *have* to trust him!"

"Not yet."

"We can't get to the sample stores without his knowing, and he already doesn't believe that we're just here for Adam's things."

"That," Cybele said, "was entirely your doing."

"I had—" Karel said, and stopped himself, glaring at her. "You said you knew what you were doing. You don't."

"Let me think," Cybele said.

"Think away," Karel said, throwing himself heedlessly into Adam's chair. "But while you're thinking, think about our situation. Somebody's going to track us here, sooner rather than later. We're on a timetable, and it's not ours."

"I know," said Cybele. "What do you suggest?"

"I suggest trusting someone. Chandar's let us stay even though he's told us they've been through Adam's things looking for proof. Why would he, unless he's hoping we can find what he didn't . . . ?"

"There's a difference," Cybele said grimly, "between potential proof and actual proof. When he's faced with proof, tangible proof, that's going to implicate the Director and who knows who else of the AOC, possibly bring down the AOC itself, lead to scandal and investigations and weaken the whole deterministic structure of Blueheart's government—justify the pastorals' anger and quite possibly totally alter the outcome of the development considerations—*what will he do?*"

"What would you do?" Karel returned. "You're not exactly open-minded about adaptation."

"That's different."

"You know the probable consequences—you've just laid them out—and you're still going ahead."

"Because of Adam."

"These people worked with Adam. They lived with Adam. They fished him out and tried to bring him back to life. Mightn't they care about him too? And even if they don't care about Adam, they're Rache's people. Don't you think they wouldn't grab the chance to help

him with both hands? Whatever color those hands are."
He leaned forward and said, "Cybele, you and Adam,
and God help us, Cesar, you're uncommon. Most people are like me: they don't see the longterm. They see
what's immediately before them. The day's necessities,
the day's pleasures, the day's loyalties. Most people
won't care about the possibility of a pastoral majority.
They'll care about a man they've worked with. They'll
care about a director of the AOC who lied, manipulated, and attempted murder. They'll care even about
you, going through fire for justice. But we need that
proof. We need to get to those stores."

She felt both reluctant admiration and resentment
of this flighty brother grown wise, willful, and eloquent.
And anger, at the challenge to her failings. "All right,"
she said. "You've learned from Teal. Implement your
learning." She pointed at the console. He did not move.
She said, "Find a way to—" and stopped at the
blanched loathing on his face.

Karel said, "You're no better than he is." The stress
of the word left her in no doubt who he meant.

She said, "I—" and he said, in a voice she had never
heard him use, "You're not the only one to whom this
matters. The only one who cares about justice. You're
not. And you have no right—"

"I know," she said, sick with the realization of what
she had demanded he do, and desperate not to hear him
say it. "I know. Karel, I'm sorry. I'm—I don't know. I
can't—I can't trust anyone." She shook her head, bewildered and blind with the pain she had kept down
beneath her anger, the pain of repeated betrayals, the
pain of vilification, the pain of being alone, right, and
unbelieved. She felt him before her, felt his hesitation
before he touched her. Started to turn away.

He put both hands on her shoulders, and said, "But maybe it takes what you have to keep going through this."

The door chimed; they started, looking huge-eyed at one another. It was Karel who went to the door, rather than trigger it from inside. The newcomer was a very tall, very young man in an exoskeletal brace.

"I'm . . . Oliver," he said. Paused a moment, waiting for a reaction. "Ringsol six system operator." He looked from sister to brother and back again. "I had to come and say I was sorry."

Cybele could not think what he had to be sorry for. But Karel stood staring at Oliver, wide-eyed, a little blankly. Oliver said, "If you want me to go, I'll go. But I had to say I am sorry."

"It wasn't you," Karel said.

"That's—kind of you," Oliver said, and Karel, fiercely, "No, it's *not* kind of me, because if it were not for your experiment, my father would not be dead." Cybele, realizing at last who this was, drew breath. Oliver stepped back, whitening. "And *I* would not have killed him," Karel said, a desperate charging at the truth. "*I* designed and released the ringsol six virus. It was I, on the unexpressed wish of my superior, Cesar Kamehameha. And we're here because we need to find hard proof that Cesar Kamehameha had a reason for such a wish. And we need help."

"You—created that virus? You, his *son*?"

"Yes," Karel said, though it cost him.

Oliver slid down the door, back against it, to a seated position. With a softly audible click, his joints locked, holding him there, propped. He said, not looking at Karel, "He was your father." Another silence. "I've thought so much about what I wanted to say to . . . that person when they caught . . . you." Karel's lips parted, and closed. Oliver continued, "But now." His voice was soft, bleak. "If you don't know what you've done, there's nothing I can say to you. If you do," his eyes flicked up and away, "there's still nothing."

Karel was very pale. Cybele gave a small, resigned shrug, and moved to join her brother. She closed a light hand on his elbow, and Karel leaned slightly against her; she could feel his tension, less a tremor than a fine vibration. She said, "We've come because Rache thinks some of his algae samples might be carrying the virus that Cesar Kamehameha released to sabotage the illegal adaptations."

"Rache?" He straightened automatically at the mention of the name, a whisper of pistons. "You mean there *was* a virus?"

"Cesar told me himself, in circumstances where he had no reason to lie. I suspect he never expected I should have the opportunity to prove it. But he used painter algae as the primary vector of infection, and Rache was collecting samples of painter algae for his studies of the blight."

He was staring at her, his long, peaked face blank.

"Cesar limited the replication cycles both in algae and human. By the time the pastoral victims presented, there should have been no unintegrated virus in them, or in the environment. It was to appear—it did appear—as an unanticipated instability in the transfection. Nobody can prove otherwise without a sample of either human tissue, or algae, containing the virus. I am certain that Cesar has ensured that there be none of the first. But he overlooked the algae." She heard the vindictiveness underlying her tone, and curbed herself. Now that they had told him this much, they must keep him. And she could not do so if she let herself seem as she had been portrayed, unstable, and malicious. She breathed out a soft, rancid breath, full of unsaid things.

Oliver said, "But why destroy ringsol six—"

"Because," Cybele said, sparing Karel, "of the body that Rache brought back. She was an illegal. She had adaptations which had never been approved, and some which had never been described. Careful, sophisticated changes, changes that showed people with skill and resources were working on illegal adaptation. Changes which would force the AOC to investigate and publicly report. Adam did enough analysis to realize that. He told me. I told Karel. Karel," not sparing him this time, "told Cesar."

"I thought—" Karel began, vehemently. Then, resignedly, "I thought you would draw a reprimand, for concealment."

"The last thing Cesar wanted was to have the AOC conducting a public investigation which would turn up the illegals' numbers. Not when these numbers threatened the balance of decision. And not when he thought he had the solution: a subtle sabotage of the illegal adaptations, such as would disillusion the adaptees with their illegal providers, and possibly the process of adaptation itself."

"So they wouldn't support non-terraforming and permanent adaptation," Oliver said, and Cybele gave him a wintry smile. The sysop stared a moment at the room's screen, which neither Karel nor Cybele had thought to activate. "So you need those samples to prove Cesar did these things. Then what?"

"What do you mean?" Karel said.

Oliver turned his eyes to the screen; an image appeared. Rache, sitting surrounded by adaptives.

Hunched forward, one heavy forearm braced across his legs, gesturing with the other hand. Everything about him bespoke husbanded, tight-focused energy. Oliver said, "Rache said, before they went inside, that he was waiting for proof. That means he's waiting for you to find what you're looking for, doesn't it? When they know that it was real. When they have proof. What will they do then?"

She stepped, quite deliberately, between him and the image, making him look at her face. "What makes people desperate," she said, "is knowing the truth and not being believed."

"Please," Karel said. "For the sake of justice, *help us*."

A long silence, then Oliver said, "Chandar will have to know that I'm taking you down to the sample stores. And he'll want to know why."

He led them through corridors to the core stairs, and down a descent of several spiral flights. Though spectrum calibrated, the light had an artificial brilliance, an artificial pervasiveness. Cybele felt the chill of the sea beyond the hull. This, much more than Rossby, was what space would be like.

Chandar was waiting for them in specimen-storage, which was a small room, with consoles and delivery slots. He said, "What's going on?"

Since he asked Oliver, Cybele let Oliver tell him, knowing that bitterness would bleed through her words, and abject guilt through Karel's. If Oliver had a flaw as an advocate, it was his shining loyalty to Rache, at whose mention Chandar's face grew taut. Cybele said, "If we do not have these samples, we have no means of proving the truth about ringsol six."

Chandar said, to Karel, "Why have you not come forward before this?"

Cybele said, "Because what happened to me would have happened to him. His reputation shredded, his credibility ruined, and to what end? Testimony, under oath, even under disinhibition, can still be disproved on the basis of an unreliable mental state."

"Because I was a coward," Karel burst out, fierce and shaking. "Because I did not want to know that I had caused my own father's death. I ran away from it and ran away from it—" He turned away, a hand over his face. It was Oliver who laid a long, featherlight hand on his shoulder.

Chander's face was tight with anger or revulsion, whether at Karel or someone else Cybele did not know. "How do I know that you will not deliberately contaminate the samples you examine to generate your proof?"

"You don't," she said, biting off the words. "But what will that achieve when there are other fractions banked elsewhere, out of my reach?"

Something of the tightness eased from his face. "How do I know that Rache, or one of his collaborators, did not contaminate the algae themselves, to discredit the AOC?"

No ready answer came to that one. Oliver said, "Surely you don't believe that?"

"It's an argument that might be made," Chandar said. "And one I find as plausible as the Director of the AOC releasing engineered viruses to undermine the illegal adaptees."

"But you believe that there are illegal adaptees."

"You're right," Chandar said, with grim humor. "That, too, is all somebody's word."

Cybele's jaw ached with tension. "Then there are several possible hypotheses. I suggest to you that we examine the samples on this list. I suggest to you that we will find a shuttle vector carrying integrating human virus. And I further suggest to you that the structure and sequence of the virus will be characteristic of Cesar Kamehameha's work, and of no one else's. It will have his signature." She stepped closer to him. "You have *nothing*," she said, "to lose by letting me do this."

Oliver said, "Think what it would mean to us here to *know* why it happened."

There was a silence. Cybele sensed that Oliver had found a lever, though she did not know its shape, or placement. Karel went to speak; she waved him quickly to silence. But the motion disturbed the stillness. For a moment, she thought she had lost, then Chandar said, "I presume you have the expertise yourselves. I see no point in bringing anyone else into this, since any ringsol six staffmember would be considered partisan and possibly suspect. We'll see what we find in the gene reads."

"Rache," Michael said.

"I'm awake," he muttered, rousing.

"'Course you are," his friend said, dryly. "I thought you'd better catch this."

On the screen, Teal Blane Berenice was dismounting from a transit capsule, flanked by four rust-clad security people. Their faces were stern, but hers was serene. Or no, not serene: serenity implied an elegant detachment. Innocent, he thought, she looked innocent, but that was not it either. There was too much presence and slightly skewed intelligence in that face. He thought of the first time he had met her, and thought he would not know that woman if he met her now. He said, to Michael, "Where are they taking her?"

"Security." He looked at Rache, a line of worry between his brows. Worry Rache could not assuage. He doubted he knew everything Teal had done to serve his ends, and he would not implicate her by discussing what he knew. But he did say, keeping his tone innocuous, "Her knowledge is a two-sided knife."

Michael shook his head. "It's too desperate, now, to rely upon self-interested restraint." He got quickly to his feet, and crossed to the console. Rache could not see, from his angle, what he was doing, and he was too tired to stand.

Lisel appeared at his side, and crouched down, resting her arms lightly on his, on the arm of the chair. Her skin felt warm, covering his. She said, "She'll be answering for Juniper's sins, poor damn woman."

"No, I think hers are originals."

He saw Athene hovering, and knew, from the shift of Lisel's arm on his, and the direction of Athene's glance, that Lisel was waving her off from below his line of sight. With grudging understanding, the girl withdrew.

"But on your behalf?" Lisel said, with a bite.

"I don't know. I haven't had a chance to talk much, with anyone."

Lisel tucked chin on hands and looked up at him. "What did you want to say?"

"To you? What is there to say?"

She grunted, and straightened, showing him long neck, broad shoulders, full breasts, and woven adornments like her daughter's. "I had no choice; I had to leave Scole. I could not have taken her to the legitimate gene engineers. And with Bede doing the monitoring, I could not have taken her elsewhere and brought her back."

"If those were the conditions you set yourself," he said, ungivingly.

"You think I should have told you? Would you have understood? I think not."

He drew a harsh breath, to argue. It knotted painfully beneath his ribs, rebuking him. He would not have let her take their daughter to illegal gene engineers, even if it meant that he force Lisel to disclose herself. He said, at last, "You were afraid I would have won that argument."

"I could not afford to let you," she said, quietly. "The cost would have been too high."

"You never," he said, deliberately misconstruing, "gave me a chance to pay." It was the one place he had the right of it, which her silence acknowledged. Whatever he would have done, whatever he would have chosen, she had not given him the chance. He could not argue further and lay claim to some pleasing course, because he now did not know what, in the brew of trust, love, self-deception, idealism, and infidelities which was his younger self, would have prevailed.

He did not feel her lift his hand. But he felt the warmth of her lips and breath upon it. "I'm not sorry," she said. "I'm not sorry that I did not involve you in our plans; I don't think you should have been. And since you don't pretend that you would have leaped to our support, I won't deny that I was glad to shut you out, in that base way you have accused me of." There was a silence. "You think your proof will save us?"

"It will make it a fairer contest."

"I'll die before I'll let myself be 'cured' of my adaptation," she said, blackly.

His hand tightened around hers. "It will not come to that."

"Your hands are cold," she noted, in passing. "What do you think it will come to, should we fail? And do not say that this is not our last chance . . . it may not be our last, but it may be our best, and you think so too, or you would not have kept us here to wait for your proof."

"If we fail here," Rache said slowly, "then our future will be no better and no worse than if we had never tried. I do not fear vengeance or vindictiveness; if they are honest with themselves, they will admit that, in our position, they would have done the same."

Lisel snorted softly, a laugh which sounded pained. "M'dear, that is precisely why I am afraid. They know what we feel. They know to fear it." She shook her head. "Maybe I am going to learn to appreciate what you feel about all these years of my secret. I know why you cannot tell me, but I wish I knew what you hoped for in your proof, so that I might know whether to hope myself."

Michael hesitated, estimating the depth of their intimacy, then crouched beside Rache. "The good news is that security has accepted my advisory about Teal's mental state, and will have her thoroughly assessed before any kind of questioning. The bad news is that they have done so—they did not say this, but it was an obvious subtext—because they think they can afford to wait a little while. They have given you an ultimatum. You have—they've obviously taken advice from an adaptive-liaison—until sunset. A deadline unambiguous to pastoral or primary."

Rache and everyone within hearing looked toward the window and the bay outside. The dock and the water were in shadow, the blue shadow of late afternoon, devoid, as yet, of the ashy depth of sunset. He heard Lisel say, "And what will they do then?"

"They'll come and remove you by force. It will be an ignominious exit, and one you cannot defend against. One I would not advise you try to defend yourself against. Indeed," he paused, and Lisel touched Rache's hand, prompting him to attend to his friend's grave face, "if you have any doubt about the timely arrival of your proof, I suggest you leave before the deadline, and wait elsewhere."

Karel said, "Cyb, you'd better see this," and Cybele drew her eyes grudgingly away from the screen to see Teal and her guard entering the security block. She merely nodded, in acknowledgment, and looked back at the screen. She heard Oliver say to Karel, "Leave her be. She can't make it go any faster."

Cybele cleared the screen, and looked across at Chandar. "This one's negative."

They were in the medical laboratory. She was working on the very analyzer on which Adam had gene-read the illegal adaptive, and set his course toward death and hers toward this. Her touch might be erasing the last of his fingerprints, those the sea had not washed away.

She erased the useless sequence with a sweep of her hand, and brought up the next. Across the room the sampler sighed softly, returning a vial, and drew in another with a muted snick. It was leading them by two samples, but its lead was narrowing as Cybele refined her search, broadening the array of identified algal alleles which could be eliminated automatically. The rest she must scan by eye. She dared not restrict her search to those human sequences she knew must be there, for fear she might miss a telling fragment.

"That's algal," Chandar said. "All of it."

She looked up, met his eyes. He looked tired, frustrated, determined not to be beaten. Despite his skepticism, he had become absorbed by the task, vexed by the challenge. His emotions, his commitment, had grown with time and effort, as hers had been blunted. Her fierce, righteous intensity had eroded. She felt only tired, frustrated, determined not to be beaten. "Next," she said.

Eliminate those sequences unambiguously algal. Study those which were left for some fragment of the interloper. Reject, move on. The sampler and analyzer was working only one ahead. "How many left?" she said, to no one in particular.

"Eighteen," said Karel, immediately. "And Cyb, security have given the pastorals an ultimatum. They have to be out by sunset."

"Sunset?" said Chandar, amused.

Her hand stalled in its motion before she saw why. She stared at the sequence before her, algal surely, so why had the subtraction not removed it, and why had it caught her eye. She requested a detailed comparison, aware that Chandar had turned his head away from the analysis screen, toward the wallscreen which showed the pastorals in the AOC. The sequence was indeed algal, but it contained a viral insertion sequence which was chimeric, a product of two natural viruses. And not a natural chimera, not interspliced to this extent.

Cesar, she thought, *I have you.*

She drew breath to speak; she moved her hand, to flick the downstream sequences into view. And she stopped.

"Sunset," she said, and her voice sounded strange to her.

"Less than an hour," Karel said.

She considered the small figures on the far screen, with an odd detachment. Karel said, "They're trying to decide what they should do. Whether to leave before security come in."

She said, trying to sound as though one thought had merely strayed into the other, "What's the status of Rache's petition?"

"Support is running around twenty-one percent, but there's still a much higher interest quotient as measured in the subjects of active discussion groups and access. That's probably what has kept the petition from being denied before this."

Chandar said, "Rache's no fool. Staying where he is is keeping the petition alive."

For how long? she thought. How long would Rache's petition last beyond surrender of the AOC? How long would the fraying pastoral unity survive beyond their stepping out onto those docks, as step they must: she could not imagine they would let themselves be taken? How long would it take to rebuild their unity, once they dispersed into the seas? *Could* they rebuild, after such failure? Or would they hide, from the AOC and each other?

She had thought she had no choice in her alliances; indeed, without them, this might have been impossible. She thought that she would have had to betray Adam's beliefs to secure justice for him. But all she need do was let an hour pass. Rache of Scole was the heart of this, and he must be nearing the limit of his strength. He could not hold them together beyond that hour. Once the pastorals dispersed, then she could bring forward her evidence, and they would have no use of it.

Rache said, looking up at them all, "I am not leaving."

"If you come back to Lovelock bay," Michael began, and Rache shook his head. Michael said, "I think you'd better explain to us why."

Rache smiled slightly and said, with a sidelong glance at his wife, "Attribute it to Juniper's influence. Blame it on a late-blooming sense of theater."

"Rache," Michael said, "this is serious."

"So am I." There was no more time to spare words or effort. He pushed himself to his feet.

"The disaster on ringsol six," he said, to the people who stood in the room, and to those who watched from beyond the walls, "was due to an effort to erase evidence of the illegal adaptives. The effort was not made by the illegal adaptives themselves, but by an agent of the AOC acting on behalf of Cesar Kamehameha. In that disaster, four people died.

"The destruction and deaths were unintended, but any mitigation of guilt has been canceled by what the AOC directorate has done since to elude discovery. I escaped lightly, with disgrace. Expert-voyager Teal Blane Berenice barely escaped with her life, in an assault intended to prevent her from investigating any further either the disaster of ringsol six, or the actions of her late sister, Juniper Blane Berenice. She is currently in custody, and I charge you," he looked directly at the unseen watchers, "to ensure that she is well treated. Whatever she has done, in aiding me, she has done no one harm, a claim few of us can equal."

Dizziness rolled over him in a wave. For a moment, he thought he would not last the immersion; then it passed, leaving only an odd ebbing murmur in his ears.

"The director of the very organization charged with safeguarding humanity and individuals from the ill effects of our ability to adapt ourselves to new environments has violated every ethical principle which that organization holds dear. He has released, into our food supply, a virus which was intended to reverse all adaptations made without sanction of the AOC." He set his feet, no longer quite aware of the people around him. "He did this rather than bring into daylight our quite indefensible crimes. We would have had no defense in law against charges of illegal adaptation, of concealment and conspiracy. Of challenging the millennial plan of settlement, and the biological unity of mankind. But rather than bring us before law, he chose to dispense his own *punishment* for our presumption."

He tipped back his head, seeing shadows, looking for light. "Ours was," he said, with a faint smile, "an appalling presumption, I agree. Instead of submitting to our destiny—to explore, to discover, to report, and then to go gently into the good night of extinction—we created a culture and society of our own, and then sought permanence. We should be obliged to plead guilty without reserve, to treachery to humanity, to the millennial plan. We would gladly do so, given the chance.

"I want," Rache said, "the chance. No, I *demand* the chance. I demand the chance to make a fair case for our survival, and I want to see the case against us fairly made. The Director of the AOC has charged us with promoting disunity, with dividing humanity against itself, with threatening us with a return to some dark age when divisions were deadly and unity to be sought at all cost. His solution is that we should cease to be, that Blueheart be terraformed, that all Blueheart is, all that we, and you, are, be sacrificed to *unity*. I say we can be united without being the same, or wanting the same. I say the seas are wide enough and deep enough for all of us, primaries, adaptives, and pastorals; we have the technology, we have the knowledge, we have the imagination, and even if the original injection did come from offworld, we have the *audacity*."

There had been a point to this, he thought, and it was not merely the final and uninhibited discharge of his thoughts. He would have lambasted any student of his presenting so disjointed an argument. And an argument should have a conclusion, other than the speaker falling down.

"I am not leaving," he said. "I have seen political influence suppress the truth of ringsol six. I will stay here, at the center, until I see the proof of what the directorate of the AOC tried to do to us. And when I see that proof, I will not let it be pushed underwater. I want a chance to make a fair case for us, and hear a fair case made against us. And I want," he said, his voice suddenly fading, "to sit down."

Oliver whistled softly. Karel murmured, "That's telling them, Rache."

Sunset, Cybele thought, if only it were sunset now, and this already over. She needed the cool, the shadow; she felt scorched by Rache's anger. It was an odd discomfort. Adam's displeasure had been penetrating, a cold, direct light probing one's unworthiness. Cesar's insight had been as sure, but it came veiled and veiling, illuminating nothing, inviting one to hide from oneself.

Rache's anger was a fierce, undirected heat. His accusations had not been intended for her, but she felt them, nonetheless.

But she was doing nothing wrong. Rache's strategy was to offset Cesar's wrongdoing against the illegals', to use the controversy to sustain discussion of his people and their place. Implicit in his argument was an indictment of the plan, and the way it had been practiced, on Blueheart. But a law is not flawed, not unworkable, because it is violated.

She need wait only a few hours, for the pastoral stance to crumble. Rache did not have the strength to hold them together. Under threat of the AOC's legal action they would disperse into the seas. Those who did not disperse would be taken into custody; she had no doubt that Cesar would seize any advantage he had.

Any advantage she gave him.

Adam, she thought, and struggled to realign herself toward that single pole. Everything she had done, she had done for Adam. For Adam, she had pursued this to its bitter end. She had served, willingly, the man who had caused Adam's death, and nearly destroyed her brother. She could not forgive herself for her ignorance, for she had given away the best of herself, her loyalty, her trust, her best thought.

She had begun this in love, and ended it in hatred. Karel was quite wrong when he said that she had Adam's depth of vision; hers had closed in to two men, one loved, one hated. She could not see past them. Karel was merely a shimmer, Rache a rumbling heat, Chandar a sketch. God did not appear. Whether adaptation contravened God's plan or not, she did not know, and she did not care. Adam spoke of a sacred law. Cesar of human survival as a species.

What did she speak of?

"Cybele." Karel, standing at her side, giving her her full name, for what, the second, third, fourth time? She looked at him in apprehension, dreading discovery. But he was not looking at the screen; he was looking at her. "The director suggests you take a rest."

Chandar said, "You won't find what you are looking for if you are exhausted."

Ah, but I have already found what I am looking for. It is what I must do with it that I do not know. She looked down at her console. If it had only come to her an hour later. Adam's voice: Time is not yours. It is God's. Was this also God's time, the time of God's choosing? His choosing that it be placed in her hands in time for this? His blessing on Rache and Rache's people, that it come to them now . . . ?

But it had not come to them, it had come to her.

"Cyb." Karel laid a hand tentatively on her arm. "Cybele, come away. You're beginning to frighten me." She let herself be led to a side workstation, sat down in it. How many seconds might that use up? A minute even. Karel crouched in front of her, hunched beneath the console, holding her hands. "It's all right," he said. "If it's there, you'll find it."

It is there, she thought. I have found it. What she said was, "I am wondering . . . if I *should* . . . find it. If I should give them," she turned unseeing eyes toward the far screen, "the use of it, for their own ends."

He looked up at her, not understanding, for a moment. And then he grasped her meaning, and his gray eyes widened in shock. "You mean withhold the proof that Rache needs?" He had spoken too loudly, audible to the others in the room; she shook her head sharply, hoping they would misconstrue her meaning as dissent, when it was merely a cautioning. He leaned up to her, and said, "Would you do that?"

She said, "Do you not care what might happen to Blueheart, because of this, because of us?"

"Cybele," he said, "why are you suddenly—" and then he looked at the console where she had been working, and his whole frame stiffened. When he spoke, it was in a whisper. "You have found something, haven't you?"

She nodded.

He did not move; his hands on hers tightened in urgency. "Cyb," he whispered. "Security have Teal. Rache has said that he has someone looking for proof. Cesar will be looking for us." His eyes searched her face. "Cybele," he said, in a low voice, "you know how ruthless he is. He has copies of all my worms and modification programs. Think where we are. Think what happened before. Cybele, there are people down here with us . . ."

"Don't be melodramatic," she said, wearily, but she could feel the tremor in his hands.

"Cybele," he whispered, "I truly am afraid of him."

"I hate him," she said.

"Then—"

How many minutes had passed, not merely minutes of day, but minutes of arc of the sinking sun? She could not tell from the part of the screen she could see beyond Chandar's shoulder. She said, quietly, "But I have fallen into error before through setting my own hatreds before my obligations; I will not do so again. I must do what is right."

"Right?" said Karel, moderated his tone as Oliver started to turn toward them. "Rache sent us to do this. He trusted us."

"There was no one else for him to send," she said. "Karel, this is beyond you and me, and Cesar; this concerns the future of Blueheart."

"No," Karel said. "This time you will not persuade me you have all the answers."

"Adam would not have wanted . . ."

"Speak for yourself," he said, his voice rising.

"Why: can you not bear to hear his name?"

She glanced at Chandar and Oliver, who were watching the screen, giving them their privacy. Oliver's back was tense within the lines of the exoskeleton; each time their voices rose, he stiffened.

Karel leaned forward, and whispered, "Yes, I can bear to hear his name. Can you bear not to speak it? Cybele, it is not up to Adam, it is up to us, it is up to you." The smallest silence, and then, averting his eyes, he whispered, "Cybele, even if you do what he wants, you can't bring him back." She stared at him, feeling as though he had speared her. He held hard to her hands, his eyes wet. "No matter how guilty you feel," he said, almost inaudibly, "no matter how much you punish yourself, no matter how different it might have been if you had made other choices, no matter how much you try to be or do what *he* wanted . . . no matter what, he will not be coming back."

For a long moment, she could not speak. She could hardly breathe. She felt as though she were already in space, and he had severed her lifeline, and set her adrift. She was suffocating, and the stars were drifting past and growing dim. He held her hands, looking up into her face. "Cybele, I know how it feels. *I know.*"

For the first time since Adam's death, she felt the pressure of tears behind her eyes, within her throat. They would come, she thought, but not now. She was not ready for them now. She said, hoarsely, "Why haven't you spoken?"

He glanced screenward, where for a moment a seascape showed the sun poised on the horizon, its bottommost curve touching the sea. "It seems a miracle to me that you do not hate me. I don't want you hating me over this. Call me a coward, but I can't . . . speak unless you do."

She gathered her feet beneath her, stood, and walked over to the screen. The two men moved apart to let her stand before it. Down one side, the sun hung on a bright band, only a slight flattening of its base showing that it had touched the ocean; there was otherwise no visible margin between sun and sea. The greater part of the screen showed the adaptives. Rache slumped back in a chair, his eyes closed, sunk in his thick-fleshed face. His chest rose and fell slowly. His red hands, spread on the arms of the chair, twitched. She could feel his exhaustion in her bones. His wife crouched beside him, her head turned into profile to look toward the window at the setting sun, and at her daughter, leaning against that window, a mahogany silhouette. Einar stood watching Rache from across the floor. He still held the broken speargun in his hands. His face was tired and empty, neither hopeless nor hopeful, a blasted peace. When she spoke, when she gave up her burden, she would have her part of that blasted peace, in face and heart, as she had had her part of his sorrow, or he of hers, but yesterday.

What was the foundation of humanity? Cybele thought. Body or spirit? Adam would have said spirit, yet he condemned these people for their bodies, and the changes they chose for themselves. But Adam is gone. It is left to me. What do I say?

She reached out and touched the screen, laying her fingertips on the space between Rache and Einar. In his face, I see a father who has lost a daughter, a son who has injured his father; I see grief, I see regret, I see remorse. In his face, I see myself.

She said, "How do I speak to them, from here?"

EPILOGUE

The apartment was high in one of Rossby's newest towers. It faced west, toward the setting sun, and sunlight splashed across Rache's face as he stepped into the study. Nobody spoke, but a moment later the windows darkened, and let him see his surroundings. Windows to the fore, overlooking the wide, yellowing sea. Viewscreens interspersed with soft-lit aquaria. All the viewscreens active, their images tracking through the undercity grottos of Rossby. All the aquaria, clean and healthy, their occupants contentedly browsing among weeds and coral, colors vibrant. On the floor beneath one rested a brush and a bucket. Offset to one side was a console, and the image on the console was not of the sea, but of dark planes and lines and lights. Rache could not make it out at a glance, inverted and foreshortened, and he did not look long, for the man seated at the console was watching him. "Thank you for coming," Cesar Kamehameha said.

He seemed, Rache thought, so little changed. So little touched by what had happened, what he had been part of, what he had done. What had been done to him. He had made no willing confession; the admissions made so public were drug-induced, after brief, savage legal argument.

They looked at each other a moment, Rache standing just inside the doorway, Cesar seated at his console.

Around them, the aerators in the aquaria burbled into the silence. After a moment, Rache walked forward. Cesar gestured over the console, and the image flipped, upright to Rache. It was of an urban cityscape; the mirrors and skypanels told Rache it was of Earth. Cesar said, "Cybele de Courcey sent me all Adam's personal logs." He folded his hands, above the image. "I do not think she meant it kindly."

"You were responsible for his death," Rache said, "in her eyes."

Cesar looked down at the inverted cityscape. "Do you feel any remorse?" one of his inquisitors had asked him, and he had said, "Yes. But no regret." "It is not the punishment she intended. I think he might have understood, better than she, why I did what I did." He paused. "How is she?"

"She will be better, Michael says, with time." She had told him what she had nearly done, down on ringsol six. He had known better than to thank her for doing otherwise.

Cesar nodded; whatever he thought, he kept to himself. "And Karel?"

"He will do well."

"I understand he works for you now," Cesar said. "And that I should offer you congratulations, on the orange-striping of your proposal." His tone was lightly ironic, reserving judgment. Very few had. Rank opportunism was the kindest that had been said. Rank opportunism; desperation; a corruption of the process; a hollow political gesture; a surrender to extremism. But, whatever was said, enough people, pastoral and primary, had indicated support of the prospect of a non-terraformed future for Blueheart, that such proposals had to be developed.

In a scant few days, he had become one of the most influential, and one of the most vulnerable figures on Blueheart. The proposal, his creation, must not fail; this he had been told several times, explicitly and implicitly. But should he fail it, or even seem to fail it, then he would be thrust aside.

Cesar said, "You realize, I will continue to do anything in my power to stop you."

And he had power, Rache thought. He had the power of his desperation and his disgrace. He was a kind of emblem. That he, Director of the AOC, should be driven to this, to outlawry and murder, was to some less an indictment of him than an indictment of the position in which he had been placed.

He nodded, there being nothing else to say. Cesar pushed himself sharply back from the console. "They asked me," he said, "if I felt any regrets." No, Rache thought, they had not; they had asked him if he felt remorse. But he did not contradict Cesar. "About the only thing I regret," Cesar said, "is the hubris of the creator. I became a genetic engineer, because the *making* appealed to me. I deluded myself in my mastery. Adam de Courcey would have pointed that out to me, readily, my moral flaw." He spoke Adam's name, more easily, Rache thought, than either of Adam's children; he resented that a little on their behalf. "Juniper Blane Berenice was the same. She, too, had the hubris of the creator; she, too, deluded herself in her mastery. And you, now. You." Over the console, over the dark cityscape, he looked at Rache. "You think you can control what you have begun. You will find that you cannot."

No, Rache thought, you are wrong. I already know what I can and cannot control. He had learned about chaos in the seas of Blueheart, on the docks of Rossby, on the barriers of Lovelock. He had learned about love, betrayal, hate, anger, loss, and despair; he had experienced disgrace, humiliation, and dispossession; he had learned he could endure and survive them all. No matter how well tended and carefully engineered, humanity retained its primitive birthright of emotions, imagination, and aspiration. And he read in the man across from him a profound fear of those things, of the traits that could not be engineered out of humanity because they were an intrinsic part. Perhaps that was what Cesar had learned from this, not that the chaos could be survived, but that the chaos was within him. He had gone far beyond his own definition of civilized, step by step. And if he could, how might other, lesser beings?

He felt, for the first time, pity for Cesar Kamehameha.

He said, quietly, "A system, and a species, must be able to adapt to survive new conditions. Human beings are not exempt from that. Our ability to transform ourselves is a new condition, to which we must adapt."

They were silent, Cesar sitting, Rache standing, while beyond the shaded window the light went ashy. Nine days, Rache thought, nine days since that sunset measured second by second from the AOC.

Cesar said, abruptly, "What of Teal Blane Berenice?" A brief pause, then, almost angrily, "She has refused reparations. I would have paid her passage to New Boots, or beyond." He sounded as though her refusal had denied him something. "An expert-voyager, reduced to a zero order interface; what is there here for her?"

Rache said, "A new life." He could not speak easily of her, any more than he could speak of Ayna. They were the irrevocable, inadmissible losses. Michael had told Rache what he understood of Teal's purpose, and yet Rache could not see how Teal's powerful, idiosyncratic intellect could be satisfied with the external world alone. There must surely come a time when she would measure her losses, and find them too great.

He stepped back suddenly, disturbed that he, who had saved Teal, seemed to regret more than the man who had almost slain her. Cesar lifted his head, catching his thought; he said, "About that, I am sorry. Tell her, if you will. It may be that I could—" but he caught himself, seeing the absurdity of his making promises to her; and of that, Rache was glad.

Cesar said, after a long moment, "So, you have your amnesty. Even the purveyors of illegal adaptation have escaped lightly. You have the resources to develop your proposal."

"We have neither of us," Rache said, quietly, "paid as fully as we might have."

The olivine eyes met and held his, looking, Rache thought, for weakness; at last, Cesar nodded. "We will talk again." He moved his hand, righting the image of an Earth three hundred years gone, seen through the eyes of the man whose death he had arranged. He did not look up again as Rache left.

He decided, by the time he reached sea-level, that clothes or no clothes, public image or no public image, he would swim back to Lovelock. The sea might cleanse the melancholy which clung to him. Pity notwithstanding, Cesar's lack of remorse chilled him. It was, Rache admitted to himself, what he had come hoping to see, some remorse, some willingness to compromise. But Cesar embodied his own belief that what he was and wanted, and what Rache and his people were and wanted, were irreconcilable. There would be no amnesty between them.

In the clear, early light of evening, the bay was littered with scraps of sail of every color and boats of every configuration, sedately mingling according to the masterful choreography of docks control. Several, he noticed, flew the red pennants which indicated manual handling, a not uncommon sight since his and Athene's sail across Manhattan bay. Two of those were racing toward the docks, close-hauled. One had the sky blue sail of *Albatross*, with its wide-winged bird. The other, narrowly leading it, was pastoral-rigged, its sail a coarse weave of ribbongrass canvas. Rache shaded his hands, narrowing his vision, so that he could see the sailors. The flapping rim of Karel's absurd hat caught his eye; he watched Karel lean outboard, sheet and tiller in hand. He was shouting not at the other boat, but at someone inside his own. Rache saw Cybele's face lift, her head shake; but even as her head shook, she glanced toward the other yacht, and pushed herself up onto the side. Karel laughed, and pulled hard on the sail. *Albatross* heeled, steadied, and surged forward. Cybele clung, shaking her head and grinning angrily into the spray.

In the other boat, Michael's dinghy, as rigged by Athene, Athene and Teal worked as one, Athene helmsman, Teal crew. They had been inseparable over the past days, Athene teaching Teal sea-lore, and discovering Rossby with her. Teal's hair, shirt, and shorts were soaked, and Athene's skin daubed with water; they had obviously capsized at some recent point. Rache could see why, the way they were handling the dinghy, trying by sheer skill, effort, and audacity to offset Karel's advantage in having the better hull. They had seen him, he thought, but none of the four could free a hand to wave.

Rache folded his arms, and, smiling, watched them come.

ALISON SINCLAIR is the author of one earlier novel, *Legacies,* and is at present studying medicine at the University of Alberta in Canada. She was previously a research fellow at the University of Leeds, having studied first chemistry and physics and then taken a Ph.D. in biochemistry. Her particular interests are structral molecular biology and neuroscience.